A bundle of adorable fun is about to drop into each of these bachelors' lives...

Bachelor...and Baby!

Bestselling authors Anne McAllister and Sherryl Woods show just how single, independent, sexy men cope when they suddenly become—dads!

We're proud to present

SILHOUETTE SPOTLIGHT

a second chance to enjoy two bestselling novels by favourite authors every month— they're back by popular demand!

October 2003

Bachelor...and Baby!

featuring

MacKenzie's Baby by Anne McAllister

The Cowboy and His Baby by Sherryl Woods

November 2003

Dark & Dangerous

featuring

A Man To Die For by Suzanne Brockmann

The Lady in Red by Linda Turner

December 2003

His Christmas Bride

featuring

The Surprise Christmas Bride by Maureen Child

A Very Convenient Marriage by Dallas Schulze

Bachelor...and Baby!

Anne McAllister
Sherryl Woods

Silhouette Books, Eton House, 18-24 Paradise Road, Richmond, Surrey TW9 1SR

MacKenzie's Baby (1997) and *The Cowboy and His Baby* (1997) were first published in Great Britain by Silhouette Books in separate single volumes.

ISBN 0 373 04954 4

64-1003

Printed and bound in Spain
by Litografia Rosés S.A., Barcelona

MacKenzie's Baby

ANNE McALLISTER

ANNE McALLISTER

RITA® Award-winning author Anne McAllister fell in love with a cowboy when she was five-years-old. Tall, dark, handsome lone-wolf types have appealed to her ever since. 'Me, for instance,' her college professor husband says. Well, yes. But even though she's been married to the man of her dreams for over thirty years, she still likes writing about those men of the West! And even though she may take a break from cowboy heroes now and then, she has lots more stories planned for the CODE OF THE WEST. She is always happy to hear from readers, and if you'd like, you can write to Anne at PO Box 3904, Bozeman, Montana 59772, USA. An SAE with return postage would be appreciated. And you can visit her website at www.annemcallister.com and e-mail Anne your comments to anne@annemcallister.com.

For Patrick, with love

Prologue

New York City, September

''Jason Neillands?'' The pediatric nurse scanned the sea of parents and offspring in the overcrowded waiting room.

Thank God, Carter thought. He'd never given much thought to the notion of purgatory, but after forty minutes, a waiting room in a pediatrician's office seemed about as close as one could get.

He scooped his nine-month-old charge away from the magazine he was shredding and followed the nurse down the corridor.

The nurse marched them into one of the examining rooms and turned, pencil poised, to look expectantly at Carter. ''And what seems to be the trouble with Jason today?''

''Er, sore throat. Can't sleep. I—he...lies awake all night.''

''Does he cry?''

''Uh, no. Not a lot, I mean. Sometimes. He's a baby, for heaven's sake.''

The nurse tapped her pencil on Jason's chart, then gave Carter a skeptical look. ''Does he have a temperature, Mr. Neillands?''

"I...don't think so." He didn't think he'd tell her he wasn't Mr. Neillands, either. Let Jack's reputation suffer a little. Do him good.

He could tell that it was all she could do not to roll her eyes at his incompetence. She contented herself with pursing her lips. "Undress him down to his diaper. Doctor will be in shortly." She went out, shutting the door with a decided thump behind her.

Doctor had damned well better be in shortly, Carter thought as he perched on the edge of the examining table. It was already almost noon. He'd picked Jason up at ten. Frances was going to wonder where the hell he'd got to with her kid. When Carter'd taken him, he'd said he was only going for a walk in the park, that they'd be back in maybe an hour.

"You won't tell her, will you, chum?" he asked the baby who stood holding Carter's fingers and balancing on his knee.

Jason gave him a dimpled grin and leaned forward to gum Carter's shoulder.

The door opened, and a silvery-blond woman in a plaid shirt and brown corduroy slacks appeared, frowning down at Jason's chart as she did so. Only her stethoscope gave her away, Carter thought with amusement.

"Well, Jason," she said briskly, "what's the troub—*Carter?*"

"Hi, Sis." He gave her a sheepish grin.

She shut the door firmly behind her. "What are you doing here? Where's Frances? Where's Jack? That *is* Jason?"

The baby, hearing his name, turned and grinned at her, then wobbled precariously and grabbed a handful of Carter's hair to steady himself.

"Ouch. Hey, easy, fella." Carter shifted the child in his

arms, turning him to sit and bounce on his blue-jeans clad knee. "Of course it's Jason. What'd you think?"

Millicent MacKenzie Moore regarded her older brother with eyes of long experience. Her expression was even more skeptical than the nurse's. "And Frances sent him to the doctor with you?"

Carter shrugged. "It...isn't him. It's me."

"Carter."

"I've been having these sore throats, Milly. Long sleepless nights."

"Carter, I'm a pediatrician."

"You're a doctor. Columbia Phi Beta Kappa. Yale Med." He grimaced. "Don't think Dad kept it a secret."

Millicent sighed. Their father's pride in her accomplishments had only been equaled by his disgust with Carter's lack of them. Not that Carter had ever cared. "You could have called your regular doctor."

"He says there's nothing wrong."

"Maybe there isn't."

"Then why can't I sleep?"

Milly's brow arched. "Guilty conscience?"

He rubbed a hand across his face. "Don't I wish."

Milly cocked her head. "Pure as driven snow, are you?"

"Close," Carter admitted. "Since Diane I haven't—" He stopped and shook his head. Even with Diane he never had.

He and Diane Bauer had been friends, never lovers. But he'd loved her. At least *he* thought he had. Diane had said he didn't. She'd said he didn't know what true love was.

What the hell did she know? he thought grimly. She'd only had eyes for Nick. Three months ago she'd married him.

"I feel lousy," he said plaintively now. "I lie awake all night. Remember when I used to have croup as a kid?"

"You don't have croup, Carter."

"Maybe I have mono."

"Didn't your doctor do lab tests?"

"Yeah, but—"

"Were they negative?"

"Yeah, but—"

"Then I doubt if you have mono."

"But there's gotta be something wrong with me. I can't sleep. I work for hours. I don't date."

Milly, heading for the door to usher him out, stopped dead and stared, nonplussed. "Why not?"

"What's the point? All the women look the same...."

"Maybe you are sick." She backtracked and reached for a tongue depressor. "Stick out your tongue and say *ah.*"

"*Ahhhhhhhh-gggghhh!* Cripes, Mil, what're you trying to do, gag me?"

She gave him a sweet smile. "Could I?"

He glowered. Jason bounced up and down and clapped his hands.

"Your throat looks fine, Carter." She checked his nose, his ears, his eyes. "Nose, eyes and ears are fine, too. Take off your shirt."

She held Jason while Carter stripped off his dark green T-shirt, then handed the baby back and laid the stethoscope against his chest.

"It's cold," Carter complained.

"Hang tough, big guy," Milly said with her typical lack of sympathy, and moved to listen to his back.

When she was done she pinched his quarter inch of spare tire and gave him one of her Mary Sunshine smiles.

"I hate to tell you this, brother dear, but I think you're going to live."

Carter tugged the shirt back on, then looked up to scowl at her. "That's all you're going to do?"

"Well, I could take your temperature, I suppose."

Carter opened his mouth and waited.

Milly just looked at him, then at the thermometer in her hand. "It's rectal, Carter," she said gently.

He bounded off the examining table. "Forget it."

She caught him by the belt loop before he could get the door open. "Hold it a minute."

"You said I'm fine."

But she didn't let go until he turned around to face her. "Physically I think you are," Milly said seriously. "Mentally, emotionally…I wouldn't be so sure."

Carter's mouth twisted. "Go see a shrink, you mean?"

"You could. But I don't think you need to unless it gets worse."

"What do you think?"

"That maybe you need a break. Since Diane got engaged and since Dad died—"

"He doesn't have anything to do with this."

"But it's only been five months." It had been a shock to them both when their robust, healthy father had dropped dead on a Bermuda golf course last April.

"It might have been years for all the contact we had."

Millicent sighed. She'd grown up a bystander to the ongoing battle between Carter William MacKenzie III and his black-sheep son. She'd hoped it might end last April. It hadn't yet. "He tried, Carter."

"He was the most trying son of a bitch I ever knew!"

"Carter!"

"He was. He had my whole life mapped out for me. Tried to tell me every damned thing to do from the time

I first took a breath. And whatever it was, I never did it well enough, did I? If he was still around, I'll bet you he'd be telling me I won't die as well as he did, either!'' Carter dropped his voice in a damningly accurate imitation of the elder MacKenzie. ```I died after sinking a birdie. You'll probably go out after a double bogey, you young fool.'''

``He's dead, Carter,'' she said quietly. ``He can't tell you anything now.''

``And thank God for that,'' Carter muttered. He bent his head, concentrated on watching Jason's chubby feet dance along the tops of his jeans-clad thighs. He didn't want to talk about his father. He never wanted to talk about his father.

Milly tapped the stethoscope against the table. ``I still think you need a break. If all you've done since Diane got engaged is work—''

``I play, too,'' Carter said quickly. ``Don't forget that.''

``I thought you weren't dating.''

``I'm not. Now. I did. After Diane got engaged, and…and later, I—I…went out a lot.'' An understatement if there ever was one. He'd felt a sense of panic, desperation for months, as if he were on some sort of merry-go-round, reaching for the brass ring and missing, then missing again. As if his life was going faster and faster, spinning away from him. He couldn't explain it, didn't try.

``But now you don't?''

He shook his head.

``What do you do?''

``Order soybeans. Shelve bags of bulgar and barley. Pack peanut butter. Inventory ninety-million varieties of organic shampoo. Keep the steel-cut oats from mating with the regular milled.'' He managed a grin.

Millicent tweaked his nose. ``Work, in other words.''

"Yeah."

"Maybe you've been working too hard."

Carter snorted. "Tell that to the old man."

Milly ignored him. "Do you want a prescription?" she asked him slowly.

Carter's brows lifted. "I thought you said I wasn't sick."

"Not that kind of a prescription."

Jason was squirming in his arms, trying to get down. Carter swung him around and settled the baby onto his shoulders. "What kind?" he asked warily.

He couldn't think of a thing he hadn't tried. Work. Play. Wine, women and song.

New York City wasn't short on stimulation of any sort. What he hadn't thought of, Jack or Frances had. Even Nick and Diane, once they'd come back from their honeymoon, had gone out of their way to keep him busy and to include him in their life.

Carter hated it. After a few attempts at dragging wholly unsuitable women along on outings with his friends or, worse, going alone as a third wheel, he stopped going at all. Being the adjunct to everyone else's happiness was worse than burying himself in soybean invoices until three in the morning.

"I think," Milly said now, considering him the way she did things under a microscope, "you need a change of scene."

"I went skiing in Jackson Hole last January. I went to Nassau in April and to Hawaii in July. I was out fishing at the folks' place in Jersey just last weekend."

"Not just a week or a weekend," Milly said. "More. A lot more."

He frowned. "You mean move?"

"Maybe not permanently." She smiled at him, blue

eyes guileless. "I wouldn't want you gone forever, you know. But for a few months, why not?"

"The store, for one thing. I know Dad didn't take it seriously, but I thought you might at least." He knew damned well his very own Jack Sprat's Health and Wellness Store was small potatoes compared to the Idaho-size business conglomerates his father had run. He hadn't expected the old man to respect it. He'd hoped for a little more from Milly.

"Of course I do," his sister said quickly. "But don't you have an assistant manager?"

"Yeah, but—"

"And isn't he competent?"

"She, but—"

"*She,*" Milly said firmly, "is probably itching for the chance to show what she can do." One blond brow arched. "Isn't she?"

"Yeah, but—"

"You don't want to give her the chance?"

"Of course I do. It's just that..."

"That if you leave you might have to get down to the nitty-gritty of what's bothering you?" Milly's eyes were gentle and knowing as they met his.

Carter sighed. If there was a virtue to being so damnably transparent, he didn't know what it was. Jason thumped him on the head.

"You haven't been off the treadmill for more than a week since you came back from Berkeley how many years ago?" Milly asked.

"Eleven," he said heavily.

"A long time," Milly mused. "Eleven years ago I was a college sophomore majoring in partying. Times have changed, Carter. You've changed. Maybe your body is telling you something your mind should listen to. Maybe you ought to try something new, get a different perspective. Figure out what's missing, what you really want out of life."

"And then I'll be back to normal?"

Milly grinned. "Heaven forbid." Then her grin faded. "Seriously, I think you should try it."

Carter rubbed a hand across his face. "Where would I go?"

Milly looked at him for a long moment, then cast aside the last vestiges of her professional persona and became fully and completely the sister who'd always adored him. She put her arms around him and gave him a hug.

"That's up to you, Carter. You'll know it when you see it. I'm sure you will. And then—" she reached up to pat his cheek "—you'll go wherever the spirit leads you. And when you get there, you'll realize what you need."

Chapter One

Boone's Corner, Vermont?

God help him, yes. That was what the sign said, and he'd been here before so he knew it was true.

But he hadn't been here to stay before. Never that. Two or three days over Thanksgiving. An evening's visit with Jack and Frances on his way to Killington. That weekend last January when they'd all come up for Jason's baptism. A couple of days this past August when he and Jack played hooky and came up to go fishing.

Short, restorative visits.

Visits that—however short—had always seemed plenty long. Unlike this one—two weeks—which promised to make eternal rest seem like a two-hour nap.

Why in heaven's name had he said he'd come?

Frances hadn't expected him to. She'd simply mentioned the problem last week as they sat on the grass in Central Park, munching corn chips, playing with Jason and watching Jack play softball.

"Cripes, you'd think it was the Series," Carter had said, watching as Jack slid headfirst into second base.

"With Jack it might as well be." Frances looked at her husband with an indulgent smile. "My husband the competitor. He's not happy that he'll miss the play-offs."

Carter raised a brow. "Where's he off to this time? I thought he was sticking pretty close to home."

He damned well would be if he were Jack. When Jack had married Frances almost two years before, Carter had thought his friend was losing his mind. As a much-sought-after, highly paid model, Jack frequently found himself in exotic parts of the globe propping up some of the world's most beautiful women.

"Nice work if you can get it," Carter had often griped. And at the time he couldn't see giving that sort of life up for anyone or anything.

Now he wasn't sure.

He found himself waking up at night, staring at the ceiling, tossing and turning in his wide lonely bed and, by this time, he'd given up wondering what luscious young woman he could call to share it with him. Now he got up and prowled around, working crosswords and playing solitaire, then picking out songs on the battered old guitar he hadn't touched since his college days. And the songs he remembered…all those lost love, hit-the-road-again, life-is-passing-me-by songs.

"*He's* not going anywhere. *We* are going up to Vermont next week," Frances was saying. "We're having a new roof put on the house."

"You're moving?" Carter felt a moment's panic at her words. Jack and Frances were his best friends. While he didn't see them as often as he once had, sometimes didn't even talk to them for a week or two, he always knew they were six blocks away. Like the Chrysler Building or the Statue of Liberty, they were a part of the landscape that he knew he could count on.

If they left…

"Not immediately," Frances said, brushing her long hair out of her face. "But we're talking about it. Jack won't be modeling forever, you know, and we would rather raise Jason in the country.'' She gave her son, busily chewing her purse strap, a fond smile. ''In any case, we need a new roof. The old one leaks. And with winter coming, we need to get it on soon. It practically took an act of God to get Benton Brothers to fit us in, and then it turned out to be during Jack's play-offs. I said I'd go alone to oversee, but he says that wouldn't be fair, that I won't be able to get enough writing done if I'm the only one taking care of Jason.''

''I'll go.''

Frances blinked, then laughed. ''With me? Somehow I don't think even Jack is that generous.''

''Not with you,'' Carter said. ''Though,'' he added with a grin, ''if I thought he would...'' He waggled his eyebrows at her and relished his ability to make her blush. ''I meant I'll go for you.''

Frances just looked at him.

''Why not? I could use a vacation. My sister's been telling me I need one. A change of perspective, she said.''

Frances's gaze narrowed. She cocked her head, looking at him. The directness of her gaze unnerved him.

He shifted uncomfortably, then looked away, reaching out to snag Jason up into his arms and nuzzle the little boy's soft dark hair.

Frances clicked her tongue. ''Ah, Carter,'' she chided gently, ''you're such a soft touch.''

''So what do you think?'' he asked her, his tone gruff. He slanted her a glance.

''That you need one of your own.''

''One what? House in Vermont?''

''No. Child.'' Frances's eyes were gentle as she smiled at him.

"Yeah, sure. But last time I checked Bloomingdale's, they were all out."

Frances punched his arm.

"Ow." Carter rubbed his arm and did his best imitation of a pout.

Frances laughed. "Poor Carter."

He scowled at her. He didn't want her pity, and as far as he could see, that's exactly what it was.

Her smile faded slowly and she cocked her head. "You mean it, don't you? About going to Vermont?"

It was a perfect chance to back out, to say he'd been kidding, that of course he didn't want to spend half of October moldering away in backwoods New England.

But Milly's advice kept echoing in his ears. "You need to sort out your life, find out what's missing. You'll know it when you see it."

Boone's Corner, Vermont, sounded as good a place as any to start.

But now, turning into Frances's lane and looking around at the steeply wooded hills, the narrow roads, recalling the town he'd cruised through in ninety seconds flat just ten minutes ago, Carter wasn't so sure.

He was a city boy, for heaven's sake. He'd been raised right smack in the middle of one of the biggest in the world.

And while there was no doubt that he was plenty savvy when it came to New York street smarts, in thirty-six years his entire experience with the wilderness could be summed up in six weeks at summer camp when he was ten, a dozen or so fishing expeditions mostly in his parents' New Jersey backyard, a score of ski trips where the self-service lodge dining room was as close as he'd come to roughing it, and six years in Berkeley, California, which, if it wasn't precisely rural, certainly had a wildness all its own.

"You'll be fine," Frances had assured him when he'd expressed second thoughts yesterday morning. "We have hot-and-cold running water, indoor plumbing, windows, doors. All of life's necessities—except a new roof."

But as far as Carter could see now, there wasn't a Chinese takeout or a barbecue joint for miles, nobody named Ray sold pizza and, if he wasn't mistaken, that was a goat munching grass in the middle of Frances's lane.

He shut his eyes, then opened them again in the hope that he had been hallucinating.

The goat regarded him indifferently, then went back to munching.

Carter leaned his forearms on the steering wheel and considered his options.

He could hit the goat, drive around the goat or turn tail and head back from whence he'd come. There was always the chance that the goat would move, of course, but Carter didn't put much faith in that. He sighed and stretched, trying to ease the kinks from the five-hour drive, trying to give the goat the opportunity to move.

The goat ignored him.

Frances hadn't mentioned goats. While he knew that she used to have some before her marriage, he'd assumed they were gone. After all, she and Jack spent most of their time these days in New York. Surely the goats couldn't run things by themselves.

If they could, they could have supervised the installation of the new roof.

The goat took a step, then bent its head again and continued cropping. Carter sighed, then tapped the horn. The goat lifted its head, looked at him once briefly, then went on with its meal.

Carter knew dogs. He knew cats. He'd even had a

guinea pig once. But goats were a mystery. One he didn't really want to solve.

"If you need anything, and I mean anything at all," Frances had told him when he was leaving, "call Annabel."

Her friend, she meant. Annabel Archer she meant. The Quintessential Earth Mother Of The Western World, she meant.

Purposeful, no-nonsense Annabel, who could wither grown men with a stare—and did—would doubtless know exactly how to deal with a goat.

Carter was damned if he was going to ask her.

He would have to see her later this afternoon to deliver Frances's birthday greetings, but that was it.

Carter edged the car forward. This time the goat didn't even look up.

Carter sighed, stopped, opened the door, got out and leaned against the side of the car.

The goat munched on. It was brown and white and spindly legged, with two curving horns that made it look almost top-heavy when it lifted its head. When *he* lifted *his* head, Carter corrected himself. There was no doubt from this distance about the sex of the animal.

He straightened, narrowed his eyes and began to walk toward the goat.

"Get out of the road," he said.

"Shoo," he said.

"Go on. Get out of here before I nail your rear with the toe of my boot," he said.

The goat must have thought Carter was a soft touch, too. He didn't move anything except his eyes, which watched Carter ever more warily the closer he came.

Carter cleared his throat. "Listen, Billy, you—"

But he got no further. The goat abruptly lifted his head, stiffened, then plunged forward, hurtling straight at him.

One minute Carter was standing in the lane, the next he was flat on his back in the dust.

"Wha' the—" He spat out a mouthful of good Vermont gravel and grimaced. It was a change in perspective, all right.

He hauled himself to his feet. The goat uttered a sound somewhere between a belch and a chuckle, ambled on down the lane and went back to his meal.

"Welcome to Vermont," Carter muttered.

He brushed off the seat of his jeans and examined the torn elbow of his shirt. It was going to be a long two weeks, he thought.

But at least the goat was standing on the verge now. The lane was empty. Carter decided he'd take his victories wherever he could find them.

FOR HER THIRTY-SIXTH birthday Annabel Archer was baking herself a cake.

She hummed to herself as she did it, crushing the allspice and grinding the nutmeg and cinnamon, then sifting them into the flour with the old hand-crank sifter she'd got at the auction in Old Man Milliken's barn last January.

In the background, on the tape her children didn't know she had, a nasal masculine twang carried on about being done wrong by and surviving.

Annabel mouthed the lyrics along with the twang. She knew them by heart, though her children thought she listened to nothing less exalted than Bach—J.S., J.C., C.P.E. and, at her most lowbrow, P.D.Q.

Libby and Leif would drop over dead if they knew their mother spent stolen moments with Waylon, Willie and their ilk. But there was something supremely self-indulgent about the whine of a steel guitar no matter whose voice accompanied it, and anyway, it was her birthday. She had a right to listen to whatever she wanted. Besides, when it came to being done wrong by and surviving, Annabel was an expert.

She added the eggs one by one, stopping between each to do a snappy soft-shoe shuffle between the table and the sink. She wondered how many other women could do it as credibly as she could in a pair of earth shoes.

Libby would have rolled her eyes and groaned, "Oh, Mom," if she'd seen it. As far as seventeen-year-old Libby was concerned, her mother could be a great source of embarrassment these days.

Life with teenagers wasn't what everyone had ever predicted that it would be. It was worse.

Not that Annabel didn't enjoy Libby and Leif. They were, despite their ages and their current despair of her, the light of her life. But sometimes it seemed as if overnight they had turned from steady, reliable sixty-watt beams into psychedelic flashing neon.

"I'm getting old," she said to the cat. "Aging, like a fine wine."

The cat smirked.

Annabel tweaked his ear. "Or a moldy fruitcake. I know. I know."

She and the cat, a formerly stray Maine Coon that Leif had found huddled in Frances's barn and had dragged home and named Goliath—which suited him—often had conversations like this. He was the only one who didn't argue with her anymore.

She picked him up and danced him around the room. He let out a moan of long-suffering protest, but he didn't struggle until the phone rang. Then he practically leapt out of her arms onto the counter where he stalked behind the mixing bowls and sat down to regard her with offended dignity.

Annabel shook her head at him. "I suppose you think you were saved by the bell," she chided as she reached for the phone. "Hello?"

"I bet you thought we forgot."

"Frances!" Annabel's face broke into a grin and she pushed a strand of hair out of her face. "No, I know you better than that. You wouldn't have the decency to let me grow old without reminding me."

"You're not old."

"Tell that to Libby."

Frances snorted. "What does Libby know? She's a mere child."

It was Annabel's turn to snort. "You haven't seen her in a while, then. You'll get a rude awakening when you do. I thought you'd be here by now. Aren't Bentons doing the roof this week?"

"They are. But we're not coming."

"Well, I can't say I won't miss seeing you, but I'll keep an eye on things."

"Not necessary. Carter's on his way."

The world seemed suddenly to tilt.

"Carter? Carter MacKenzie?" Annabel couldn't quite hide the disbelief in her voice. She hoped she did a better job with the dismay. "You're kidding."

"Not a bit."

"He wouldn't come up here. Not voluntarily. What'd you do, doctor his martinis?" There was no other way Annabel could imagine a clever, smart-ass big-city boy like Carter MacKenzie agreeing to spend two days, much less two weeks, in the wilds of Vermont.

"He said he wanted a vacation."

"He's run out of Club Meds?"

"I think he wants a different sort of vacation this time."

Annabel doubted that.

"Why is it I get the feeling you don't like Carter?" Frances teased.

"Use your imagination," Annabel said gruffly. "He has all the depth of a mirror and all the sincerity of a used-car salesman."

Frances laughed. "He's not that bad."

Annabel made a doubtful noise.

"Truly," Frances said. "I don't know of a better friend. He's loyal and kind and he thinks Jason is the cat's meow."

"Jason is the cat's meow," Annabel said. "It doesn't take much insight to see that."

"You're just prejudiced. Really, Annabel, give him a chance."

"I probably won't even see him."

"He's delivering your birthday present."

Frances was famous for her gifts. She always put such thought into them. Annabel supposed it was because Frances was a writer that she had such a gift for empathy. But her presents were always so clever and apt that Annabel often wondered what she was revealing to her perceptive friend.

Last year, for example, Frances and Jack had simply moved in for the weekend, pressing into her hand a plane ticket to New York, the key to their apartment and an envelope full of tickets to the best New York shows. Annabel had protested.

"It's too much. I don't need this," she'd said, even as they'd bundled her onto the plane that night.

"You do," Frances had said implacably. "More than you'll ever know."

And Annabel, coming back five days later revived and

refreshed, had admitted that Frances was right. "It was sort of fun really," she'd allowed, which didn't begin to cover how much she'd enjoyed the solitary bliss and cultural immersion they'd provided for her.

Frances didn't say, I told you so.

"You're sending my birthday present with Carter?" Annabel didn't know if she liked that. "What is it?"

"You'll see."

"You got them to put me on the cover of your latest book?" Annabel teased. Frances wrote historical romances, which Annabel only read because her best friend wrote them. It was a bone of contention between them. "It doesn't hurt to dream," Frances would say. But Annabel didn't agree. "I don't need dreams," she would reply. "I like my reality just fine."

"Whoops, gotta run," Frances said now. "I promised Jack I'd meet him for a quick bite before his game and Jason's still sleeping. Talk to you later." And she was gone.

Annabel stood with the receiver against her ear for another half a minute before she slowly set it down again. What would it be this time?

Something discreet, she hoped. The last person she wanted sharing in her birthday surprise was Carter MacKenzie.

She'd spent only a few hours in his company. They were more than enough. He was everything she'd told Frances he was, plus he had the charm of a toad.

How, she'd asked Frances more than once, could a man own and run a health-food store when he spent most of his waking hours eating junk food?

"He strives for balance in his life," Frances had told her, grinning.

Balance? Annabel doubted he knew the meaning of the word.

He certainly went to excess when it came to women. Every time Annabel had seen him, it had been in the company of a different one. All of them beautiful.

"I suppose he strives for variety, too," she'd groused.

"His time will come," Frances had said confidently during the summer. "He's ready for it to happen. I really thought it had with Diane."

Annabel had only met Diane Granatelli née Bauer once, at Thanksgiving a year ago. She didn't know her well, but what she did know, she liked. Diane was the one woman she'd seen Carter with who seemed to have a brain in her head.

She wasn't at all surprised when Diane married someone else. She told Frances so.

Frances had clucked her disapproval and said that Annabel didn't understand him. Annabel was willing to concede that. She had no desire to, either.

She finished stirring the cake and popped it into the oven, then sat down at the table and began to poke cloves into the first of a half a dozen oranges.

Every pomander she made now would buy one shingle when she resided her house next summer. That was a lot of pomanders, granted, but she had wreaths and dried flower arrangements and herbal teas to sell to make up the difference, and anyway, equating pomanders with shingles was an incentive. It made what seemed an impossible task possible. Annabel had learned long ago to take things one step at a time.

It would be an hour before Leif got home from school, and Libby wouldn't breeze in until six because of cheerleading practice. She could at least finish this one before things got too hectic.

The doorbell rang. She grimaced, then sighed and jabbed one last clove into the orange, then went to answer the door.

It was Carter, all right. But after that, all bets were off.

Certainly he wasn't standing there looking lean and clean and sexy with his usual cocky grin on his face. On the contrary, he was dirty, disheveled and grim.

"Is that your goat?"

Annabel blinked, then looked in the direction in which he'd jerked his head.

There in the lane beyond the grassy yard, tethered to the bumper of his car, was a reluctant, defiant, noticeably irritable goat. Not just any goat, either.

"Arnold!"

"Ah." Now she caught a glimpse of his smile, albeit the sardonic one. "You do know him." The smile twisted. "Somehow I thought you might."

"Where did you get him? Why do you have him tied onto your car? What have you done to him?" Annabel's voice rose as she pushed past him and hurried down the steps into the yard.

"What have *I* done to *him?*" Carter was following her, breathing down her neck. "That goat damned near killed me! First he blocked the lane, then he mowed me down, then he ran in front of the car and I practically squashed him. Then he followed me all the way to Frances's house. He got up on the porch and wouldn't let me in the damned door!"

Annabel would have liked to have seen that. She smothered a smile as she realized the reason behind Carter's dusty jeans and torn shirt, the smudge of dirt on his cheek and the glint of fire in his eyes.

"He thinks he's a guard goat."

Carter's eyes narrowed as if he thought she might be

making fun of him. Annabel tried to look demure. She couldn't recall the last time she'd managed it—probably twenty-five years at least.

"Well, keep him tied up from now on," he said gruffly. "If I get him in my sights again, I won't think twice about flattening him."

At that Annabel did laugh. "You? The same man who wouldn't eat the turkey last Thanksgiving because he saw it beforehand still wearing feathers?"

Carter scowled. "I'm not planning on eating your damned goat."

"And a good thing, too," Annabel said fiercely. "Come on, Arnie." She reached for the rope and began untying it. "Let's get you settled."

She led him around the back of the house toward the small hillside pasture where he belonged, making a mental note to tell Leif to latch the gate—at least for the next two weeks.

Arnie was used to running free between her house and Frances's, and he didn't bother people he knew. But he was particular about strangers, and Annabel didn't want him being the excuse for Carter MacKenzie landing on her doorstep time and time again.

She shut the gate with a flourish and latched it carefully, then turned and gave Carter a smile. "There. Satisfied?"

He looked from her to the goat, then back again. It was pretty clear to Annabel that he didn't have a much higher opinion of her than of the goat. He grunted and turned back toward his car.

Annabel followed him, wanting to get her birthday present. "Frances says you're staying for a couple of weeks," she said politely, more because she knew Frances would expect it of her than because she wanted to make conversation.

''Just while they get the new roof.'' Carter sounded irritable and put-upon, and Annabel wondered again why he'd allowed Frances to talk him into coming in the first place. He headed straight for his car and opened the door, starting to get in.

''Wait!''

Carter turned. ''Wait?''

Annabel's mouth opened and closed. She felt like an idiot. ''A-aren't...aren't you...forgetting something?''

Where's my birthday present? she wanted to say, and felt like a veritable child for wanting to say it.

She wouldn't care about it if it weren't from Frances. Who got excited about receiving a dog-eared copy of *1001 Knock-Knock Jokes* or the fuzzy yellow sweater in the window at Beecham's that was, coincidentally, also just Libby's size?

But Frances never gave those sorts of gifts. Hers were special. Knowing. Aimed directly at the woman Annabel was. They came with full forethought and no strings attached.

''Forgetting?'' Carter's brows were pulling together.

Annabel's fingers knotted into fists. ''Frances said...er, you were...er, bringing my...birthday gift?''

Carter scowled. ''She told you?'' He sounded horrified.

Annabel drew herself up stiffly. ''Well, I don't see that it's any skin off your nose,'' she said irritably. ''She only asked you to bring it, didn't she?''

The look he gave her was wary. Finally he shrugged and took the two long strides that covered the distance between them.

''She said to give you this,'' he muttered and, taking her by the shoulders, he pulled her close and brought his mouth down over hers.

"YOU DID *WHAT?*" Jack Neillands stared at his wife in amazement.

Frances shrugged equably. "Told him to give her a kiss."

"Carter? Kiss Annabel?" Jack started to laugh.

"What's wrong with that?"

"Mother Earth and the Big Bad Wolf?"

Frances looked affronted. "A lot you know. They're perfect for each other."

Jack just looked at her, stupefied. "You're out of your mind."

"Marriage has gone to my head," Frances agreed, putting her arms around him. "I want everyone to be as happy as we are."

Jack kissed her. It was a long, lingering kiss, but when he looked up, he was shaking his head. "Yeah, sure. But Carter and Annabel? This isn't one of your books, you know."

"I know," Frances said serenely.

Jack cocked his head and looked at her. "Come on, Fran. What did you really give Annabel for her birthday?"

Frances smiled. "She'll know."

Chapter Two

She knew. She was aghast. No, that was too mild. She was fuming. Furious. Frantic.

She was punching out Frances's phone number almost before Carter had driven down the hill and turned off the lane onto the highway.

Frances wasn't home.

Annabel banged the phone down, made a tiny sound of suppressed rage and flung herself about the kitchen, practically caroming off the walls.

Damn Frances anyway! How dared she? And Carter! Heavens above, why, of all men, Carter?

A kiss was bad enough. She could still, even now, feel the hard, warm touch of his lips on hers! But it wasn't just the kiss, and Annabel knew it.

It had to do with Frances's last book, with a kiss her hero had given her heroine—the kiss that awakened her to love. And Annabel had rolled her eyes.

"Spare me," she'd said.

But Frances had simply laughed at her. "It happens."

"Sure." Annabel had scoffed. "Like it happened to you."

"Well, no. It took Jack a bit longer to convince me. But that doesn't mean it can't happen."

Annabel had shaken her head. ''I'll believe it when I see it.''

And now Frances had sent Carter to kiss her! To fall in love with her? And she with him?

And how did she think it was going to happen? Like magic?

Oh, damn Frances anyway.

The door banged. ''Hi, Mom!'' Leif tossed his backpack onto one of the chairs, sniffed the air, then beamed. ''Cool. Birthday cake. What kind?''

''Hmm? Oh, spice.'' Annabel ran a hand through her hair, knocking out the pins distractedly.

''When can we have some? Can I have the bowl when you make the frosting? I got a B on my math test and Mrs. Street says I do too understand ratios, but I don't think so. How come Arnie was in the pasture? I let him out.''

Used to this sort of after-school conversational barrage, Annabel let Leif's questions and comments flow over her in a wave, none of them penetrating except the last.

''You what?'' she yelped. ''You let him out? Oh, hell.'' She went flying toward the door, leaving Leif staring after her.

''What's wrong?''

''MacKenzie,'' Annabel threw over her shoulder. That was what was wrong. In spades.

Damn it, where was that goat? Her eyes darted back and forth, taking in the empty pasture, the small barn and shed, the ominously silent garden. Where on earth had he gone?

Where did he always go? she asked herself with resignation.

Her shoulders slumped. Arnie, like all males, was a victim of his hormones. Where else would he go but where he could find a bit of female goat companionship? To Frances's. She shut her eyes.

"What's goin' on, Mom?" Leif wanted to know. He was practically running to keep up with her.

"That miserable Carter MacKenzie is staying at Frances's until the roof is on," she told him, even as she headed out through the woods toward Frances's place. "He had a run-in with Arnold earlier today." And if he had another one, he'd be back.

"Carter? Here? Really?" Leif was clearly delighted. There was nothing miserable about Carter as far as he was concerned.

Annabel shot him a baleful, over-the-shoulder glance. "He said he'd flatten Arnold if he got in his way again."

"Naw, he wouldn't do that," Leif said with the same assurance she'd felt. "Carter's a good guy."

Annabel's lip curled into a snarl. "Fine," she said. "If you think so, you go get him back."

"Sure." Leif gave an equable shrug and headed off toward the trail that led over the hill to Frances's house. "No problem."

Annabel watched him go, shaking her head. No problem? That's what he thought.

What on earth had Frances told Carter besides that he should give her a kiss?

Had she confided in him? Surely not.

Carter would no more allow himself to be a target of Frances's misguided matchmaking—especially with Annabel Archer—than she would.

And there was no doubt in Annabel's mind that matchmaking was what Frances intended.

And Annabel, in her naiveté, had actually asked for it!

"Where's my birthday present?" she'd asked him. She wanted to sink through the floor at the very thought. She was glad Leif was home to go get Arnold. The last thing she wanted today was another encounter with Carter MacKenzie. Though she didn't see how another could possibly be worse than the last one!

She watched Leif disappear over the top of the hill, then turned and went back into the house. Leaning against the door, she pressed her fist against her lips, trying to forget the feel of Carter's lips.

This was her haven, the two-story log house with wide plank floors and tiny-paned windows that she and Mark had found all those years ago—the abandoned building, which she had made into a home with hand-hooked rugs and homemade pottery and loads and loads of love.

It had seen her work and seen her play, seen her laugh and seen her cry. But always she had loved it, always she had felt warm and safe here, protected against the vicissitudes of a capricious world.

Now, with the tingle of Carter's lips still vivid in her mind, suddenly it didn't feel quite so safe at all.

THE GOAT WAS BACK.

Carter, about to go outside again and get into the car to head into Boone's Corner for groceries, took one look and stopped dead in the doorway.

There was no way he was going out to tangle with that cloven-footed ruffian again today. When he'd taken it back to Annabel, he'd glossed over his experiences with it.

He hadn't mentioned the way it had flattened him twice, the way it had followed him up on the porch, nosing its way in while he was unloading the car, how he'd gone upstairs and come back down to find it in the kitchen, how he'd had the devil's own time getting it out.

He'd never told her it had stood on the porch and butted its head against the front door so hard he'd finally had to come out and chase it through the woods to capture it. And he certainly hadn't mentioned the way it had nailed him in the rear end the minute he turned his back on it even after he'd tied it to the bumper of his car.

He wasn't about to admit any of that—especially to Annabel Archer.

It was bad enough he'd had to kiss her.

Ordinarily Carter liked kissing women. In his top ten favorite things to do, it was right up there in the top two. But not, for heaven's sake, Annabel Archer!

She'd made him feel like some gawky schoolboy who, on a dare, had allowed himself to be talked into stealing a kiss from the disapproving spinster teacher.

He rubbed a hand across his mouth, wishing he could forget the touch of his lips on hers. Her mouth had been surprisingly soft. Her lips had been slightly parted, from surprise, not encouragement, but still he'd felt a split second's temptation to slip his tongue between them.

And get it bit off, no doubt.

He was lucky to have escaped with his life. What on earth could Frances have been thinking of? Of all the women she could have asked him to kiss…!

And what in the hell sort of birthday present was that? Or was it just a joke? Probably her real gift was in the mail.

It must be living with Jack that was making Frances so feisty, he thought grimly. She had to know that he and Annabel Archer were like fire and ice. The less they had to do with each other, the better.

But Annabel was not his immediate problem. He raked a hand through his hair and contemplated the goat. Arnold.

Who in their right mind would name a goat Arnold? Mephistopheles, more like. Or Satan.

Perhaps Annabel Archer was a witch and Arnold was her familiar.

Never a violent man, Carter found himself wishing for a shotgun now. How the hell was he going to get out to his car and get groceries with that damned goat patrolling the place?

"Arrrr-neeee!"

Carter's head jerked up, his eyes flicking away from the goat toward the wooded hillside. He spied a small figure wearing jeans and a lumberjack shirt trotting down the trail.

"Arrrr-neeee!"

He grinned. A savior. And by the grace of God, not Annabel, either.

He waved at the boy loping down the trail toward him. "He's here, Leif," he shouted from the doorway. "I've got him."

A small exaggeration and perfectly excusable under the circumstances, Carter decided. He gave another wave and walked out onto the porch.

Arnold lifted his head and met Carter's gaze straight on.

"Arnie!" Leif admonished, skidding to a stop next to the goat.

"Watch out," Carter warned.

"Don't worry," Leif said, looping a lead around the goat's neck and giving him a hug. "It's all right. Arnie wouldn't hurt a flea."

Carter opened his mouth, but no sound came out. Arnie? Harmless? Impossible.

But wasn't that Arnold, right this very minute, nuzzling Leif's cheek, rubbing his head against Leif's hair?

Carter tucked his hands into the back pockets of his jeans, wincing against the bruises his palms touched. Arnold nibbled playfully at Leif's ear. Leif rubbed noses with him, then looked over at Carter and flashed him a grin.

"Ma said you were gonna flatten him if you found him loose again. But you didn't. I knew you wouldn't. You wouldn't ever do that, would you, Carter?"

Carter's fingers, still in his pockets, crossed. "Er, no. Of course not." It wasn't precisely a lie. He probably couldn't flatten Arnold if he tried. He didn't say he wouldn't try.

Leif beamed. "I didn't think so. Ma exaggerates," he confided and gave Arnold another hug.

"Mmm."

"But if you really don't want him around, I guess we can put him in the pasture." Leif looked at Carter hopefully.

Carter, uncurling his fingers and easing them out of his pockets, winced again. "I kind of think you ought to," he ventured. "I'm not used to goats being on the road, you see. I might...accidentally...run over him. Or something."

Leif looked suddenly worried. "I guess we should, then, huh? Till you're gone, I mean."

Carter's smile was one of profound relief. "I'd appreciate it. I'd hate to be the one to do old Arnold in."

"You wouldn't," Leif said confidently. "How long you gonna be here?"

"Till the roof is on. A couple of weeks, I guess."

"Swell. You wanta come to the spaghetti supper at school next Friday?"

"I—"

"It's a good cause. We're supporting the swim team. Me an' Libby aren't on it, but Mom says if you live in a small community, you gotta do these things. Besides, it's sorta fun."

"Well, I—"

"Tickets are only four dollars. How many times can you get a good meal with seconds for only four dollars?"

Carter gave Leif a sidelong look. He looked for all the world like Oliver Twist hopefully holding out an empty gruel bowl. "You aren't by chance getting a cut from each ticket you sell, are you?"

"Me?" Leif looked momentarily guilty, then grinned unrepentantly. "No. Not unless you count that whoever sells the most gets two tickets to the last Red Sox game of the season."

"Ah. In that case, I don't see how I can refuse."

"Me, neither," Leif said cheerfully. He fished in his pocket and came up with a slightly crumpled sheaf of tickets. He peeled off one. "I don't suppose you'd like to take a date?"

"Who? Arnold?"

Leif shrugged. "I dunno. Ma, maybe?"

Carter's stomach gave a lurch. "I don't think—"

"Naw. You can't take her," Leif said. "She's already got a ticket. Besides, she's going with Aaron."

Carter frowned. "Who's Aaron?"

"He's a friend. He's the county ag agent."

"Ag?"

"Agricultural." Leif enunciated the word carefully, as if Carter might never have heard it before. "Jack calls him the sheep-shit expert."

Carter grinned. Now he remembered where he'd heard the name before. Aaron had once, in Jack's estimation, been a contender for Frances's affections. Clearly, even having won, Jack wasn't being a gracious winner.

Carter was prepared to be, especially if it meant he didn't have to squire Annabel Archer to a spaghetti supper. He took out his wallet to pay Leif the four dollars, but that meant getting within butting distance of Arnold. Halfway down the steps he stopped.

"It's okay," Leif said. "I won't let him hurt you."

"I thought you said he wouldn't hurt a flea," Carter reminded him darkly.

"He wouldn't. But he has opinions, y'know." Leif tugged hard on the rope, pulling a reluctant Arnold back as Carter came forward warily. "An' sometimes he doesn't have good ones."

"Neither do I," Carter said sourly. He held out the money, took the ticket and backed away.

"Thanks. Don't go. Let Arnie get to know you."

Carter gave Leif a skeptical look.

The boy shrugged disingenuously. "How's he gonna learn to like you if you run every time you get close to him?"

"I wasn't running," Carter said somewhat stiffly.

"I know that," Leif said quickly. "But don'tcha want to make friends with him?"

Making friends with a goat was not high on Carter's list of priorities, but if it would allow him free passage to and from his car, there was perhaps something to be said for it. He took a cautious step forward.

Arnold lunged.

"Hey!" Leif, goggle-eyed, hauled back on the rope with all his strength. "Cool it, Arnie. Hey, old fella. Be nice."

Nice? Carter felt a sardonic laugh coming on. "Maybe we should forget it."

But Leif shook his head. "Naw. I got him now. Stick out your hand and let him get to know you."

With about as much enthusiasm as he had mustered when he'd had to kiss Annabel, Carter held out his hand.

Arnold stared at him suspiciously.

"You oughta give him a treat. You got anything to eat on you?"

Carter shook his head.

"In the house?"

"I was just going to go for groceries when you came."

Leif lifted his shoulders. "Ah, well, maybe he'll like your shirt cuff or something."

Carter hoped not. He wouldn't have been surprised, though. Arnold was still watching him warily. The feeling, Carter could have told him, was mutual.

"Go on," Leif urged the goat. "Give him a nibble, Arnie."

Carter's teeth came together gently but firmly. He held his breath. Shut his eyes. Waited.

All at once there was a cold, wet slurp, a tiny nip. His eyes flew open.

"See! I told you! He likes you! I knew he'd like you!" Leif hugged Arnold. "Do it again!"

Carter wiped his hand on the seat of his jeans. "Let's don't overdo it, huh? Give him time."

Leif sighed. "Yeah. I guess you're right." He gave the goat another enthusiastic hug. "Good boy, Arnie," he praised.

"Good boy," Carter echoed faintly, then began to move toward his car. "See you later. I've got to get some groceries now."

"You can eat with us."

"No!"

Leif's eyes widened at the force of Carter's tone.

"I mean, no, I wouldn't want to put you to any trouble."

"It's no trouble," Leif said magnanimously.

"You aren't cooking the dinner. Are you?"

''No, Ma is. But she's always inviting people. The more the merrier, she always says.''

''I don't think she means me. Your mother and I...'' How, Carter wondered, could he explain the more or less instant antipathy he and Annabel Archer had obviously felt?

''It's her birthday. She made a cake, and...''

''*She* made a cake? She made her own birthday cake?'' Even for Annabel Archer that seemed somehow unfair.

Leif shrugged. ''She makes better cakes than Libby 'n' me. I made her a paper-towel holder in shop class. Solid walnut.''

''A paper-towel holder?''

''It was that or a three-legged stool.''

''You made the better choice.''

''I thought so. Anyway, she'd want you to come. If I tell her I invited you and you refused, her feelings will be hurt. And if you're worried, 'cause there might not be enough, don't. There's plenty. Ma's cooking Chinese. Chicken Almond Yuck or something. Come on, Carter. What do you say?''

He wasn't going to get away with saying no; he knew that much. He also knew Annabel wasn't going to be any more thrilled than he was that he was coming to her birthday dinner. He sighed.

''I'll even put Arnold in the pasture till you go back home.''

A corner of Carter's mouth quirked. ''Is that your final offer?''

Leif considered for a moment. ''You can have my fortune cookie. We eat at six. Libby's home from practice by then. You'll come.''

It wasn't a question. They both knew he would.

"*DINNER?* You invited him to *dinner*?"

"Don't yell, Ma. I only did what you're always doing—taking pity on the poor and homeless...."

"Carter MacKenzie is neither poor, nor homeless. Far from it!" Annabel was still yelling, even though she was making a distinct effort not to.

It was true, what Leif was saying: she did drag home strays for dinner; she did exhort her children to care for the less fortunate; she did stress neighborliness and helpfulness as admirable virtues.

But Carter MacKenzie? Coming to dinner? On her *birthday?*

"Very funny, Frances," she muttered, turning away. What sort of direct line to God did Frances have that she could pull such strings? Annabel gritted her teeth.

"What?" Leif asked. Cherubic, solemn eyes followed her.

"Nothing." Annabel opened the silverware drawer with a crash. "You'd better add another place setting then," she said with bad grace.

"Okay." Leif gathered up chopsticks and a plate, then frowned at the table already set for three. "What about Ernie and Bert and Eb? Aren't they coming?"

Ernie and Bert were really Sisters Ernestine and Bertha, the remnant congregation of a once-thriving convent whose nonretired members had gone off to save souls in more populous areas. Bert and Ernie had, with a little help from Jack and the Holy Spirit, turned the convent into one of the most sought after bed-and-breakfast establishments in all Vermont.

It was a rare birthday that they didn't help celebrate. And the same was true of Ebenezer Toot, owner of Boone's Corner's general store.

"Bert and Ernie have a houseful of stressed-out businessmen. And Eb had a root canal this morning. He says he may never eat again.'' Annabel was feeling much the same way, and it had nothing at all to do with root canals.

Leif dug his toe into the braid of the rug. ''I s'pose I could go back an' tell him not to come.''

Oh, right, Annabel thought, *and have him think I'm an even bigger witch than he already does.* She sighed and raked her fingers through her hair. ''No. That's all right. I was just…unprepared, that's all.''

''How come you don't like Carter?''

''It isn't that I don't like him,'' Annabel began, then remembered that besides exhorting them to feed the less fortunate and doing so herself, she also exhorted them not to lie. ''Well, you're right, I don't like him,'' she admitted. ''He…makes me uncomfortable.''

Leif cocked his head. ''Why?''

How to explain that without going into things she had no intention of going into tonight or any other time? ''He's…unpredictable.''

From the very first moment she'd seen him, she'd been wrong about him. It was exactly what she'd told Frances—she didn't understand Carter MacKenzie, could never get a handle on how he would behave.

Most men were an open book to her. There were the strong, silent types. The tough, macho types, the bookish, earnest types, the devil-may-care types. There were even, few and far between, the to-die-for romantic-hero types like Jack.

And there was Carter MacKenzie.

She'd never met a man she couldn't pigeonhole. Until him. Cocky. Calm. Quiet. Quick. Cool. Charming. He had more applicable adjectives than the minister's cat, and all of them contradictory.

And sometimes he looked at her as if…

No. She shook her head firmly. He couldn't remember.

She barely remembered herself. It was years ago. Aeons. Another lifetime. They had been other people then. At least, *she* had been.

About Carter she wasn't sure.

Deliberately Annabel sighed. "Never mind. Everything will be fine," she said when Leif still looked worried. "I'm just fussing. Mothers do."

"Not you," Leif said.

"Perhaps I'll start."

"No." Leif shook his head.

"Thanks for the vote of confidence."

Leif wrinkled his nose. "What's that?"

She smiled and ruffled his hair. "Your faith in me. Come on." She opened the refrigerator. "If we're going to have company, I'm going to need some help. You can slice the mushrooms."

IT'S ONLY DINNER, Annabel thought as six o'clock arrived and with it, Carter. How difficult could it be?

She'd forgotten about Murphy's Law. And Libby.

If anything that could go wrong, would, in the normal course of events, how much more likely was it to do so if one took an already trying situation and introduced into it one's seventeen-year-old daughter?

Not precisely, Annabel realized almost the moment Libby walked in the door to find Carter leaning against the kitchen counter, a rhetorical question.

If she'd thought the fifteen minutes she'd spent making small talk with Carter before Libby's arrival had been fraught with tension, it was nothing compared to the increase she felt when the door banged open and Libby appeared on the threshold.

"Carter?" It was very nearly a squeal. Libby's normally

flushed cheeks took on an even rosier glow and she flew straight across the room, shedding books and jacket as she went, to fling her arms around him.

Carter, to give him credit, didn't fling his arms around her. But he didn't look displeased at the attention, either. He was grinning as he caught Libby by her upper arms and held her out to look her up and down.

''My God, a woman! You've become a woman.'' His grin grew even wider. ''And what a woman, too.'' There was just the right amount of male appreciation in his tone to make Libby glow.

Annabel's teeth came together with a snap.

''Wash your hands, Liberty,'' she said and returned her daughter's steely glare with one of her own. ''You're late.''

Libby shrugged unapologetically. ''Old Puterbaugh kept us late. If I'd known Carter was going to be here, I'd have skipped practice and come straight home.''

She linked her arm in his and looked up to give him an adoring smile and bat mascara-encrusted lashes at him.

''I thought you wouldn't miss a cheerleading practice for God or the orthodontist,'' Annabel said dryly, recalling a conversation she and Libby had had less than a week before.

Libby gave an airy wave. ''Oh, well, you know…for Carter…''

Annabel rolled her eyes. ''Come on,'' she said before things deteriorated further. ''Let's eat.''

At least, she told herself, she didn't have to worry about keeping the conversational ball rolling. Libby and Leif took care of that, regaling Carter with tales from school, anecdotes about their friends, their follies, their fun. And Carter seemed as willing as she was to sit back and let the kids take the lead.

Did he know what Frances was plotting? she wondered. He couldn't, Annabel was certain. If he had, she doubted whether he would be within ten miles of here.

Poor thing, Annabel thought, then promptly squelched the thought. She wouldn't waste any sympathy on Carter MacKenzie.

She slanted him a wary glance but, perversely, she found that he seemed to be on his best behavior and, in fact, was as wary of her as she was of him.

He focused entirely on the children, barely sparing her a glance throughout the meal.

Why should he? Annabel thought. Watching Libby make a fool of herself would be enough distraction for anyone.

Her daughter had become no less giddy with the serving of the meal. She was clearly enchanted to find Carter there, and obviously eager to throw herself at him.

"Two weeks? You're going to be here two weeks? Super!" Libby clapped her hands. "You can come watch me cheer."

Carter looked less than enthusiastic.

"Libby, I don't think..." Annabel began dampeningly.

But it did no good, for Libby just shot her a disdainful glance. "I don't expect you to come, Mother. I know how you feel. But not everyone hates football."

"I don't hate—"

"Mother *hates* football," Libby confided to Carter, who raised his brows, turned his head and gave Annabel an assessing look.

Annabel met his gaze defiantly, daring him to say something snide. He didn't say a word.

"She thinks it's a secular manifestation of the aims of the military-industrial complex." Libby recited the words as if they were a direct quote. Annabel's fingers tightened on the chopsticks.

"She thinks I should stick myself out here in the weed patch all day, pottering about with sprouts and things, cultivating my own garden." Another apparent quote. Libby sighed and rolled her eyes. "I might as well be dead."

She might soon be, Annabel thought, her fingers itching to wring Libby's slender neck.

It wasn't that what Libby said was so far from the truth. Annabel was not wild about football. She might, once, have even, in a rash moment, equated it with military strategy. It didn't mean she would prefer her views to be expressed in quite those same terms to the man on the street. Or to Carter MacKenzie, damn it.

What Carter thought of her daughter's pronouncements she had no idea. He simply murmured politely at intervals and kept his head bent over his plate. Only occasionally did she catch him glancing her way. Hastily she averted her own gaze.

"Time for fortune cookies," Leif said at last. He passed them out, handing two to Carter. "You get mine."

Carter handed it back. "One fortune's enough for any man."

Libby was already biting into hers. She pulled out the paper and gave a little squeal. "Look what it says! I'm going to get my heart's desire."

"You're gonna marry Tom Cruise?" Leif asked.

She shot him a withering look and turned to Carter. "What does yours say?"

Carter unfolded his. "Same thing."

Leif came and peered over his shoulder, then ripped into his own. "So does mine."

So did Annabel's. She didn't think it was very likely to happen, however, especially since today hadn't been anywhere close to her heart's desire. "I think we just happened on to a very optimistic fortune-cookie company," she said.

Libby looked crestfallen. Leif said, "We got rooked." Carter looked as if he felt about the day much the same way she did.

Annabel prayed it would end quickly.

Libby rattled on even after the meal had ended, but Annabel wasn't even listening now. She stood at the sink, rinsing off the dishes, breathing a sigh of relief.

It was over. Any minute now he'd leave. She looked hopefully toward the door.

"Time for presents and cake," said Leif.

"Presents? Cake?"

He stared at her aghast. "You forgot it was your birthday?"

"When you get to be her age..." Libby said airily.

Annabel made a strangled sound, coloring furiously at the first glint of Carter's amused grin. "Right. Get the dessert plates, Liberty," she said tightly.

Libby did. She also made a production of decking out Annabel's cake with thirty-six candles.

Leif shut off the light and led them in singing "Happy Birthday."

It was an occasion that frequently made Annabel squirm. She had never really enjoyed being the cynosure of everyone's attention, even when everyone was composed of no one other than her children.

But tonight, when the singing also held the sound of Carter's surprisingly true baritone, she felt even more like ducking beneath the tablecloth.

Still, she apparently hadn't been immune to all those years of proper etiquette that her mother had despaired of having had any effect on her. She managed a creditable smile and a slightly raspy "thank you" at the end.

She even managed to blow out the candles in one determined breath, wishing, as she did so, that Frances would get what was coming to her.

"What'd you wish, Ma?" Leif demanded.

Annabel shook her head. "Never mind. It won't come true if I tell you."

"I know what I'd wish," Libby said, batting her lashes and giving Carter a come-on smile that made Annabel's teeth ache.

"Cut the cake, Libby," she said and slapped the knife handle into her daughter's hand.

Libby cut the cake. Leif scooped ice cream onto the top of each piece. Annabel handed a piece to Carter without even looking at him. She had always sensed a certain ironic amusement in his eyes whenever he had seen her and her children in the past. She could just imagine what he must think of them after this evening.

The cake would have been good if she'd been able to taste it. As it was, she choked it down, keeping her eyes on her plate the entire time.

"Time for presents," Leif said the moment they were done with the cake.

Annabel would have protested, but he was already on his way to the closet by the front door. She simply waited, willing herself not to make a fool of herself, when he came back with the small stack of gaily wrapped packages.

"Open this one first," Leif said, thrusting a big rectangular box at her.

Obediently Annabel did and exclaimed with enthusiasm over the dark-stained walnut paper-towel holder she found inside. "It's wonderful," she said, smiling at her son. "Just what I needed."

"I know. Libby made a dumb bookshelf. An' she kept it," he added loftily. "But I knew you'd like this."

"I do." Annabel leaned over quickly and kissed him, and Leif, blushing, ducked his head and shot a quick glance at Carter, then shrugged and kissed her.

Libby rolled her eyes. But seconds later she proffered the next box on the pile. Annabel took it. It wasn't nearly as heavy as Leif's box and when she shook it gently, she heard only a soft rustling sound.

"You know what it is, don't you?" Libby demanded, her eyes alight with excitement.

Annabel shook her head and began to unstick the tape and ease off the paper.

"Rip it, Ma," Leif urged.

But Annabel wouldn't. She took her time removing the paper, then folded it and set it aside before slipping the lid from the box. Inside was a pair of wildly flowered jeans remarkably like the ones that Libby's best friend, Alice, had been wearing recently—the ones Libby had practically swooned over.

"Heavens." Annabel cleared her throat.

"Aren't they great?" Libby's eyes sparkled. "Don'tcha just love them?"

"They're…really something." Annabel took them out and, smiling brightly, held them up against her. "They might," she ventured, "be a tad on the small side."

Libby's face fell. "Do you think so? It was the only size they had left. But if you can't wear an eight…"

Annabel couldn't ever remember wearing an eight. "I'm sure they'll be fine," she told her daughter. "And if they shrink—" she shrugged "—perhaps you can still wear them even if I can't."

"Do you think so?" Libby's eyes shone. She gave her

mother a hug. "Thanks, Mom. But I will take 'em back if you want."

And Annabel, hugging her back, shook her head. "No, Lib. They're fine. Just fine. I love them."

And when Carter gave what for all the world sounded like a muffled snort, she looked over Libby's shoulder and glared at him.

"Come on," Leif said now. "You got one more." He shoved another good-size, lightweight box into her hands.

She frowned at it. "I told Ernie and Bert not to get me anything this year."

"It isn't from Ernie and Bert, Ma," Leif told her. "It's from Carter."

Annabel's head came up with a snap. Her stare collided with Carter's.

"*Carter* brought you a present?" Libby sounded as amazed as Annabel felt. Her gaze traveled from her mother to Carter and back again. She frowned, too.

Annabel shook the box gently, as if too energetic a motion might set it off. She heard only a soft rustling sound. Crumpled newspaper, probably. Wrapped around a bag of herbal tea leaves, no doubt. That was the best construction she could put on it. What if he'd gift wrapped a random selection of Arnold's goat droppings? She wouldn't have put it past him.

"So open it," Leif demanded, clearly not smitten with any similar fears.

Annabel sighed. Bending her head, focusing strictly on the box, she began to peel the paper away. Her fingers weren't nearly as adept as when she'd unwrapped Libby's. She tore the paper almost at once, then, fumbling, nearly dropped the box. At last the paper was disposed of and she sat with the box on her lap. Carefully, unsure what to expect, she lifted the lid.

It was a shawl. A shawl in vibrant blues and greens, knitted of the finest angora. Her fingers curled into its softness, kneading it, then lifting it to rub against her cheek. She was speechless at the unexpectedness of the gift.

For all her practicality, Annabel could still appreciate beauty, and when the two were united, she couldn't resist.

"Oh, wow!" Libby exclaimed.

"Cool," said Leif. "Try it on."

Self-conscious, Annabel stood and unfurled the shawl, then settled it around her shoulders and struck a dramatic pose, her cheeks burning. "There. What do you think?" She looked at her children, not at Carter.

"Fantastic," Libby said.

"Great," agreed Leif.

In the silence that followed, Annabel had to look at Carter. He was still sitting in the wing chair, his loafer-clad feet crossed at the ankles, his long legs stretched out, his fingers laced across his flat belly. He was leaning back, looking up at her from beneath hooded lids. Annabel, meeting his gaze, felt as if she were wearing less clothes, not more.

"Well?" she demanded irritably.

A corner of his mouth lifted at last. "Yes," he said.

It wasn't a query, it was a pronouncement. It was approval. The smile reached the other corner of his mouth. He hauled himself to his feet and took the three long steps he needed to stand in front of her.

"Happy birthday, Annabel Archer." He bent his head and kissed her on the lips and this time, for an instant, his tongue did touch hers.

Then he was striding toward the door. It opened and he was gone.

"ANNABEL CALLED while you were gone," Jack said to his wife.

Frances's brows lifted. "Oh?"

"She said, thank you."

Frances looked at him suspiciously. "She said, *thank you?* And that's all?" In her wildest dreams Frances had never thought it would be that easy.

"No." Jack spooned a mouthful of mashed bananas into his waiting son's mouth. "She said the shawl was beautiful."

"What shawl?"

"That's what I said. And she said, the shawl we gave her."

"But we didn't give her a shawl."

"I told her that."

"And what did she say?"

"Nothing. She stammered around a bit, then hung up."

"Did she mention Carter?"

"Not once."

"Curious," Frances said. "Curiouser and curiouser."

IT DIDN'T MAKE SENSE. It only made sense if Jack and Frances had given her the shawl, had sent it with Carter to be delivered at dinner...if the kiss given earlier had been given only to tease, to annoy, to throw her off. It was a beautiful shawl. She'd loved it on sight, had known it was "her," exactly the way Frances, seeing it, would have known it was her and bought it for her birthday.

But she hadn't.

Carter had.

Presumably.

Which meant what?

Lying awake, restless and remembering as she stared up at the shadows that splashed across the ceiling of her moonlit bedroom, Annabel wished she knew.

Chapter Three

It didn't make sense.

Kissing Annabel Archer *once* because Frances had asked him to, well, all right. Carter had always helped out his friends. A guy did what a guy had to do.

But *twice?*

Carter thought he needed his head examined.

He was clearly in far worse shape than he'd thought.

He lay back against the pillows, his arms folded under his head, and stared at the ceiling, remembering his folly, remembering the warm, sweet taste of Annabel Archer's mouth.

It had nothing to do with Annabel Archer per se, of course. It was just that he'd been far too long without a woman. He could have felt that sharp, insistent hunger with any woman. He *would* have, he was certain.

And, he thought savagely, with any other woman, chances were he could have satisfied that hunger by now.

Instead of which he was lying here alone, supremely *dis*satisfied, with only the sound of a barn owl and the occasional bleat of a sheep in the pasture beyond the window to keep him company.

"Thanks, Milly," he muttered. "Thanks a whole hell of a lot."

He rolled over and punched his pillow, tried to sleep. But his eyes refused to close. In the moonlight he could see the photos on the dresser. Three of them.

One was an unposed blowup of Jack and Frances at their wedding, with Jack looking as if he couldn't believe his good fortune and Frances positively glowing with her love for him. The second was of Jason at six months, already in possession of the cocky grin and masculine charm that would doubtless make him a lady-killer in his prime. Carter's mouth twisted in rueful acknowledgement of his godson's inherent talent.

If anyone had told him a year ago that he would be absolutely nuts about a nine-month-old baby, Carter would have laughed in his face. But it was true.

Granted, he'd spent plenty of time doing what he'd told Milly he'd done—chasing women. But he'd spent a damn sight more time playing with Jason, going for walks with Jason, giving piggyback rides to Jason. And when he was with Jason, he wasn't even thinking about finding a woman to replace Diane in his life. He was far too consumed with the moment.

He'd never thought he'd be a good father. Heaven knew he'd had a bad enough example from his own. C.W. had had lots of expectations for his son, but very little time. The only way to get his attention had been to annoy him. Carter had perfected the art. He couldn't see that it had done him a damned bit of good.

In the first few years of his own meager attempt at entrepreneurship in New York, Carter sometimes fantasized that his father would walk into Jack Sprat's Health and Wellness Store, look around and smile. He dreamed that C.W. would nod his head and say, "Yes. This is sane. This is manageable. It's not a conglomerate, but I like it. You could teach me a thing or two, son."

He never had. Then Carter had allowed himself one or two brief fantasies in which he and C.W. ironed out their differences at the end. A sort of sappy deathbed reconciliation scene that would prove to him once and for all that, in spite of everything, his father had loved him.

He hadn't got that, either.

He didn't know what he did have, except a lot of misbegotten dreams and fantasies, a thriving health-food store that he cared about more than he wanted to admit and a few good friends whose lives were changing and deepening and who seemed to be rapidly leaving him behind.

He wanted a child. A wife. He wanted commitments. Responsibilities.

Things that had terrified him less than a year ago were now at the top of his list of priorities.

And, God help him, today he had kissed Annabel Archer. Twice.

He punched his pillow again, rolled over again. Sighed. Rolled back over and contemplated the third picture.

It was another enlarged snapshot, taken on the afternoon of Jason's baptism. They were standing just inside the church, Jack and Frances hovering behind, looking nervously at the couple staring down at the infant they held between them. He and Annabel Archer.

At the time it had been all he could do to bring himself to stand next to Annabel Archer, to smile politely at her, to slip away at the earliest opportunity before she could fix him with her basilisk stare or impale him with a cutting remark, before he succumbed to the urge to knife her with a remark or two of his own.

He didn't know what it was about Annabel that brought out the worst in him. He didn't know what it was about Annabel that brought out anything in him!

The need to give her something for her birthday, for example. He certainly hadn't intended to.

But while he was in town getting the groceries, he'd seen the shawl. He'd been thinking about Leif's paper-towel holder, about her baking her own cake, and he'd found himself wondering, for the first time, what life must be like for Annabel.

She'd always seemed as tough as old boots to him. He'd told Frances he was afraid to give her a kiss.

"Afraid?" Frances had scoffed. "Of a softy like Annabel? Oh, good grief."

But Carter had never considered her a softy, and he'd said so.

"She's had to be tough because she's had a tough time," Frances had told him. "But that isn't the real Annabel. Inside she's a marshmallow."

Perhaps it had been to test that marshmallow theory that he'd found himself buying the shawl, wrapping it himself, trying to guess what her reaction would be. He'd imagined scorn, disdain, a perfunctory "How nice" before she set it aside.

He'd never dreamed she'd curl her fingers into the wool and rub it against her cheek, never imagined her color would heighten so much that her freckles would fade into the general rosiness and that her wide hazel eyes would actually sparkle.

It had been a hell of a shock.

Such a shock that he had kissed her. Again.

"I KNOW WHAT you're up to," Annabel said to Frances the next morning.

"*Moi?* Up to?"

"And it won't work," Annabel went right on determinedly. She had scarcely slept all night, but she wasn't admitting it to Frances.

"Don't get so testy," Frances said. "It doesn't become you."

"And Carter MacKenzie does?" Annabel retorted.

"I think he might."

Annabel felt as if steam were coming out of her ears. "Didn't you ever listen to anything I said? I don't want a man in my life. I don't need a man in my life."

"That's what *I* said," Frances reminded her. "You told me I ought to reconsider."

"Well, you should have, and I'm glad you did. Jack is right for you."

"Yes. And if you give Carter a chance, I think you may find that he's right for you."

Annabel made an inarticulate muttering sound. "I told you yesterday, I think he's as shallow as a plate. And he doesn't have any better an opinion of me."

"Carter needs a woman—"

"Fine. I'll find him a woman, just so long as I don't have to be it."

"The *right* woman," Frances said patiently.

"Don't worry. I can do it."

"Oh, Annabel." Frances sounded sad.

"Leave it to me," Annabel said and rang off before Frances could come up with anything else.

The best defense, Annabel knew—and not from watching Monday Night Football—was a good offense.

And that meant finding Carter a woman. Not precisely an easy task in a town the size of Boone's Corner, Vermont. And even if she expanded her sights to include Gaithersburg to the north and Pock's Hollow to the south, she didn't have a much bigger selection. But it was certainly preferable to waiting and seeing what other tricks Frances had up her sleeve.

She sat down at the table and began to make a list.

In three hours she managed to come up with four names: Patty Willits, Tracey Forrester, Beth Hayes and Marilee Newman.

And even that was stretching it a bit. Patty was the vet's assistant. She tended to check the teeth of anything breathing, which Carter might or might not find entertaining. She was also rather young. Barely twenty-two. And still a bit spotty, come to that. Carter, used to women as lovely as Diane Granatelli, wouldn't hesitate to turn up his nose.

Annabel crossed Patty off the list.

Tracey Forrester was even younger, also chubbier, though less spotty. She worked at the grocery in Gaithersburg, where she chewed bubble gum and talked a mile a minute, both at the same time. When she wasn't talking, she still managed a sunny smile to greet every winter snowstorm and every station wagon full of summer tourists.

If Annabel smiled that much, she was sure her jaws would ache.

She tried to imagine Carter with Tracey.

She crossed Tracey off the list.

Beth Hayes wasn't a Tracey Forrester. She taught geometry at Libby's school. She was single and spare and as socially square as the angles she taught. As far as Annabel knew, she'd never been married or had a date. Even Aaron Leggett hadn't shown the slightest interest.

If Aaron didn't, how could she expect Carter to?

Another pencil slash.

Marilee Newman. Tall. Even taller than Annabel. With long, bleached-blond tresses that reached almost to her waist and a tan that would make Miss California seem pale. Marilee was an associate at Winterwood and Walden, Attorneys at Law, Gaithersburg's only legal firm.

Annabel didn't know if she'd been married or not. She frankly couldn't imagine "not" being a possibility given Marilee's attractiveness to the opposite sex, but she didn't know Marilee well enough to have found out.

Marilee had moved to the area only a year before, and since she had no kids Annabel's kids' ages, nor any inclination to move beyond the circle of friends she met at Toastmasters and the AAUW, she and Annabel had rarely met.

Annabel had no idea if she would appeal to Carter or not. Physically, Annabel thought, she stood a good chance. Beyond that, who knew?

And how was Annabel supposed to effect an introduction, anyway? She somehow couldn't imagine Carter taking her meddling well. She began to regret ever telling Frances she'd find him a woman.

Let him find his own woman, Annabel thought irritably.

Or perhaps Frances wasn't infallible, after all. Maybe he wasn't even interested in finding one. And if he was, so what? She didn't care. As long as he wasn't interested in her, he could have any woman he liked.

CARTER SPENT THE DAY by himself.

There was, he was pleased to note, no Arnold to contend with—which meant that there was no Annabel, either. He was even more pleased about that since he still hadn't figured out how to deal with her.

There was also no sign of Bentons. He was less happy about that. A phone call netted him an answering-machine message that said to call back after five or to leave his number and someone would return his call. He did the latter, and he would have done the former, but shortly after three his frenzied pacing was broken up by a knock at the front door.

"Hi!" It was Libby. She wore a happy-face grin and her long dark hair was windblown. She looked so young and fresh and vibrant that Carter couldn't help smiling back.

"Hi, yourself. I thought you'd be cheering." He stepped back and allowed Libby to pass through into the living room, glad for a friendly face. Libby, unlike her mother, had never been a problem.

She tossed her book bag onto the table and draped herself casually on the sofa and smiled expectantly up at him. "Oh, no, not every day."

"My mistake." He waited for her to explain what had brought her calling, but she didn't. She just smiled. "Can I get you something to drink? Milk? Er—" he tried to think of something appropriate "—soda?"

"I suppose it is a little early for a beer." Her nonchalance made Carter blink. "So I guess I'll have a cup of coffee. If you don't mind?" Her voice dropped a note or two, became husky. Seductive?

Surely not.

Carter swallowed. "Coming right up." He headed toward the kitchen to look for the coffee. Libby got to it before him.

She gave him a wide smile and a pat on the cheek. "I'll fix it. You sit down. You've probably been working hard. What did you do all day?"

She knew exactly where the coffee filters were, too. And the measuring spoon.

Carter, helpless in the face of such efficiency, still feeling the warmth of her palm against his cheek and wondering if it could possibly mean what he thought it meant, sat.

No, he thought. It couldn't.

He tried frantically to remember what Jack had told him about Libby. It didn't seem to be nearly enough all of a sudden.

She was thinner than her mother, coltish almost. No hips to speak of, and what breasts she had were camouflaged under a baggy green Celtics sweatshirt. A sweatshirt wouldn't hide Annabel's breasts, Carter was certain.

Annoyed at the direction of his thoughts, he turned them abruptly, concentrating on the girl at hand and the question she'd just asked.

"I went to town," he told her. "Looked around. Visited with Ernie and Bert. Stopped in and talked to Eb."

"How exciting," Libby drawled.

Carter shrugged. "He's a character."

Libby wrinkled her nose. "But he never goes anywhere, does anything. Nobody does here. It's all so *boooooring*. You know what I mean?"

Carter didn't completely agree. But then he thought about his own reaction to Boone's Corner when he'd arrived yesterday. He tried to imagine what it must be like for Libby, who, as far as he knew, had spent her life here. He remembered his own rebelliousness at her age and he'd grown up in the most exciting city in the world. "I know what you mean."

"I knew you'd understand," Libby confided. "Mom doesn't. She thinks Boone's Corner is the Hub Of The Western Cultural World."

Carter could well believe that. He laughed.

Libby thumped the coffeemaker together, adding the coffee and setting it on the stove. "She *loooooves* it here. She won't even go to Boston."

''Well, if you aren't used to them, haven't been in them—''

''Mom was *born* in Boston.''

That surprised him. There was no big-city sophistication about Annabel Archer. At least, he'd never seen any. He shrugged. ''Maybe she got fed up.''

Libby snorted. ''Maybe? She won't even talk about it. It's like I'm speaking Martian whenever I ask. But it couldn't have been very exciting, could it? I mean, not with my mother.''

''Probably not,'' Carter said in all truthfulness.

''So, tell me about New York. Is it wonderful?'' Her eyes glittered eagerly. ''I want to go there so bad.''

''It's okay. Plenty to do. Most of the time, at least.'' He wasn't about to share his current aimlessness with Libby. She wouldn't be able to understand it in a million years.

''I bet it's super. Next summer Frances says I can come down and visit them, if Mom lets me.''

''Why wouldn't she?''

Libby rolled her eyes. ''Contamination.''

''Well, yeah, the pollution can be pretty bad some days, but—''

''Not *air* pollution, Carter. Mind pollution. You know—'' Libby's voice broke into a singsong chant ''—how's she gonna keep me down on the farm after I've seen NYC?'' She gave him a stunning smile. For a second he could see Annabel in her again. Something in her eyes. Not the smile. He wondered if Annabel had ever in her life smiled at anyone like that.

She must have, he thought, if she'd managed to marry someone and have two kids. Or maybe not. Maybe she had simply intimidated some poor sod into marrying her.

The latter seemed a damned sight more likely, Carter decided.

"What do you take in your coffee?" Libby asked him.

"Nothing."

"Me, neither," she said giving him a conspiratorial smile. She handed him his mug and took a healthy gulp of her own. Her eyes bugged. Her adam's apple bobbed frantically and she lurched over to spit it into the sink.

"Too hot?" Carter asked.

"Ah...just a little." Libby waved her hand in front of her mouth and gave a sheepish little grin. "I guess I... forgot."

"Mmm." More likely she never drank the stuff.

"I just have more important things on my mind today," she said, sipping carefully this time. She set down the mug, looked at him and batted her eyelashes.

She didn't look at all like her mother when she did that! Carter couldn't imagine Annabel batting her eyelashes at anyone. Not in a million years.

He fought down a smile and took refuge behind his coffee mug. "More important things?" he prompted.

"Like seeing you again."

It was Carter's turn to choke on the coffee.

Hastily Libby patted him on the back. "Are you all right?"

Eyes watering, throat burning, he nodded his head. "Fine," he croaked.

"Good." She gave him one more long sultry look, then settled down at the kitchen table so that their elbows nearly touched. Her knee nudged his thigh.

Abruptly he stood up and set the mug down with a thump. "You gotta go."

"What?"

"I mean, I don't want to keep you. Your mother will worry. It's getting late."

"It's a quarter to four."

"Right. You shouldn't be late for supper."

Libby sighed. "I normally don't get home from practice till six, Carter."

"I thought you said you didn't practice every day."

"Well, er, not all days. But..." The two of them stared at each other. It was hard to say which of them was the more flustered now.

"Well, *I* ought to put together some supper even if you don't." He headed straight for the cupboard and began setting cans on the counter.

It was far too early to start fixing anything from a can unless he wanted to eat with the proverbial chickens, but what else could he do? He sure as hell wasn't going to sit there and let a seventeen-year-old flirt with him.

He might consider himself hard up—he might even be looking to get involved—but he sure as hell wasn't looking to get involved with Libby! And have Annabel Archer as a prospective mother-in-law?

God help him.

Libby was at his side in a moment. "I love to cook."

"So do I," he lied.

"Great. We have something else in common."

Carter shut his eyes. Swell. "I can manage." But she wasn't taking no for an answer. It was going to be easier to let her cook than to get rid of her, and it might be safer.

"Be my guest," he said and retreated to the table again.

"There's chili, applesauce, soup, canned spaghetti, tuna, rice, noodles...." She turned and smiled at him. "What would you like?"

The way she was looking at him and the soft, seductive

tone of her voice made him wonder if she was talking about dinner. He wasn't about to ask.

"How about chili and rice. It's a complete protein."

Libby made a face. "You sound like my mother."

Just what he wanted to hear.

Libby set about preparing the meal, sashaying her non-existent hips to and fro past him at eye level, slipping behind him to get a pot for the rice and letting her breasts brush against his back, then leaning across the table in front of him to reach the saltshaker.

Carter edged forward, then back, all the while trying to make intelligent responses to her running commentary about the misery of living in rural Vermont and the supposed joys of the big city.

He began to think dealing with Arnold might be preferable.

Ten minutes later when the doorbell rang, he practically ran to answer it.

It was Leif. Carter nearly dragged him into the living room.

"I can't come in," the boy said. "I just stopped to warn you. I had to bring Arnold down."

Carter wondered if perhaps he was becoming psychic. If he decided he'd prefer an earthquake or some other magnificent natural disaster, would it happen?

"You *had* to bring him? Why?"

"It's fall."

Carter shook his head, uncomprehending.

Leif gave him a patient, long-suffering look. "He makes babies in the fall, Carter. You know, has sex," he added when Carter still stared at him in stupefied silence.

"I know what you mean," Carter managed at last, strangling on the word. He jammed his hands into his pockets. Visions of Arnold among the nannies filled his head. His own months of frustration loomed to haunt him. He shook his head desperately. ''Yeah, fine. You go ahead. Do whatever you want.''

Leif grinned. ''It's not me. It's Arnie.''

''I *know* that!''

Leif glanced into the kitchen and frowned. ''What's Libby doing here? How come she's not cheering?''

''She says she doesn't have to.''

''She does,'' Leif told him matter-of-factly. He cocked his head and considered first his sister, then Carter. ''Ho, boy, Carter,'' he said, grinning as he turned to go back down the steps. ''You better watch out. You could be in big trouble!''

Carter grabbed him. ''What's that supposed to mean?''

''You know.'' Leif was still grinning.

Carter was afraid he did. ''She wanted to cook,'' he growled. ''So I let her. Big deal.''

''For her,'' Leif agreed solemnly.

''It doesn't mean a thing.''

''Tell her that.''

Carter raked a hand through his hair. ''Get out of here, you little monster!''

Leif laughed and scampered down the steps.

Libby appeared in the kitchen doorway. She wore an apron now, which, Carter supposed, was intended to make her look even more domestically appealing. She shoved a strand of hair back away from her face. ''Dinner's nearly ready. I've made a salad, too.''

She'd also set the table, and it was immediately clear to Carter that he wouldn't be dining alone. ''You shouldn't have gone to so much trouble.''

She smiled. ''Oh, it was no trouble. I'll do it every day if you like.''

"No, that's okay," he said hastily. "I wouldn't want to take advantage—"

"You wouldn't be taking advantage. I'd love to do it. I need to practice cooking."

Carter shook his head adamantly. "So do I."

Libby paused. "Well, then, maybe you can cook for me sometime."

Carter felt as if the neckline of his T-shirt had become suddenly tight. "Maybe…sometime."

Before Frances, Jack had at times complained about the way women hovered around him, breathed on him, batted their lashes at him. Carter had been singularly unsympathetic. Until now.

Libby was looking at him expectantly, obviously waiting for him to sit down. Seeing no alternative, Carter sat.

Over the course of the last twenty years, Carter had had dinner with plenty of females. He had danced his share of duty dances, gone on his share of disastrous blind dates. And he could never remember having been more uncomfortable or trying to be more careful not to show it.

There was ingenuousness to Libby's attentions that made him worry terribly about the possibility of hurting her.

Not that he wanted to encourage her, for heaven's sake. But he didn't want to shut her down rudely, either. She was so young, so untouched.

He got the definite sense that she was trying out wiles on him that, if he reacted wrongly, could have an adverse effect on all her future relationships with the opposite sex.

A conscience, Carter? he chided himself. *At your age?*

But that was, in fact, what it must be. He couldn't imagine that he would have behaved with such avuncular circumspection a few months ago.

God, he must be getting old!

ANNABEL WAS GETTING frantic and she suspected it showed. ''What do you mean, she didn't go to practice?'' she demanded into the telephone. ''Libby always goes to practice. She hasn't missed a cheerleading opportunity since she was born.''

''Well, she missed this one, Ms. Archer. Just said she wasn't coming and took off. I think she took the school bus home.'' Libby's best friend Alice sounded earnest and absolutely truthful. She was also, as Annabel's inquisition went on, beginning to sound upset.

Not half as upset as Annabel. It was seven o'clock and she hadn't seen hide nor hair of her daughter.

''Well, if she'd taken the school bus, she'd have come home, wouldn't she?'' Annabel asked. It seemed like a reasonable assumption to her.

''I guess so, Ms. Archer,'' Alice said miserably.

''She didn't say where she was going?''

''No.''

''Or what she had to do?''

''No. Nothing. She acted sort of mysterious.''

Mysterious? What did that mean? ''If she comes by, you tell her to call me at once,'' Annabel instructed and hung up.

What, Annabel wondered as she stood staring out the window into the darkness, could have been suddenly more important to Libby than cheerleading?

She spotted Leif coming across the yard with Arnold and let out a sigh of relief. At least one of her children was accounted for. And her goat. She hadn't wanted Leif to take Arnie up there at all, but Leif had been adamant.

''I gotta,'' he'd said. ''I need 'em for 4H.''

So Annabel had let him go. ''Don't bother Carter,'' she'd warned.

And Leif had nodded. "I never bother Carter. We just talk and stuff. I'll explain about Arnie."

Annabel thought she would have liked to hear that.

Leif banged in through the door. "Mmm. Smells good. Am I late?"

"No later than Libby," Annabel said distractedly. "Damn that girl. She didn't go cheerleading. She didn't come home. She probably went shopping in Gaithersburg with Mary Kate and didn't tell me. I'll wring her neck if she has."

"She's at Carter's."

"What?"

He turned then and shrugged, drying his hands, grinning at her. "She's with Carter. She cooked him dinner!"

Annabel felt her mouth opening and closing like a fish.

"She's in love with him," Leif said. "What an idiot."

"In love with—? She didn't go to practice so she could go cook dinner for Carter MacKenzie?" Annabel knew her voice was on a steady rise. She knew she practically ended the sentence at a shout. She didn't care.

Libby? Her darling, defenseless daughter? And *Carter MacKenzie?*

Oh, God. Please God, I didn't mean it. I didn't mean he could have any woman if he'd leave me alone. He can't have Libby!

She pulled on a jacket and was heading out the door almost before she knew what she was doing. Halfway up the hill she stopped.

What was she going to do? Bang on Carter's door and demand Libby's release?

He was hardly holding her prisoner. Annabel wasn't entirely certain about Carter's role in the afternoon's events, but she wasn't a complete fool. She knew that Libby wouldn't be there if she didn't want to be.

And barging in and making demands was the surest way to alienate her daughter that Annabel could think of.

Oh, damn, she thought. Why was parenting always so difficult?

She stood on the hillside, weighing her alternatives.

Her eyes went to the top of the hill, to where the path led down the other side toward Frances's house, to Libby. To Carter. Her mind fast-forwarded to how big a fool she could make of herself if she went that way.

Her gaze turned back toward her own snug log home where Leif stood in the lit doorway, watching her. She could be a fool if she went that way, too.

She raised her eyes to the heavens. It was a vast black canopy sprinkled with stars, immense but not unfriendly. Looking at it, Annabel felt the years roll away. She felt as she had at twenty, at twenty-five, young and vulnerable and uncertain.

When she was young, back when Libby was in first grade and Leif only a toddler, Annabel had often come up to sit on the hillside in the evening when the children were asleep to get a better perspective on her life.

It seemed as though all she had time for during the day was to work like a demon. But at night she would climb the hill to sit quietly and reflect, albeit briefly, on her day. She would think about what was—and then about what might have been.

And at the end, before getting to her feet and going back to her everyday life, she would raise her eyes skyward to find that star somewhere to the right of the Big Dipper, the one she used to wish on as a child, the one she knew better than to wish on anymore.

It was always there, constant and reliable. When she no longer had her parents, when she no longer had Mark, she still had the star.

She didn't know its name, its constellation, its astronomical significance. She only knew it focused her, steadied her, kept her from making a fool of herself. It had always been there to balance her when she hadn't been sure if she could cope, when she'd contemplated throwing in the towel and running back home to Daddy.

She hadn't looked for it in a long time.

As the children got older, as what might have been faded into a simple determined acceptance of what was, as she grew up, she'd stayed in her kitchen at night, reading, working, humming to herself. Satisfied. Comfortable.

She wasn't comfortable tonight.

She hugged her arms across her chest and stared upward, finding the star. It gleamed faintly in the night sky, steady and reassuring.

''Now what?'' she asked softly, though whether she was talking to the star or to God or simply to herself, she wasn't certain.

She tucked her hands into the pockets of her jacket and stood still, watching, waiting.

There was a sudden crackling behind her. She spun around to see two shapes moving down the hillside toward her.

''Libby!''

''Mom? What are you doing up here?''

Annabel, seeing the second shape materialize into Carter, took a slow, careful breath. ''Enjoying the evening. Looking at the sky.''

''That's all?'' Libby sounded suspicious.

Annabel gave her daughter a look of wide-eyed guilelessness. ''What else would I be doing?''

Libby flicked an instant's gaze over her shoulder at the man who'd stopped just behind her. ''N-nothing, I guess,'' she said brightly. "I...I suppose maybe I should have called to tell you. I was at Carter's."

"Leif said. And yes, I would have appreciated a call."

"I fixed dinner," Libby went on. "And we did the washing up together. Then we took a walk. Around by Milliken's old place. You know? The trail that crosses the bridge."

Annabel nodded. She knew. She and Mark had often lingered, kissing, on that bridge. Her eyes narrowed as she looked at Carter. Had he been kissing her daughter?

"Then he said he'd walk me home," Libby went on. She glanced at Carter again. She was smiling. Swooning.

Near to melting, Annabel thought, annoyed. "How thoughtful," she said tonelessly.

"My pleasure," Carter said.

She looked at him sharply. He sounded pleased. She gave him a steely glare.

Carter met her gaze with a stubborn one of his own. "Would you rather she'd walked alone?"

"This isn't New York City. But I appreciate your concern." She took Libby by the arm and began herding her down the hill. "Thank you for seeing her home, Mr. MacKenzie."

"I enjoyed it, Ms. Archer," he drawled, then after a moment, "Come again, Libby."

Over my dead body, Annabel thought.

"Tomorrow," Libby promised, blowing him a kiss.

Chapter Four

There was no help for it. As much of an idiot as it made her feel to do so, Annabel had to intervene.

It was one thing to have Carter MacKenzie preying on her—not that he was, of course. It was entirely another to find him lusting after her seventeen-year-old daughter! He might not like the selection of local ladies, but he was going to have to make do.

She didn't say anything more to Libby. She simply sat stonelike in the living room and listened while Libby babbled on for the remainder of the evening, extolling Carter's manly virtues. His muscular arms. His strong jaw.

His hairy chest?

Annabel clenched her teeth. Just how Libby knew he had a hairy chest, she managed not to inquire.

She even mustered up a smile when Libby said how glad she was that he'd come and wasn't he such a good friend to Jack and Frances for doing so.

"Indeed."

"Don't you think he's handsome?"

She hadn't, if the truth were known, given it a lot of consideration. The less she thought about Carter MacKenzie, the better. "I suppose he's turned out well enough."

Libby gave a little squeal. "Did you see a picture of him when he was little?"

"No. I did not."

"But—"

Annabel flapped her hands. "It's just a matter of expression, Libby. For heaven's sake, stop pestering me. Go do your homework."

"I did it."

Annabel's hands came to a halt in midair. "All of it? Without being told? When?"

"At Carter's. He helped me."

"You asked Carter to help you with your homework?"

"Oh, no. I didn't really want to bother him with it. But...well, he offered. We had this rotten long trig assignment and he helped me with it all."

Having done so, he rose in Annabel's estimation a tiny bit. Or he did until she realized that he might merely have done so to give Libby a reasonable excuse for coming there in the future, some plausible reason to offer her mother for spending time with him.

"You needn't bother him with your homework."

"I'd better bother somebody," Libby said, "or I'm going to flunk trig."

And heaven knew, Annabel wasn't going to be able to prevent that. As far back as ninth grade, Annabel had begun opting out of anything having to do with numbers.

It wasn't that she couldn't do them; it was simply that she hated them. And once she'd finished geometry, she'd said, "That's it," and had never looked back.

Her father had told her it was a huge mistake. But almost everything she did was, according to Edward Lodge Archer, a huge mistake. Annabel hadn't thought ignoring mathematics was one of them. Until tonight.

''Well, there must be someone else who can help you...Eb? Ernie?''

''Ma,'' Libby said patiently, ''they didn't have trig when Eb was a kid. And I don't think math is Ernie's thing.''

''Well, what about Aaron?''

Libby cocked her head. ''Oh, good idea. And he can come over every evening to help me.''

''Sarcasm does not become you, Liberty.''

''You suggested it.''

''My mistake. Is Carter really good at it?'' She couldn't imagine it, somehow. It seemed too much like work for Carter to excel at it.

''Yeah, he is. And he explains it well, too. Lots better than old Morrissey at school.''

''Why'd he have his shirt off?''

Libby blinked. ''What?''

Annabel could have torn out her tongue. ''Never mind.'' She tried to leave it alone. She couldn't. ''You said he had a hairy chest.''

''He does.''

''How do you know?''

''I did his laundry.''

''And he *undressed?*''

''I...accidentally spattered some chili on his shirt when I was cleaning up, so he took it off and I said I would wash it.''

Annabel's gaze narrowed. She looked at her daughter carefully. Accidentally? she wondered.

Libby looked away, reaching out to snag her backpack off the table. She rustled inside it for her math book and pulled it out.

''See?'' She waved a neatly set out paper full of equations in front of her mother. ''He knew everything about the law of cosine and all that business about secants and cosecants.''

Annabel, who knew about as much about cosines and secants as she did about lateral forward passes was reluctantly impressed. ''And you understand it now?''

''Oh, yes.'' Libby nodded her head enthusiastically. ''He should be a teacher. He was amazing.''

''Good.'' Annabel wasn't really sure if it was good or not. It was perhaps, at best, a mixed blessing. She wondered if God looked more kindly on men who taught girls trigonometry as they seduced them. She didn't think mothers did.

Still, he clearly hadn't seduced Libby yet, though, she suspected, not from Libby's lack of trying. With luck, perhaps she could forestall it before it became a sure thing.

''Very nice,'' she said briskly. ''Now, since you're such a whiz at laundry, you can bring your dirty clothes downstairs so I can get an early start tomorrow.''

Libby looked as if she might have argued, then, as if she was considering all the other avenues the conversation could have taken.

''Right,'' she said and, giving Annabel a sunny smile, she bounded up the stairs.

''WHAT DO YOU MEAN, you won't be able to get here this week?'' Carter scowled at the telephone in his hand, listened to the droning explanation on the other end, sighed and rubbed a hand around the back of his neck.

He'd got up this morning to another ominous silence. But this time he'd managed to do more than exchange messages with the elusive Benton Brothers. In fact, he had Luther Benton right at that very moment on the other end of the line.

"You told Mr. Neillands you'd be here this week," he said when Luther's excuses finally ground to a halt.

"Can't. All that rain we had couple of weeks ago, it set us back."

"And you couldn't have called and told him?"

"It's long-distance," Luther said, as if that was all the explanation necessary.

"I bloody know that!" Carter exploded. "It took me five hours to get up here!"

"We can be there next week, I reckon."

"You reckon?"

"Well, ain't nobody can say what the weather's gonna do, can they?"

"No," Carter muttered. "Ain't nobody can do that."

"Well, then," Luther said, "you see what I mean. Next week, week after. Don't fret. We'll be there 'fore the snow falls."

"It's the rain, not the snow they're trying to keep out."

"Ayuh. That, too."

Carter quietly strangled the phone in his hands, then took a deep breath and made up his mind. "You've got the roofing shingles in stock?"

"We're roofers, ain't we?"

"Fine. I'll be down this morning to pick them up. I'll put on the roof myself."

His decision wasn't as altruistic as it might appear at first glance. It was basically self-preservation.

"Tomorrow," Libby had said in response to the invitation he'd issued simply to annoy her mother. He'd known damned well what Annabel was doing on that hillside, and it wasn't looking at the stars. She was afraid he was after her daughter.

The truth was, her daughter was after him! And he didn't know how many more visits from Libby he would be able to handle as well as he'd handled the first one. Through dinner and washing up, he'd held her off. The question about her studies that had resulted in their foray into trigonometry had been pure blind luck. The walk had been less lucky. He could see real dangers lurking in the moonlit path, the old stone bridge, the now-deserted but still-comfortable farmhouse. It was not a place to go with Libby.

Seductive teenagers were a mystery to him—a mystery he wanted to preserve forever. Being on the roof, he thought, might give him the edge he needed.

Bentons were surprisingly cordial when he showed up. Probably, he thought sourly, because they fully expected him to call them up to rescue him in the midst of his folly a few days hence.

They smiled and snickered behind their hands, helped him load all the shingles into the back of his Blazer and sent him on his way with a hearty "Good luck, fella."

If they didn't actually add, "You'll need it," it didn't matter. Carter could hear the words echoing off the mountainsides as he drove home.

He needed it sooner than he thought.

There, sitting on the front step, waiting for him, was Annabel Archer. Bloody hell.

He parked the car beside the barn and got out. She had watched him drive without moving at all. But when he began walking toward the house, she stood up and came toward him slowly across the yard.

Like gunslingers, Carter thought.

He felt decidedly unarmed. He wasn't sure what she wanted, but he was willing to bet it had something to do with Libby. She obviously didn't trust him an inch.

"Here," she said and thrust a paper into his hand.

He took it, frowning. "What's this?"

"A list of local eligible women."

His head jerked up. He stared at her, amazed. "You're joking."

"I'm not. This one is a vet's assistant." Her finger jabbed at one name on the page. "This one teaches. This one works in a supermarket down the way. The last one's a lawyer. Not many, I realize. But old enough—" her voice hit the word *old* with a definite authority "—and certainly a better bet."

He cocked his head, regarding her carefully. "Than Libby, you mean?"

She looked momentarily taken aback that he would be so blunt. Then, "Yes," she hissed.

She reminded him of a mother cat defending its off-spring. Her cheeks were flushed; her eyes flashed fire. She looked ready to burst into flame in a moment. Even her gingery hair seemed to glow.

He couldn't help grinning. "But Libby's lovely," he teased.

"Libby is seventeen!"

"She'll be eighteen in four months."

"She told you that?" Annabel looked horrified.

Carter shrugged equably, beginning to enjoy himself now. "Who else?"

Annabel's mouth opened. And shut. He could almost see her making the effort to calm herself. He wanted to tell her it wouldn't work.

"Damn it!" She exploded. "It won't work!"

"What won't work? Me and Libby?" He tried to keep the smile off his face.

"That, too," Annabel snapped. "But I meant me, trying to be rational. Trying to appeal to your good nature, your sensitivity, your common sense! I should have known!"

She was almost shouting now. ''You don't have any common sense!''

''How clever of you to have noticed,'' Carter said mildly.

''Damn,'' Annabel muttered under her breath. ''I shouldn't even have come.'' She spun away and started to stalk across the gravel toward the trail.

He caught her arm and spun her back to face him. ''Hold on.''

''Why should I? It was a mistake to come.''

''You're sure of that?''

Fire flashed in those amber eyes again. ''What do you think?'' she asked scornfully.

''I think I'm in big trouble if the only woman in the world who supposedly appeals to me is seventeen.''

Annabel just stared at him, but her gaze went from angry to merely suspicious. ''Meaning?'' she asked after a moment.

''Meaning I'm not after your precious daughter.''

'''Come again, Libby,''' she quoted in a deliberately seductive singsong voice. ''That wasn't you?''

Carter laughed a little self-consciously. ''Not in that tone of voice.''

''But you invited her back.''

''I was being neighborly. What'd you expect me to do, throw her off the property? Sorry, lady, that's your forte, not mine.''

The color in Annabel's cheeks grew even deeper. ''I try to be neighborly, too,'' she said in a grudging tone. ''Maybe I haven't been very pleasant...to you.''

''Yeah, well, I sort of said it to annoy you, too,'' Carter admitted.

Annabel's brows arched.

''You looked so disapproving.''

"I was. I *am,*" Annabel said.

"Well, stop worrying. Libby's safe with me."

Annabel shifted from one foot to the other. "Thanks," she muttered. Then, "I'm sorry if she bothered you."

"No bother," Carter said quickly. "She's a good kid."

"But she is a kid," Annabel said firmly.

"I know that," he said. "But she's very nearly an adult, you know. She isn't going to be a little girl forever."

"Do tell."

He grinned. "I thought you'd probably already figured that out."

"I'll try to keep her away," Annabel promised.

"It won't work."

"Why not? You can't be that wonderful." The moment she said it, her face flamed.

Carter gave her an amused look. "I haven't had many complaints."

"I didn't mean that," Annabel said tightly. She tried to pull her wrist out of his grasp but he didn't let go.

"I know what you meant," he said easily. "It's just that—" he shrugged "—I enjoy baiting you."

She scowled. "Why?"

"You get so mad. And it makes me feel a little better," Carter added after a moment. "Most of the time you're damned intimidating."

Annabel's grin was like sunshine, dazzling enough to make Carter blink.

"I think I've created a monster," he muttered. "It isn't becoming, you know."

Annabel smiled. "Who wants to be 'becoming'?"

Not her, obviously. And just as well, too, he thought. When she smiled Annabel Archer was really surprisingly pretty. It made him want to kiss her again.

"Let's see this list," he said.

SHE INTIMIDATED *HIM?*

She didn't know whether to believe him or not. It was a mark of her basic lunacy that she even had to think about it, Annabel decided. When had Carter MacKenzie ever stood there and told her the simple, honest truth?

But heaven knew she wanted to believe him. It would make life so much easier to feel she had a foothold on the slippery cliff of their relationship.

What relationship? she asked herself.

A few days ago she would have denied the possibility of ever even having one.

But after the past few days…after his cordiality toward Leif, after his gift of the shawl, after his soothing of her fears about his interest in Libby…there might, she conceded, be a remote possibility.

She spent the rest of the afternoon winding Spanish moss around heart-shaped wire forms, trying to think about how she was going to decorate them. Instead she thought about Carter.

She thought about his impish grins, his outrageous comments, his deliberate teasing. She thought about his lean, whipcord body and the way his hair flopped across his forehead and the way he had to shove it back.

Not a good idea, thinking about things like that.

She thought instead about the list she had given him. Was he, even at this moment, consulting it?

He'd certainly snatched it quick enough. It just went to prove that Frances was right about him wanting a woman.

That was all right, Annabel told herself, as long as the woman wasn't Libby. Or her.

That last thought, long suppressed, definitely unbidden, came out of the blue and hit her squarely between the eyes.

No, she thought. Oh, no. She couldn't be so stupid as

to entertain such a ridiculous possibility as herself and Carter together, could she?

She sat quite still, staring down at the creation in her hands. A heart. Wire and moss, tiny dried roses, baby's breath and a bow. Delicate. Fragile. But sturdier than it looked. Far, far sturdier than the heart of an adolescent girl had been years ago.

No, of course she couldn't consider it. She wouldn't let herself.

Once had definitely been enough.

HE TOOK PATTY WILLITS to a movie. She laughed in all the wrong places. She was censorious about his penchant for junk food. He got the feeling that every time he opened his mouth, she was checking his teeth.

He took Tracey Forrester to the spaghetti supper. She giggled. Incessantly. She hung on his arm. Her presence seemed to have the effect of making Libby scowl at him all evening. But what was worse, he had the dubious pleasure of watching while Annabel, obviously ignoring him, smiled and laughed with Aaron on the other side of the room.

He made it a point to go over and speak to her. She was cordial, welcoming even, as if she had mended her ways after he'd commented on them. But it didn't feel real or as if she meant it.

Perversely he found he liked it better when she sniped at him. He was so irritated by her polite words and cool welcome that when he got home at ten, he went up on the roof and, with the flashlight in his teeth, pounded in an entire row of shingles. Then he took a long walk, a cold shower and went to bed.

He didn't get a lot of sleep. At first his mind was filled with thoughts of Patty and Tracey and Libby. But once he fell asleep, they vanished and Annabel Archer haunted his dreams. She sicced her goat on him, then metamorphosed into Libby and batted her eyelashes at him. But when he made a move on her, she walked away.

In the morning, shortly past six, he called Milly to complain.

"It's not working," he said the moment she picked up the phone.

"Carter?" She sounded sleep muddled and confused. "Is that you? What didn't work? Where are you?"

"Godforsaken Corner, Vermont, trying to get some perspective on my life. What you said I should do. And it's not working. At all!"

There was a silence while Milly sorted through that. "What happened?"

"Nothing. Everything. There's this woman—she haunts me. And her daughter—"

"Both?" Milly sounded more awake now.

"No! Not both. The daughter's after me. She's a kid, for heaven's sake! And the woman doesn't want anything to do with me. I just damned well see her everywhere and I think about her and…and I…I…" His voice trailed off.

"You what, Carter?"

"I don't know," he muttered, anguished.

"Sounds like it's working to me," Milly said quietly. "Tell me about this woman."

"She's a witch."

"Really? That sounds promising."

Carter snorted. "She's Frances's friend. Frances made me kiss her."

"Made you kiss her? Heavens."

"Oh, shut up."

Milly giggled softly. "Sounds like she's really getting to you, big brother."

"She made me a list of eligible women," he grumbled.

"Did she? How enterprising. Why?"

"She's afraid for her daughter. Thinks I'll seduce her."

"Did you come on to her?"

"Of course not! I'm not a cradle robber."

"Then why would she think…?"

"She just doesn't like me."

"Why not?"

"How the hell should I know? Maybe she's got it in for tall, handsome guys. I don't know. She's unnerving as hell."

Milly laughed.

"It isn't funny. The way she looks down her nose at me, glares at me, gives me these disapproving stares all the time—she's just like Dad."

Milly sighed. "I doubt if she's at all like Dad, Carter."

"You haven't met her," he said darkly.

"I'd like to. Did you ever think she might be giving you the names of these women because she's equally unnerved by you?"

"That'll be the day."

"You might be surprised."

"Yeah. Sure."

"You're such a skeptic, Carter," Milly chided. "I think it's great."

"What's great?"

"That you're interested in her."

"Interested? In her?" he practically yelped.

"Who else? She's all you've talked about."

"Not because I'm interested. I told you, she hates me. And I don't like her, either. Why would I want to get involved with someone who reminds me of Dad?"

"You tell me," Milly said quietly.

Carter scowled at the phone. "It's not like that," he muttered.

"And I'm telling you, I don't believe it. Tell me more. Have I met her? Is she young and single and eminently eligible?"

"No, you haven't. And she's middle-aged and widowed. With two kids," he reported dampeningly. "Not my type at all. I told you that."

"But she still has the power to torment you? My, my."

"You're a sadist, Milly."

"I'm a sister."

"Same thing."

"Poor Carter."

"Poor Carter is right. I came up here for rest and relaxation, and all day long I'm plagued by kids and goats and a woman who hates my guts, plus I'm putting on a new roof, for heaven's sake."

"Are you?" Milly sounded impressed. "Well, that's one way to get a new perspective."

"Very funny."

"Not funny. Good. You sound livelier, Carter. Something must be happening."

Something was, but Carter wasn't sure he liked it. He wasn't even sure he believed in it. God knew he didn't want to.

"What's her name?"

There was no use pretending he didn't know who Milly was talking about. "Annabel. Annabel Archer."

"Sounds vaguely familiar."

"You probably heard Jack or Frances mention her."

"Maybe." There was a pause, then, "Oh, cripes. I've got to get going. I have rounds at the hospital this morning. Call me soon?"

"Sure."

"And, Carter? Think about what I said—about your Annabel maybe feeling a bit intimidated, too."

"She's not *my* Annabel."

"Yet."

Chapter Five

His Annabel.

Lord, what a thought.

It made him want to pull the pillow right over his head. It made him want to turn tail and run as fast as he could.

It was true, he realized as he lay there in bed and stared up at the ceiling, what he'd told Milly about her reminding him of his father.

While clearly there wasn't much of a physical resemblance to the hawk-nosed, barrel-chested steamroller who'd sired him, she and C.W. had a lot of other things in common. They certainly seemed to share the same disdain of him, the same minimal bored tolerance for his antics, the same penchant for cool dismissal.

And he felt the same about them: he wanted to rattle them, unnerve them, get under their skin.

It had been easy with his father. All he'd had to do was go his own way, do what he liked, disparage the power and the glory that came with the MacKenzie name, and C.W. was ready to strangle him. Even when he made an effort to keep the old man happy, it was to no avail.

Carter had found that out quite early.

"It's a good school. It was *my* school," his father had

trumpeted as he'd sent Carter off to Kenwood Prep at the age of thirteen. "They respect MacKenzies there."

They threw Carter out in less than two months.

"Smoking?" his father had roared. "Shinnying up the flagpole in your underwear? What in hell were you thinking of, you young fool?" C.W. had bellowed at him when he was sent home in disgrace.

Carter, as stubborn as his old man, didn't reply.

There was no way he could explain that still-immature thirteen-year-olds didn't command the respect that company CEOs did, no way that he could tell his father the only way a skinny little kid could earn it from his peers was to take foolish risks, act tough, never show the slightest fear. He had tried…had done the best he could.

For C.W., Carter's best was never good enough. Not in school, not in football, not in dating. He was told so time and time again. So, to his father's face, he always simply pretended he didn't care.

So did C.W. Having a son like Carter—who didn't command immediate respect by his size and authority, who not only didn't make first-team quarterback, but who actually rarely got to play, who never dated the right girls—was irritating in the extreme.

As time went on, C.W. did his best to ignore the son who bore his name.

Carter resented that even more than he resented his father's fury.

So he did things to get the old man's attention. Things designed to infuriate and annoy. Things that would get a rise out of him and which would prove to Carter that his father was at least aware of his existence, even if he didn't love him.

For some reason Annabel Archer made him feel much the same way.

He didn't understand why she disliked him. He didn't expect adulation from every woman he ever met. But he could be charming. He could be fun. He was good for a few laughs, a night on the town, a roll in the hay.

And if they weren't interested in that, he knew it instinctively and was quite willing to be a good friend.

But not with Annabel Archer?

He'd sensed her disapproval from the moment they'd met. She'd given him a stiff smile and a snooty stare when Frances had first introduced them.

He'd commented on it, teasing her—or trying to. But that had only made her stiffer and snootier. She'd uttered a bare monosyllable, then walked away.

She might as well have thrown down the gauntlet.

He'd never learned not to accept a dare.

Every time they'd met after that, he'd done his best to say outrageous things to her, to tease or harass her. It had become a minor goal in his life to discomfit Annabel Archer.

And until recently that had certainly been enough.

It was all Frances's fault, he thought morosely. If she hadn't had to redo her damned roof, he wouldn't be up here. He wouldn't be thinking about Annabel, dreaming about her.

He was willing to bet Annabel never dreamed about him.

He thought about what Milly had suggested, about the possibility of Annabel being intimidated by him.

"Not bloody likely." He gave a bitter laugh. Annabel wouldn't be intimidated by a tank.

She's no better than the old man. Forget her, he told himself.

But how could he forget her when she lived just over the hill? When her children were at his door? When her goat was in his pasture? When her cool, deliberate antagonism irritated the hell out of him? When her smile made the sun come out?

CARTER MADE IT A POINT to meet Beth Hayes. He'd asked Ernie and Bert about her. They said she was sweet, lovely, intelligent, kind. Good, he thought. She sounded a perfect antidote to his fixation on Annabel Archer. After the first two he began to wonder if Annabel hadn't been setting him up.

He skulked around the school parking lot for two hours to casually run into Beth as she walked to her car. And she seemed surprised at his story about Frances having mentioned her and telling him to be sure to look her up.

"I scarcely know Frances Neillands," she protested. She looked at Carter doubtfully.

"She knows you. Says you're a great teacher. I suppose one of the kids in your classes must've said it. Libby Campbell, I think."

"Libby? She got a *D* in geometry."

"Oh, well...maybe it wasn't Libby then." Carter began to wish he'd thought up another story. "Anyway, I was wondering if you'd like to go out Friday night."

"Well, I... There's school, you know? A football game and..."

"Swell. How about going to the game?"

She sighed. "I...suppose we could do that."

She might be sweet and lovely and kind, but she sure as hell wasn't enthusiastic. Carter feared he was making a mistake. But he could hardly retract the invitation. Besides, Libby was coming out of the building just then, and he didn't want her input into this conversation.

"Come on," Carter urged. "It'll be fun. I'll pick you up at six. We can have a bite of supper first."

Beth Hayes sighed. "I suppose."

IF PATTY HAD GUFFAWED all through the movie and Tracey had chattered and giggled all the way through the spaghetti supper, Beth Hayes never cracked a smile.

She rarely spoke, either. Carter did his best to be charming, but if he couldn't metamorphose into a geometric figure, he reckoned he didn't have a chance.

He hoped things would improve when they got to the football game. Libby had told him she was cheering, had been delighted to hear he was coming, had even accepted his coming with Beth Hayes with equanimity.

"Oh, her," was all she'd said.

But despite Libby's dismissal, he still held out hopes. Beth was svelte and elegant looking. And even if she didn't laugh and talk, her very presence would let Annabel know that he wasn't repulsive to other women.

His plans, though, went awry from the first. Even when they got to the game, Beth scarcely said a word. Worse, she kept a good two feet away from him all the time. It was cold enough to merit having someone to snuggle up next to, but when Carter tried, she quickly edged away, tucked her duffle coat more tightly around her and gave him a frosty look. "I am a teacher."

The look he gave her must have made his bafflement obvious. She managed a slight smile. "I'm sorry, but it wouldn't do, you know. I must set a good example for my students."

Carter glanced around at the students, most of whom were huddled so close together that it was hard to tell where one began and the other left off.

"Right," he muttered.

Beth gave him a prim smile. "I knew you'd understand."

He understood, all right. He understood it was going to

be a long night. He stared back down at the field, hunching his shoulders against the wind, and wondered if Annabel was laughing at him.

He had been looking for her since they'd arrived. He'd looked for her right down front where she could see Libby cheering, but he didn't find her there. And though he periodically craned his neck and scanned the rest of the bleacher crowd, he didn't find her there, either.

"Hi. Can I sit with you?"

Carter turned to find Leif standing behind him, grinning.

"If you don't want me to, that's okay," Leif said quickly when Carter didn't answer at once.

"Of course you can sit with us. Why not?"

"Swell." Leif studied the amount of space between Carter and Beth, decided it was sufficient, then clambered down to sit between them. "Cold, isn't it?" He shivered cheerfully, hugging his arms against his chest.

"Yeah." Carter hesitated a moment, then put his arm around the boy, drawing him close. "That help?"

Leif grinned, huddling closer. "Yep."

They sat that way for the rest of the half, snug and warm against the cold north wind. It had been years since Carter had gone to a football game. He couldn't remember one, in fact, that he had gone to for purposes of enjoyment. MacKenzies went, according to C.W., to play. And win.

This was different. Easier. Far more relaxing. Leif asked innumerable questions and Carter surprised himself by knowing the answers. He bought Leif a soft drink and himself a cup of coffee. Beth declined anything.

"You sure you're comfortable?" he asked her now and then.

She always said, "I'm fine," and moved farther down the wooden bench.

At halftime Beth glanced at her watch, then at him, and back at her watch again. "Would you think me terribly rude if I asked to go home? It's not that the game isn't interesting, or…or that you aren't, but…"

"You have a lot of papers to grade?"

She nodded eagerly. "How'd you guess?"

"Instinct. Come on, I'll take you home," Carter said with an alacrity that would have made his socially proper mother wince.

He deposited Beth Hayes on her doorstep, bade her a quick farewell and was back in his car before she shut the front door. He considered, for a moment, not even going back to the game.

It wasn't as if he dearly loved football. Nor was he going to enjoy Annabel's knowing smirks. But Leif was waiting, saving him a seat, and he didn't want to disappoint the boy. Besides, he was enjoying it.

Leif was right where he had left him, but since Beth had left, now he could ask, "Where's your mother?"

Leif blinked, as if the question surprised him. "At Eb's. She always goes to Eb's. Like Libby said, Ma doesn't like football."

"But Libby cheers."

"Yeah. That's Libby's choice. That's what Ma says anyway. That we have to make up our own minds about things, make our own choices in life. She brings us to the game, then she goes and plays checkers with Eb. We call her when the game's almost over and she comes to pick us up."

It was apparently simple and clear-cut to Leif. It boggled Carter's mind. In his own experience, his parents had not encouraged their children to make up their own minds. Exactly the opposite, in fact.

If Carter William MacKenzie III didn't like something, then no one liked it. Period.

Apparently Annabel wasn't completely like his father. She didn't raise her children the same way, at any rate. In fact, he rather admired the way she raised her children. They were nice kids, fun to be with, forthright, eager, charming, funny.

He supposed they might have inherited it all from their father, but honesty compelled him to admit that Annabel might have had something to do with it. It was a disconcerting thought.

He didn't have time to dwell on the notion, though, for right then the Gaithersburg Gators scored a touchdown and Leif dragged him to his feet to cheer.

"Cool!" Leif exclaimed. "Do you think they might win? Do you? They haven't won a game in years."

"Maybe tonight." Carter was grinning, too, feeling the same sort of exhilaration that Leif felt. Eager, joyful, alive. He was glad Beth had left, grateful that Annabel hadn't been there to see her leave.

He sent Leif down to buy popcorn and Snickers bars, then they drank hot spiced-apple cider. Halfway through the fourth quarter Carter found himself explaining the virtues of zone defense, the Gators scored another touchdown, Libby leapt around, cheering madly, Leif said, "You really know a lot about football," with sincere admiration, and Carter felt better than he'd felt in months or, maybe, years.

"Did you go to lots of games with your dad?" Leif asked him.

"Some," Carter said. But they hadn't been fun. Not the way this had been.

He didn't want the game to end. But when it did, he wasn't abandoned to go home to Jack and Frances's alone.

"Come with us," Libby said, hanging on to his arm, grinning up at him. "We always go out after for donuts."

He didn't even stop to think. "I'd like that," he said.

He'd forgotten about Annabel.

When they got out to the parking lot, there she was.

She was wearing his shawl.

The sight of her standing under the lights, her gingery hair windblown, the blue-green sea of the shawl swirling around her, almost took his breath away.

"We won!" Leif yelled. And Libby grabbed her by the hands and swung her around.

Annabel grabbed for the shawl, laughing, looking flustered as she glanced at him. It made Carter smile.

"We missed you," he said.

"I'll bet."

"He brought Ms. Hayes," Leif told her. "She went home at halftime."

Annabel looked at Carter, her brows arched.

He spread his hands. "What can I say? She must have found my charm too much for her."

Annabel's mouth twitched. Then she gave up trying to fight the grin and laughed. "Oh, undoubtedly."

"Come on," Leif said. "I'm starving."

Carter looked at him, horrified. "I fed you popcorn and candy and—"

"Shh!" Leif glared at him. "Not in front of Ma!"

Annabel gave him a mock-stern look. "You know what I think about junk food."

Leif's smile was ingenuous. "We gotta make choices, Ma."

Annabel pretended to strangle him. "What did I ever do to deserve you?"

Leif giggled. "If you don't know, I won't tell you."

Annabel's face flushed. "Come on, then. Let's go."

"Carter, too, Ma," Leif said.

Annabel looked at him. For just an instant their gazes met.

"Carter, too," she said.

ANNABEL HADN'T BEEN prepared for Carter. She'd heard from Ernie and Bert that he'd asked about Beth Hayes. She'd convinced herself he'd have invited Beth to drive toward Rutland to one of the inns for a quiet, romantic meal.

Seeing him coming out of the stadium with Leif and Libby was a shock. If she'd known he'd be there, she wouldn't have been wearing the shawl, for heaven's sake. And she wouldn't have left her hair to hang loose as though she were some sort of hippie. She'd have bundled it back neatly and skewered it in place with a wood-and-leather thong.

But, she told herself as she followed the taillights of Carter's Blazer through the streets of Gaithersburg toward Maggie's Muffin and Doughnut Shoppe, it could always be worse.

He could have invited Libby to go out with him after the game, instead of Libby and Leif inviting him to join them.

Her stubbornly rational side argued that there were better case scenarios, too. He could have declined to join them, could have at least said he'd follow her instead of allowing both kids to act as "navigators" and come with him.

He could, Annabel thought, exasperated, have hung on to his date and not been available at all.

Had Beth Hayes really left him at halftime? Had he really cared as little as he seemed to?

Annabel pulled into Maggie's small gravel parking lot

alongside Carter's Blazer with all these thoughts still buzzing in her head.

Leif bounced out of the car immediately. Libby still sat in the front seat, talking animatedly. Carter was listening intently. Annabel wondered what Libby was saying—and what he was thinking.

She got out of her car and slammed the door.

The sound made Carter look over at her. He grinned at her and opened the door of the Blazer. "Come on. We'll have to ask your mother," Annabel heard him say to Libby.

"Okay," Libby replied. "But if you manage, I'll be your slave forever. I'll get your laundry so clean, it will blind you."

Annabel decided to ignore the "slave forever" line. It did not bear discussing. Nor did she say, "Ask me what?"

Seventeen years and eight months of motherhood had taught her that there was no use asking for trouble. Unencouraged, it found her soon enough.

"Carter says he'll take us to Boston a week from Saturday," Leif told her without preamble. "So Libby can go shopping, and after we can go to the Red Sox game. Can we go, Ma? Huh? Can we?"

"Leif!" Libby looked as if she'd like to strangle him.

It wasn't Leif Annabel wanted to strangle. She felt as if she'd taken a blow to the gut.

"Boston?" she said to Carter. "You want to take them to Boston? You asked if they'd like to go with you to Boston?"

"No," Carter corrected mildly. "They want to go to Boston, and they said you don't. I said I'd take them if you like."

Annabel didn't like.

She didn't want her children going into Boston. Not

with her, not without her. She was doing her absolute best to raise them the way she thought they ought to be raised, and that didn't include forays into Boston where their heads could be turned by things that didn't matter, where their minds could be swayed by people who didn't have their best interests at heart.

She opened her mouth to say so and knew she couldn't. Not to Carter.

Carter took the greatest pleasure in making mincemeat of her at every opportunity. Carter thought she was a reactionary, granola-crunching leftover hippie. He wouldn't understand. Not a bit.

"Tell you what," he said after a moment when she didn't reply. "Why don't we just go in and have muffins or doughnuts or whatever, and you can think about it."

"Please, Ma?" Leif looked at her with absolute longing in his eyes.

Annabel's jaw clenched.

"Leif." Libby nailed his shin with her toe. "Shut up."

Annabel stood straight and waited for Carter to add his pressure to theirs, waited for all three of them to gang up on her. He didn't speak.

Instead he took her elbow, steering her gently toward the brightly lit shop front. "Come on. Let's eat."

Annabel ate. She sat there, determinedly chewing her muffin, waiting, marshaling her arguments. But while Leif continued to look at her with beseeching intensity, Libby held her tongue, and Carter didn't talk about it at all.

In fact, he seemed to have forgotten all about it. He regaled them with tales of his first attempts to sell muffins at his health-food store. Muffins, he insisted, that were made from grass clippings, soybeans and banana peels.

"Very high in potassium," he told them.

He told the story with such seriousness that Leif and

Libby were taken in completely. Annabel sat back, choking on her own muffin, and tried not to laugh.

She shouldn't encourage him, she told herself. He didn't need an appreciative audience. But she didn't think what she did would make any difference. Carter MacKenzie would always do whatever he pleased.

"Even Ma wouldn't eat one of those," Leif said, then looked at her. "Would you, Ma?"

"Oh, I don't know," Annabel said. "I think they sound rather good."

"As good as the one you're eating now?" Carter asked.

"I don't know if I'd say that."

"Let's see." And before she could respond, he reached out and drew her hand with muffin in it toward his mouth. His lips touched her fingers. She felt the faint scrape of his teeth against her hand. She snatched it away at once.

For a second their eyes met, and Annabel was surprised that Carter's eyes slid away as quickly as hers.

"I don't know," he said at length, his voice rough through the mouthful of muffin. "I think I actually like the ones I sold better."

Annabel, fingers still tingling, dropped the rest of hers on her plate, then wiped the crumbs off her hand on the napkin. "I'm not surprised," she said somewhat stiffly.

Leif, who had watched it all with consummate interest, spoke up. "So, Ma, what do you think about—"

"—a bite of a doughnut?" Carter cut in before Leif could finish.

It didn't matter. Annabel knew what he was going to ask. "No, thank you," she said.

"But, Ma—"

Carter dug into his pocket and came up with a couple of quarters. "Go play a video game and let your mother eat her muffin in peace."

Leif started to protest, when suddenly he winced and bent to rub his shin. He shot Libby a hard glance. "Okay," he muttered.

"Oh, look," Libby said with great heartiness. "There're Tina and Vicky."

Tina and Vicky, as far as Annabel could see, had been there since they'd walked in. But Libby pushed back her chair. "I just want to go talk to them for a few minutes." And she was gone.

Carter and Annabel sat at the table alone.

"Very clever," Annabel said. "They know I'll say no to them, so they've conned you into doing the asking."

Carter didn't pretend not to know what she was talking about. "Are you going to say no?" He didn't sound challenging, just curious.

"Of course I am."

He shifted in his chair, leaning back comfortably, one arm resting along the back of the chair Leif had vacated. "Why?"

"Because they don't need to go to Boston!"

"You're right," he said. "They don't." He pushed some pumpkin-muffin crumbs around his plate with his forefinger, then licked his finger.

Annabel watched him irritably. She wanted to eat her own muffin crumbs, but she could still feel the touch of his lips on her hand. There was no way on earth she was bringing that hand up to her mouth. Even if he agreed with her about Libby and Leif and Boston.

"They have everything they need in life right here," she went on as if he'd contradicted her. "There're shops here. Clothes. Tapes. Posters. Everything a teenager could possibly want. And Leif can listen to the game on the radio. Or see it on television."

Carter nodded again.

"It's important for them to learn to bloom where they're planted," Annabel said after a moment, knowing she sounded like a sixties' slogan even as she said it. "Boston isn't necessary!"

"No." He cocked his head and smiled slightly. "But it can be fun."

Annabel glared at him.

"I'd forgotten how much," he said almost wistfully. "It's been ages since I went to a football game. And I always used to hate 'em because I always had to go. But tonight I liked it." He looked up to meet her gaze, and she was surprised by the guilelessness in his eyes. "I'd like to go to a baseball game like that."

"So go," Annabel muttered.

"It'd be more fun to go with someone. Someone who wanted to go. Someone who didn't think I should be the first baseman," he added wryly.

"Someone thought you should have been?"

"My father. He was a sports freak. He was good at it."

Though it remained unspoken, Annabel heard the admission that Carter wasn't. It surprised her.

"I know Boston can be fun," she conceded, out of sorts, remembering in spite of herself exactly how much fun it could be.

On the far side of the room she could hear the zing and ping of Leif playing the video game. Nearer she could hear Libby's eager laughter and Tina's squeal. Her children were fine, right here, both of them.

"I thought you'd be at the game tonight," Carter said after a moment.

"I don't like football."

"Yeah. I remember Libby saying so. But I thought you'd be there anyway because she was cheering."

Annabel straightened, lifted her chin and looked down

her nose at him. "Are you implying that I'm a bad mother because I didn't come to a football game?"

He shook his head. "You have the greatest kids I've ever met. They're bright, funny and independent. And I think they owe it all to you. You let them make their own choices in spite of the way you feel."

The video game whizzed and banged, the cash register whirred. Annabel didn't hear a thing. All sound but the echo of his words seemed to stop. She stared at him.

Carter lifted a quizzical brow. He cocked his head and returned her stare.

"Damn," Annabel muttered under her breath.

"What's that?"

"You know very well what I said. I said *damn.*" She grimaced wryly. "Isn't this what's known as being hoist by my own petard?"

Carter's mouth quirked into a grin. "And are you?"

She pursed her lips, annoyed, outfoxed, impressed at how neatly he had done it. "What do you think?" she grumbled.

He smiled. "That you're a good mother, Annabel Archer."

"HOW'S THE ROOF?" Jack asked Frances when he got home.

Frances looked up from her computer and gave him a bright smile. "Carter's doing it."

"Give me a break."

"He is. I called this afternoon and talked to him. He was on top of the roof even as we spoke."

"The wonder of cordless telephones," Jack marveled. He kissed her, then crossed the room and flopped down on the sofa, beat. "And was Annabel up there with him?"

"Well, no. But that's hardly unexpected. You can't make wreaths on top of a roof."

"I'll bet he hasn't even seen her since the first night."

"Of course he has. That's why he's doing the roof."

Jack's brows drew together. "Say what?"

"So he has the excuse of staying longer," Frances said patiently. "Honestly, Jack." She shook her head. Sometimes men were so dim.

CARTER KNEW what was missing in his life. He knew what he wanted: Libby and Leif.

He wondered if Annabel would trade him.

Would she consider his stereo a fair swap? Or would he have to throw in his Blazer and the custom-built dining-room set Nick Granatelli had made for him, as well?

He knew they wouldn't come cheap.

He knew, if he was honest, they wouldn't come at all.

Annabel Archer had what he wanted. He didn't stand a prayer of getting them.

He could always marry her, he supposed. That was about the only way he could see getting them.

He wondered what she'd say if he suggested it.

Most likely she wouldn't say anything, just laugh.

Even that wouldn't be so bad, he thought now, hunkering down on the roof, feeling the warmth of an Indian-summer sun on his bare back. He liked Annabel Archer's laugh.

She ought to do it more often. She was far too serious, too intense. Like his father.

No, not really.

She cared about her children, her friends, her pets. She tried to take care of them all. He remembered what Frances had said about her being a marshmallow. He was beginning to believe it.

He wondered what had made her so resilient, so independent, so necessarily tough. He wanted to ask her. He knew she'd never tell him. No more than she'd ever trade her kids for all the accoutrements of his fast-lane life.

"You want kids? Go have your own," she'd tell him.

And he knew she wouldn't be interested in going through all that again. He knew she wouldn't be interested in him.

Hadn't she, for God's sake, given him a list of eligible women?

MARILEE NEWMAN was like a breath of fresh air. Bright, articulate, funny. She left the first three on Annabel's list in the shade.

He called on the pretext of wanting some advice about property he was considering for purchase. It seemed smarter than saying that Frances had raved about her. She was, according to Eb, one of those lawyers who end up owning the county because they have their fingers in every real-estate pie.

The only drawback was, if it was true, his father would have loved her.

They made a date for dinner on the following Sunday. "Let's combine business and pleasure," he said.

Marilee agreed enthusiastically.

Carter looked forward to it avidly. Eb had said she was "a looker," too. He wondered if she liked children, if she had any of her own.

He tried to think about Marilee, about what sort of questions he could ask about real estate that would make him sound knowledgeable. He ended up thinking about how to explain the use of the two-point conversion to Leif and the virtues of subtlety in eye makeup to Libby. He dreamed about their mother.

THE TRIP TO BOSTON was better than he'd dared to hope. Even liking Libby and Leif, even wishing that they were his, he knew he hadn't spent a lot of time with them. Over the long haul he might hate them. They might hate *him.*

It was great.

They were, among other things, a damned sight more entertaining and fun to be with than Tracey or Patty or Beth Hayes. Leif was such an amazing combination of innocence and knowledge, of fact and opinion, that Carter found himself asking question after question just to enjoy that boy's candid responses.

And when Libby forgot she was trying to be a seductive teenage femme fatale and was her normally exuberant naive self, he was equally charmed.

He relaxed in their company, having a far better time with them, he realized, then he'd had not only with Tracey and Patty and Beth, but better than he'd had with any woman he'd dated since Diane.

He took Libby to an area of trendy boutiques, then stepped back and watched her set forth. She dragged both him and Leif from shop to shop, oohing and ahhing, trying first this piece, then that one.

But she wasn't easily parted from her money. She was, he saw quite soon, her mother's daughter. She studied things carefully, examining shirts and sweaters, hats and wallets, necklaces and earrings. She weighed this tape against that one, even asking Leif's opinion once or twice.

"I want to think about it," she said at last. So they went to an arcade where Leif zeroed in on the video games. He and Libby found out one of Carter's weaknesses. He could actually get intense when he played Double Dragon II.

"You're good at it," Leif said, amazed when Carter's initials made it into the top-five high scorers.

''Don't tell your mother,'' Carter grinned. ''Come on.'' He herded them toward the door. ''We've got to make tracks if we're going to get to the game on time.''

''Wait!'' Libby grabbed his hand. ''Let's get our photos taken.''

It was one of those four-photos-for-a-dollar machines that spewed them out in a matter of minutes. Carter shrugged. ''Why not?''

Libby orchestrated the whole thing, arranging the three of them in the booth, putting in the money, then leaning back between them, all of them grinning and mugging for the camera, then shifting facial expressions with each one.

''I'll wait for them,'' Carter said when they were finished. ''You go back and get what you want.''

She ended up with three tapes, two T-shirts and an outrageously floppy felt hat that somehow suited her coltish charm.

''What do you think?'' she asked Carter, who walked in with the pictures as she was trying it on.

He gave her a thumbs-up. ''You look sensational.''

''What about my mom?''

''She'd look sensational, too.''

Libby punched him. ''You know what I mean.''

He did and told her that he was sure her mother would think it was great. But he'd meant what he said. The hat would suit Annabel to a *T*.

They got to the Sox game as the first inning began. Leif was in seventh heaven from the moment they'd arrived.

''Oh, man! Isn't this great?'' he said at the first glimpse he caught of the field. And once they'd descended the steps to their seats twelve rows back on the first-base side, he kept turning to Carter, then to Libby, his eyes glowing, his grin enormous. ''I'm seein' the Red Sox. Right up front. I can't believe it.''

Carter lounged back against his box seat and smiled.

"Carter?" Libby tapped him on the shoulder.

He turned and she handed him a small paper bag.

"I would have wrapped it," she said, "but I didn't have time or the paper."

He stared at the bag. "What is it?"

"Open it."

He did. Carefully. Slowly. Unfolding the bag, then shaking it slightly. The black sport-style wallet Libby had been examining in the shop lay in his hand. He opened it up. In the first pocket she had put one of their pictures.

The three of them, jammed together, grinning their heads off.

They looked like a family. He swallowed hard.

"I just wanted to say thanks," Libby said. She gave him a shy smile.

He looked up, met her gaze, felt his throat tighten and wondered if he gave Annabel fifty-million dollars and his soul whether she'd think it a fair exchange. "Thank you," he said softly. "I'll cherish it."

"It isn't much, but I just wanted to tell you that…you remember those fortune cookies? Well, you did it. You gave me my heart's desire."

WHERE WERE THEY?

It was nearly two in the morning. There was no reason—no *good* reason—they shouldn't have been home hours ago. They were supposed to have gone shopping first, then to the Red Sox game, then come home.

Even stopping for dinner on the way, they should have arrived no later than 11:00 p.m.

The game had got over before 5:00. She'd watched the whole thing on television and had ended up with a lopsided wreath as a result. But the lopsided wreath was the least of her worries right now.

Where were they?

She knew it had been a mistake, knew she shouldn't have let them go.

"What can I bring you?" Carter had asked when they'd left this morning at dawn.

"Them," she'd told him. "Safe."

And Carter had said, "Scout's honor." She doubted if Carter had a passing acquaintance with any sort of honor at all.

"Where are they?" she asked Goliath for the umpteenth time.

Goliath chirped mournfully and wove between her legs, rubbing his head on her calf. Annabel reached down and plucked him up into her arms, crooning along with Waylon, who had been keeping her company for the past hour and a half.

He wasn't doing as good a job as he usually did. It was one thing to have been done wrong by and to survive. It was quite another to feel so helpless, so alone.

Libby and Leif were all she had in the world. And they were missing.

"They aren't missing," she told herself aloud. "They're just late."

But being late was enough. It scared her. They were the center of her universe, the reason for her being.

After Mark's death she'd had to fight her instincts every time one of them wanted to go out of her sight. If they were close by she'd believed she could protect them. But in her heart she'd known that wasn't true.

She hadn't been able to save Mark. She'd been right there, less than twenty feet from him, and she hadn't been able to save him.

No one could have—except the man who'd been drinking the day he'd roared down the highway on the wrong side of the road. If only he hadn't come around the curve just then.... If only Mark hadn't seen that nest of baby cardinals and wanted a closer look.

Annabel had been over all those "if onlys" a hundred times—a thousand times—before. She couldn't change the past. She had learned to live with it.

She just didn't think she could stand to live with it ever happening again.

"Please, God, no," she whispered now, a sudden awful vision of another such driver out on the road tonight, of Carter momentarily distracted, of...

She fought the vision, fought her memories. She felt cold, her hands clammy, her throat constricted.

A flicker of light swept across the living room.

Headlights.

Annabel ran to the door and flung it open as the Blazer came to a stop in front of the house.

"Where have you been?" Even with relief flooding her, Annabel still couldn't mask the sound of panic in her voice. She practically flew toward the car.

Carter looked surprised. "We stopped to eat. We got to talking...."

"Talking? I thought you were dead!"

"I told you I'd take care of them. We weren't in a big hurry. You didn't say..."

"I should have said," Annabel said tersely. She peered past him in the dark. She could see Leif sound asleep in the front seat. Libby was curled in the back, totally oblivious.

"Come on," she said to them now. "Lib! Leif! You're home! Let's go. Say thank you to Mr. MacKenzie and come in the house!"

They came awake slowly, muttering and stretching. Libby uncurled slowly. Carter stood rigidly by the door.

''Mr. MacKenzie?'' His voice was low and hard, questioning her.

Annabel ignored him. ''Leif! Come on!''

Leif groaned and opened the door. He looked at her blearily and stumbled out. Libby followed, gathering bags in her arms as she went.

''Thank you, Carter,'' she said and hugged him around the packages in her arms. ''It was the most wonderful day of my life. It really was.''

''Mine, too,'' Leif said. And even he reached out and gave Carter a hug.

Annabel stared at them. She remembered her fears and felt a pain deep within, a loss, a panicky sense of not being in control. ''Go on to bed,'' she said sharply.

She waited to speak until the front door had shut behind them. Then she turned to Carter. ''Thank you for taking them.'' She kept her voice steady and well modulated, her furious panic controlled. ''Good night.''

He took three steps, caught her arm and pulled her back around to face him. ''You were frightened.''

Annabel tried to pull away from him. He held on. ''It's late. It's very late.''

''We were having a good time. We stopped for dinner in Hanover. We got to talking. They're great kids.'' His mouth curved in a wistful smile. ''The best.''

''Yes.'' She didn't want to discuss it. It was over. They were safe. Her world was intact. She managed a thin smile. ''Thank you for taking them.'' She turned to go, but he didn't let her loose.

''Why were you so scared?''

''I told you. It got to be so late. I envisioned disasters. It's a part of the package that comes with parenthood.

Protectiveness. Panic. All the best parents do it. I suppose I'm a bit worse than most. They're all I have." She looked away, embarrassed by her confession.

"I understand. I'm sorry."

She looked up at him, startled. She hadn't expected an apology. Not from him.

"I was having too good a time to bring them back," he confessed. "Look." He pulled out the wallet and showed it to her, opening it so she could see the picture. "Libby gave it to me."

Annabel just stared at it. It was so warm, so unposed, so natural. The three of them—Carter and Libby and Leif—with their arms around each other and big grins on their faces. She closed her eyes.

She wanted...

No. She didn't. She couldn't.

"Very nice," she managed.

"Thanks for sharing them with me," Carter said quietly.

She smiled slightly. "You're welcome."

"I really am sorry."

"It's all right. You didn't realize...."

"No."

"You will." Her eyes met his. "When you have a child."

WHEN YOU HAVE A CHILD....

And there was wishful thinking for you, Carter thought as he lay in bed and stared at the ceiling.

He thought about Libby and about Leif. He thought about Jason. He thought about the joys and trials of parenthood. He thought about his own father and what a consummate mess that had been.

For years he hadn't wanted a child, hadn't wanted to wish his sort of childhood on anyone.

But now…

He thought about Diane marrying Nick and about all his dreams that had shattered along the way.

He thought about Tracey Thingummy and Patty Whosits. He thought about Beth Hayes and, before then, the legions of women he'd dated with no thought beyond a night's fun and games.

He thought about Milly telling him that he needed to figure out what was missing.

"Oh, yeah, Mil," he said softly into the darkness as he rolled over onto his side and hugged a pillow against his chest. "I know."

But what good did it do?

IT WAS BARELY LIGHT when something woke him.

A sound.

Not birds. Not a truck changing gears on the hill. Not Arnold having his way with a nanny.

Something high-pitched. Intermittent at first. Then louder. Stronger.

Carter frowned, stretched and sat up. "What the hell?" he muttered, rubbing his eyes, raking his fingers through his hair. He glanced at the clock. It was 6:30.

He got to his feet, pulled on a pair of the briefs Libby had so painstakingly laundered for him, then a pair of cord jeans.

He stumbled barefoot and shirtless down the stairs.

It was louder now. Furious. Turning into a full-blown wail.

Wail?

Carter flung open the front door.

There was a baby in a box on the porch.

Chapter Six

Carter blinked. Shook his head. Closed his eyes and opened them again.

There was a baby in a box on the porch.

Yelling its head off.

Waving its arms in the air.

Not a hell of a bad idea, Carter thought.

He edged closer, half expecting it to vanish. It didn't. It screamed on.

He was right next to it now, peering down into its red, enraged face, marveling at the noise that broke the stillness of the morning.

''Hey,'' he said softly, hunkering down beside the box, rocking it gently. Then, more loudly, ''Hey, baby. Hey, it's okay.''

But clearly, from the baby's perspective, things were far from okay. It screwed up its tiny face and continued to scream.

''Come on, now,'' Carter said, fumbling with its blankets, trying to get a secure grip on it before he lifted it into his arms. He thanked God for all the times he'd held Jason, rocked him, soothed him.

If it weren't for Jack and Frances's son, he'd have no idea at all what to do with a screaming infant.

The moment he lifted the child, there was silence, then a faint hiccuping sob. Dark eyes opened to regard him curiously. And looking down into them, Carter smiled.

"It's okay," he said again, hugging the blanket-wrapped baby gently against his bare chest, rocking back and forth on his heels, swaying slightly. "Shh, now. Everything's going to be fine. I don't know who you are or what the devil you're doing camping out on the porch, but we'll figure it out. Don't you worry. Everything's going to be fine."

The baby was totally still while he was speaking. The moment the words dried up, the crying began again.

Carter muttered under his breath. "You're hungry, aren't you? Starving probably." Still holding the baby close with one hand, he squatted again, and groped around in the box, which had been padded with blankets into a sort of makeshift bassinet. He found a bottle, happily still somewhat full, and a piece of paper.

There was rather a lot of writing on it. Loopy and girlish from the look of it, and far too much to do more than glance at in the dimness of the early-morning light. He stuffed it into the waistband of his jeans.

The baby began another long wail.

"Hang on, kiddo." He noted two paper bags sitting on the porch swing, which, he hoped, would hold the rest of the child's worldly possessions. He'd find out later. First things first. Tucking the bottle under his chin and wrestling the box under his one free arm, he carried the baby, the box and the bottle into the house.

There he dumped the box unceremoniously to the floor, then carried the baby and the bottle over to the rocker. He sank down into it, nestled the baby securely in the curve of his arm and offered it the bottle.

Blessed silence—broken only by the occasional whimpery hiccup and a soft slurp-slurp.

"There now, that's better, isn't it?" He smiled down at the unblinking dark eyes regarding him. "Told you so, didn't I?"

There was another soft hic...a tiny sniff.

"Right. Now let's read this and see if we can find out who you are and how you got into this mess."

He pulled the paper out and spread it on his thigh. Then, reaching over, he flipped on the table lamp, bathing them in soft light.

He was right about the handwriting. Whoever had written it even used tiny circles to dot her *i*'s and swooping curves crossed all the *t*'s. "Dear Frances," he read. "This is Conan."

He looked down doubtfully at the child in his arms. "Conan?"

The baby gave an audible sniff, then sucked on.

Carter considered the tiny hands, the cherubic cheeks, the dark downy hair. Well, maybe, he conceded. Even with a name like Conan, you had to start somewhere.

"Okay, Conan," he said. "Now we know who you are and who was expected to receive you. Let's see what else we can find out." He read on. "He was born May 24th. He's the most wonderful baby in the world, and that's why I'm bringing him to you." Carter doubted that Frances would agree. Jason was the most wonderful baby in the world to her. He kept reading. "You remember me telling you about Jerry Higgins? He's Conan's father."

Carter looked down at the baby again. "Conan *Higgins?*"

Conan blinked solemnly.

"Oh, brother." He continued reading. "Him and me are trying to work things out, but it isn't easy. He just got laid off and he took off on me. I can't take care of Conan by myself. I work all day as a waitress and at night I am an usher at a theater. Even with tips, I can't hardly make enough for Conan and me to live on. I can't pay anybody to take care of him. My mother would of, but she got sick last month. You know how bad the rest of my family is, so you know I got nobody else. Just you. I'm trying to find Jerry. When we get settled, I'll come and get Conan. I will miss him just awful but I know he will be happy with you. Love, Maeve. P.S. I have listed what Conan can eat on the other side. I will love you forever for taking him."

Carter glanced at the other side, then let the paper fall from his fingers. He considered the words, the child, the implications.

"God," he breathed. It was pure prayer. Nothing else.

He eased the blanket farther away from the baby's face and looked down at the child in his arms, so tiny, so trusting.

Conan Higgins. A child with more baggage than it seemed possible for a four-month-old to have—a child who was supposed to be loved and cared for by Frances who was hundreds of miles away; a child who, at the moment at least, was totally and completely dependent upon him.

"Be careful what you pray for," he remembered his father threatening when he was a child. "You just might get it."

The old man was probably laughing his head off right now.

But Carter didn't have any time to spare thoughts for his father. "What do you think, Conan?" he asked the baby. "You think we can batch it till your mom gets back?"

Conan looked at him, reached out a hand and waved it uncertainly toward Carter's face. Then it fell again, coming to rest against Carter's hand, wrapping around Carter's fingers. Holding on.

FOR TWO HOURS and twelve minutes, give or take a second or two, Carter reigned in supreme and confident pseudo-fatherhood, smiling down at the infant in his lap.

Then Conan woke up.

"I know you're wet," Carter said to the screaming infant. It was basic psychology, right? Acknowledge the problem. It was no great deduction. Conan had leaked right through diaper, sleeper and blanket to leave a warm wet spot on Carter's lap.

Carter scratched at the spot, adjusting his jeans as best he could. Then he carried the baby upstairs and hunted frantically through Jason's bedroom for something to remedy Conan's situation, finding, at last and to his great relief, half a dozen disposable diapers in a bag at the bottom of the closet.

"All's well," he told Conan. "Supplies have been uncovered."

He thanked heaven—and Jack and Frances—for his knowledge about diapering babies. In scant moments Conan was clean and dry. A quick search of the bags on the porch revealed clean, dry sleepers and playsuits. With slightly less dexterity he wrestled Conan into one of them.

"Now," he told the baby, "you wait here while I change." He laid Conan on his back in Jason's crib. Conan screamed.

"All right. Never mind. Come with me."

Conan didn't scream when Carter put him down in the middle of the unmade bed. He looked around curiously, then let his gaze follow Carter as he rummaged through the neat stacks of laundry Libby had arranged on top of Jack's dresser.

Carter stripped off his jeans and briefs, washed off, dressed again, this time adding a sweatshirt before he sat down next to the baby to put on his socks and shoes.

"So what do you think?" he said. "Should we call Frances and tell her?"

But even as he said it, he knew he wouldn't. Not yet.

There was nothing Frances could do. Oh, perhaps she could reach this Maeve girl. Now that he thought about it, Carter seemed to recall having met her once. She was one of several girls Frances had known during her teaching days in Boston, girls she'd stayed in touch with, had tried to give some options to.

Obviously Maeve had made her own choices.

It was equally obvious that Maeve wasn't where she could be reached yet, even if she were headed back to Boston. And she might not be. For all Carter knew she could be headed in the opposite direction entirely—hot in pursuit of the peripatetic Jerry Higgins, with whom she hoped to "work things out."

"We'll just hang loose a little while, buddy," Carter told the baby, picking him up and laying him on his own knees so that they faced each other. "Maybe you can help me with the roof. 'Never too young to learn the ropes,'" he quoted in a tone so like his own father's it made him cringe. "But you don't have to be a roofer if you don't want to be," he added and bent to kiss the baby's nose.

There was no way, Carter soon discovered, to put the baby in his box on the roof. There was also no way he could leave Conan on the ground in his box while he proceeded with the shingling.

But that was only one of his problems. He also had to

figure out how to fix oatmeal with Conan in one arm, then eat it with the baby trying to grab the spoon.

How the hell did mothers and fathers, whichever stayed home with Junior all day, cope?

How had Annabel done it?

His respect for her was growing by leaps and bounds.

He could, of course, call her and ask her. But he didn't want to. Maybe he was too stubborn. Maybe he had too much pride. But he didn't want to go running for help at the first sign of difficulty.

"We can manage, can't we, fella?" he asked Conan.

Conan burped.

Carter considered the matter, and tried to visualize Frances with Jason. Of course, he knew Jason had slept sometimes. But just as clearly he knew that Jason had demanded his share of Frances's time and attention. And during all that time and all that attention, surely at least occasionally she'd had the use of her arms. How else could she have written two more books?

She'd had some sort of sling that snuggled Jason against her body in sort of reverse papoose fashion, keeping him close and leaving her hands free.

Well, Maeve hadn't provided any such gear, but Carter was nothing if not resourceful.

"I can create something useful out of damned little," his father had boasted to him as, throughout Carter's formative years, one enterprise after another prospered under strict MacKenzie tending.

"So can I," Carter muttered, less to Conan than to himself. He scavenged through Frances's drawers for material that would do the trick.

But he couldn't work on it immediately because Conan was awake and wanted attention.

"You're spoiled. You know that?" Carter told the baby in his arms.

They had a bottle of juice and some cereal. Carter took him down to see the goats and up the hill to inspect the sheep. He came back with the intention of putting Conan down for a morning nap.

But Conan wasn't sleepy. He batted the bottle out of Carter's hands, he wriggled in Carter's arms, he giggled, he bounced.

That was when Carter had gone deep into his subconscious to dredge up every nursery rhyme he knew.

So far they'd done at least twenty run-throughs of "The Grand Old Duke of York," twice that many of "Pat-a-Cake" and "This Little Pig Went to Market."

"How about '99 Bottles of Beer on the Wall'?" he asked the cheerful cherub.

Conan grinned at him.

Carter grimaced in return. He shifted in the chair, feeling itchy and irritable. Was parenthood paling so quickly?

But when he acknowledged the problem, it seemed less one of parenthood than of his jeans.

They hadn't felt quite right for a couple of hours. He moved to ease the scratchy discomfort. It didn't help.

He sighed and got back out of the chair again, pacing around the room, showing Conan the photographs on the sideboard. "This is Jack," he said. "And this is Frances. This is Jason. You'd like him." He went on at length for another half an hour, then he carried Conan upstairs and sat down in the rocker in Jason's room.

This time Conan went out like a light.

And this time Carter didn't sit solemnly for almost two hours admiring the child in his arms. He got up and carefully settled the baby on his stomach in the crib. Then he tucked a tiny quilt around him and, with one last backward glance, he stole out of the room.

He'd never been a whiz with a needle and thread. Still, he'd been a bachelor living on his own for half of his life. He could sew on a button if he needed to. The principle was the same, wasn't it? How hard could it be?

Of course, he couldn't try out his invention until Conan woke up, but once he did, the baby fit neatly and securely in the sling.

Carter grinned down at the silky hair and the warm cheek pressed against his chest. ''Look, kid. Both hands.'' He waved them in front of Conan's face.

He climbed up on the roof that way. It was a little harder going up the ladder. And once he got there, he had to make sure he had all the shingles, nails and tools he needed before he settled down, because he couldn't scramble around with the ease he'd been used to.

But it worked!

''Take that, Dad,'' he muttered and hammered a shingle into place.

That's where they were when Leif appeared that afternoon.

He waved at Carter from the top of the hill, then loped down and climbed the ladder. It wasn't until he reached the top that he stopped and stared. ''Cripes! It is a baby! Where'd you get it?''

Carter positioned another shingle. ''On the porch.'' He took in Leif's disbelieving expression and added, ''Would I lie to you?''

Leif grinned. ''Maybe. Whose is it?''

''Somebody named Maeve.''

''I know her! She used to come to see Frances. She was sorta cool.'' He peered again at the baby. ''Cripes. She's like only a year older'n Libby. How come she brought it to you?''

''She thought she was bringing him to Frances. She's got some problems to work out.''

''You gonna keep him?''

''For now.''

''You know what to do with babies?'' Leif was skeptical.

''More or less.''

''You're pretty brave, Carter. Or pretty stupid.''

Carter grinned ruefully. ''Thanks.''

''What's his name?''

''Conan.''

Leif laughed and took another long look at the baby, then at Carter. ''You're gonna have your hands full. Bring him over tonight. Show Ma. She'll flip.''

''I've got a date.'' Even as he said it, he realized he also had a problem. Wondering if Marilee Newman liked children had suddenly become more than an academic question. He wondered what she'd think of going out as a threesome.

''Who with?''

Carter told him.

Leif's eyes got big. ''Wow. She's foxy.''

''She's what?''

Leif reddened. ''Aw, you know. She's got big...an' she's real...and her eyes...''

''It's business.''

''I thought you said it was a date.''

''Date to talk about business.''

''Yeah, sure.'' Leif was having none of it. ''So, who's baby-sitting?''

''I haven't thought about it,'' he admitted.

"I will—at our house. If Ma's there. Ten bucks. What'd'ya say?"

"*Ten* bucks! You shyster!"

"Children are our most precious resource." Leif gave him a cheeky grin.

"I took you to Boston and I didn't charge your mother a cent!"

"She gave me money and told me not to impose on you."

"I bought your dinner and your ticket to the game."

"Yeah. Well, okay. Tonight it's on the house." Leif cocked his head. "Did you really think I was gonna charge you?"

"I never know what you Archers are going to do," Carter grumbled.

"Campbell. I'm a Campbell." Leif corrected. "Ma's an Archer."

Of course. A woman as stubborn and independent as Annabel Archer wouldn't ally herself with any man. Carter shifted irritably and scratched. Conan began to grumble a little, sucking on his fist, making a grizzling sound.

"I think he's hungry," Leif said.

"Probably," Carter agreed. "Let's call it a day."

"You wanta come see the fort me and Roger built by the old mill?"

"Not today. Gotta feed my friend here."

"Tomorrow?"

"Yeah, okay."

All the time he was mashing a banana for Conan, he considered his options: he could call off his meeting with Marilee; he could take Conan with him; he could get Leif—and thereby Annabel—to baby-sit.

He eliminated the second at once. Even he wasn't a big

enough idiot to take a baby on a first date. He set Leif to feeding Conan while he went to call Marilee.

But she was in a meeting.

"May I take a message?" the secretary asked.

Carter couldn't imagine explaining over the phone that he'd come up with a baby overnight. He sighed. So much for options.

"Leif," he said. "You've got a job."

"WHAT DO YOU MEAN, you're baby-sitting for Carter?" The thought stopped her cold. Annabel knew Leif wasn't kidding. She could see that from the expression on his face.

"He found a baby on the porch this morning. It's Maeve's."

"Oh, heavens." But her feelings of sympathy for Maeve were overshadowed by a shaft of pure relief that the child was not Carter's.

"He's got a date tonight," Leif went right on. "With Marilee Newman. So we're going to baby-sit. Neat, huh?"

Annabel sat down.

Leif looked at her oddly. "You don't mind, do you, Ma?" he asked a little worriedly now.

She dredged up a smile. "Of course not." What she minded was that Carter was going out with Marilee Newman.

She tried to talk herself out of caring. Why should she? And why shouldn't he? she asked herself. It had been her own idea, for heaven's sake. She'd given him Marilee's name!

But try as she might, she couldn't face the prospect with complete equanimity. She kept remembering the picture of him with Libby and Leif, kept thinking about how frightened she had been, how tempted she had been the moment he'd come back to throw her arms around him and hang on tight.

No, she thought. Oh, no.

He was going out with Marilee Newman.

She drew a careful breath. "I'm looking forward to it."

She was, too, after a fashion. She was curious about how Carter had handled this unexpected windfall. She remembered saying to him just last night, "When you have a child," never thinking it would be so soon.

Not that it would last, of course. But she knew how much he liked children. She'd seen it with Libby and Leif, with Jason. Marilee Newman was the right age to be thinking about starting a family. She wondered if that was what Carter had in mind.

"Does Carter like the baby?" she asked Leif.

Her son looked at her as if she were out of her mind. "Like him? I guess! He made him this pouch an' everything."

Annabel amused herself with visions of Carter as a marsupial until he arrived on their doorstep, when she found out she wasn't far wrong.

She opened the door to find him standing there in jeans and a crewneck sweater, dark green, the same color as his eyes. His hair was brushed, his loafers shined. And wrapped around his middle was some sort of cloth contraption from which she could see poking out little bits of snugly wrapped baby.

"Amazing," she muttered. He looked so fatherly, so natural.

"What?" Carter sounded defensive.

She shook her head, smiling. "Nothing. Come in. I understand you've become a father."

"Only temporarily." He sounded almost regretful. "He's Maeve's. Did Leif tell you?"

"Yes. But not why she left it with Frances. At least, I presume she intended it for Frances and not you."

"She did. But we're not doing so bad, are we, fella?" Carter bent his head and spoke in a soft voice to the baby. Annabel, watching him, felt a quickening stab of something—Envy? Jealousy?—she didn't know.

"Maeve and her husband or boyfriend—she doesn't say which—are having some problems and need a little time and space. Hence, Conan. I appreciate you taking him on such short notice."

"I had more notice than you did."

"Yeah, well...these things happen."

He didn't seem at all upset by his unexpected fatherhood. In fact, he seemed unwilling to hand the baby over. Only when Annabel asked, "What time is your date?" did he glance at his watch, grimace, then begin undoing the straps.

Annabel moved to help him, easing the baby out of its snug pouch and cradling it in her arms. It felt so familiar, so natural. It had been so long. She stepped away quickly, trying to squelch the urgent maternal feelings growing inside her.

"Leif said he'd take him back over to Frances's at bedtime," Carter was saying. "I brought along some food and a bottle. Also diapers and a clean stretch suit. An extra pair of plastic pants. And a rattle." He put each object in turn on the table.

"You're very thorough."

He gave her a strained smile. "I'm trying. I hope he doesn't give you any trouble."

Annabel shook her head and smiled at the baby in her arms. "He won't."

"You can call me. At Rossi's."

"I doubt if Marilee would appreciate a phone call in the middle of a date."

Carter looked uncomfortable. "It's okay," he insisted.

"I hope we won't need to."

"Yeah, well, me, too." He shifted his weight from side to side again, as if something was bothering him.

Didn't he trust her? Annabel wondered. "I do know how to take care of babies, Carter."

He gave her a rueful grin. "Yeah. Better than I do, I'm sure. It's just...just..." He shrugged, hesitated, then backed out the door. "I'll go. Thanks."

Annabel, with the baby, walked him to the door, watched him go down the steps, felt an odd little tugging ache somewhere deep inside her. "No problem," she said. "We'll enjoy it," she said. "Have...a good time."

MARILEE NEWMAN was the woman of his dreams. The one he'd been waiting for all his life. Somewhere back in his subconscious, years ago, he'd dreamed her up—tall, slim, with long blond hair, sculpted cheekbones, classic jawline, full mouth with supremely kissable lips.

She was already at Rossi's when he arrived. Perched on a bar stool, sipping a club soda, her grape-colored wool skirt hiked up just enough to give him a glimpse of a tiny bit of thigh, her wavy hair curving to cup her cheek, she made his heart kick over, made the itch he'd been feeling all day grow worse. And worse yet when she looked him up and down and smiled.

Thank God he hadn't brought Conan. First things first.

He smiled. "Ms. Newman?"

"If we're going to have dinner together, I think you'd better call me Marilee." Her voice was slightly huskier in person than it had been on the phone, less businesslike, more caressing.

And she had a dimple, too, God help him. Just the tiniest indentation in one cheek appeared as she moved to make room for him at the bar.

Carter drew a steadying breath and held out his hand, enjoying to the hilt the warm, firm pressure of hers. "Marilee. I'm glad to meet you. At last."

One curving eyebrow lifted. "At last?"

"I feel as if I've been waiting all my life." If Annabel could hear him, she'd be gagging on her carrot juice.

Marilee laughed. "Better and better. Tell me about this property you want to buy and what you want to do with it. Tell me about you."

Carter could make small talk with the best of them. He was never averse to offering a personal anecdote or two. He ordered a Scotch. They moved from the bar to their table, with Marilee alternately offering sound purchasing advice and at the same time asking Carter questions about his background.

He tried to answer. He kept thinking about Conan. And Annabel. Was he taking his bottle? Would she remember to burp him? Had he left her enough diapers?

"And after Berkeley, what?" Marilee asked him.

"Huh? Oh, I spent a year traveling." Working his way around the globe, taking whatever jobs he could find, infuriating his father who wanted him to come home and get to work.

"Sounds like fun," Marilee said. "You must've been a regular rolling stone."

"I guess." The thought depressed him. He didn't want to roll. He wanted to settle down. He tried to focus on Marilee. She was beautiful, all right. And intelligent. Savvy. Was she really the one?

Had he remembered to give Annabel the jar of peaches?

"—leaving New York?"

"What?" He looked up, startled.

Marilee was looking expectantly at him. "Thought I'd lost you," she chided. "I just wondered if you were really serious about leaving New York."

Was he? He didn't know. He'd always lived in cities. They were comfortable as long as you knew the ropes. But he had to admit he'd rather enjoyed the last week. "I like Boone's Corner," he said, surprising himself.

Marilee smiled at him. "Good."

The food at Rossi's was good, the conversation better. It was serious, yet at times downright playful. Clearly Marilee Newman wasn't averse to a little flirtation. Nor, it seemed, was she averse to getting to know Carter better.

He tried his best to get to know her. It was perverse, he told himself, that when the right woman finally came along, he would find himself preoccupied by a baby and the world's most irritating woman. He shifted uncomfortably, trying to ease the continual itch that had been plaguing him all day.

He must have done something right, though, for after dinner, when he thought she'd want to hop in her car and leave, instead she suggested that they continue their conversation at an inn.

"There's a great piano bar. We could forget real-estate law and just talk. Like you said—" her lower lip jutted slightly, tempting him "—get to know each other."

"You don't have to be in court early?" he asked.

"Not until ten."

So they went to the piano bar. The conversation all but stopped, however. The piano was soft and moody and, the moment they got there, Marilee took his hand and said, "Let's dance."

What was a guy to do?

She was tall and she fit into his arms as if she belonged there. Her lips were bare inches from his.

Kiss me, they urged him. And he would have, wanting to see if her kisses would set him on fire the way Annabel's had. But the gentle press of her body against his set off a fiery feeling that wouldn't quit.

Carter was used to fiery feelings when it came to beautiful women, but this one was getting out of hand.

It had been building all day, nagging, itching, even before his proximity to Marilee. He didn't know what the hell was causing it. He only knew that Marilee made it worse.

She could make it better, too, he thought ruefully. But not tonight.

They danced three dances. He couldn't last any longer.

''I, uh, need to get home,'' he said when the music finally stopped.

Marilee cocked her head and gave him a teasing smile. ''Got to get up early to work on the roof tomorrow?''

Carter flushed. ''They're predicting rain in the afternoon.'' He didn't know whether they were or not.

Marilee sighed. ''Fair enough.'' She picked up her coat from the back of the chair and Carter helped her into it. ''Will I see you again?''

''Do you want to?''

''Oh, yes.''

He smiled. ''Dinner on Wednesday?''

His life would probably be back to normal by Wednesday. Maeve would probably have retrieved Conan by then, and this ridiculous itch—whatever it was—would be gone.

''I'll look forward to it,'' she said as he walked her to her car.

''Same time, same place?''

''Oh, I know a better place,'' Marilee said, her dimple returning to tantalize him. ''Mine.''

Carter wanted to scratch. He gritted his teeth. ''Sounds great. I'll bring some wine.''

''And you can help cook.'' The dimple deepened.

''I'll cook with you any day, Miz Newman,'' he drawled.

She laughed that husky, sexy laugh and blew him a kiss. ''Till Wednesday.''

ANNABEL WAS NOT sentimental.

She did not cry at weddings. She had let her children race off to kindergarten without a moment's qualm.

And if she'd kept the best of their baby clothes, it was more a matter of frugality and the fear that if she got rid of them, somehow God would find a way to get her pregnant again, than of a need to remember the days when Leif and Libby were so small.

So she couldn't understand this fascination with Conan.

But fascinated she was. Besotted, more like.

Why else would she have insisted on feeding him his bottle when Leif was perfectly capable of doing it? Why else would she have played pat-a-cake when she should have been poking cloves in oranges and saving up money to shingle her house? Why else would she have told Leif that she would carry the baby back to Frances's and stay with him until Carter got back?

Why else, except to recapture those moments when she had felt young and strong, steady and sensible, calm and collected, as if she had all the answers to the meaning of life?

Well, she might be doing it because of Carter.

If she was honest, there was that.

Carter MacKenzie.

She couldn't seem to get away from him. It was odd—annoying—how much time she spent thinking about a man she didn't even want to like.

She owed the whole direction of her life to Carter MacKenzie, and he hadn't a clue. Even now he was oblivious to it, wandering on through his own, dating this woman and that one. Lost, Frances said. Searching, Frances told her.

While he had inadvertently set Annabel on a course toward the best years she'd ever known.

She looked down at Conan, sound asleep in her arms. She stroked his petal-soft cheek and crooned lullabies to him. She remembered Libby as a babe in arms, recalled the chaos that had been her life then, of Mark's despair and flight, and still the comfort and sense of rightness she'd found holding her daughter close late at night.

She thought about Leif, born five years later into very different circumstances, to parents who'd weathered plenty of storms and had found faith in each other again.

She thought about Mark. About loving him and losing him. About finding and losing again.

She thought about the years since. Nine of them. Long years in some ways. Mere hours, in others, it seemed.

She was thirty-six now. Twice the age she'd been when Libby was born. Not twice as smart or twice as clever. Just twice as old.

And, she thought ruefully, sometimes she feared she knew no more about where her life was going than Libby knew about hers.

She knew the folly of dreaming. Of false hopes.

But as she looked down at Conan, snug and secure in her arms, she knew one thing. She had no real regrets. Her father had always expected her to, had waited all these years for her to admit she was wrong, to come back home.

But she hadn't been wrong. She still wasn't.

She had loved Mark. She loved her children. If Mark had lived, there would have been more.

''Babies like you,'' she said to Conan.

She looked down at the tiny child and a smile curved her mouth. ''Just like you.''

No, she didn't regret it a bit. She'd do it all over again.

Chapter Seven

Carter took the front steps in one bound, listening, as he had been since he'd opened the door of the Blazer, for sounds of Conan screaming.

All was quiet.

He slowed then, proceeding more cautiously, not wanting to wake the baby—not wanting to wake Leif, either, if the boy had fallen asleep. It was past eleven and high time he was home in bed.

Carter knew he should have called, should have told Leif he'd be late. But he'd had no idea when Marilee had suggested the inn with the piano bar that it would be so far or that it would take so long.

He eased open the door and crept into the entry, slipping off his shoes before he padded into the dimly lit living room.

Annabel was asleep on the couch.

He stopped dead and stared.

She lay with her head pillowed on one arm, her gingery hair spread out against the arm of the couch, her body curled beneath the soft sea-colored shawl. Her lashes lay like half-moons against her cheeks. He'd never noticed before how long and thick her lashes were. He'd never had the chance, he mused. Usually her eyes were wide open and flashing amber fire at him.

But her eyes were shut now, and he allowed himself a moment to appreciate her long-lashed beauty for the first time. He also appreciated her lips, slightly parted, full and soft and reminding him of the night he'd arrived, the night he'd kissed her.

He made a soft, strangled sound. Annabel woke up.

"Oh!" She blinked, sat up, rubbed her eyes and started to stand, but she did so too quickly and she lost her balance, sinking back onto the sofa.

"You okay?"

"Fine." Her voice sounded soft and rusty, quite unlike the customary drill-sergeant responses he expected from her.

He smiled.

"I just fell asleep a moment ago," she said, standing again, this time managing to stay upright. With one foot she was groping around on the floor for her shoes.

"I'm sorry I'm so late."

She stopped groping and gave him a sidelong glance. "I trust you had a good time." Her voice was getting back to normal. Starchy and disapproving.

He stiffened. "I did. I can't figure out why you put her fourth on your list." He tried to sound outraged as he took a step back. He was too susceptible tonight, too much in the mood for things that would never happen. And he itched. Still.

"I put her fourth because I didn't know her, that's all." Annabel found one shoe, stuffed her foot in it, then felt for the other. "I'm glad you liked her," she said tersely.

"You don't sound glad."

Annabel gave an inarticulate mutter. "I'm thrilled."

She glanced at her watch. "Good grief. What'd you do, have a seven-course meal?"

"We went dancing. A discreet little piano bar. I didn't know Vermont had such interesting places."

"Trust you to find them." She bent down and was reaching under the sofa for her other shoe. In seconds she'd be gone.

"Did Conan behave?" he asked quickly.

"Oh, yes. He was a lamb. He ate his peaches and drank his bottle. We played games and Leif wrestled with him...." Her starchiness faded even as she spoke.

"Leif wrestled with him?"

"Oh, you know. Little-boy stuff. Lots of noise and not much else. Like you and Jack this summer."

Carter scowled at her. "That was not little-boy stuff."

"Oh, right." Annabel had found her other shoe and was heading for the door.

"I'll walk you home."

"Don't be ridiculous."

"It's close to midnight. You're a woman out alone."

"In the middle of the woods. This is not a discreet piano bar full of men on the make. Who do you think is going to jump me? Arnold?"

"I'll walk you home."

"Don't be an idiot, Carter," she said gruffly. "I'll be fine." And giving his cheek a condescending pat, she opened the door and walked out without looking back.

Carter stared after her. "You're a bossy witch, you know that?"

She turned, grinned, gave him a little wave. "You'd better believe it."

He watched her until she was across the yard and starting up the slope, until he had almost lost her in darkness. "Annabel?"

"What?" Her voice floated back to him.

"...Thanks."

HE HAD THIS FAINT mottled red rash in places he'd rather not associate with rashes. He had a baby who thought 2:00 a.m. was playtime. He paced the floor. And hummed. He played the guitar. And sang. He did pat-a-cake and peekaboo and thought he'd lose his mind.

He tried to focus his thoughts on more pleasant topics: Marilee's throaty laugh and long legs, the way she had smiled at him, had said that next time they'd eat at her place. He remembered far more vividly Annabel asleep under her shawl, Annabel starchy and disapproving, Annabel's spitfire response.

He itched. He scratched.

"Come on, Conan," he pleaded. "We've got a long day tomorrow. Miles and miles of roof."

Finally at 3:00 a.m., when Carter had very nearly given up hope, Conan smiled, closed his eyes and went back to sleep.

"Thank God."

He had a new appreciation of why Jack sometimes looked bleary-eyed in the mornings. He sank back against the cool sheets and shut his eyes, reached down and scratched.

A million impressions kaleidoscoped in his mind, inundating him, spinning around, becoming a whirling mass of emotions, sensations, thoughts. He tried to stop them, order them, sort them: Conan in the box, Conan on the roof, Conan in his arms, smiling; Leif handing him the shingles, Leif feeding the baby; Marilee laughing, Marilee looking deep into his eyes while they danced; Annabel.

In the end, oddly, there was only that one.

Annabel.

"CARTER CALLED," Jack told Frances when she came in from walking Jason in the park.

"Anything new?"

"Two things. First, he's met his idea of the perfect woman."

"Ah." Her smile widened.

Jack grinned. "Her name is Marilee Newman."

"What? Who? Who in heaven's name is Marilee Newman?"

"Some lawyer from Gaithersburg. Annabel gave him her name." He almost laughed at the look on Frances's face.

But then the look changed, became thoughtful, then slyly knowledgeable. Frances nodded her head, smiled smugly.

Jack gave her a worried glance. "What?" he demanded.

"Defense mechanism."

"Huh?"

"Never mind. What's the other bit of news?"

"Oh." He wasn't sure whether he ought to grin about this bit or not. "He's become a father."

Frances just stared.

"Remember Maeve—"

"Maeve?" Frances was shocked. "No! He couldn't have! Carter would never—"

"Relax. *He* didn't do anything. Except find Maeve's baby on the doorstep. *Our* doorstep. She's taken off after her boyfriend or husband or whatever he is, and baby was a burden. She left him for you. Carter's got him."

Frances grinned. "I'll bet he's doing fine. Isn't he?"

"As a matter of fact, he seems to be. He was enjoying it."

"I knew it."

"You really think they'll be okay? The two of them?" Jack didn't feel all that confident himself.

"I think they'll be fine."

"What about Maeve?"

"She's a pretty bright girl. She obviously thinks she can work things out, and if Carter is willing to hang on to the baby while she tries, why not? They deserve a chance. All of them."

"And you don't think you should maybe…step in? Arrange things?"

"Oh, no." Frances shook her head. "I wouldn't have the faintest idea how things should work out for them."

"Not like you do with Carter and Annabel?" Jack teased.

"No," she said. "Not at all like that."

SO HE'D DINED and danced with Marilee Newman. He liked her. He was probably even taking her out again.

Annabel accompanied all these enthusiastic thoughts by banging her mixing bowls down on the counter and slamming the silverware drawer. She also reached over and changed the tape in her stereo. She'd started with Beethoven, gone on to Waylon before nine, and now at ten-thirty she knew if she was going to get anything done today, she'd moped long enough. She needed stimulation.

"How about this?" she said to Goliath.

He shot off the counter at the first crash of John Philip Sousa.

"Sorry," she said to his departing tail. "But it's time for desperate measures."

Ten times, at least, she had reached for the phone to call and see how Conan was, to find out if he'd slept through the night, if he'd taken all of his bottle, if he was awake then and, if so, what he was doing.

Nine times, thank heavens, she'd put the receiver down

without making the connection. The tenth she made herself dial Aaron Leggett, instead.

"I was wondering," she said without preamble, "if you would like to go see the Woody Allen movie in Gaithersburg tonight?"

Aaron stuttered for at least ten seconds before saying, "S-sure."

"Shall I meet you there?"

"I'll pick you up. We can have dinner."

Annabel thought that dinner might be too much, then thought it might not be nearly enough. "Why not?" she said recklessly.

"See you at five-thirty," Aaron said.

Annabel put the phone down and found that she breathed a little easier. Until five seconds had passed and she found that the sight of Arnie, looking grumpy in the pasture, made her think she should take him down to Frances's. And that made her think about Carter and…

"Stop it," she said to herself aloud.

She didn't want to think about Carter. He was well and truly taken care of at last.

He was plenty busy now with Conan and with the roof and with Marilee Newman. He wouldn't be at a loose end. All his available time was taken up.

She needn't worry about him being around disconcerting her anymore. She needn't worry about Frances's meddling.

If she needed to worry about anything, Annabel decided, she needed to worry about why she cared.

ALL DAY it had been getting worse.

The itching.

The scratching.

The rash.

He'd expected to get up in the morning and find it gone.

It was still there, less red than when he'd showered the night before, but there, all right, from somewhere just south of his navel down to the tops of his thighs. Carter scowled at it, wondering what Milly would say if he showed it to her.

Probably tell him it was a psychosomatic allergic reaction to fatherhood or some ridiculous thing.

He'd never ask her in any case. He might on occasion bare his soul for Milly's inspection, but he'd be damned if he'd bare the rest of him!

Still, he had to do something. It nagged at him continually, made him quick-tempered and irritable, made it nearly impossible to sit up there and work on the roof for any length of time, made him squirm even when he was stretched out on the sofa giving Conan a bottle.

And every time he checked it, hoping against hope that it was lessening, growing fainter, he found it getting worse. Redder. Blotchier.

Leif came over after school so they could go see the fort he and Roger had built.

"You ready to go?"

The very thought of walking all that way made him wince. "Taking Conan might be a hassle. We could wait until—"

"It's no problem. Not with that sling thing you made. I'll carry him."

"It's almost time for his nap."

Leif stared down at Conan, lying on his back in the middle of a blanket, giggling, wide-eyed. Leif shrugged. "We can wait."

Carter managed a surreptitious scratch, then sighed. "Never mind. We'll go now."

The walk was less than a mile. Another day it would have been marvelous. The trees were at the height of autumn color and the day was clear and bright, warm in the direct sun but blessedly cool in the shade of the trees. They followed a narrow path behind Frances's property, then across the back of Annabel's. They went over three stone walls, up a hillside, along the side of the stream. Leif chattered. Conan gurgled. Carter itched.

He'd never had anything like it save the time he'd been cutting trees on his father's place in New Jersey and had got poison ivy all over his arms. This wasn't poison ivy—not unless he'd been shinnying up trees naked in his sleep.

By the time they got back, he was frantic. He handed Leif a bottle of milk. ''Feed him this and put him down in the crib, will you? I'm going to grab a shower.''

Still scratching, Carter escaped up the stairs. By the time he came back down, Conan was asleep and Leif was reading a magazine.

''Thought you'd have gone,'' Carter said, glancing at his watch. ''Didn't you say your mother wanted you home by 5:30?''

''Not tonight. I can stay as late as I want. It's just me and Lib. Ma's going out.''

Carter scowled. ''With who?''

''Whom. With Aaron. Who else?''

''What for? Where? Why?''

''Dunno. She doesn't usually. She says she doesn't want to encourage him.''

''She doesn't want to marry him?''

Leif made a strangling sound. ''Gimme a break.''

Carter grinned his relief. ''So eat with me. Libby, too.'' He'd prefer it, actually. Having some company might take his mind off the red blotchiness that was driving him nuts.

Wishful thinking.

He didn't actually think Libby and Leif noticed his distraction. Even Libby, who professed no interest in babies, took a turn at giving Conan a bottle and playing peekaboo with him.

"He is kinda cute. It might be kinda neat to have a baby around."

"You're a little young."

"Maeve's only a year older," Libby countered, following him into the bedroom where he put a sleeping Conan into his crib.

"And you think she's doing a bang-up job, do you?" He bent and dropped a light kiss on Conan's ear, then turned and left the room, shutting off the light.

Libby followed, sighing. "I guess not."

"It's hard to be a parent when you're just a kid yourself."

"But if you meet the right guy—"

"It isn't only the people, Libby. It's the situation, the timing. It's all got to be right. Don't rush."

Libby looked up at him, her eyes, so like her mother's, wide and bright. "Don't get serious, you mean?"

Carter felt like an elderly uncle. "Something like that."

"About you?"

"You were interested in an old man like me?"

Libby laughed. She punched his arm lightly. "Oh, Carter."

He rubbed it. "I'm flattered."

"You are not." She started down the steps alongside him, then caught his arm, stopping him. "What about you? Are you ever going to get serious?"

"I try to now and then."

"Not that kind of serious, idiot. About a girl. A woman."

"Sure. When the time's right. If the right one comes along."

"When is it right? What makes the right one? How will you know?"

Trust a seventeen-year-old to ask the question of a lifetime. He gave a helpless shrug.

"What do you want in a wife?"

He didn't think he'd ever had a conversation like this with anyone, even Milly. He looked at Libby, wondering what she would ask next, wondering how he could even begin to answer the questions she'd already posed.

There was Diane, of course, whom he'd thought he loved. She'd said he didn't, and at the time he couldn't see it, but in retrospect, he was beginning to see that she was right.

He'd loved what Jack and Frances had—the sharing, the closeness, the commitment, the warmth. He wanted that for himself. And Diane seemed the best person to have it with.

But it wouldn't have worked. He liked Diane, maybe even loved her the way he loved Milly. He liked the way Marilee Newman looked. He liked her smile, her sexy laugh.

But real love? Honest-to-God enduring, adult love?

Love that made you want to laugh and cry, dance and sing, love that made life seem brighter, warmer, holier? Love that called forth the absolute best that a person had to give and made the world a better place?

"I don't know," he said at last.

The look she gave him bordered on exasperation. "Well, really, Carter. How can you expect to find the right woman if you don't have any idea what you're looking for?"

He raked a hand through his hair, then mustered a grin. "Don't you have to do your math?"

"Not tonight. Honestly, Carter, how can you be so good at math and so bad at life?"

He stopped grinning. It wasn't really funny.

"Men." Libby sighed and shook her head. "Come on, Leif. We've got to go."

"Half an hour," Leif promised. "I'm reading *Road and Track.*"

"Leif—"

"Let him finish," Carter said. "I'll send him along shortly."

Libby opened her mouth to protest then shrugged. "Okay. But if he's still there when Ma gets home…"

It wasn't to let Leif finish the article that Carter wanted him to stay. It was because he wanted a favor.

"Listen," he said when Leif had finished the article and was putting on his jacket. "You know those potions your mother makes? The ointments and stuff? Does she have any for rashes?"

"Rashes?" Leif frowned. "Like poison ivy? Probably. She's got stuff for everything unless it's really bad. Then she sends us to the doctor."

"Could you bring some over?"

"Sure. After school tomorrow."

"How about tonight?"

Leif's eyes widened a fraction. "Tonight? Yeah, I guess."

"Thanks. You're a pal."

He almost gave up. It was close to ten-thirty when at last he heard the knock on the door. He strode quickly out from the kitchen and jerked it open.

"I thought you weren't—*Annabel?*"

Her cheeks were flushed with the cold. Her hair was

flying in untamed wildness. She rushed right past him into the living room. "Let me see this rash."

WHY WAS HE STARING at her like that?

He looked almost horrified. Panicky. And here she'd been giving him credit for being such a surprisingly experienced hand at surrogate fatherhood.

Or, Annabel thought, maybe he wasn't panicking unnecessarily. Maybe Conan was really ill.

"Let me see the rash. Before I know what to do, I need to see it. Is it keeping him awake? Does he cry? He didn't have any rash last night." She said this last almost accusingly.

Carter just looked at her. There was a line of color along his cheekbones.

"Oh, for heaven's sake," she said when he still didn't speak. "Never mind. Frances says Jack goes nuts when Jason runs the tiniest fever. I suppose you're the same. I'll take care of it myself."

She flung off her coat and headed up the stairs. Conan wasn't crying at least. She'd reached the doorway when Carter cleared his throat.

"Annabel." His voice sounded ragged.

She turned, her hand on the knob.

"It isn't Conan."

"What?"

"It isn't Conan that has the rash." Pause. "It's me."

"You?"

He glared at her. "Babies aren't the only people who get rashes, you know."

"I know that. I—Leif said you needed ointment for a rash. He said Conan. I thought he said Conan. Did he say Conan?" She felt like a fool.

"Sorry," she said. She would have gone right back

down the stairs but he was standing on them, cutting off her avenue of escape. "I misunderstood."

They stared at each other. Neither moved. From the other side of the door Annabel heard Conan sucking softly in his sleep.

"I was worried about Conan. I thought he was sick."

"He's fine. D'you want to see him a minute? Since you're here, I mean."

"That'd be nice."

He motioned for her to open the door, and together they crept softly into the room. Conan was sound asleep, his fist in his mouth, his face turned toward the wall.

Annabel leaned over and peered down at him, marveling at his beauty, at his innocence and trust. She remembered other babies, other nights. When Carter came to stand next to her, their hands brushed.

Quickly Annabel stepped back. "Thank you." She moved quietly toward the door. "He's lovely."

Carter nodded. "I hope Maeve and Jerry can make a future for him."

"Me, too."

They looked at each other then and smiled. In complete accord for once, Annabel thought, amazed.

"So. Let's see if we can help you."

Carter blinked. "Huh?"

"Show me your rash," she said.

SHE WASN'T LOOKING at him as she spoke. She'd clattered down the steps and had gone to get something out of the pocket of her coat. "What is it?" she asked him over her shoulder. "Poison ivy? Contact dermatitis? Athlete's foot?"

"Uh—well—"

She had two jars in her hand. She was setting out some

small vials of powder. When he still stammered, she turned and looked at him expectantly.

"Carter?"

No one had ever called Carter MacKenzie bashful. Women had never complained that he was reticent about shedding his clothes in front of them.

But now?

Here?

In front of God and Annabel Archer?

He wanted to die.

Annabel seemed to realize this. She also seemed to realize he wasn't just going to push up his sleeve or reach down and slip off his shoe.

She looked faintly alarmed. "It's...?"

He nodded. He could almost see her become professional, detached.

She swallowed.

He did, too. It became a war between his pride and his rash.

His pride surrendered. He dropped his pants.

ANNABEL FELT, for all the world, as if she were a doe trapped in the headlights of an oncoming car.

She couldn't move. Could only stare. And what she was seeing wasn't the rash.

"So what is it? And how do I get rid of it?"

Annabel pulled herself together. "I...er...the light isn't good right here. Could you, um, maybe come over and lie down on the couch?"

Carter gave her a fulminating glare.

She switched on the reading lamp and stood waiting. "I can't see it over there."

He gritted his teeth and somewhat clumsily he made his way over and stretched out on the couch. Annabel focused the light. She could see the rash very well now. She could see considerably more than the rash. She took a slow, steadying breath, then forced herself to concentrate on the medical aspect of the sight before her.

It looked red and itchy and basically unhappy. It went from an inch or two below his navel to the tops of his thighs. And it seemed to go right around...

"Is it on your, er, bottom, too?"

"Yes."

"And how long have you had it?"

"Couple of days."

She glanced at the sparkling white briefs pushed down below his knees. "New underwear?"

He scowled. "What? No."

She reached down and plucked the fabric between her fingers. "No? They look whiter than white."

"Thank your daughter the laundress."

"Libby washed them?"

"She washes all my clothes. Remember? It's her mission in life."

"I see."

She was seeing a hell of a lot, Carter thought grimly. He'd never felt more exposed in his life. Serve her right if he had some airborne venereal disease. He looked away at the far side of the room. "So what is it?" he demanded.

"It looks," Annabel said mildly, "like diaper rash."

His humiliation was complete. He glared at her, outraged.

She was grinning, damn her. "Contact dermatitis, Carter. Your skin's probably become irritated by whatever detergent Libby's using."

"But it's not in my shirts. Or my jeans."

"Maybe it's bleach."

"I'm allergic to bleach!"

"There you are, then."

Carter said a rude word. He said several of them. Then he sat up and started to pull up his pants.

Annabel moved out of his way. "You go run the bath water. I'll get the oatmeal."

"What in hell do you want to eat oatmeal for?"

"I don't want to eat it. You're going to take a bath in it."

"Annabel," he protested.

"I thought you ran a health-and-wellness store. Don't you know anything?"

"I don't know anything about bathing in oatmeal, for cripes' sake. Is that brought to us by the same people who think we want to wash our hair in wheat germ and honey?"

"Probably," she said, but she was on her way to the kitchen and there was nothing he could do but head up the stairs to comply.

He ran the bathwater and waited, scratching. Finally, unable to stand it, he stripped off his clothes and got in.

He no more than got into the tub, than the door opened and she walked right in.

"Hey!"

"What? Oh, am I supposed to close my eyes now?"

He scowled. "I suppose you're used to walking into men's bathrooms."

"Sure. I do it all the time. Here." She dropped a cheesecloth bag filled with oatmeal into the bath water. "Sorry it took so long. I had to find some way to confine the oatmeal. Swish this around. It should take some of the itching away if you sit there awhile. I'll take care of these." These were his underpants. She picked them up, waved them at him and vanished out the door.

She was right about the oatmeal. He swished it around

and, after a while, it did seem to help. But the water was cool to begin with and he was getting goose bumps just sitting there, so he pulled the plug, got out and dried off carefully, trying not to start up the itching again.

Then, towel wrapped around his waist, he opened the door and padded into the bedroom.

Annabel was already there.

''Here. You can wear this.'' It was red and flannel and it didn't look promising.

''What is it?''

''Jack's nightshirt.''

''Jack's *nightshirt? Jack's* nightshirt? Jack wears nightshirts?''

''Not ordinarily, I understand. But Frances got him one. For research purposes.'' Her face was absolutely straight, except for a momentary twitch of one corner of her mouth.

Carter muttered under his breath.

''Well, you don't seem to have anything suitable.'' Annabel cast a scathing glance at his belongings. ''And you can't sleep in your underwear. It's in the wash. It'll have to go through at least twice, then be line dried tomorrow.'' She held out the nightshirt again.

''I sleep naked.''

''Fine.'' She shrugged indifferently. ''Come on, then.''

''Come on? Why, Annabel Archer, I thought you'd never ask.''

Chapter Eight

It was the challenge in his words that did it.

If he hadn't given her that seductive grin and almost taunted her—dared her—she would have simply handed him the ointment and walked away.

Heaven knew it was her first instinct.

But she couldn't.

It was odd, Annabel thought, the way life twisted and turned on itself, letting you walk away from situations, allowing you to believe you'd survived without confrontation, permitting you the false belief that you'd escape unscathed.

And then, whatever you'd run away from was back, staring—or in the present case, leering—you in the face.

And it was equally odd the things you thought of when it did.

Right now, for instance, faced with Carter MacKenzie wrapped in a towel, she was thinking of her father and Erik Erikson.

On the surface, not too likely. But if she analyzed it, which for a few moments she did, it made perfect sense.

Edward Lodge Archer met life head-on. Always had. Always would. And it galled him no end that his only child, Annabel, was such a wimp.

"You've got to get back on the damned horse, girl," he railed at her when his attempt to put his eight-year-old daughter on the most spirited horse in his stable had ended with Annabel in the dust.

But Annabel hadn't got back on. She'd mutely shaken her head and stumbled away. She'd never liked horses that much anyway.

She'd done the same thing when he'd taken her water-skiing. Plowing headfirst into the water wasn't Annabel's idea of fun. So what if you eventually got good enough to skim along at breakneck speeds, thumping madly along behind a maniac boat driver? If that didn't thrill you, why go through the pain?

And when someone clearly didn't want to dance with you at a yacht-club dance, when someone made it abundantly clear, in fact, that he thought you were the biggest turkey there, why force him—and yourself—into a clearly unpleasant situation?

What was wrong with avoiding problems?

Edward Archer and Erik Erikson knew.

You had to face problems to come away the conqueror, according to Edward Lodge Archer.

You had to pass through each successive stage of life before you could move on to the next one, wrote psychologist Erikson. No skipping. Ever. You stuck right where you were until you went through each and every one.

Annabel looked at Carter, at the low-slung towel. She knew now exactly what was underneath it. But she couldn't walk away yet. The gauntlet had been flung down.

Obviously Carter MacKenzie was a stage she was destined not to miss.

"Very funny," she said. "Now lie down so I can put this on you."

The seductive leer vanished in a flash. "Put what on me?"

"Ointment. It's what you asked for, isn't it?"

Something flickered in his gaze for just a moment...panic, apprehension? Annabel wasn't certain. But whatever it was, she was glad of it. If he was even slightly off balance, so much the better. Better the two of them than just her.

Carter seemed to grind his teeth.

Annabel waited, determined.

"Right," he said.

HE NEVER THOUGHT she'd do it.

One more time he'd misjudged Annabel Archer, he thought grimly as he lay facedown on the bed and felt the first touch of her fingers as they spread the cool cream against his fiery skin.

The gentleness of her touch almost made him moan. He swallowed hard.

"What is it? What sort of cream?" He needed to talk, to ramble incoherently, anything to forestall the inevitable physical response building inside him.

"Calendula cream." Her voice was husky. There seemed to be a vibrato in it when she spoke, or maybe he just imagined it. He didn't know anymore. Didn't even know his own name.

Her fingers were working a kind of magic on him. They moved rhythmically, soothingly over his tender hips and buttocks, then slipped down to stroke between his legs, not soothing him at all.

"Did you make it?" His voice was ragged.

"Yes." There was a slight catch in hers, too. "Does it help?"

"Yeah." But he thought the cure was likely worse than the disease. He fought down the urge to whimper.

Her fingers moved on, sending soft shivers through him, making him crazy. Finally they stopped, came to rest lightly on his hip. "You can...roll over now."

He went rigid.

Roll over?

God! Didn't she realize? He looked up at her.

She was peering down at him, apprehension in her wide dark eyes. "Carter?" She sounded a little worried.

She wasn't the only one.

He shut his own eyes. There was no way on earth he could roll over. Not without disgracing himself entirely. Or not without reaching for her, taking her, making her a part of him.

Make love to Annabel Archer?

How incredible was that?

But damn it, he wanted to! Wanted *her!*

And Annabel? Did she want it? Yeah, sure. One move and she'd give him a bloody nose. Or worse.

His fingers curled into fists against the sheet. He sucked in a breath and bit down on his lip.

"Go away, Annabel," he muttered into the pillow.

"I'm not—"

"Go away!"

"You don't want...?"

He lifted his head and turned his glowering gaze on her. "Oh, yes, Annabel," he bit out. "I damned well do!"

He didn't move, just watched as she stood, then set the jar on the table by the bed.

She looked down at him, her gaze making him burn as it traveled with incredible slowness up the length of his body until at last once more their eyes momentarily locked.

She smiled, a faint and oddly wistful smile as she backed away. But the most disconcerting thing of all came when she turned and left the room.

Had he really heard her whisper, "Me, too?"

"DID YOU EVER HAVE a midlife crisis?" Annabel asked Sister Bertha the next morning. They had been making a new batch of goat's milk soap since seven o'clock, a project that required more than one set of hands. And while Bert discoursed at length on most of the important issues in the world, Annabel replied in monosyllables, if at all.

To Annabel, after last night, the most important issue in the world was what she felt about Carter MacKenzie and, more important, what she was going to do about it.

She had been determined to face him, to touch him, and to walk away unscathed. And she had walked away, all right.

But unscathed?

Dream on, sweetie, she told herself.

Whatever God and Erik Erikson had in mind for her in the Carter MacKenzie stage, it was obvious she wasn't through it yet.

"A midlife crisis?" Bert laughed as she poured the soap into the molds. "Did I ever! But they didn't call it a midlife crisis in those days. They called it Vatican II."

"I'm not sure it's the same thing."

"Of course it is," Bert said briskly. "It's a matter of confronting who you thought you were, learning who you really are and where you're really going with your life."

Yes, it was that, all right. "But I thought I already knew," Annabel said a bit plaintively.

"And...?"

"Now I don't."

"Carter."

Annabel looked at her sharply. "How did you know?"

"I've got eyes."

Self-conscious, uncomfortable to know she'd been so obvious, Annabel made a production of tapping the molds gently on the counter to release air bubbles. But finally she had to ask, "What do you see?"

"That you're interested." Pause. "And he is, too."

"Interested? In me? I don't think so."

Bert tsked. "Look again."

But Annabel shook her head. Even if he'd actually almost said he wanted to make love with her last night, she knew very well that it wasn't because he loved her. It was merely a physical response to her touching him. When she thought about it now, she could feel the blood burn in her cheeks.

How had she dared?

She was lucky he hadn't pushed the issue. Or had she been wishing he would? Was that what was behind her recklessness? Had she been hoping he'd take the matter out of her hands, leave her no choice?

The very thought made her wince. It was so very much against her principles, so totally against everything she had ever claimed to believe about the way relationships ought to be conducted between women and men.

What had Bert just said? That going through a midlife crisis was a matter of confronting who you thought you were, learning who you really are…

Annabel gave a little moan.

"Something wrong?" Bert asked.

"No. Not at all. Just…thinking."

She did a lot of thinking that day, about herself, about the past, the present and the future. About Carter.

She wished she had someone to talk to about it. About him. She wished now that she'd confided in Frances the first time Jack had brought Carter to the house. But she hadn't. What was the point? she'd asked herself. Why rake up past disasters?

And, indeed, at the time there had seemed little point. Especially since Carter clearly had no recollection of her.

Afterward, even when she saw him again at Thanksgiving or at Jason's baptism, she had said nothing.

She never thought she'd be subjected to him on virtually a daily basis. She never thought Frances would dream of matchmaking. And she certainly never thought that her reactions to Carter would have remained the same.

Was it natural perversity, she wondered, that made her so constantly aware of him—as aware now as she had been that fateful night at Marblehead?

She could remember it all so well, as if it were yesterday, not nineteen years before.

She hadn't wanted to be there at all. The yacht club was one of her father's bailiwicks. It had nothing to do with her.

She didn't like yachts any more than she liked waterskiing. Nor did she like going to dances where she stood on the sidelines thinking about the book she'd rather have been home reading while she watched other girls twirl competently around the room.

All in all, to Edward Archer she must have been a most unsatisfactory child.

She was a dreamer, given by fate into the hands of a doer. And while her mother might have felt a modicum of sympathy for the unsuitable daughter she had given birth to, Christina Archer had no power to protect her daughter from Edward's plans. Indeed, why should she want to?

It wasn't as if Edward abused the child. It wasn't even

as if he didn't care. Probably, Annabel thought now, he cared too much.

But whether he cared or not, he certainly didn't understand her, didn't want to try.

He never accepted that she found little joy in the social whirl that was his life and breath. He never understood that what he found inspiring, to his daughter produced only dread.

Most importantly, he never saw that she wasn't every young man's ideal.

"You'll be the belle of the ball, my Annabel," he told her, with unpardonable optimism, the evening of the Marblehead affair.

He took in his tall, gangly daughter, her long gingery hair crimped and twisted into an uncharacteristic halo of curls, her curvy figure accentuated in a frilled and flounced, rose-colored gown her ever-hopeful mother had chosen, and nodded his head in approval.

Annabel merely shook hers. She knew better. There were girls who attracted the boys the way honey pots did bees. There were others who, in the words of one of her more perceptive teachers, might "find the right man someday."

Implied, but not stated, was that someday wouldn't be soon.

Annabel didn't care. She knew that someday her prince would come. She was quite confident that she would know him when he did.

She was willing to wait, even if her father was not.

Marblehead, as far as Edward Archer was concerned, was Annabel's launching pad. After an indifferent, inauspicious—not to say totally disastrous, in his eyes—childhood, she would redeem herself here.

Being a debutante was, happily for Annabel, passé. Few

of the girls she knew were obliged to go through the continuous round of parties, teas and formal dances that had brought women of earlier generations into society's folds.

But just because she didn't have to go through the formal rigmarole, she didn't get off scot-free.

On the contrary, her father made it quite clear that, either at Marblehead or one of the several other dances she was going to that year, she would meet the man who would, a few years hence, marry her. Under Edward's careful tutelage, he would take over Archer Industries and, of course, provide Edward Archer with the requisite handsome grandchildren, thereby insuring the succession.

Annabel doubted it sincerely.

Of course, she didn't tell her father that. She never told her father anything. One didn't talk to Edward Archer. One only listened and, at the appropriate moment, nodded one's assent.

She expected a boring evening. She was prepared for nothing more than a duty dance with her father, another with Michael Peters, the son of her father's golfing crony, a few glasses of watered-down punch and a couple of tasteless cucumber sandwiches.

And then she saw Carter MacKenzie.

Love bloomed.

Well, not love precisely. Even Annabel wasn't enough of a romantic to believe in that.

But infatuation, certainly. Interest. Heightened awareness. A tingling. A sense of something momentous about to occur.

Years before she had expected him, her prince was here.

He was laughing, his head thrown back, a lively grin on his handsome face.

Yes, Annabel thought. Oh, yes.

But it was his liveliness more than his good looks that

attracted her. Handsome young men in tuxes, their manners as polished as their shoes, were a dime a dozen in Annabel's stuffy world. But this one made a difference to the very air.

The room had seemed flat and stale until he'd come in. Now there was life, excitement—promise—in the air.

"Who is he?" she asked Lolly Talbot, one of the twirlers who would undoubtedly know.

Lolly looked. "Carter MacKenzie. Daddy's in oil. Chemicals. Steel or something. New York, Palm Beach, Cape Cod. Good catch."

Annabel wasn't fishing. She wouldn't have cared had he been destitute. It was the inner man who mattered, not how many companies his father ran or how many mansions he owned.

She looked at Carter again, who was now being introduced to somebody's mother, and saw that the laughter had vanished. He was looking polite and slightly bored, but there was still that energy in him, leashed now, controlled. As if he wasn't really interested, as if he was but waiting…waiting…

Like her.

She wanted to dance with him, to talk to him. She wanted to know what made him laugh, what made him frown, what would make his heart sing the way hers had the moment he came into the room.

She hadn't the slightest hope of doing so. Unless…

He was dancing with Wendy Ferguson. The same Wendy Ferguson who had copied Annabel's sociology homework for an entire semester. The same Wendy Ferguson who would have been caught smoking before chapel had Annabel not deliberately crashed into her and knocked the cigarette into the pond. The same Wendy Ferguson who spent the weekend with Willy Carstairs last March and told her parents she was with Annabel Archer.

Wendy owed her. A lot.

She got up, moved over near to where Carter was standing and tried to look as if she were having such a good time that he should come and share it with her.

He didn't.

She followed him to the punch bowl and waited for him to see her and fall under her spell the way she had fallen under his. But he only edged past her in the crush, then tripped over her feet on the way back.

He did, however, give her a glance and vague smile.

Annabel stood, rooted, smiling back at where he'd been.

"Do take a cup and move along, dear," said one of the matrons irritably. Sighing, Annabel did.

But as the evening wore on and he never approached her, she grew more and more desperate. She felt as if she were Cinderella at the ball, watching midnight come ever closer and never getting a chance at the prince.

She knew—just knew—if the dance passed without her getting to know Carter MacKenzie, her life would be irrevocably different.

She sought out Wendy Ferguson in the powder room.

"You want to dance with Carter? Why?"

But even if she'd been inclined to, Annabel couldn't have answered that. "M-my father," she offered after a moment. "He'll think I haven't been making an effort."

"Whatever."

They left the powder room separately, Wendy first. When Annabel came back into the ballroom she spied Wendy across the floor, talking earnestly to Carter MacKenzie.

While Annabel watched and tried to appear not to, she saw Carter frown and scan the room. Wendy turned and nodded her head in Annabel's direction. Carter looked right at her.

Self-conscious, Annabel pivoted slightly and tried to look bright, zestful, interesting, as if she were deeply involved in the discussion about tropical fish between the two Harvard juniors who were standing right there ignoring her.

The music started up again. Couples moved out onto the floor. Annabel lost sight of Wendy and Carter, but she knew the deed had been done.

Now she only had to wait.

She made herself as conspicuous as possible, standing instead of sitting, smiling vacantly and tapping her foot in time to the music. But Carter MacKenzie never materialized in front of her. She didn't see him anywhere.

She waited through three more dances. In vain. The evening was drawing to a close. The lights were dimming, the music becoming softer and more romantic with each piece.

And then she knew. He was waiting for the last dance. The special one.

He had seen her and he had known, just as she had, that they would need more time than a simple dance with each other. They would need hours and hours. Days. Was a lifetime too much to hope for?

"We'll wait for you out front after," her mother whispered in her ear.

"Don't."

Christina Archer blinked. "But—"

"It's all right." Annabel fabricated a story. "I'm going with Wendy. We...we arranged it a little while ago."

"Wendy Ferguson? But I thought she and Willy Carstairs were..."

"Oh, well, they are," Annabel said brightly. "We all

are. Going out for a postdance breakfast, and then back to Wendy's. I'll be fine, Mama. Really.''

And Christina, relieved at last that her ugly-duckling daughter had found some friends to go out with, could only smile and give her consent. ''Well, of course, darling. I'll tell your father. He'll be so pleased.''

Of course he would. But whether Edward Archer was pleased or not didn't matter to Annabel in the least.

She spotted Carter just then, going into the alcove that led to the rest rooms. She didn't know if he'd seen her or not. She gave her mother's hand a quick squeeze and headed off in his direction.

She stopped just outside the alcove, determined not to go after him, but quite equally determined to be readily available when he reappeared.

She didn't lean against the wall. She didn't sit down. She stood quite straight and tall, waiting, dreaming.

In mere minutes, she told herself. In scant seconds...

''The things one does for mothers.'' She heard his voice around the corner, coming closer as he replied to another gruff masculine one. ''I told her no. God knows I didn't want to come.''

''Pretty slim pickings,'' his friend grumbled.

''Not a looker among 'em,'' Carter agreed. ''I said I'd dance with Wendy and Bitsy, but that's it.''

''What about that girl Wendy asked you to dance with?''

Carter snorted. ''The gingerbread girl? The one with the Orphan Annie hair and the dress that looked like it was made for Petunia Pig? No way. A guy's gotta have some standards.''

He came around the corner then—face-to-face with Annabel Archer.

She didn't move. Didn't blink.

He opened his mouth, closed it, swallowed, ducked past.

And Annabel fled, cursing her romantic idiocy, into the cool silence of the soft April night.

Minutes later she met Mark.

IT WAS ODD, she thought now, how wrong—and how right—she'd been that night. Right about the fact that Carter would change her life from that day forward; totally wrong about the means through which he would do so.

For instead of finding in him the man of her dreams, she had fled the suddenly oppressive building and run smack into Mark, who worked there, one of the minions in charge of maintaining the grounds.

Mark Campbell had no fortune in chemicals, no future in steel. And his only connection to oil, he'd told her with a grin, was a father who ran a filling station in Indianapolis.

But Annabel could talk to him, could relax with him. And, as the hours wore on, she let down her defenses and became herself with him.

In fact, she spent the night with him, cuddled in his arms in the bunk of some rich man's yacht.

It had been a reaction to her rejection by Carter, certainly. But as crushed as Annabel had been by Carter's words, she wouldn't have gone as far as she had if there hadn't been something wonderfully right between herself and Mark.

It was the day she left childhood irrevocably behind, the start of a course of action that had ruptured her ties with her family and had brought her here.

Face-to-face with Carter once more.

But now she was a woman, an adult with her feet planted firmly on the ground. She wasn't angry or hurt by

Carter anymore. In fact, damn it to hell, she actually liked him.

But Annabel was no longer a dreamer. She entertained no illusions.

Carter could still affect her, no doubt about that. He still called forth in her that same shivery awareness that he'd been able to elicit almost nineteen years ago.

He also seemed to feel some sort of awareness himself.

Where would it lead? Annabel wondered.

To bed?

It was a mark of her years, she guessed, that allowed her to consider such a possibility dispassionately.

Would she do it? she asked herself.

It might be the only way to get through her preoccupation with him—the stage of her life that was Carter MacKenzie.

Yes, she imagined it could lead to that.

One thing she knew it would never lead to—happily ever after.

Sometimes Annabel might still be a fool, but she'd never be a big enough fool to believe that.

CONAN SLEPT through the night.

Carter didn't. He spent it twisting and turning, writhing and restless. He cursed himself for his idiocy. Could rolling over and exposing his desire for her possibly have been any worse than this?

"Me, too," she'd said.

Or had she?

God, he wished he knew!

He was still awake at Conan's first mutterings shortly past six. He got up, naked and shivering in the early October morning, groping about for something to wear. His underwear was, of course, in the washer. The thought of wearing his jeans without it made him wince. Jack's night-shirt lay on the dresser. He remembered Annabel holding it out to him, challenging him.

He remembered his challenge back to her.

And her response. Her touch.

The memory stirred him. He shivered again. Ached a bit. He reached for the nightshirt and tugged it over his head, then went to get the baby.

He moved in a sort of daze—warming milk for Conan, changing him, then carrying the baby back upstairs, crooning to him softly all the while. It was too early to get up. He was too tired. He crawled into bed and cradled Conan close, nuzzling the baby's soft hair as he fed him his bottle. He wondered what Milly would say if she could see him now.

Lying back against the pillows, he closed his eyes. He felt bleary and disoriented, frustrated and sleepy.

But for the first time in months he felt challenged. Alive.

Chapter Nine

Annabel knocked, but no one answered.

She waited, then opened the door. ''Carter,'' she called, but still no one came.

His Blazer was parked right where it had been last night. He couldn't have gone far.

She and Bert had finished with the soap half an hour ago, and Bert, promising to be back to wrap the bars on Thursday, had headed home.

It was almost eleven, and Annabel had more than enough to do. She had orders for wreaths that needed making, ornaments to fashion, goldenrod to pick, a dozen Christmas centerpieces to start. She should be starting to think about them, getting some ideas in her mind, planning.

But in her mind all she saw was Carter.

All she could think about was Carter.

She wanted to see him. She didn't want to see him.

She needed to talk to him. She never wanted to talk to him again.

It had taken her only a few minutes after Bert's departure to know that she wasn't going to get anything done until she faced him again.

Besides, she had promised to hang out the wash. She was as bad as Libby, trying to come up with an excuse!

Now, of course, it was so late that she had no doubt he'd hung the wash out himself. But when she came over the hill, she saw no string of underwear flapping on the line. No one answered her knock. No one came to her call.

She called again, then walked in, curious, frowning.

She looked in the kitchen for signs of habitation, found none except a pan of now-cool water on the stove, which earlier he might have used to heat Conan's bottle.

A faint gurgling sound made her turn and retrace her steps into the living room. "Carter?"

Another gurgle. A coo. From up the stairs.

He hadn't left the baby alone, had he?

She took the stairs two at a time and hurried into Jason's room. Conan wasn't there.

Just as quickly she walked down the hall to the other bedroom and stopped quite still.

Conan lay on his back, waving his arms, kicking his feet. He was perfectly safe, fenced in by a wall and a huddled comforter.

And under the comforter, sleeping soundly, was Carter.

He was curled up, his reddish-brown hair tousled and drifting across his forehead, one red flannel-clad arm tucked under his head, the other still loosely grasping the empty bottle he'd been feeding to Conan. So—she smiled—he'd put on the nightshirt after all.

She moved closer, bemused, and simply stood there, taking advantage of the opportunity to study him. Were there, in his sleeping features, vestiges of the boy he'd been?

His mobile mouth was softened, lips parted, reminding her of a younger Carter. His high cheekbones and slightly beaky, once broken nose were the same, as well. Tiny lines fanned out from his eyes, aging him, but not unattractively.

It was his eyes that were different. And that was because now dark lashes hooded their normal mocking green.

Last night, she remembered, she had seen a different look in them.

Desire.

She had felt it herself then, felt the stirring of it again now as she stood here simply looking at him.

However long her ill-begotten attraction lasted, it had certainly survived the night.

Conan kicked again, burbling, smiling at her, and she smiled at him, wondering how long he'd been awake. Not long enough to wake Carter, that was clear. He still hadn't moved.

Had he had as restless a night as she'd had?

Probably worse, she reflected, recalling the red itchy skin that had plagued him as well as the frustration she'd heard in his ragged voice.

She reached across Carter's sleeping form and scooped the baby into her arms.

"Come along, laddie," she said softly. "We'll get you changed and fed, then you can help me hang out the laundry."

The next hour seemed rather like a déjà vu to Annabel. The sloppy spooning up of baby cereal with its accompaniment of drools and dribbles, kicks and lunges was so familiar, so comfortable. It came back as naturally as if she still did it every day of her life.

She rinsed out the bowl, then hummed as she put the laundry into the basket. Balancing Conan on one hip and the basket on the other, she went outside.

The day was clear and cool, warm enough for shirtsleeves in the sunshine, but Annabel was glad of a sweater when she stood in the shade, and glad she had dressed Conan in a furry jacket that Jason had outgrown.

She set the basket on the ground, then tied Conan against her middle with the sling Carter had made. She moved from the basket to the line, back and forth, making Conan giggle when she swooped down to grab another piece to hang on the line.

"You like that, do you?" she said to him, laughing a bit herself, bending her head to drop a light kiss on the top of his. She danced him around the yard, doing chain steps and double steps, making him crow with glee. And when she stopped, he hiccupped and looked surprised, then giggled again.

Annabel gave him a gentle hug.

That was the problem, she thought, with having had her children when she was scarcely more than a child herself. She'd never fully appreciated them.

Oh, she'd enjoyed them enough, had played right along with them. But she had also been so worried about doing a good job, about being a responsible mother so that no one could possibly say she wasn't—making sure they ate the right vegetables and didn't watch the wrong television shows—that she'd missed some of the sheer joy that came with relaxing a bit, sitting back and sharing their enthusiasm in simply being alive.

She heard a scraping sound behind her. "Good morning. Or is it afternoon?"

She turned, startled, and looked up.

Carter had opened the bedroom window and was leaning on the sill, his hair tousled, his chest and arms still covered in red flannel as if he'd come straight from bed.

Annabel licked suddenly parched lips, clutched Conan against her front as if he were a shield.

Carter was smiling at her, a hint of amusement in his gaze. She wondered how long he'd been watching her.

She felt faintly foolish that he might have seen her antics, then deliberately shrugged it off. A sense of fatalism took its place.

"*Qué será será,*" she muttered under her breath. Then she met his gaze. "It's morning—barely—sleepyhead," she replied, and she couldn't resist smiling, too.

"How about breakfast?"

"Conan's already eaten."

"I meant us."

Us.

Nineteen years ago Annabel would have swooned over the very thought.

Don't, she cautioned herself. "That sounds...fine." She tried to sound positive, upbeat, cheerful.

Carter grinned. "Don't sound so worried. I can cook."

It wasn't his cooking she was worried about.

HE'D WATCHED HER for a good five minutes before he opened the window and spoke to her.

He'd seen the bounces, the turns, the swoops and the flourishes. He'd watched her gingery hair glint almost bronze in the sunshine as Annabel Archer swirled herself and Conan around the yard.

It was an Annabel he might very well have denied existed a few days ago. She certainly bore no resemblance to the one he'd first met. Where was the stiff, judgmental woman who'd always looked down her nose at him, who made him feel as if he were a schoolboy, and not a particularly well-behaved one, either?

He didn't feel especially well behaved at the moment, come to that. If he hadn't been wearing this damned nightshirt and nothing else, he might have gone down and joined in.

Which would have got him where?

He grimaced. Precisely, he thought.

There was no telling where, given their history, he and Annabel might end up.

But he was beginning to think bed might not be such a bad place to start.

THE THING TO DO, Annabel told herself, was to be matter-of-fact, sensible.

She was attracted to him. She should admit it.

Yeah, sure, she thought, and have Carter say that was nice but he sure as hell wasn't attracted to her.

If she was going to admit anything, she thought, she ought to admit to herself that his rejection of nineteen years ago could still hurt.

But was he the same man he'd been nineteen years ago? Heaven knew she was not the same woman.

She watched him now, flipping pancakes with aplomb, not the least bit self-conscious that she should be sitting there while he wandered around the kitchen in Jack's nightshirt.

She couldn't imagine his eighteen-year-old self doing any such thing. So maybe he wasn't the same man, she conceded. But that didn't make his reaction any more predictable.

Her own was becoming disgustingly predictable. The simple sight of those hairy calves peeking out below the hem had her remembering last night, remembering the strong length of his legs, the bony knees, the muscular thighs, the…

And she'd berated Libby!

HE WISHED TO GOD she would stop watching him.

Of course, he acknowledged, there wasn't a lot else in the kitchen of consuming interest.

Conan had, fifteen minutes before, drifted off into his morning nap. The morning paper had been read, the table set, the orange juice poured.

He was the only thing moving, as he flipped pancakes and shifted from one foot to the other on the bare wood floor.

So Annabel watched him.

He was glad the floor was cold. It made his feet cold, which in turn provided a certain amount of coolness to his calves. He wished like hell the coolness would reach further up. He wished he had put on his jeans, underwear or not.

He needed…

He wanted…

He looked around desperately. Out of the window he spied Arnold with one of Frances's nannies doing precisely what he wanted to be doing with Annabel. It was the last straw.

He scraped up the half-cooked pancakes and slapped them onto the plate. He carried them across the room, holding them strategically as he went. He stuck them right in front of Annabel.

"Dig in. Don't wait."

"But—"

"I'll be right back."

Annabel took in the heightened color in his face, the hastiness of his departure and frowned.

A few minutes later he reappeared, this time dressed in jeans and a flannel shirt. A line of color still ran along his cheekbones and he didn't say a word, just went straight to the griddle and, ignoring her, poured out more puddles of batter.

She watched him, intrigued, wondering…

Was she having the same effect on him that he had on her? Was he as attracted to her as she was to him?

If so, were they ever going to be able to get on with their lives unless they got past it?

A younger Annabel wouldn't have done it.

A less frantic Annabel would never have dared.

But this Annabel was thirty-six and desperate.

She wanted her sanity back. She wanted her sense of focus and direction, her calm and peaceful life.

''Carter,'' she said to his back, ''do you think maybe we should just forget the pancakes and go to bed?''

IF HE LIVED TO BE A hundred, Carter was sure he'd never win a bet on the next words to come out of Annabel Archer's mouth.

Heaven help him, he'd have lost a bundle on those.

For a moment he didn't even realize that he was pouring batter all over the griddle, the stove and the tops of his toes.

''Here,'' Annabel said. ''You're making a mess and a half. Let me do that if you're so desperate for pancakes.'' She whisked the bowl and spoon out of his hands, set them aside, mopped up his spill efficiently and poured neat little round puddles of her own.

He watched numbly, mind reeling.

She glanced at him, her hands on her hips. ''Don't look so shocked.'' Her chin came up; there was a note of challenge in her voice.

''No. Of—of course not. I just…just…'' He looked at her dazedly and shook his head.

Annabel sighed and flipped the pancakes. "This is all Frances's fault."

"Frances? What's she got to do with it?"

"The kiss," Annabel said sweetly.

"It was just a kiss."

"It was a setup!"

He stared at her.

"Don't you realize it yet? This is all her fault. She created this situation. She threw us together and then challenged us. It was like someone saying, 'Don't think of elephants. Whatever you do, don't think of elephants!'"

Carter grinned. "'Whatever you do, don't think about going to bed with Carter MacKenzie'? That sort of thing?"

Annabel's flush deepened. "Exactly." She turned back to the pancakes, scraped them into a pile and dumped them onto the plate, then thrust them at him. "Here. Eat."

He took the plate, held it a moment, then let his eyes rove slowly down the line of her nose, past the thin-pressed lips, the stubborn jaw. His gaze slid leisurely over the swell of her breasts, the line of her legs. He set the plate on the counter.

"I think I'd rather go to bed."

ANNABEL HOPED he couldn't notice that her knees quaked as he followed her up the stairs. She hoped he couldn't tell from her flushed cheeks and damp palms how really nervous she was.

Had she really suggested going to bed with Carter MacKenzie? Out of the clear blue? Just like that?

Yes.

And had he taken her up on it? Just like that?

Right again.

Oh, Annabel, what a big mouth you have!

She shut her eyes, her fingers tightened on the banister. It wasn't too late to turn back, she told herself.

She didn't really want to go to bed with Carter MacKenzie, did she? She didn't really want to know intimately the man who had been the source of her humiliation all those years ago, did she?

Yes.

She wanted to know him, *needed* to know him, to solve the mystery of his attraction and get back to the important things in life.

And did she want him to know her?

Her palms were damp, her cheeks flushed. The very thought frightened her. Once more her knees trembled. She chewed on her lip.

Perhaps Conan would cry, the phone would ring, Arnold would come rampaging up onto the front porch.

She took the steps slowly, deliberately, stalling. But there was no rescue, only the sound of Carter's bare feet on the floor behind her, only the heat of his body when she paused in the doorway to the bedroom.

"Second thoughts?"

The barest hint of challenge, real or imagined, was enough to send her right on through. "Of course not," she lied. But at the side of the bed, she stopped once more.

It was so big, so broad, so rumpled. As if it had already known a night of passion, of love.

It won't be love, she told herself. It was a scientific inquiry, an exploration of phenomena. Nothing more.

Quickly she reached down and picked up the nightshirt Carter had discarded. She folded it automatically, smoothed it against her breasts, held it like a shield against her.

Carter reached out and lifted it from her hands, setting

it on the dresser. His own fingers lingered, smoothing it, too. Then slowly he turned to face her.

His eyes were so green, so deep. It didn't seem fair that a man so shallow should have such wonderful eyes. Or was he really shallow? She wasn't sure anymore.

He wasn't smiling. He looked, if anything, even more serious than she did. As if he didn't want to be here any more than she did. As if he were just performing a duty. The thought made Annabel wince.

"What's wrong?" he asked her.

"Nothing."

"You always act like this when you go to bed with someone?"

"I don't often just 'go to bed' with someone."

"I didn't mean..."

"It was perfectly obvious what you meant."

They glared at each other. Annabel could see a pulse ticking in Carter's temple. His lips were a hard line. Her own lips were pressed together tightly.

He sighed and thrust his fingers through his hair. "So do you want to or not?"

"How charming. Is this the way *you* always act when you go to bed with someone?"

"Cripes, Archer, I don't know whether to strangle you or kiss you."

She shrugged. "Don't ask me."

"Ah, hell," Carter muttered and reached for her.

He didn't strangle her, but he might as well have. He robbed her of all her air.

He'd kissed her before. Twice. Three times. Annabel didn't remember.

They weren't all that memorable, she'd told herself. Carter MacKenzie was no great shakes as a kisser.

Think again, sweetheart, her reeling mind managed to convey before she lost all coherent thought.

This was no quick peck, no brotherly buss. His lips met hers with a hunger that astonished her. They asked for—no, demanded—a response.

And Annabel, lost to propriety, rationality and simple common sense, gave him one. She couldn't help it.

Her fingers came up to close on the soft flannel of his shirt. Her hips surged forward to press against his. And her lips opened, parting under the urgent quest of his tongue, tasting of him with the same eagerness with which he tasted her.

When he pulled back, she was speechless.

"That," Carter said hoarsely, "is the way I act when I go to bed with someone."

Annabel swallowed again.

"Shall I continue?" His soft voice challenged her. "Or not?"

Are you woman enough?

He didn't say the words. Annabel heard them loud and clear.

"Yes."

Her fingers fumbled with the hem of her sweater. Carter couldn't seem to get his shirt buttons undone. He muttered his frustration.

"Let me." Annabel reached for them at the same time his fingers touched her sweater.

"I'll help you," he said.

They stopped, stared at each other for an instant, offered hesitant smiles.

Annabel unbuttoned his shirt. Carter eased the sweater over her head.

He had much better luck with the buttons on her shirt than he'd had on his own. Annabel stood mutely while he worked, but her fingers came up to rest softly against his now-bare chest.

He skimmed the shirt off her shoulders, letting it drop to the floor. Annabel bent automatically to pick up both his shirt and her own.

Carter took them and tossed them aside. Then he stood, silent, wetting his lips as he gazed down at her breasts inside the ivory lace.

Annabel was not ordinarily given to frilly underwear. Sturdy, not sensuous, was generally the order of her day. Who was she going to do a striptease for? she asked Libby when her daughter suggested some sexier lingerie.

Libby took matters into her own hands. For Christmas last year Annabel had opened a gaily wrapped ivory lace bra, her size, not Libby's 32A.

She glanced down at it now self-consciously.

Carter reached behind her and undid the hook, then drew it forward, letting the straps slide down her arms, his fingers following, the backs of his hands brushing her arms, the tips of his fingers gliding lightly over her breasts.

Annabel looked away, then ventured a quick glance back at him. He looked utterly serious, intent. The bra fell to the floor.

Annabel didn't pick it up.

With slow deliberation Carter leaned forward and touched his lips to hers.

This kiss was totally different. Slow and sensual. A quiet start, then steamy, seeking. Simmering. Smoldering.

It set off an answering heat in Annabel that started somewhere deep inside and curled downward into the center of her, making her burn. She felt a shudder run through her.

Carter pulled back. His eyes were dark, the skin on his cheeks taut and flushed. He was breathing quickly. His fingers went to the top button of his jeans. Annabel saw a fine tremor in his hands as they tried to open it.

"Please. I want to."

Was that her voice? Her words? Had she dared say such a thing?

Carter's hands dropped to his sides. His fingers clenched lightly. His hooded eyes watched her. He held his breath.

Annabel did, too.

She moved closer, slipped her hand lightly beneath his waistband and eased it open. Her fingers brushed his hard belly and the line of silky hair that arrowed down his abdomen. She felt him tense as she moved on to the next button…and the next.

She undid them all with studious concentration, then hooked her thumbs in the belt loops and gave a gentle tug. The jeans slid down his hips to his knees. He kicked them off.

He wasn't wearing any underwear.

It was nothing she hadn't seen before. He was the same man he'd been last night. He even had the same rash, although it was slightly fainter now.

But last night he'd been discomfited, irritable, tetchy. Today he was aroused. By her.

Annabel couldn't stop looking at him.

"My turn." Carter's voice was ragged.

She blinked, momentarily disoriented, then lifted her eyes to meet his, all her nervousness returning as she realized what he intended.

He bent his head. His fingers went to the snap on her jeans and popped it easily. Annabel started to take a breath, but his hands didn't move away. They remained, the backs of his fingers brushing lightly to and fro across her belly, fanning the flames within her, making her ache.

She'd thought she would hate for him to undress her,

to expose her body to his gaze. Now she only wanted him to hurry.

But he wouldn't. His fingers were maddeningly slow as they plucked at the tab of the zipper, then lowered it. They were painstakingly gentle as they slid inside the denim and pushed the fabric down her hips.

She tried to kick them off as he had done, but hers were cut narrower and she couldn't shed them without help.

Carter dropped to his knees, skimming his hands down her thighs and calves, taking the denim with them, lifting her feet one at a time. The calluses on his fingertips made the soles of her feet tingle. Off balance, Annabel tottered, then righted herself by catching hold of his head.

It was the first time she'd ever touched his hair. Her fingers curled in its thickness. She felt the silky softness of it brush her thighs. She trembled.

Then he settled back on his heels and his hands slid slowly back up her legs.

Annabel waited, tense, scarcely breathing, expecting his fingers to continue their climb, to hook in the waistband on her panties and slip them down.

Instead one finger lightly traced the leg opening, then another did the same. He lifted his head and looked up at her. She swallowed. His fingers continued their light tracery, moved slowly, teasingly up until they'd slipped under the cloth barrier. Touched her. Knew her. Learned of her readiness, her need.

Annabel's fingers clenched in his hair.

In mere seconds he peeled off the last barrier to her nakedness, and bore her back onto the bed. His eyes glittered green fire now. The skin was taut across his cheekbones, his breathing came shallow and quick.

She lay in his embrace, reveling in the feel of his firm, hair-roughened flesh, in the sinewy strength of his arms as he pulled her against him, kissing her eyes, her cheeks, her hair.

At eighteen she'd had the barest notion, the faintest fantasies of what going to bed with Carter MacKenzie would be like.

At thirty-six she found that reality was beyond compare.

He was as impatient as she was, but controlled. He let his hands rove her body with excruciating thoroughness, stroking, inciting, making her yearn for more.

Her own hands sought him just as eagerly, skating lightly over his ribs, learning the rough strength of his thighs, then at last, finding the center of his desire.

A tremor shook him. He bit his lip, groaned and shifted so that he knelt between her legs, ready.

And Annabel was ready, too. She held him gently to draw him to her, but he shook his head.

"Not yet." His voice cracked. His fingers trailed down the smoothness of her belly, touched the soft hair at the apex of her thighs, slipped beyond it.

Annabel sucked in her breath, held perfectly still...then melted under the rhythmic, knowing stroke of his fingers.

Her own fingers trembled, reached out and clenched handfuls of the sheet. Her back arched. She gasped. "Carter!"

He came to her then. Hot. Hungry.

She welcomed him, opened for him, savoring his silken strength as he slid inside, meeting his thrust, arching into it, making him groan.

His weight rested on his arms. They shook. He shut his eyes, then opened them again.

And Annabel met his gaze. She loosened her hold on the sheet and lifted her hands, setting them lightly against his back, smoothing him, stroking him, learning the feel of the bunch and flex of his muscles under her touch.

She tried to be analytical, objective.

She tried to fathom her attraction, his mystery.

She couldn't begin to.

She was lost.

Lost in the hunger of his gaze, in the sweet slip of his body into hers, in the hunger and passion that flamed between them. Her fingers clenched against his buttocks, her toes curled. She tossed her head from side to side.

And all the while Carter moved. Slowly at first, then faster. Finally frantic, desperate. Wanting. Needing. ''Anna...bel!''

Annabel was with him, meeting him, feeling the explosion growing inside her. One last thrust and then a shudder. Her body splintered, her mind reeled.

Carter collapsed against her, trembling, his back slick with sweat, his breath hot and quick against her shoulder.

As her own breathing slowed, as she gathered her scattered wits about her, tried to muster all those logical, objective, analytical thoughts, attempted to put Carter MacKenzie behind her, Annabel really only knew one thing.

She hadn't got over him in the least.

Chapter Ten

Making love with Annabel Archer wasn't what he'd expected.

Not at all.

He'd expected complaisance, competence, a cool, composed coupling. Nothing to write home about.

He'd burned. Gone up in flames, more like.

And so had Annabel Archer—he thought.

But if she had been as affected as he'd been, why, Carter asked himself, had she so blithely bounded out of bed to fetch Conan the moment he yelled?

Why had she hummed with such carefree exuberance while she changed him?

Why had she left again right after, giving Carter just a nonchalant goodbye wave and nothing more?

He needed to think.

Strapping Conan against his chest, he clambered back up onto the roof and set to work. The sunshine warmed his back as he worked. Conan gurgled and burbled, wriggling and cooing.

Normally Carter would have stopped work and bounced the baby on his knees, tickling him and reciting the nonsense rhymes that seemed to lurk somewhere in his memory ready for recall at a moment's notice.

Today he didn't even think about Conan. The baby was there, a part of the environment. But nothing more. Carter moved rhythmically along, laying the shingles and hammering, his mind consumed with Annabel.

Annabel in bed. Annabel making love. Annabel kissing him, holding him tight.

But other Annabels, too. The one who good-naturedly listened to Leif's innumerable knock-knock jokes, who could act pleased about the gift of a pair of ridiculous jeans. The Annabel who hung out the clothes while dancing with the baby, who crooned lullabies and cooked Chinese and dealt masterfully with goats. The Annabel who could spit fire at him and argue with him, then love him with such intensity he'd burned.

It didn't make sense.

Maybe he was having a relapse.

He wondered if he ought to call Milly.

And tell her what? That he'd made love with a woman for the first time in months and now he couldn't stop thinking about her?

What's wrong with that? Milly would ask him.

And Carter wasn't even sure there was something wrong. But he'd never felt quite like this after making love before—as if some fundamental chord deep inside him had, for the first time in his life, been touched.

And by Annabel Archer?

Good grief.

He worked like a demon all afternoon, stopping only when Conan fell asleep, and then only long enough to tuck the baby into the crib before heading back to the roof once again.

But even physical labor and lots of it didn't settle his mind. Or his loins.

He still had the rash, of course, and it still itched, though less than it had, thank goodness. He did his best to attribute his state of unrest to that.

Carter was only ever marginally successful at lying to himself. This wasn't one of those times.

He wondered when he'd see Annabel again. Would she come back over this evening? Did he dare just sort of casually drop in on her?

The thought made him laugh. To think that he was actually plotting ways to be in her company. It boggled the mind.

He thought about Frances. Had she really been trying to match him up with Annabel as Annabel had claimed?

Obviously Annabel thought the idea preposterous.

Carter found her reaction annoyed him. Was he as unlikely a marriage prospect as all that?

The phone was ringing when he got down off the roof.

Annabel?

He hurried to answer it.

"Carter." The voice was undeniably female, actually quite sexy. "It's Marilee," she said after a moment when he didn't reply.

"Oh, right! Marilee! How are you?"

"Looking forward to Wednesday," she said in that throaty voice of hers.

"Wednesday?" He couldn't get a grip on it.

"Dinner. You didn't forget!"

"No. Not at all."

"Well, I called to tell you I'm doing chicken marengo, so if you still want to bring the wine, get a white."

He felt like saying he couldn't come. He didn't want to. Not now. Not after loving Annabel.

Why not? he asked himself irritably. It wasn't as if Annabel really gave a damn about him. She'd been positively cavalier in the aftermath. She'd practically sprung out of bed to get Conan. She'd scarcely spared him a glance when she left.

"Carter?"

"Er, sure. Fine." Pause. "Can I bring anything else?"

"Just yourself." Another throaty chuckle. "You don't know how much I'm looking forward to it."

He hung the receiver up slowly, trying to sort things out. It made sense to go out with Marilee, he thought. She was gorgeous, talented, witty—everything he'd ever wanted, ever dreamed of.

And Annabel?

What about his relationship with her?

They were adults. Consenting adults.

LIFE, ANNABEL TOLD herself, hadn't changed a bit. She still had work to do, children to raise, goats to tend. She had pomanders to poke and a siding job to save for. Her oven was just as dirty as it had been last night, and if she needed to keep her feet on the ground, she could always contemplate how many hours it would take to clean it.

But she couldn't help smiling. A lot.

It was foolishness—this business with Carter—and she knew it.

There was no future in it. She knew that, too.

But it was fun. It was different. It was lovely, charming, sexy, beautiful.

It had been far too long since her life had held all those things together.

As long as she remembered that, as long as she saw their lovemaking as a lark, an affair and nothing more, she could handle it.

Like the series of allergy shots she remembered from childhood, developing a resistance to Carter would apparently take some time. It would, she thought with a smile, be a blessed sight more pleasant a way to develop resistance than the allergy shots had been.

She knew it wouldn't last. She was a big girl now. She didn't believe in fairy tales. Goodness knew, Carter was no knight in shining armor, no prince come to rescue her from her dreadful plight.

Her plight wasn't all that dreadful. In fact, life was damn good.

Making love with Carter—however briefly—just made it better.

In the afternoon she took Eb's standing order down to the shop and helped restock his shelves. She took Leif to Gaithersburg for his trombone lesson and picked up Libby to go to the dentist.

She did the laundry, dyed soaps and untangled Arnold from the thicket behind the barn. The washing machine overflowed. She called the plumber, went back and got Libby from the dentist, picked up Ernie and Bert's order at the bakery, dropped it off, then shopped for the groceries for supper. The washing machine cost $84.70. The parts wouldn't be in until next Thursday. Maybe the plumber could come back a week from Monday. He'd have to see.

A normal, average day.

But better than wonderful really because while she shelved and drove and wrapped and dropped and coped, she remembered her morning with Carter.

She smiled.

She cooked lasagna for supper, the kids' favorite. She made a chocolate cake.

''Chocolate? Not carrot?'' asked Libby. ''What's the occasion?''

Annabel smiled.

It wasn't until Libby was tucked up with forty pages of

government to read and outline, until Leif had finished his homework and gone to sleep, until she had mopped up the water in the basement and had decided, by brief experimentation, on a natural cranberry dye as a possible coloring agent for the soap, that she actually sat down, put her feet up on the hassock, closed her eyes and wondered what Carter was doing at that very moment.

A few seconds later when the phone rang, she found out.

"Where've you been?"

Just the sound of his voice set off tiny nerve endings all along her spine. She flexed her toes. "Don't ask."

"Why? What happened?"

"Nothing out of the ordinary. Not since this morning anyway," she added, still smiling.

"Shall we do it again?"

"We could, I suppose."

"When?" His eagerness was flattering, heady. Dangerous.

Annabel opened her eyes.

Deliberately she grounded herself in the holey sneakers under the table, the trig book on the counter, the comfortable bulk of Goliath curled in the best chair in the house.

Those were the things that would last. Not her affair with Carter MacKenzie.

"You could make a house call," he suggested. "Put a little more ointment on my rash."

A tempting thought. "I can't," Annabel said. What would she tell Libby if she suddenly took off?

There was another pause. "Chicken, Annabel?"

She sat up straight. "Like hell!"

CARTER WAITED. And waited.

She never came.

Finally, sometime just past one, he gave up, climbed the

stairs, checked on a soundly slumbering Conan and fell frustrated into his bed.

He was exhausted. He couldn't sleep. Images of Annabel played with his mind, teasing him, touching him. His rash bothered him, but he was too tired to get up and put the ointment on it.

So he lay there and itched—and wished.

His dreams, when he finally managed to sleep, were vivid and erotic. They did everything to him that Annabel wasn't there to do, except to satisfy him. Until the last.

The last dream was different. Gentler. Cool at first, as if a soft breeze caressed his heated skin. Then soft. Her fingers playing with his toes, then moving on to his calves, smoothing and stroking, brushing lightly against the backs of his knees, sliding slowly up under the hem of the nightshirt to caress his thighs.

He twisted under her touch, moaned at the injustice of it, knowing it was a dream. But still her touches went on. Feathery light. Maddeningly slow. Driving him to the brink.

He fought his way to consciousness and flipped over, furious with himself.

In the soft morning light, Annabel sat on the edge of the bed, smiling at him, all ginger hair and golden freckles.

He blinked. Blinked again. Made a little disbelieving sound at the back of his throat.

The comforter had been shoved to the foot of the bed and he lay covered only by the nightshirt. Annabel's finger traced tiny circles on his knee. "I'm making a house call."

He reached for her, but she pulled back, still smiling, and shook her head. "You're the patient, remember?"

"And what are you?" His voice was rusty.

"The doctor, of course."

Carter hesitated, then slowly let his arms fall to his sides. He watched her warily as she got up and reached for the jar of cream on the nightstand, then came back to kneel at the foot of the bed between his legs.

She picked up his left foot, flexing his knee as she settled the foot in her lap.

"I don't have a rash on my toes!"

"The best doctors are the most thorough, Carter. Who knows what I might find?"

She found that he was ticklish. He squirmed as her fingers explored his toes, as her nails traced gentle lines along the sole of his foot, scratching lightly, first on his left foot, then on his right.

"Annabel!"

She touched a finger to her lips. "Shh. You'll wake the baby."

Even as she spoke her hands moved on, circling his ankles, then tripping lightly up his calves. She leaned forward and kissed his kneecaps.

He jerked at the touch of her tongue. "What the—"

"Just testing reflexes. I didn't bring my hammer."

His fingers twisted in the sheet. "Annabel," he warned, but still she ignored him, her fingers edging beneath the hem of the nightshirt, lifting it, pushing it up until she exposed the beginnings of the rash at the top of his thighs.

"Ah, yes." One finger trailed lightly along the bottom edge of the redness. "I begin to see the problem."

"You can't possibly see the problem!"

She gave a light laugh. Her fingers strayed briefly beneath the bunched-up nightshirt, finding and acknowledging the true source of his distress.

"We'll get to that," she promised, her fingers leaving

him, their absence making him ache. She edged up closer so that she sat between his knees. "First things first."

Her fingers dipped into the jar, then began to spread the cream along the tops of his thighs. It was so cool and blissful at the same time that it made him feel hotter and hungrier than ever. He bit his lower lip, watched her from beneath hooded lids.

She looked so serious, so intent, her head bent, her eyes cast down as she watched her fingers move, noting his response to them. Only the faint tremor in her touch gave her away. His own body was perilously close to giving everything away.

"Annabel!" He muttered her name again, tensing, resisting the sensations she was arousing.

She lifted her head, smiled at him. "I think I missed my calling. I had no idea a doctor's life could be so interesting."

"We could make it a lot more interesting," he said huskily.

A gingery brow arched. "Oh? How?"

"Let me take your clothes off."

"Oh, no. We couldn't do that. I'm the doctor. Doctors don't take their clothes off. That wouldn't be fair."

"Not fair? This is fair?"

"You don't like it?" Her hands stilled, then pulled back.

"Annabel!" Her name whistled through his clenched teeth. His hips arched, seeking.

She took hold of the nightshirt again, easing it clear up so that now it bunched around his waist, exposing him totally. He was on fire. She didn't touch him.

He tried to lie still, not to squirm. She was frowning now, bending her head closer, then she lifted her gaze and met his, her expression quite grave.

"Goodness," she said quite solemnly, "have you had that swelling long?"

"Too damned long," Carter growled, the last threads of his control beginning to unravel as her soft fingers touched him once more.

Annabel made a tsking sound. "Dear me. It looks serious."

"It *is* serious!"

"Perhaps I should call for a second opinion."

"Not on your life, lady. You're the doctor. You know what to do about it." And please, he thought, desperate, aching, his whole body rigid under the gentle brush of her fingers. *Please do it. Do it now!*

She bent slowly and brushed a kiss across his lips.

"I think I have just the remedy on hand." With quick efficient movements, she set the jar of cream aside, reached up and stripped off her shirt, slid out of her jeans and came to him, giving him hungry kisses, nipping at his nose, his chin, his ears.

And Carter, who had never in his life been so ready for loving, gave himself up to it. To her.

He kissed her fiercely, ferociously, unable to get enough of her. His arms went around her, drawing her down so that now she straddled him. With his hands, with his hips, with everything in him, he urged her to complete their union.

And the second she did, he felt as if he had come home, as if this embrace was the one he had been looking for, this the haven he had been seeking, the love he'd always hoped for and despaired ever to find.

His climax hit him so swiftly, so fiercely that he felt a moment's panic that he had gone too fast, taken everything for himself, leaving Annabel behind. But it wasn't so.

She was with him, her body as consumed by the force of their union as his.

After, he felt her lift her head and kiss his chest, then look him in the eyes. "What do you think?" she asked huskily. "Are you cured?"

Not nearly, Carter thought. And when she sank against his chest, he kissed her hair and held her close and wondered how he could have been so blind.

GREAT SEX, Annabel decided, could blow your mind. She'd never realized.

Sex with Mark had been lovely. It had been warm and tender—once, that is, they'd figured each other out. But it had never completely shattered her, had never left her reeling the way she reeled under Carter's touch.

She sat in the rocker in the living room, cradling Conan in her arms, giving him a bottle, smiling at him, smiling at the memories of the past hour and a half, at the thought of Carter's naked body under the shower right now upstairs.

It was dangerous the way she was coming to feel about Carter, the way she wanted to be with him, to touch him, to feel him tense under her fingers, to feel the hunger of his lips on hers. It was like playing with explosives. A good way to get hurt.

The moment she thought it, she denied it.

Love would hurt. If she loved Carter, it would hurt. She didn't. She was simply, briefly, enjoying him.

And a good thing, too, she thought moments later when the telephone rang.

"Is this Frances? This is Marilee Newman," the voice said at her answer. "Tell Carter I've changed my mind. I'm making beef Wellington tomorrow night. If he hasn't already got the wine, tell him to get a red. Thanks.'' She rang off without giving Annabel a chance to reply.

Annabel sat quite still. She looked down at Conan, listened yet again to the running water upstairs. Her throat felt funny. Kind of tight.

If she'd *loved* him, she would have cared.

It was ever such a good thing she did not.

Conan finished his bottle and batted it aside. Annabel heard the water shut off, heard Carter's footsteps making the floor creak overhead as he moved around the bathroom.

The door opened and he padded down the hall. Moments later he came down the steps and smiled that bewitching smile.

''I washed all the ointment off in the shower. I don't suppose you'd like to maybe...apply another dose?'' His grin beguiled her.

Annabel shook her head. She swallowed carefully. ''Can't. Conan wouldn't approve. You can do it yourself.''

''More fun when you do it.''

For a fleeting moment she wished—oh, God, she wished—it had been more than lust, more than great sex between them.

But it wasn't. Wouldn't ever be.

''I agree,'' she said. ''But that's the breaks.'' She got up and carried Conan with her into the kitchen to wash out his bottle. ''By the way,'' she said over her shoulder. ''Marilee Newman called. She said to tell you to bring a red wine instead.'' She waited half a second before adding, ''Do you by any chance need a baby-sitter?''

Probably she was a fool for asking, but she had to show him that it didn't matter—that *he* didn't matter. She wouldn't let him hurt her again. The problem was hers, not his. He'd never pretended to love her.

She concentrated on the bottle, running the water, swishing it around, rinsing it again.

"Er, yeah, I guess," she finally heard him say behind her. She turned to see Carter standing in the doorway to the kitchen. He wasn't smiling.

"What time?"

"Um, about six. Shall I bring him over?"

"Sure. At bedtime I'll bring him back here." She dumped out the water and set the bottle on the counter upside down, then handed Conan to Carter. "I've really got to be going," she said, wiping her hands on the sides of her jeans. "Lots to do."

Carter followed her to the door. "You don't mind? Baby-sitting while I...while I..."

"Go out with Marilee? Heavens no. It was my idea, wasn't it?"

HE WENT OUT WITH MARILEE. He smiled at her jokes, he praised her cooking, he brought red wine instead of white. He made a deliberate effort to enjoy himself. She was a charming woman—even more charming than she'd been the first time he'd met her.

He didn't care.

He was thinking about Annabel, remembering her blasé attitude, her easy dismissal of his date, the nonchalance with which she'd greeted him earlier in the evening, taken Conan from his arms and given him a blithe smile.

"Have a wonderful evening," she'd said.

"I will," he'd answered with gritted teeth. If she didn't care, neither would he.

Nice try, Carter, he told himself ruefully.

"What? What did you say?" he asked Marilee. It was the fifth time he'd lost the thread of the conversation since they'd left the table and adjourned with brandy glasses to sit on the sofa in front of the fire.

He turned to her, gave her a game smile and tried to look interested.

"It doesn't matter," she said lightly, curling her feet underneath her, smiling at him. "I was just talking real estate. Were you really thinking of buying property up here?" she asked him, a speculative look on her face. "Or was it just a ploy?"

"Er," Carter said. "Um..."

"I thought so." She leaned toward him and brushed her lips across his. "I'm so glad."

He sat up straight, blinked several times, eased his collar away from the back of his neck. "Yeah, me, too."

"Collar too tight?" Marilee's fingers were eager to solve the problem.

"N-no. It's fine." Carter pulled back. "You know," he glanced at his watch, "I really should be going now. You have to get up and go to work tomorrow."

"It's early yet."

"Yeah, well, it isn't just for you. I— There's this baby."

Marilee's eyes got huge. "You have a baby?"

"No. Not I—but—"

But he'd seen enough of Marilee to know that mentioning the circumstances of his acquaintance with Conan would not be a good idea. Marilee would doubtless find Maeve's behavior reprehensible. She was a good lawyer, a thorough one. She might even know of a law against it. Child abandonment came to mind.

"I promised to baby-sit," Carter lied. "I nearly forgot."

"At this hour? For who?"

"Er, no one you know. And like you said, it's early

yet.'' He got to his feet and plucked his jacket off the back of the armchair, shrugging into it.

Marilee looked at him with a mixture of hurt and suspicion. Carter felt vaguely guilty. He should have begged off, should never have come at all.

It was all Annabel's fault that he had. If she hadn't been so damned cheerful about his going out with Marilee...if she hadn't been so eager to baby-sit so he could—as if their morning together had meant nothing more to her than a good-time roll in the hay, so to speak—he would have called Marilee and told her he couldn't make it.

Damn Annabel, he thought grimly.

He took hold of Marilee's hand. ''Thanks for the wonderful dinner. I enjoyed it. You're a fantastic cook.''

She smiled a little ruefully. ''I'm glad you liked the dinner at least.''

''I liked the company, too,'' he said. ''I'm afraid I'm just...preoccupied tonight.''

''Apparently.'' Marilee walked him to the door. ''It's been...interesting, Carter.''

It was his turn to look rueful. ''You're being kind.''

''Perhaps.''

''I'm sorry.''

''Me, too. But, hey—'' she gave a little shrug ''—that's life. We're grown-ups, right? We know not everything goes the way we want it to.''

''Yeah,'' Carter said.

WE KNOW NOT EVERYTHING goes the way we want it to.

Her words echoed in his head as he walked to his car, as he got in and started the engine, as he drove home to Conan. And to Annabel, who didn't love him.

There was, he supposed, a certain amount of poetic justice in her casual approach to their intimacy.

Heaven knew he'd been casual enough for most of his life. It wasn't until he'd met Diane Bauer that he'd ever even considered a less-than-casual approach to women.

But Diane hadn't meant to him what Annabel did. He hadn't thought about her night and day. He hadn't dreamed of her, needed her, loved her.

Diane had told him he hadn't, but he hadn't really understood. Now he was beginning to.

Because for the very first time he thought it was happening to him.

He had, somehow or other, fallen in love with Annabel Archer. Without wanting, without knowing, certainly without trying.

But definitely with passion. With exuberance. And increasingly with every little corner of his soul.

And she thought he was a good lay.

Chapter Eleven

He was in a less-than-cheerful frame of mind when he got home.

He didn't know what to say, how to act. He flicked off the ignition and jerked open the car door. Stuffing the keys into his pocket, he strode toward the house.

Would she be smiling? Welcoming him with open arms? Ready for another tumble in the sheets?

The thought made him grit his teeth.

He didn't damned well *want* another roll in the sheets. No, that wasn't true. He wanted one, but he wanted it to matter. *He* wanted to matter.

To Annabel Archer?

Fat chance.

He banged the door open with unnecessary force, ready to make up a thousand lies about a wonderful evening with Marilee. So what if it wasn't true. She didn't have to know. A guy had to preserve his pride, didn't he?

But he never got to say a word.

Annabel was standing in the middle of the floor looking at him, stricken. Her face was blotchy, her freckles more pronounced than ever. Her eyes were decidedly red.

"What is it? What's wrong?"

For a moment she didn't speak, just shook her head, her lips pressed tightly together, her fingers knotting.

"Annabel!" He crossed the room and grabbed her by the arms. "Damn it! What happened? Is it Conan? Leif? Libby?"

He'd never seen her look like this. He didn't know what had happened, but whatever it was, he knew it was serious.

She seemed to stiffen under his touch. He could feel her begin to compose herself, pull her emotions in, straighten up, draw a deep breath.

"It's...my father...he's had a stroke." Her voice was almost steady. He felt her begin to shake, and he pulled her hard against him, holding her.

He didn't know anything about Annabel's father. She'd never mentioned him before. But from her reaction he decided they must be close.

"Is he—I mean, how...how bad...is he?"

"Bad," she said, her mouth against his jacket. "Mother would never have called me otherwise. He wouldn't have let her."

"He'd try to protect you from knowing?"

Annabel shook her head. "He wouldn't want me to know."

"Why not?"

She looked away, out the window into the darkness. "We don't...speak."

"Ever?"

"Not for nineteen years."

"My God." All his impressions changed in an instant. *Not speak for nineteen years?* He couldn't imagine it. He and his own father had yelled at each other every chance they got.

He suddenly realized how little he really knew about

Annabel. She might have been found under a cabbage leaf for all he knew. And he wanted to know everything.

But now was not the time.

"What are you going to do?"

"I don't know." Her fingers twisted together. She bent her head.

"Should you go see him?"

"The shock would probably kill him."

Carter looked at her closely. There were tears on her eyelids, trembling, about to fall. She blinked rapidly.

"I doubt that," Carter said gently.

"You don't know my father."

Carter didn't think he wanted to. Anyone who could reduce Annabel Archer to tears sounded like a bastard and a half. "I know you."

She pressed her forehead against his shoulder, shaking her head. He held her, his lips brushing against her hair, wishing he could make the whole painful episode go away.

The phone rang. Carter gave her a quick hug and went to answer it.

It was Leif. "Is my ma still there? Did she tell you my grandmother called looking for her? Did she say why? Was that really my grandmother?"

"Yeah, she told me. Yeah, it was." Carter didn't know what else to say.

"What's going on?"

"She'll talk to you when she gets home."

"Is she...okay?"

"Yes." He wasn't sure it was the truth, but he'd do everything in his power to make it so. He hung up the phone and went back to Annabel.

"Leif," she guessed, her voice a monotone.

"He's worried about you."

"I'm fine. Everything will be fine." She reached for her coat. "I've got to go."

"I'll walk you back."

"Conan—"

"Conan will be fine."

"You don't know—"

"I know what my priorities are. I'm seeing you home."

They walked quickly, in silence. Annabel's hand was cold and dry in his. She didn't speak. Nor did Carter. He didn't know what to say or what to do. He needed to wait for her.

Leif was at the door when they arrived. "She called again. My grandmother." He seemed almost to test the word as he spoke it, as if he might have got it wrong.

Annabel's hand clenched around Carter's. "What'd she say?"

"To call her." Leif thrust a piece of paper at her. "This is the number."

Annabel snatched it and hurried to the phone. Carter followed her in and shut the door, leaning against it. Leif watched his mother punch out the number.

"What's wrong?" he asked Carter.

"Your grandfather's had a stroke."

"I didn't know I had a grandfather, either. Holy cow. Is he gonna die?"

"I don't know."

Annabel had got through and was talking now in a low, intense tone. Her face was pale, her freckles vivid.

"I hope not," Leif said. "Not when I just found out I got him."

Annabel's voice rose slightly. "I don't know! What'll he think if— I know, Mom. I know. But if he doesn't even *know*...yes." She bowed her head. "Yes. All right." Her voice faded almost to a whisper now. "All...right."

She let the receiver drop back onto the hook and stood staring at the floor. Then slowly she raised her eyes and met Leif's gaze.

Carter saw the boy hesitate, bite down on his lip.

"Oh, baby," Annabel said and in three steps came to take him in her arms. She buried her face in Leif's fair hair, hugged him close. Leif put his arms around her, held her.

Carter envied them their love.

Annabel lifted her head and met his eyes. "I have to go. I have to go, and I don't know how. It's been so long. Too long. But I can't let him go without...without trying."

Carter nodded. He understood. Oh, God, how well he understood! He wished he'd had the chance.

"I'll go with you."

SHE SHOULD HAVE SAID NO.

She should have had the guts to handle it on her own, shoulder her own burdens, fight her own fights.

She couldn't.

She needed Carter.

She needed his support, his calm, his steady presence, his wry humor.

She didn't think she could get through the next few days otherwise.

She had been stunned by her mother's phone call. Communication between Annabel and her parents had been virtually nonexistent since the night she'd announced she was marrying Mark.

Christina Archer, to give her credit, had tried to mend the breach between father and daughter. But she had no success. Edward Lodge Archer would tolerate no view other than his own, and his view was that Annabel had ultimately and completely let him down.

"Him or me" might be too simplistic a way to think about the choice her father had given her. Doubtless he had couched it in finer, more sophisticated terms. But ultimately it had come down to the same thing.

And for Annabel there had been no question.

She'd picked Mark and her unborn child.

"Go, then," Edward had said. "Marry him. Make your bed and lie in it. But don't come back to me as long as you have him. Don't expect me to save you from your folly. As long as you persist in this, I no longer have a daughter."

She'd never seen her parents after that night. She'd married and buried a husband. She'd given birth to two beautiful children. She'd supported herself and them for eighteen years. And she'd done it all without a word from Edward Archer.

Someday, she'd told herself, there would come a time to face the past, to test the pain, to see if the wound had healed.

But never had the time been now.

Never until tonight...until her mother's desperate phone call told Annabel that tomorrow might well be too late.

"Please come," Christina had said. "Don't let this go on between you."

And if he still refused to make peace with her?

Christina did not believe he would.

Annabel was less certain. She was afraid to contemplate the possibility.

But with Carter behind her, Carter's hand in hers, her father's ultimate rejection no longer had the power to terrify her.

Carter might not love her—she didn't expect him to love her—but at least he cared.

He got up at the crack of dawn, not even waiting for Conan's summons. He had his own gear packed and most of Conan's by the time the first warbles from the back bedroom were heard.

A clean diaper, a warm bottle and a quick change of clothes and Conan was ready to travel. Stowing the baby and the gear into the Blazer, he set off for Annabel's.

She was in a dither.

He'd never seen Annabel in a dither, indecisive, muttering, putting this into her bag, taking that out again. He didn't take time to appreciate the novelty of it.

"Hold Conan. I'll do it," he told her.

And while she sat on the couch, crooning softly to Conan, Carter packed for her. He also packed for Libby and Leif.

"What are you doing with all that?" she demanded when he reappeared coming down the steps carrying suitcases filled with their clothes.

"I don't need all that."

"It's not all yours. It's mine, Conan's, Libby's and Leif's."

"Libby's and Leif's? They're not coming!"

Carter just looked at her. "You think they're going to stay here?"

"If I tell them to. I'm their mother!"

"Exactly. And you love them and you want what's best for them."

He didn't have to argue very hard.

She pressed her lips together. "I don't want them hurt."

"No one will hurt them. I won't let anyone hurt them. I'll keep an eye on them while you're at the hospital. I don't know where you grew up, Annabel. I don't care. But I promise you, I can handle it."

She looked almost startled. But then she nodded, a tiny

smile twisting her mouth. "I can't imagine anyone better equipped."

He didn't know what she meant by that.

He just bundled her and the baby into his car, called Bert and asked her to feed the goats and keep an eye on things, called Jack and Frances and left a message on their answering machine just in case Maeve contacted them about Conan, then went back and got into the car.

"Where are we going?"

"First to pick up the kids from school, then Boston."

He remembered Libby saying her mother had been born there. He remembered how little she wanted her children exposed to it. He supposed it must have something to do with the places she had lived growing up.

There were some rough parts in Boston. Some seedy neighborhoods, some less-than-savory streets. He thought he understood.

But when they arrived on the outskirts, Annabel aimed him through the suburbs, past the factories, beyond the row houses and the narrow dirty streets. They came into rolling wooded hills, lush lawns, palatial estates.

"This exit," she told him.

He frowned. There was nothing here save money and influence, Harvard accents and well-limbed family trees. He'd even been here himself a time or two, under duress, at somebody or other's dance or deb ball in the days before he'd learned the fascinating art of rebellion.

But he wasn't questioning Annabel now. He didn't have to. As they wove through the tree-shaded lanes, catching occasional glimpses of scrupulously manicured lawns and rambling Colonial-style mansions, the kids did it for him.

"You lived *here?*" Libby's tone was accusing as her eyes followed one after another of the curving driveways up into the wooded hillsides that protected most of the houses from view.

"Holy cow," Leif muttered. His head swiveled as he caught a glimpse of a three-story building set back into the hillside. "Look at that. Is it a house or a school?"

"A house, stupid," Libby said. "These are all houses. Aren't they, Mother?" There was just a hint of challenge in her voice.

"Yes."

Leif whistled.

Carter didn't say a word. He glanced over at the woman by his side, taking in her plaid flannel shirt, her faded jeans, her scuffed earth shoes. Earth Mother my foot, he thought, and reassessed everything he knew about Annabel Archer yet again.

"Take a right at the next drive," Annabel directed. Her fingers were knotted in her lap.

Carter slowed down. "This the road to the old homestead?"

She sighed. "I'm afraid it is."

"Are you okay?"

"Fine."

"You look like you're about to throw up."

"Thank you very much." But he saw the corner of her mouth twitch.

He grinned. "I'm a great flatterer."

Annabel's smile faded. "Not always."

"Huh?"

"Never mind."

He didn't have time to pursue the matter for they went around the curve in the road and there across a wide, shimmering pond, lay an immense three-story rose-colored Georgian brick with four gleaming white pillars.

Carter stopped the car.

"That was the house you grew up in?" asked Libby. Her eyes were like saucers as she looked from the house to her mother and back again.

"Yes."

"Hol-eeee cow," breathed Leif.

And Conan, who had slept like the proverbial baby since early in New Hampshire, opened his eyes at the sudden cessation of movement and looked around.

He gave a tiny whimper and started to cry.

ANNABEL KNEW precisely how he felt.

The first glimpse of Archer's Lodge—her father's pun on his middle name—was always intimidating to be sure.

But it wasn't the house that daunted Annabel. She knew about the cracks in the plaster, about which corner had settled and which chimney smoked.

It was the past that loomed before her, all the memories of expectations and failures, of battles lost and wars not won. And she wondered not for the first time why she had even bothered to come.

Nothing would have changed. Certainly not Edward Lodge Archer.

And to subject Libby and Leif to all this?

And for what?

Her fingers twisted in her lap. A strong warm hand covered them, squeezing them lightly, then just holding on.

She glanced over. Carter gave her a quick smile.

Oh, Carter. She wanted to put her arms around him and hang on, lay her head against his shoulder and cry.

He was being so strong, so steady. And she was taking such advantage of him.

She'd half expected a roar of outrage when he discovered where she'd lived, the circumstances in which she had grown up. She had knowingly misled him about her background ever since she'd met him. And she hadn't had the strength to explain how things really were either last night or this morning. She'd expected he would ask questions on the way in, but he must have realized how fragile she felt.

He hadn't said a word.

Even now the look he gave her was solicitous as he simply asked, ''Are you ready? Shall we go on?''

Annabel drew herself together, then nodded. ''I don't know if my mother is at the hospital or home. But the kids can stay here while I go to the hospital.''

''Don't we get to go to the hospital?'' Leif asked.

''Not yet.''

She might not totally be able to protect them any longer from the knowledge of their grandfather's existence, but she was going to do whatever she could to keep them from experiencing the same sort of rejection she had felt as the recipient of her father's cold, disapproving stare. She wasn't taking them anywhere near him until she knew they were welcome.

As Carter pulled up in front of the house, the door was flung open. Disapproval was the last thing on the face of the woman standing there.

''Mother.'' Annabel just stared at her, seeing the result of nineteen years of sadness on a woman she remembered as sunny and gay. She blinked back tears, then opened the door slowly and got out.

This was, she realized, going to be harder than facing her father would be. She could still get angry at him, could easily justify her actions with him. She'd never been angry at her mother.

Christina Archer might have been weak, she might have failed to overcome Edward's flat edict that Annabel was henceforth banished, never to be permitted home again, but she'd never said an unkind word about Mark, had never berated Annabel for making her choice, had never said she no longer had a daughter.

But Annabel had acted as if she'd never had a mother. She'd hugged her hurt tight against her, refusing contact with the woman who had borne her. "Him or me," she'd said in effect.

And Christina had paid the price.

And now?

Annabel stood quite still, her throat aching, her eyes stinging. "Mom?"

"Annabel!" Her mother came down the steps two at a time to sweep her daughter into her arms.

"Oh, Mom." Annabel buried her face in her mother's hair, hugged her tightly, struggling to hang on to her composure. Losing.

It was several moments before she could step back and swipe at her eyes. "Come," she said when her mother, too, took a step back and looked up at her. "Meet your grandchildren."

Libby and Leif had stopped their oohing and ahhing and now sat in the back of the car, silent and unmoving. Libby held Conan in her arms, staring down at him, trying to look as if she wasn't paying attention to every word her mother said.

Annabel didn't blame her. She didn't blame Leif, either. Neither they nor she knew precisely what to expect.

Carter eased out from behind the wheel and opened the door for Libby, taking Conan from her, offering soft words of what Annabel could only guess was encouragement. Libby gave him the baby and got out to stand next to him. Leif came out the other side and stood holding the open car door.

"This is Libby," Annabel said quietly. "And this is Leif."

Christina reached Leif first, stopped in front of him and simply looked at the boy who was only an inch shorter than she, who had her own fair hair and freckled skin, yet who looked at her solemnly with Mark Campbell's blue eyes.

She smiled and held out trembling hands to him.

Leif took her hands in his, and that was all she needed. She drew him close and rested her cheek against his hair, then brushed her lips against his forehead, once and then again. "Oh, Leif, I'm so glad you've come."

It was a minute or more before she stepped back, still holding his hands, and looked over to meet her granddaughter's eyes.

Annabel watched grandmother and granddaughter and hurt for them both. Innocent victims of a father-daughter battle, they had never known the closeness they might otherwise have shared. Christina, she thought ruefully, would have loved a cheerleader.

Would she have changed things if she could? she asked herself. Had she stayed away after Mark died only for spite?

No.

She'd put the obituary announcement in the paper she knew her father read. If they had come to the funeral, if they'd sent flowers, even a card, she would have tried again, would have braved her father's scorn for her mother's love.

She'd never had a word.

She wasn't Edward's daughter for nothing. She wasn't going to beg. Not then. Not now.

But as she watched her mother's first hesitant steps toward the child whose very life had caused the rift, she wished there could have been another way.

"Libby," her mother breathed and held out her arms. "I'm so happy to see you at last."

For a long moment Libby hesitated. She was no fool. If she and her mother hadn't actually discussed the reasons for the breach between Annabel and her parents, it didn't mean Libby didn't suspect what it was.

Annabel knew she'd been wrong not to have talked to Libby before now, knew that very shortly she would have to. But in the meantime she hoped her daughter would give her grandmother a chance. She gave Libby an encouraging smile.

Libby gave her a faint one in return. Then she took one step, then another, and allowed herself to be enfolded in her grandmother's arms.

Then, still holding her granddaughter's hand, Christina looked at Carter. She hesitated a moment, then held out her hand to him.

"Mark," she said. "Thank you for coming."

Annabel stared. *Mark?*

She'd called Carter *Mark?* She didn't know? She'd never been told? All this time and Christina never even knew that much about her daughter's life?

Oh, God, Daddy, couldn't you at least have told her?

She shook her head. "This isn't Mark. Mark...died nine years ago."

Christina went white. "Died? But...I thought..." She looked from Annabel to Carter, shaking her head.

"This is Carter, Mom. Carter MacKenzie. He's a...a friend." She didn't know how else to describe him. "And this is Conan," she went on quickly, more from desperation than anything else.

"I...I see," Christina murmured, though in fact Annabel didn't think she saw much at all. How could she when for at least nine years she hadn't known the truth?

"How's Dad?" Annabel asked.

"I don't know. They don't tell me much. They say he's 'stable,' that he's 'resting comfortably,' is feeling 'as well as can be expected.' How can you tell?"

"I'll go now. Can the kids stay with you?"

"Of course. I'd be delighted." She beamed at her grandchildren, who gave her slightly wary smiles in return. "Come along, both of you."

"Isn't Carter staying?" Leif asked Annabel.

"I'm going with your mother," Carter said, and Annabel didn't realize how much she'd been counting on him until that moment.

"But—"

"Moral support," Carter said. "You'll get your turn. Will you take care of Conan till I get back?"

"Sure." Leif reached for the baby, handling him with an expertise that made Annabel smile. He gave his mother a worried look. "You okay, Mom?"

"Fine." She ruffled his hair, gave Libby's hand a squeeze, kissed the tip of Conan's nose. "We won't be long."

Carter unloaded Conan's car seat and the bag that contained his gear, handing it to Libby. "That'll do for now," he said. He went around and held the door open for Annabel.

She got back into the car and stared straight ahead.

THEY HARDLY SPOKE all the way to the hospital. Carter knew enough not to offer platitudes. Annabel apparently could think of nothing coherent to say. She seemed to retreat further and further from him the closer to the hospital they came.

When, at last, they arrived, she made no move to get out of the car. Her face was chalky white, her knuckles even whiter. She looked as if she were going to face a firing squad.

"You don't have to do this," Carter said.

"Yes. I do."

He understood what she meant. He didn't know everything that must have passed between her and her father, but he could guess.

He wished—oh, God, he wished—that he'd been given the same opportunity, that he'd been there on that golf course, that he could have told his own father that he loved him, that just once he could have heard those words from his father's lips.

"All right," he said. "Let's go." He got out and came around to join her, tucking her arm through his and pulling her against his side, needing to protect her in whatever way he could.

He kept her there while they walked down endless corridors, held her hand while she talked to this nurse and that one, felt her tremble beneath the touch of his fingers when at last a nurse pointed them toward a private room at the end of the hall.

She took three steps, then stopped; her fingers strangled his.

"It's okay," Carter said. "It'll be fine."

She shook her head and took a deep breath. He could see her struggling, could see the fear in her eyes.

"He's your father. He loves you."

Annabel bit her lip. Her fingers tightened on his and he squeezed hers in return.

"He does," Carter repeated. "He does." As if it were a mantra. And as he spoke, he drew her with him down the hall.

She came slowly but steadily, hesitating only for a moment outside the room, and with just the briefest glance at him, she pushed open the door.

Carter intended to stay where he was—not wanting to intrude—but when she didn't let go of his hand, he followed her in.

Annabel's father lay in a high bed next to the window. He was painfully pale, his cheeks sunken, his lips cracked. But Carter knew him now by name, by reputation and, even devastated by the stroke, Edward Lodge Archer was a formidable man.

He could have given old C.W. a run for his money, Carter thought. Probably had.

The old man's eyes were closed as they approached. Annabel stopped beside the bed and cleared her throat.

''Daddy?''

His eyes opened then, slowly. He focused. Frowned. His eyes were a glittering amber-hazel that reminded Carter of an agate marble he'd had as a child.

''Hello, Daddy.'' Annabel managed a smile.

Edward Lodge Archer's lips parted slightly. Carter could hear the labored intake of breath, then the wheeze as he spoke. ''Go…away.''

Chapter Twelve

She left. Turned and, without a backward glance or even the slightest hesitation, marched straight out the door and down the hall.

Carter stood staring after her, speechless.

He looked from the rigid waxen features of her father to the rapidly retreating back of the woman he loved.

"You bloody damned fool!" he yelled at her father "How could you say that?"

The nurses came on the run.

Carter didn't care. He'd had his fill of crusty old men, of opportunities lost, of chances never taken. He pulled away from the nurse who had hold of his arm and bent over the bed.

"She loves you, you blind idiot. She's your daughter, for God's sake!"

"Mr.—Mr.—Whatever your name is! Please, lower your voice!"

The nurse had his arm again, aided by another one. They were both dragging him toward the door.

"Come along. Let's go now. You really must behave. Mr. Archer is very ill!"

"He can damned well die for all I care!" Carter knew his voice was caroming off the walls. "As far as I'm concerned it'd be no big loss! But before he does he ought to think about making peace with his family. Not everyone gets to, damn it. Did you ever think about that, you old bastard? You're lucky you have the time!"

"That's enough." The nurses had him almost out the door now. "This is a hospital! You're disturbing the patients. If you don't leave quietly at once, we'll have to call security."

Carter took one last look at the man in the bed. The nurses pushed. He held fast. His eyes met Edward Archer's.

"Don't worry," he said. "I've said it all. There's nothing left to say."

SHE MUST'VE BEEN SITTING in the car a good five minutes before Carter came.

Of course, she could hardly have expected him to participate in her dramatic exit. He had no stake in what was going on between her and her father. He had simply been there for support.

No doubt that's what was taking so long. He was busy placating the nurses, being polite to her father, smoothing over the troubled waters she'd left behind.

Thank God for Carter.

She'd been right. Her father's rejection had hurt, but it wasn't devastating. Not with Carter there.

She looked up and saw him now, walking toward her, his hands stuffed into his pockets. His head was bent. He scuffed the leaves as he came. With every scuff of his foot, with every step he took, Annabel felt as if the clouds were lifting, as if the gloom was being swept aside.

Even the darkest clouds—even the deepest pain—went away when Carter was there.

He got into the car and rested his hands on the wheel for a long moment, then looked over at her. "I'm sorry."

"It's hardly your fault. I really shouldn't have expected anything else." She gave him the best smile she could manage.

"You deserve better," he said tersely.

"Heaven help us if we get what we deserve." She turned then and leaned toward him, kissing his cheek. "Thank you. I appreciate your being there."

"Will you?" Carter muttered enigmatically. "I wonder." He started the engine. "Where to?"

"Back to get the kids, I suppose. Then home."

"What about your mother?"

"My mother and I will talk."

Annabel didn't know what sort of understanding they would come to, what form their relationship would take. She only knew that from here on, it wouldn't be wholly determined by her father.

If her mother was willing to see her, there was no way she was going to let her father keep them apart.

Christina was, to say the least, disappointed when she heard about Annabel's encounter with her father. "Oh, my dear. I'm so sorry. I never thought..." She sighed and wrung her hands.

"Nothing's changed. He's a stubborn man, Mom. He doesn't want me there."

Christina pressed her lips together. "I had so hoped..."

"Don't. There's no point."

"I suppose not." Christina's gaze went to her grandchildren outside exploring the garden. Leif was swinging from a tree. Libby, with Conan in her arms, stood watching him. They were laughing.

There was no laughter in Christina's face as she turned

to her daughter. "I don't want to lose them, Annabel. I don't want to lose you."

"You won't."

"But your father—I don't know what to do about your father."

"You can't do anything," Annabel said. "He did it himself."

Christina sighed. "I guess he did."

"If you want to see your grandchildren, you're always welcome. If you want to come and see me, I'll always want to see you," Annabel told her.

"Oh, my dear," Christina murmured and put her arms around Annabel, holding her close.

The phone rang and Annabel felt her mother jerk. Then, pulling herself together, Christina went to answer it.

"When?" Her fingers clenched on the receiver. "Now? I'll come right away." Christina dropped the receiver back onto the hook and looked at Annabel, anguished. "It's your father. They want me to come."

HE SHOULD HAVE KEPT his big mouth shut. There was always the chance that the old man might have come around if he hadn't shot off his mouth as if he were some raving lunatic. He should have been rational, sensible, coherent. All of the above.

Carter sighed, and stared at the white line curving through the Vermont mountains as he drove. When had he ever been any of the above?

That had always been his father's complaint.

"You never think," C.W. would bellow at him. "Never! You only feel!"

You're right about that, old man, Carter thought.

He felt like hell.

Why should that surprise him? Hell was exactly what he deserved.

He wondered if C.W. was chortling in the hereafter at the idea of his son finally agreeing with something he'd said.

Somebody might as well be getting some joy out of it. It wasn't going to be him—or from the look of things, Annabel.

He'd left her and the kids at her mother's, looking distraught.

"I can't leave," she'd told him. "What if…what if…?"

She didn't have to say it; he already knew the only *if* that mattered. If her father was dead, she could thank Carter for having been the one to dispatch him.

He didn't tell her that.

He couldn't have borne seeing the look on her face, the dismay, the disgust, the disdain.

Everything his father had always felt for him. In spades.

"I'd rather come home with you, but—"

He understood that she was just being kind, just saying thanks for having come along, not really aware of what a botch he'd made of things, not aware at all of what he'd done that was going to be the cause of even further pain.

For regardless of what she said, he knew her father's words this afternoon had hurt her.

He'd seen her instant of recoil, as if she'd been slapped. And then he'd seen her pull herself together, begin to rationalize, to pretend she didn't care.

He understood her reaction all too well. He'd done it often enough himself.

He also knew what a lie that facade of difference was.

"I understand," he told her.

He'd allowed himself one chaste kiss on her cheek.

He'd given Libby a hug, and Leif one, too. Then he'd carried Conan out to the car and started the long, lonely trip back to Vermont.

"THERE WAS A MESSAGE on the machine when I got home," Frances said when Jack came in the door. "From Carter."

"How's the roof coming?"

"He says he can't work on it for a while."

"Why not?"

"He's gone to Boston. Taking Annabel home to her parents." She was smiling.

"I didn't know Annabel had parents."

"Neither did I. But you can hear it yourself. I kid you not."

"WHY COULDN'T CARTER stay?" Leif asked.

Annabel, distracted, pacing the hospital corridor she'd just walked out of scant hours ago, anticipating the worst, wished desperately she knew the answer to Leif's question.

She shook her head. "I don't know. The roof, I guess. Conan." *Marilee Newman.*

She didn't mention Marilee, of course. She might not be the actual reason that Carter had left.

All Annabel knew was that he had.

Ever since they'd driven away from the hospital she had felt him withdrawing from her, distancing himself.

Who could blame him? she thought grimly. She should never have pitched him into this mess. It could only embarrass him, make him regret they'd become friends.

It was better, anyway, that he'd left. If her mother came out with the news she expected, Annabel would never be able to brave it out. She'd go to pieces, she knew she would.

And Carter would have had to deal with that.

"Is he gonna die, Ma?" Leif asked. "Your father, I mean."

"I don't know."

"How come we've never met him?"

"Leif!" Libby admonished.

But Annabel took him by the hand, then reached for her daughter's, leading them both over to the orange plastic bench by the wall. "It's time we talked about that."

She didn't start at the beginning—she couldn't tell them about Carter—but she did start with her moonlit encounter with their father. She told them about Mark's warmth, his strength, his innocence as well as her own.

"We were children," she said simply. She looked at her daughter. "I wasn't any older than you."

"Oh, Ma." Libby's eyes brimmed.

"I don't want you to think I regret it," Annabel went on. "I don't. I never have. But it wasn't easy. Not for your father or for me."

"He left you, didn't he?" Libby asked.

Something else Annabel had never talked about—the four years when she had been alone.

"We were big responsibilities, you and me," she said to her daughter. "Heavy burdens for such a young man. He didn't know where to turn. He didn't have a job, didn't have any skills to speak of. I said we could manage with the sheep, the goats, a little farming, my herbs and things. We argued. He drove off. I didn't hear from him for a month. And then I got a postcard from Pensacola. He'd joined the navy."

"You got his picture in the album," Leif said. "In his uniform. I saw it."

Annabel remembered the day she had put it there. It was on Libby's second birthday. It had come the day before in her daughter's birthday card.

It was the first communication she'd had since Mark's postcard almost eighteen months before. The card, of course, was for Libby. In it he'd put a check. ''I can't go shopping at sea,'' he'd written. ''But it doesn't mean I've forgotten. Please get her something so she'll know her father loves her. And you.''

Until then, Annabel hadn't hoped. After that she hadn't dared. Not at first anyway.

But on his next shore leave, Mark had come to see her. Theirs had been a tentative meeting. ''I didn't know,'' he'd told her, ''if you were even still out here. I thought you might have gone home to Mommy and Daddy.''

Annabel hadn't even considered it. She hadn't wanted to face her father's certain rejection. She might be struggling to make ends meet, but she and Libby were doing all right. She liked her independence, liked being responsible and making ends meet, liked the feeling that she could make it on her own.

But she liked sharing life with Mark even better, and she told him so.

Uncle Sam did his part in making sure they didn't have a lot of time together until Libby was four and a half. But as soon as Mark was out of the service, he came to Vermont.

''Did you mean it?'' he asked, and she knew from the hesitancy in his voice and the wary look in his eyes that he was afraid she might not.

''Oh, yes,'' Annabel had told him.

She smiled now at her son. ''And then we had you.''

''And your parents...'' Libby began somewhat hesitantly ''...they still never came around?''

"No. But," Annabel had to admit this, "I probably wouldn't have been very welcoming if they had."

"Because they hurt you."

"Yes. And I wanted to hurt them in return," Annabel replied. "And I think I hurt us all instead."

"It wasn't your fault," Leif said.

Annabel gave him a hug. "Thank you for saying so."

"It's true," he insisted. "They were rotten."

"But it was a long time ago," Annabel told him. "And we've all paid the price. We'll see your grandmother sometimes now. And I don't want it to come between you. The fault was mine and my father's. Not hers."

"She's nice," Leif allowed.

Libby nodded. "She is."

"I'm glad you like her," Annabel said.

"She said maybe she could come and see us sometime," Leif reported.

"Maybe she can."

"What about your father?"

But Annabel never got to answer that, for just then the nurse opened the door to his room.

"Ms. Archer? Come quickly. Please."

CONAN CRIED the last half hour of the trip. Carter's head ached, his nerves were shot, his emotions in tatters. He felt like crying, too.

When they finally pulled into Jack and Frances's yard and the yard light came on, he sagged against the steering wheel until Conan's yelling urged him on. It was all he could do to unload Conan's gear and his own. He set it on the porch, then turned to go back to get the baby.

Arnold came ambling around the corner of the barn.

"Damnation!"

Arnold cocked his head.

Conan was screaming his head off. Hungry, no doubt. Also very likely sopping wet.

Carter took a step off the porch. Arnold came a bit closer. He made no pretense of cropping the grass, showed no feigned interest in tree bark—his interest was all in Carter.

"It isn't as if you don't know me, you old reprobate," Carter muttered, coming slowly the rest of the way down the steps. "You see me every damned day."

Arnold stood still, his feet planted squarely, regarding the man who walked steadily toward the car.

"Don't tell me you haven't noticed," Carter went on. "I'm the one on the roof, the one you always check to see is there watching before you go after one of your girls in the pasture." He couldn't be sure, of course, that Arnold was deliberately flaunting his prowess with the ladies, but it was the interpretation Carter had early on given Arnold's glancing smirk in his direction.

"I'm impressed," he said now. "You're a damned sight more successful with females than I am." He had almost made it to the car now.

Arnold still watched.

Conan screamed.

"Maybe I should take lessons from you," Carter told the goat. He reached the car, opened the door and realized there was no way he was going to get Conan out of the car without exposing his backside to Arnold.

"So that's what you were waiting for," he muttered.

Oh, well. What the hell. What else could go wrong today?

Deliberately Carter turned his back on the goat and bent over Conan, unbuckling the strap that held his car seat in place. At every instant he was prepared to be catapulted forward from one of Arnold's powerful butts.

He felt a quiet, curious nudge to his elbow. He turned, car seat and screaming baby in his arms. Arnold was standing next to him, scowling as only a goat could scowl. He was regarding Conan with a mixture of goatish worry and distaste. Then he looked at Carter, his wide expressive eyes quizzical, not hostile in the least.

"He's hungry," Carter explained, and didn't think it odd that he should be offering explanations to a goat. "And wet. I have to change him." Cautiously he began to move toward the house.

Arnold walked right alongside him, keeping pace. When Carter went up on the porch, he did, too. When Carter balanced the car seat against his hip and opened the front door, Arnold stepped aside politely and waited. Carter went in and Arnold followed, nosing curiously around the house, then peering directly into the screaming baby's face when Carter set the car seat on the kitchen table.

Conan shut up abruptly.

Carter looked at Arnold, amazed. "How'd you do that?"

The goat belched and nuzzled Conan's belly, tugging at his blanket.

"Here now. Quit that." Carter cast about hastily for something to offer Arnold in place of the blanket. All he could find that was edible was a banana. Did goats eat bananas?

He held it in front of Arnold's face. Arnold nibbled at it delicately, then curled his lip and took a bigger bite.

"Right," Carter said. "Why don't you just come with me, then? Enjoy your banana on the porch."

He didn't imagine he had a snowball's chance in hell of getting Arnold to come along quietly, but apparently once the baby had stopped crying, the goat lost interest. He allowed Carter to slowly chivvy him out the door, across the yard and through the gate into the pasture with the nannies.

Carter had no idea if he was supposed to be there or not, but Leif wasn't around to ask. And there was no way he could take Arnold home.

He shut the gate and hung over it a moment, watching Arnold as he worked his way through the banana. "'Night, Arnie," he said.

Then he made his way back to Conan, shaking his head.

But it had to say something about the quality of his day, he thought as he was changing Conan, that the high point was not getting knocked on his rear by a goat.

Conan, changed, was a happier camper. He waved his arms and gurgled while Carter spooned cereal into his mouth. He blew oatmeal bubbles and they dribbled down his face. Carter wiped them off with the edge of the bib.

"You're a slob," he told Conan. "Your manners need work. Tomorrow you're going to have to do better. How can I let you out in the civilized world otherwise." He remembered his mother saying exactly the same words to him.

Conan made a distinct raspberry sound.

Carter smiled at him. "My feelings exactly." He finished feeding Conan, then put a bottle on to heat. He walked the baby around the kitchen as they waited, savoring the solid warmth of Conan's tiny body nestled against his chest, the weight of the baby's head as it came to rest on his shoulder, the soft sound of Conan sucking his thumb.

He picked up the bottle, dried it off and carried it and the baby into the living room. Only the one light beside the sofa was on. Carter sat in the rocker as far away from it as he could, settling in, relishing the dimness, the peace.

He didn't have much else to relish. Only Conan. The

baby lay snuggled in his arms, one chubby hand pressed against the bottle, the other gripping the front of Carter's shirt.

Carter looked down into the dark watchful eyes, saw them cloud with sleep, fight to stay awake, then lose. The bottle slipped out of Conan's mouth. His lips moved, then stopped, remaining parted, almost smiling.

Carter continued to sit there, rocking. He couldn't just get up and carry the baby upstairs. He couldn't let go that easily. It was comforting, sitting there holding Conan and rocking. Carter needed comforting tonight.

He dozed there till well past eleven. He was roused by a knock on the door.

Annabel?

His heart leapt before he became rational and realized it couldn't possibly be. But then…who…?

He got up carefully and moved to lay Conan, still sleeping, on the couch, buffering him with a pillow so he wouldn't roll off. Then, at the second knock, he went to answer the door.

It was a plump fair-haired girl about Libby's age. Behind her there stood a weedy-looking young man with wild hair.

"I'm Maeve," she said. "And this is Jerry."

HE DIDN'T NEED THIS.

God knew, on top of everything else that had happened today, Carter didn't need to confront Conan's wandering parents.

"Who're you?" Maeve demanded, apparently noting for the first time that he wasn't Jack.

"My name's MacKenzie. I'm a friend of the Neillandses. I'm putting on their roof."

"Where's my baby?" There was panic in Maeve's

voice now. She pushed her way past him into the living room, stopping only when she spotted Conan asleep on the sofa.

"Is *this* where you've been keeping him?" she demanded, rounding on Carter, furious.

"No, by God, it's not where I've been keeping him," Carter snapped back at her. "But a hell of a lot you'd care anyway, going off and leaving him like that!"

"I thought Frances—"

"Think again. Frances and Jack are in New York. But did you think to inquire? You might have left Conan with anyone—with *no one*— dumping him on the porch like that! Like he's some kind of parcel!"

He should have been calm, should at least have not yelled. Heaven knew he should have learned his lesson by now. He plowed straight ahead. "He's fine, no thanks to you," he told the two of them harshly.

"I didn't mean..." Maeve said faintly. "I saw the car, and...I never thought..."

"Well, you need to start thinking," Carter told her in more modulated tones. "You have a child. Not just when you feel like having one, but all the time. And you have responsibilities toward that child."

"I know that." She met his eyes for just a moment, then looked away.

"It...was my fault." Jerry's voice was gruff.

Carter's gaze swung to fix on the boy.

Jerry rubbed a hand through his hair, making it stick up even farther. "I panicked. I ran. I lost my job and I didn't see how I could get another one. She...came after me. I'm coming back. I'll take care of him while she's working. It'll be okay. I'm going back to school, too. And I'll try to find part-time work. We worked it out."

''Nice for you,'' Carter said. ''It might not have been so nice for Conan.''

''I'm sorry,'' Maeve whispered.

''Me, too,'' Jerry said. He craned his neck, trying to catch a glimpse of the blanket-wrapped child. ''Is he all right? Really?''

''He's fine,'' Carter said. ''I just got him to sleep. I was holding him when you knocked.''

Maeve started toward him, then hesitated, looking again at Carter. ''Can I—''

''Go ahead.''

She started to, then stepped back. ''No. Jerry, you do it.''

Jerry looked as if she'd asked him to wrestle Arnold to the death. But he gamely moved forward and bent to scoop Conan up in his arms.

Carter moved, too, wanting to push Jerry out of the way and show him how to pick up the child. He shoved his hands into his pockets, told his feet to stay welded to the floor.

Jerry bobbled the baby momentarily, then got a hold on him, rather as if he were a wide receiver and Conan a football. He peered down into his son's face, jiggling him, waking him.

Carter wanted to gnash his teeth.

''See, look. He remembers me.'' Jerry was beaming. He bent his head and nuzzled his nose against Conan's. ''How ya doin', son?''

And Carter felt his throat close tight.

''I really am sorry,'' Maeve said to him. She put her hand on his arm so that he couldn't walk away. ''I've always depended on Frances. She's meant so much to me. Like an aunt, I guess. I knew her when she taught at my school when I was just in junior high. She saw me getting involved with the wrong crowd and tried to steer me away. I didn't always listen, but I always knew she'd be there when I needed her.'' She colored slightly. ''At least I expected she would. Thanks a lot, Mr. MacKenzie. You're really special, too.''

Carter managed half a smile.

''Come on, Jerry,'' Maeve said. ''We've bothered Mr. MacKenzie long enough. Where are Conan's things?'' she asked Carter.

''I'll get them.'' He made his escape up the stairs to Jason's bedroom. He gathered up the small pile of Conan's clothing, his extra blanket, leaving behind only the footed sleeper Annabel had given him that had belonged to Leif. He stood for a moment looking down at the empty crib. His eyes stung.

He turned and walked quickly back down the steps where Maeve met him at the bottom. He piled everything into her arms. ''His extra bottles are in the kitchen. Hang on, I'll get them.''

He put the bottles, the jars of strained peaches and pears, the half-gone box of cereal into a grocery sack. He carried that back into the living room. Jerry was already putting Conan into the car.

Maeve stowed the sack in the back, then got into the passenger side and rolled down her window. ''I don't know how to thank you,'' she said.

Carter leaned one hand on the car door and looked at the baby, wide-eyed and curious in the back seat. He looked back at Maeve. ''I think you do.''

''I'll take the best care of him in the world,'' she promised. ''Would you like to...see him sometime?''

Carter hesitated. How much pain could a grown man stand? he wondered. But would not seeing Conan ever again be better?

"Yes."

Maeve patted his hand. "You can be his honorary uncle."

UNCLE CARTER.

He supposed there was justice in it. He supposed, if he looked hard enough, he could even find some small consolation. It was better, he told himself, than nothing.

But he couldn't muster up much enthusiasm, because right now nothing was exactly what he felt he had.

He'd done what Milly had suggested: he'd gone away, taken a look at his life. He'd discovered quite a lot of things about himself that he'd only just begun to suspect.

He would have been a good parent.

He'd first begun to consider the idea when he'd been entrusted with Jason, when Jack and Frances had smilingly but quite seriously bestowed on him what Jack called "godfatherhood." He'd confirmed that feeling in the past few weeks in his dealings with Leif and Libby. And with Conan.

He sat now in the rocker. Alone. In the dark.

And he remembered the solid warm body he'd held against his only a few short hours ago. He ached for the loss.

He ached for another loss more.

He knew he'd never really had Annabel Archer. She'd never loved him the way he'd grown to love her. But he missed her anyway. He wondered if she would even speak to him again when she found out what he'd done.

What could she say to the man who'd killed her father that he might conceivably want to hear?

Most of his adult life he'd found fault with his own father—especially with C.W.'s inability to form and maintain relationships. He knew now that he had no room to talk.

The old man had been right after all. Carter did screw up everything he touched.

He'd finish the roof. It'd take another day or so. Then he'd be off.

He'd go a long way away this time. To the farthest ends of the earth. Maybe join a monastery.

Not the Trappists. They lived in communities. The Carthusians would be better. They couldn't ruin relationships—they lived by themselves in little huts.

He could get a really good perspective on his life then, Carter thought. But he wouldn't have to look for what was missing. That he already knew.

Annabel.

The other half of his heart.

Chapter Thirteen

''Is he—'' Annabel's eyes flew to her mother's. Christina, standing beside the hospital bed, one hand gripping the bed rail, looked very pale.

''He wants to talk to you.''

Hesitantly, feeling as if she were negotiating a mine field rather than a linoleum floor, Annabel crossed the room.

Her father looked much as he had earlier, pale, waxen, a shadow of his former self. His eyes met hers as she approached, but he didn't speak until she was right next to his bed.

Then, with considerable effort, he raised himself slightly and his lips began to move. His voice was hoarse, ragged, and the words came out one at a time. *''Who...the...hell... was...that?''*

''Who? Who was what?''

''Man...yelled at...me.''

Annabel could only stare at him.

His adam's apple was working in his throat. His left hand clutched fretfully at the sheets. ''Man...with...you. Yelled...old bas...tard.''

Annabel's mind was whirling, trying to make sense of

what he was saying. His hazel eyes were snapping with impatience. That much hadn't changed a bit.

She shook her head. "Some man yelled at...you, Daddy?" She didn't think mental confusion was part of his diagnosis, but she had to admit, she didn't have the faintest idea what he was talking about.

"The man with you," the nurse told her. "He was, well, yelling at Mr. Archer."

"Carter?"

"'S'name?" her father demanded.

"The man who was with me was Carter MacKenzie, but surely you're mistaken! He wouldn't—"

Her father coughed weakly. His head sank back against the pillows. "Might've...known," he rasped.

Annabel stared at him. "What?"

"Brash...arrogant...know-it-all. Son...of...a...bitch." He stopped and took a breath. "Jus'...like...'is father."

THEY ARGUED, of course. How could you not argue with the man who called the man you loved a son of a bitch?

The man she loved?

Loved?

Well, yes, of course. It was crystal clear now, for all the good it did her.

But Annabel didn't even stop to think about that until after. She made some concessions to her father's health. With her mother looking on and the nurses alternately tittering and wringing their hands, she had to.

But she didn't let him get away with it.

She told him in no uncertain terms that Carter was a far better man than he had ever been, that Carter knew what it was to be a friend, a father.

"He loves children who aren't even his own," she told him finally. "Unconditionally."

Edward's jaw stiffened. He glared at her, then, slowly, his gaze slid away. His hand worked again fitfully on the sheet. ''Was…wrong,'' he mumbled.

''What?''

''Said—'' his voice broke with the effort ''—I was…wrong.'' His eyes came back to meet hers. They weren't flashing anymore. They looked shadowy now, sad almost. ''Shouldn't…have done…what I…did. Too hard.''

Annabel stared at him, stunned. An apology from Edward Archer?

But he wasn't finished yet.

''He's right…y'know…M'Kenzie…said I got to… make peace. Tell…the truth 'fore s'too…late.'' He looked at her. ''Sorry.''

His hand clenched again. Annabel reached out and took it in her own. Their fingers curved around each other's. Annabel, mind reeling, throat aching, hung on.

''Anna…bel? Love…you.''

Carter had accomplished this?

Carter had yelled at her father?

''Good…man,'' her father went on, his fingers slowly, weakly kneading hers. ''Better'n…'is old man. More… fire. Guts.''

''Yes.''

''Marry him?''

''What?''

''Deaf?'' The hazel eyes were snapping impatiently at her again. ''Said…you going to…marry him?''

Don't I wish, Annabel thought. *Haven't I wished for years and years?* But she had nothing to offer Carter except a house with a mortgage, a goat who couldn't stand him, two children to drive him crazy and a wife who had neither youth nor beauty nor exceptional talents, whose only claim to his attention was that she'd imposed on him tremendously and that she'd dreamed about him for nigh on twenty years.

Carter wasn't interested in her. Not as a wife. He could have virtually any woman he wanted. Like Marilee Newman.

She gave her father's hand a gentle squeeze. ''I'd like to, Daddy,'' she said with absolute honesty. ''But I'm afraid Carter has other plans.''

''YOU BLEW IT,'' Jack told Frances cheerfully when she came in from taking Jason to the park.

His wife cocked her head. ''I beg your pardon.''

''Milly called while you were gone. Said she'd called Carter. He's back in Vermont, by the way. Roofing. She asked him how Annabel was. He hung up on her.''

SHE DIDN'T WANT TO GO and see him.

It would hurt. He would want to pick up where they'd left off in the bedroom earlier in the week—or he wouldn't.

And she didn't know which would be worse.

Because there was no way on earth she could go to bed with him now. Not loving him. Not knowing that he didn't love her. While she'd been able to keep the knowledge of her feelings at bay, she'd stood half a chance of not making a fool of herself.

No more.

And if he didn't want to—well, perversely enough, that would hurt, as well. It would mean he was moving on, ready now to find someone new. A woman he could really love, who would be able to start a marriage afresh, without encumbrances.

Marilee Newman?

A good bet. But if not her, then any one of a legion of women. Carter had always been good at finding women, she thought wryly. There'd never been any doubt about that.

Still, she had to go by and see him. Had to say thank you.

How did you thank a man who had given you back your father? What words could express the gratitude, the joy, the satisfaction Annabel felt?

She didn't know.

She only knew she had to try.

She was quiet and distracted all the time the kids were getting ready for school. They were kind and solicitous, careful with her, as if she were some fragile piece of porcelain, all too capable of being cracked.

She knew they thought she was suffering from the aftermath of the reunion with her father and mother, of the soul-baring talks that all of them had just shared.

She let them think it. Telling them how she felt about Carter, and more especially about the futility of those hopes, was more soul baring than she could stand.

She waited until they were safely on the school bus. She waited until Bert had come, wrapped soaps, chatted and gone. She waited until Aaron had stuck his head in and asked if she wanted to go to a movie and she had gently declined.

Finally she could wait no longer.

HE SAW HER the minute she came over the top of the hill. He was sitting on the roof, three rows away from being finished with the whole reason for his being here. And he had been hoping he would get done—and gone—before he had to talk to anyone else.

And here she came.

She looked remote, distracted, unhappy. What else? Her father had just died, hadn't he?

And even though the old man had sent her away with what was probably close to his dying breath, it didn't mean she'd be rejoicing. She'd probably heard from one of the nurses what had transpired.

She was probably coming to tell him off.

He didn't blame her a bit. All the same, he sat very still and hoped she wouldn't look up.

Dream on, sucker, he told himself an instant later when her eyes lifted and her step faltered. She picked her way down the rest of the trail, then crossed the yard, stopping where she could look up and see him.

"Carter?"

"I'm really busy. Gotta get this done before it rains." There was maybe one cloud in the sky. He set to hammering again, positioned another shingle, hammered some more, moved on.

When he glanced up again, she'd disappeared. He breathed easier.

"Fine," he heard her voice a moment later, and looked up to see her climbing onto the roof. "I'll talk to you up here."

He bit down on the nails he held between his teeth. He shrugged, facing the inevitable, wishing it would hurry up and be over. He wanted to say he was sorry about her father, sorry about his part in it, but he was too much of a coward. He set another nail and began to hammer.

"You did it, you know," Annabel said quietly.

So much for vain hopes. He shut his eyes. His knuckles went white around the hammer. He bowed his head and took a slow breath before he could look up again and meet her eyes.

She was smiling. Not a thousand-watt grin, but still a smile.

He didn't understand. He shook his head. "I didn't mean—"

"You gave him back to me."

Now he really was confused. He sat back on the roof and spat the nails into his palms. "I don't know what you mean. I lost it in there. I yelled my bloody head off, said things I don't even want to think about now and—"

"And got through to him."

"I...killed him."

She started, laid a hand on his knee. He flinched and she drew back abruptly. "On the contrary. I think you brought him back to life."

Carter stared at her. "That—that phone call. From the hospital... Didn't he...didn't he die?"

Annabel shook her head. "He made the nurse call my mother, wanted her over there right that minute. She thought it was the end, too. So did I, so the kids and I went with her and hung about in the hall. He wanted her to find me." She stared off into space for a moment, then smiled again, that same gentle smile.

"He thought he'd driven me away for good, and wanted me back. Wanted to 'make his peace,' with me. That's what he told me when they let me in." Her gaze met his. "Because of you."

Carter sat very still, letting the words sink in. His jaw tightened, his throat felt blocked. He hadn't killed him, then? His yelling had actually done more good than harm?

"He said you were a brash, know-it-all son of a bitch, just like your father."

"What?"

Annabel shrugged. "That's what he said. He seemed pleased."

Carter wasn't. He was horrified. ''I'm like my old man?''

''That's what he said. Except that you were better. He said you had more—more fire. More guts.''

Carter digested that. It mollified his feelings a bit. There was a certain amount of truth to Edward Archer's assertions, God help him. He'd never wanted to acknowledge it before, but now he had to.

He and C.W. were both stubborn, both opinionated, both passionate in their beliefs. That was why they'd gone head-to-head so often. Less similar men might have found ways to accommodate each other.

It wasn't the first time he'd heard it said, either.

Even Milly had told him so. ''One jackass braying at another'' was the way she'd described them.

But he'd ignored her. What did sisters know?

Besides, he'd been jealous of her, if he was going to admit the truth. Milly had always been able to twist their father around her little finger, had always been able to smile and get good grades and say the right thing. And Carter had always yelled and fought and then pretended it didn't matter.

Just like his old man.

''I thought I'd killed him,'' he said to Annabel now. ''I really thought I'd done him in.'' He felt weak with relief. She wouldn't hate him now. Was that enough?

He sighed and placed another nail. It would have to be. There was certainly nothing encouraging in the way she was looking at him, nothing that might give him the faintest hope that she'd come to see him as being more than a physical significance in her life.

And he couldn't be that. Not the way he felt.

It would kill him.

"Thanks for telling me," he said and began to hammer again, hard, expecting her to go.

Please God, she had to. She wasn't going to sit there and come on to him, torment him, expect him to make love to her, was she?

But she made no move to leave.

"Where's Conan?" she asked after a moment. "He surely can't be sleeping through all this hammering."

"He's gone. Maeve and Jerry came. Took him," he said through the nails in his mouth. He bent his head, concentrating on the shingling.

"Oh, Carter." She sounded as sad as he felt. She put her hand out again, as if she would have touched him. But then she jerked it back. "I'm so sorry. I know how much you'll miss him."

"Yeah," he said gruffly. "But, hell, that's the way things go. He had to go back."

"Did they settle things?"

"They damned well better have! I told 'em he's a baby, not some parcel they can just set aside whenever they don't feel like dealing with him! I told 'em—" He stopped abruptly, embarrassed by his vehemence.

"You were right," Annabel said gently. "I hope they take it as well as my father did."

He hammered in another nail. For Conan. Pounding some sense into his parents' heads. "It's great being right about everybody else's life," he said bitterly. "I feel like some damned oracle."

"You're a perceptive man. Sensitive. Caring."

Too damned caring, Carter thought.

"You were good for Conan. You were good for Libby and Leif. You'll...be a good father someday, Carter."

"No."

"Doesn't...doesn't Marilee want any kids?"

"Marilee?" He frowned at Annabel. "What's she got to do with it?"

Annabel shook her head. "I—I thought… You said she was so wonderful! You went out with her after…after we—" She broke off, looking away, the color high across her cheekbones.

"I didn't want to!"

She looked at him then. "Why not?"

"After making love with you I'm supposed to want to go out with somebody else?"

"She called. She said you had a date."

"Yeah, made days before…before—" Oh, hell, why was he doing this? Why was he opening his mouth? Telling her things he didn't want to tell her?

"—before we made love," she said quietly.

He looked out over the wooded pasture, at the brightly colored trees, the brilliant blue of the sky. He looked down at the toes of his sneakers, at the roof between his feet.

"Did it…matter?" She sounded doubtful.

"Hell, yes!" He couldn't stop himself. He would never learn. There was no hope. "It mattered to me. It sure as hell didn't matter to you!"

"What?"

"You didn't give a damn," Carter insisted, his teeth biting down on the nails. "You bloody offered to babysit!"

"Well, what was I supposed to do? You had a date!"

They glared at each other.

Then Carter set down his hammer. He spat out the nails. He turned on his knees and faced her squarely with far more confidence than he felt. "Do I matter, Annabel?"

He felt time stop.

Then Annabel's eyes met his, warm and unguarded. Infinitely gentle. "Oh, yes."

He didn't know if he believed in fairy tales or not. He didn't know if he was dreaming some impossible dream and might at any moment awaken. He only knew it was the answer to his prayers.

He reached for her, pulled her into his arms and knew a sense of relief when she came so willingly, putting her own arms around him, holding him, kissing his jaw, his cheeks, his ears.

Then Carter kissed her. He kissed her with everything he had in him—all the hurt and all the sadness and all the thwarted hopes, and all the joy and all the gladness and all the satisfaction that came from finding at last his heart's desire.

"I love you," he whispered.

And Annabel shook her head. "I don't believe it."

So he had to show her again. And this time, when he pulled back and asked, "Do you believe it now?" she nodded shakily.

"I—I want to," she said. Her voice wobbled, sounded tight, as if her throat hurt.

"Please believe it. I've never said anything truer in my life."

Annabel smiled, a watery smile. "And we know you tell the truth at all costs, don't we?"

Carter winced. "I should learn to keep my mouth shut."

"I don't think so," Annabel told him, and proceeded to show him one reason why he shouldn't.

"You're shameless," he told her. He was laughing and trembling at the same time.

"Possibly," Annabel said. "But I don't do that with just any man. Only with you. Because I love you, too."

He didn't realize how badly he'd needed to hear the words until she said them.

He couldn't remember anyone—save perhaps his

mother—ever having said them to him. They seemed rare and beautiful, and Annabel must have sensed it because she laid her hand on his cheek, touching her lips lightly to his.

"I've loved you forever," she told him. "Almost twenty years."

He didn't know what she meant. "Twenty years? You were a child."

"We were both children. And besides being a child, I was a bit of a romantic fool."

"What are you talking about? Twenty years? We only met maybe three years ago, because of Jack. And you hated my guts from the first moment you saw me."

"Ah, yes," she admitted. "But that was because it wasn't really the first moment." She blushed and looked down. "I've never told anyone else this. I probably shouldn't even tell you. It makes me sound like an idiot."

"Tell me."

"It was at a dance at Marblehead. I was seventeen. Gawky. Tongue-tied. Bookish. A dreamer. I should have stayed at home, but Daddy insisted I go. To meet my prince, he said. If not there, then at some other dance shortly thereafter. He was always a bit unrealistic when it came to his expectations for me." She made a wry face. "It must have rubbed off on me because I had unrealistic expectations of my own the moment you walked in. I was convinced you were my prince." She gave a self-conscious laugh. "You thought otherwise obviously."

"Oh, God." Carter felt the blood drain from his face. "You? You were her? The gingerbread lady?"

"'With the Orphan Annie hair and the Petunia Pig dress,'" Annabel quoted. "Yes. And my only hope of salvation has been believing you didn't remember it at all. And you do!" She almost wailed this last.

Carter rubbed a hand against the back of his neck. ''I ought to remember. My mother overheard me, too. Gave me holy hell all the way back to New York. Told me I was rude, inconsiderate, obnoxious, hateful and a few thousand other things equally as bad.''

He looked right at Annabel, seeing for the first time a remote resemblance to that awkward young girl. ''My mother was right. I was rude, inconsiderate and obnoxious. I'm sorry.''

She put out a hand, brushed his hair away from his forehead, touched his cheek. ''I think I've recovered from the trauma,'' she told him softly. ''It was childishness on both our parts. I shouldn't have been such a ninny.''

He kissed her. ''Forgive me?''

''Oh, yes. In fact I owe you.''

''For your father, you mean?''

''And for Mark. I ran out of the dance straight into his arms. Fell in love. Got pregnant. Married him. I owe you the past nineteen years of my life.''

''Good God.''

''They've been good years, Carter.''

''I hope the rest of them will be even better,'' he told her unsteadily. ''Will you...marry me?''

He waited a long time for her answer.

An interminable time.

He sat very still, his head bent. He remembered when he'd asked Diane. Her gentle smile, her tender touch, her soft ''Oh, Carter, I can't.'' He relived it all now, didn't know what he'd do if it happened again.

''Are you sure, Carter?''

His head snapped up. ''You think I'm asking for the hell of it?''

''But I'm old!''

He laughed ''No older than I am.''

"I've got kids."

"I've noticed."

"An unfriendly goat. A cat. Responsibilities."

"Commitments. Yes, I know. I envy you your responsibilities, Annabel." He took her hands in his. "I want to share them. All of them. Will you let me?"

Her eyes seemed to become suddenly brighter, brimming with tears. "Oh, Carter. Oh, heavens, yes!"

She launched herself at him, practically knocking them both off the roof. Only a hand out to stop their headlong tumble saved them. And then he was kissing her again, and salvation seemed assured.

"Carter," she said when they'd stopped to breathe, "would you like to have a baby?"

He went quite still. He hadn't really thought about it, hadn't dared. Even when he was mentally rearranging the world according to his own desires, he'd never got Annabel pregnant. "Would you?" he asked hoarsely.

She nodded. "Maybe it's silly, but I was such a child when Libby was born, I hardly got a chance to enjoy her. And with Leif I was a widow so soon after… I love babies, Carter. I loved having Conan. I might be too old, but—"

"Stop with this old business." He'd felt old himself only hours ago. He didn't feel it anymore. He felt as if all possibilities were open to him. He felt young, untried, new. Amazing, he thought, what love could do.

"We're not old. We've got a lifetime ahead of us, Annabel. And I'd—" his voice wobbled "—I'd love to have a baby with you." He kissed her lingeringly. "Or two."

Annabel, starry-eyed, smiled at him. "You're such an optimist."

"I have my reasons." Carter hugged her close. "We might think about going down now. Perhaps getting started."

"We can't."

Carter felt a sudden alarm. "Why not?"

"Look." Annabel pointed down into the yard. Arnold was staring up at them. He wasn't wearing a lead. "I don't know if I can keep him away from you."

"Don't worry. Arnold will approve. He and I have an understanding."

Annabel cocked her head quizzically.

Carter grinned. "Over the past few weeks we've taught each other a thing or two."

FRANCES LOVED a good wedding.

It was so satisfying seeing people who belonged together realize what she'd known all along.

"Nice, wasn't it?"

"Different," Jack conceded. "I can't believe they let the goat in the house for the reception. I guess I'm lucky you didn't bring the sheep to ours."

"You wouldn't have noticed if I had," Frances said, snuggling back against him in their bed.

"Probably not."

"I don't think Carter and Annabel noticed, either. They had eyes only for each other."

Jack grunted.

Frances tucked his arm up against her breasts and turned her head to brush a kiss across his lips.

"I told you so," she said.

HE WAS BORN the following August.

He weighed eight pounds three ounces, was twenty-one inches long. And what hair he had was red.

"What else did you expect?" Annabel asked her husband, who simply looked at her with tears of joy in his eyes and shook his head.

"He's beautiful," he told her, stroking her cheek. "You're beautiful."

And Annabel, who had months ago stopped arguing with him about that, smiled and kissed his hand. Then she looked down at the baby in her arms, whose dark blue eyes seemed already to have a hint of green as he tried to focus on her.

"Welcome to the world," she told him softly. "Welcome home, Carter William MacKenzie, the fifth."

She heard Carter's sharp intake of breath, prepared herself for the explosion, for the adamant rejection of the name, of saddling their son with the generations of baggage that went with it.

She heard him swallow and saw his hand drop to rest lightly on the baby's red hair.

"All right," Carter said. Then he lifted his gaze and smiled at her. "But he's going to be his own person."

In his eyes she saw that the battle was over, that love had won. "Of course," Annabel said and touched her lips to his. "I thought we'd call him Joe."

* * * *

The Cowboy and His Baby

SHERRYL WOODS

SHERRYL WOODS

lives by the ocean, which, she says, provides daily inspiration for the romance in her soul. She further explains that her years as a television critic taught her about steamy plots and humour; her years as a travel editor took her to exotic locations; and her years as a crummy weekend tennis player taught her to stick with what she enjoyed most—writing. 'What better way is there,' Sherryl asks, 'to combine all that experience than by creating romantic stories?'

Chapter One

Damn, but it was cold, Cody Adams thought as he chased down the last of the herd of cattle he was rounding up. Texas had never been this frigid, not even in the middle of January. He was surprised half the livestock hadn't flat-out frozen in the harsh Wyoming winter. They'd lost a few head of cattle, but nothing like what he'd anticipated the first time the temperatures had dropped below zero and the snow and ice had swirled around him.

The bitter cold and the frequent blinding snowstorms did serve one useful purpose, though. They kept him so busy—kept his brain cells so frozen, for that matter—that he hardly ever thought about home. He'd freeze his butt off and suffer frostbite on most any part of his anatomy for the blessing of a blank memory. He didn't want to think about Texas or his family. Most of all, he didn't want to think about sneaky, conniving Melissa Horton and the way she'd cheated on him.

It had taken him a long time to block out the image of his longtime girlfriend wrapped in his best friend's arms. Even now, more than a year later, that terrible, gut-wrenching moment sneaked up on him when he least expected it and reminded him that that kind of pain might hide out, but it seldom went away.

With the last of the herd rounded up and dusk falling, Cody gestured to one of the other hands that he was leaving and headed back toward the small but cozy line shack he'd insisted he preferred to the bunkhouse. He'd claimed it kept him closer to the cattle for which he was responsible, but the truth was, he craved the isolation.

For a man who had been a very social creature back in Texas—okay, a notorious flirt—it was quite a change and, for the time being, a welcome one. It was the only surefire way he could think of for staying out of trouble and avoiding the sort of heartache that falling for some woman just about guaranteed.

His boss, impressed by the fact that for years 28-year-old Cody had been running White Pines, his family's ranch back in Texas, hadn't argued with his idiosyncratic decision. Lance Treethorn had insisted only that a phone be installed so he could reach Cody on business. He was the only one with the number. He rarely used it. Cody dropped by the ranch house often enough to stay in touch.

On the tiny porch Cody stomped the snow off his boots, gathered up an armload of firewood and went inside. Within minutes he had a fire roaring and had shucked off his skeepskin jacket. He stood in front of the blaze, letting the heat warm his chilled body. Unfortunately, it couldn't touch the cold place deep inside him.

He'd been standing there for some time, lost in thought, when he noticed the stack of mail sitting on the table in the kitchen area of the one-room cabin. It was sitting atop a foil-covered pan that he suspected from the sinful, chocolaty aroma, contained a batch of freshly baked brownies. He grinned and ripped off the foil. Sure enough, brownies. Apparently, Janey Treethorn had been by again.

The fifteen-year-old daughter of his boss had a giant-size crush on him. Thankfully, though, she was painfully shy. She limited her overtures to dropping off his mail, always with a batch of brownies or his favorite apple pie. In the summer it had been fresh fruit cobblers. She was usually careful to stop by while he wasn't home. On the one occasion when he'd caught her, she'd blushed furiously, stammered an apology for intruding, and fled on horseback before he could even say thanks.

Unable to resist, he grabbed one of the brownies and ate it as he sorted through the few pieces of mail she'd left, putting the bills aside to be paid later. A small blue envelope caught his attention. Turning it over, he recognized his sister-in-law's handwriting.

As always, when anything came from a member of

his family, his heart skipped a beat. Letters were rare enough to stir a pang of homesickness each time one arrived. Jordan's wife had been dutifully writing to him once every two weeks or so from the moment she and Jordan had gotten married. For a man who swore he wanted nothing to do with anyone or anything back home, it was downright pitiful how he looked forward to Kelly's chatty letters and the family gossip she shared with such humor and telling insight. This one was more than a week overdue. Since the others had come like clockwork, he'd been trying not to admit just how worried he really was.

He could tell right off there was something different about this one, too. It was stiffer, more like a card than a letter. He grabbed a second brownie, then carried Kelly's latest correspondence with him back to his chair in front of the fire.

When he ripped open the envelope, a tiny square dropped out of the card inside. He grabbed for it instinctively and found himself staring at an infant swaddled as tight as a papoose in a blue blanket. He caught himself grinning at the sight of that tiny, red, scrunched-up face.

So, Jordan was a daddy, he thought, amazed by the shaft of pure envy that shot through him. He'd known the baby was due any day now. Kelly had kept him apprised of every detail of her pregnancy, including his older brother's bemusement at the natural childbirth classes she'd insisted he take with her. He wondered if Jordan had made it through the delivery or if he'd fainted at Kelly's first big-time contraction.

He closed his eyes against the tide of longing that rolled over him. He was missing so damned much, he thought, once again cursing Melissa for the betrayal that had made staying in Texas where he belonged impossible.

He was missing seeing his other brother Luke and his wife Jessie's little girl grow. Angela had turned two back in December. Kelly had sent a picture of her with her face streaked with icing and her fist in the middle of the chocolate birthday cake with its two, fat pink candles. He'd tucked it in his wallet, along with the snapshot of Kelly's daughter from her first marriage, Dani, a little con-artist-in-training who could persuade penguins to buy ice, if she was of a mind to. Now he opened his wallet and inserted the tiny picture of this latest addition to the family.

He stared at the brand new baby one last time and wondered if he'd ever see him. He'd been named Justin James, according to the information on the birth announcement.

"We're going to call him J.J.," Kelly wrote in the note accompanying the card. "We can't wait for you to see him. Jordan swears he hasn't slept a wink in the past week. I don't know how that can be, since I'm the one up every time the little monster screams in the middle of the night. I haven't noticed Jordan pacing the floor alongside me. I think he's been sleeping with a pillow over his head deliberately, so he can claim he never hears J.J. crying. He swears he only wakes up after I've already left the bed. The silver-tongued devil says it's missing me that wakes him. He thinks a line like that will make me more sympathetic to him. Fat chance.

''No, seriously,'' he read on, ''your big brother has been a huge help. I think he's a little awed by fatherhood...or maybe it's just that mountain of diapers he's expected to wash every night.''

Cody chuckled at the image of his button-down brother, the big-time oil company executive, changing diapers and warming bottles. Maybe he was taking to it better than any of them had anticipated, including Jordan himself.

''We're scheduling the baptism for the end of the month and we expect you to be here,'' the letter continued. ''No excuses, Cody. It's time to come home.''

It's time to come home. Kelly's words echoed in his head, taunting him, reminding him that nothing would ever make this beautiful, sprawling Wyoming ranch into home. Lance Treethorn was a kind, decent man. He'd become a good friend. His daughters were real little angels and they treated Cody like one of the family. Even so, it wasn't the same. Not that a little thing like being homesick mattered. Even though his heart ached for the life he'd left behind, he knew he could never go back. He'd rather eat dirt than get within a hundred miles of the traitorous Melissa ever again.

It had been over a year since he'd left Texas, eighteen months to be exact, but not even time had cured him of the rage that had sent him away from everyone and everything dear to him.

Mention Texas and he didn't think of his beloved White Pines, didn't think of his parents or his brothers, much as he loved them all. The only image that inevitably came to mind was of Melissa Horton. Sometimes not even an entire bottle of the best liquor in the store could blot out the memories of the woman who'd betrayed him with his best friend.

Even now the vision in his head of Melissa was so vivid he could practically feel the silky texture of her skin and the soft flow of dark auburn hair through his fingers. He could practically smell the sweet summer scent of her.

But along with the sensual memories came the blinding rage, as powerful now as it had been on the day he'd left Texas for good. Accompanying that rage was the anger and frustration of realizing that he was, in part, responsible for what had happened. Maybe if he'd told her he loved her, she wouldn't have turned to Brian Kincaid in the first place. Maybe if he'd had a clue just how much she mattered to him, instead of taking her for granted, he wouldn't be lying awake nights aching for her. He'd been a fool. She'd been a cheat. Quite a pair, the two of them. Maybe he deserved to be this miserable. She certainly did, though he had no idea if she was. She could be happily married to Brian now, for all he knew.

Before he'd realized what he was doing, he'd ripped the note inviting him to the baptism of Jordan and Kelly's baby to shreds. He couldn't allow himself to be tempted back, not even by something as important as this. He would not go back to Texas. Not now. Not ever.

The decision was firm, but it left him feeling heartsick and more lonely than he'd ever felt in his life. He was almost glad when the ring of the phone shattered the silence. He grabbed the receiver gratefully.

"Hey, boss, what's up?" he said, knowing it would be Lance Treethorn on the other end of the line.

The widowed father of three young girls, Treethorn had his hands full with trying to run the ranch and raise his daughters to be proper young ladies. He'd succeeded with the oldest. Janey was as prim and proper and dutiful as a father could ever want, but the two younger ones, ten and twelve, were terrors. Cody didn't envy the thirty-five-year-old man trying to get them raised and married without calamity striking.

"We got the herd rounded up today," he told Lance. "We only lost one more to the cold."

"Thanks, Cody, but I didn't call for an update."

Something in Lance's voice triggered alarm bells. "What's wrong?" he asked at once. "Are there problems with the girls?"

"No, it's nothing like that. We're all fine, but you had a call here at the house."

"I did?" He'd given the Treethorn number only to Jordan, with a direct order that it never be used except for a dire emergency. He knew his brother would never break that rule. His heart thudded dully as he waited for whatever bad news Jordan had imparted.

"Call home," his boss told him. "It sounded pretty urgent. Your brother asked how quickly I could get a message to you. Obviously Jordan still doesn't know you have a phone in your cabin."

"No," Cody admitted, grateful that his boss had

never asked why he insisted on having such a buffer between him and his family. Lance was the best kind of boss, the best kind of friend. He was scrupulously fair. He lent support, but never asked questions or made judgments. There had been no hint of criticism in his voice when he'd commented just now on Cody's decision to keep his private phone number from his family.

"I'm sorry he bothered you," Cody apologized anyway.

"You know damned well it's no bother. I just hope everything's okay at home. Give me a call if there's anything I can do to help."

"Thanks, Lance."

Cody hung up slowly, thinking of the tiny picture that he'd placed in his wallet only moments earlier. Had something happened to Justin James? Or to Kelly? Why else would Jordan call? Damn, but he hated being so far away. What if… He allowed the thought to trail off.

"Stop imagining the worst and call," he muttered out loud, finally forcing himself to dial his brother's number, knowing that this call, whatever it was about, would shatter whatever distance he'd managed to achieve from his past.

Jordan picked up on the first ring. His voice sounded tired and hoarse.

"Hey, big brother," Cody said.

"Cody, thank God. I was worried sick you wouldn't get the message for days."

Jordan, the most composed man Cody had ever

known, sounded shaken. The alarm bells triggered by Lance's call were clanging even louder now. "What's wrong?"

"It's bad news, Cody. Real bad."

Cody sank onto a chair by the kitchen table and braced himself. The last time Jordan had sounded that somber was when their brother Erik had been killed in an accident on Luke's ranch.

"Is it Dad?" he asked, hating even to form the words. Harlan Adams was bigger than life. He was immortal—or so Cody had always tried to tell himself. He couldn't imagine a world in which Harlan wasn't controlling and manipulating things.

"No, he's fine," Jordan reassured him at once, then amended, "Or at least as well as can be expected under the circumstances."

"Dammit, Jordan, spit it out. What the hell has happened?"

"It's Mother," he began, then stopped. He swallowed audibly before adding, "She and Daddy were out riding this morning."

He paused again and this time Cody could hear his ragged breathing. It almost sounded as if Jordan were crying, but that couldn't be. Jordan never cried. None of them did. Harlan had very old-fashioned ideas on the subject of men and tears. He had set a tough example for them, too. He hadn't shed a single tear when Erik died. He'd just retreated into stony, guilt-ridden silence for months after the loss of his son. The rest of them had coped with their grief dry-eyed, as well.

If Erik's death hadn't caused Jordan's cool, macho facade to crack, what on earth had?

"Jordan, are you okay?" he asked.

"No. Mother took a bad fall, Cody."

Cody felt as if the blood had drained out of him. Hands trembling, he grabbed the edge of the table and held on. "How is she? Is she..."

"She's gone, Cody," Jordan said with a catch in his voice. "She never woke up. She was dead by the time the paramedics got to the ranch."

"My God," he murmured, stunned. Forbidden tears stung his eyes. Ashamed, he wiped at them uselessly. They kept coming, accompanied by a terrible sense of loss. "Are you sure Daddy's okay? Why aren't you with him?"

"Luke and Jessie are over at White Pines now. Luke's got the funeral arrangements under control. Kelly and I will be going over right after I get off the phone. I wanted to stay here until you called back. How soon can you get here?"

Cody noticed his brother asked the question as if there were no doubt at all that he would be coming home. "I don't know," he said, struggling between duty and the agony that going home promised.

Disapproving silence greeted the reply. "But you will be here," Jordan said emphatically. "I'm telling Daddy you're on your way."

Cody rubbed his suddenly pounding head. "I don't know," he repeated.

"Look, this is no time to be indulging in self-pity, little brother," Jordan snapped impatiently. "Daddy needs you here, probably more than he needs any of the rest of us. He'll need you to take up some of the slack at White Pines while he pulls himself together. He's always depended on you. Don't let him down now.''

Cody said nothing.

Jordan finally broke the silence with a sigh. ''We're scheduling the funeral for Saturday,'' he said. ''Be here, Cody.''

He hung up before Cody could reply.

Cody sat in the gathering darkness, silent, unchecked tears streaking down his cheeks. He had no choice and he knew it. Mary Adams might not have been the kind of warm, doting mother a child dreamed of, but Harlan Adams had worshiped her. He could not let his father go through this kind of grief without all of his sons at his side. It was the kind of loyalty that had been ingrained in him since birth. As badly as he wanted to pretend it didn't matter, he knew better. Nothing mattered more at a time like this.

He took some small comfort in the odds that said he would probably never even see Melissa. He doubted she would have the nerve to show up at the funeral. She certainly wouldn't have the audacity to show up at White Pines afterward. It would be okay. He could slip in and out of town before temptation overtook him and he sought out so much as a glimpse of her.

At least, that's what he told himself on the long, sad drive back to Texas after he'd cleared his departure with Lance. He'd chosen to drive to delay his arrival as long as possible. Maybe to come to grips with what had happened in private. He'd spend a few days with his family to grieve. A few days to do whatever he could for his father. A few days to spoil his nieces and hold his brand new nephew. A few days to soak up enough memories to last a lifetime.

With all that going on, Melissa would be the last thing on his mind.

The very last thing, he vowed with grim determination as he finally turned into the lane to White Pines.

He slowed his pickup and looked around at the land that he loved, the land he'd hoped one day would be his since Luke's mile-wide independent streak had sent him chasing after his own dream and his own ranch and Jordan was only interested in oil.

Even in the dead of winter, it was starkly beautiful, at least to him. He was home and suddenly, despite the sorrow that had drawn him back, he felt at peace for the first time since he'd driven away more than eighteen months before.

Melissa Horton took a break from her job behind the lunch counter at Dolan's Drugstore and perched on a stool with the weekly newspaper and a cup of coffee. Her attention was riveted to the story of Mary Adams's tragic riding accident.

The 55-year-old woman had always been incredibly kind to her. Melissa had figured Mary pitied her because she'd been mooning around Cody for most of her life. Once Mary had even tried to give her some advice. It had turned out to be lousy advice, but Melissa was certain Mary had thought she was doing her a favor.

Mary had sat her down one afternoon over tea and told her that Cody was taking her for granted. Not that that was news. At any rate, Mary had claimed that the only way Melissa would ever win him would be to make him jealous. Tired of being ignored except when it suited Cody, and taking the well-meant advice to heart, Melissa had tried to do just that by going out just once with Cody's best friend.

What a disaster that had been! Had she chosen anyone else, maybe the plan would have worked, but she'd foolishly selected the one man she'd figured wouldn't get hurt. Brian had known her heart belonged to Cody. He'd known their date meant nothing, that it was only a ploy to shake up Cody. He'd even tried to argue her out of it, warning her it could backfire, but her mind had been made up. She had risked everything, certain that Mary Adams was right. She'd seen it as the only way to get Cody to finally make a commitment to her.

She should have guessed that Brian understood Cody even better than she did. Every time she thought of the anger and hurt in Cody's eyes that night, it made her sick to her stomach. He had stared at them for the space of one dull, thudding heartbeat. He'd looked not at her, but through her. His gaze riveted on Brian, he'd said, ''A hell of a friend you turned out to be.''

He had spoken with a kind of lethal calm that had been more chilling than shouted accusations. Then he'd turned on his heel and walked away. He had taken off the next morning and never once looked back.

For the past eighteen months she'd had no idea at all where he was. Brian hadn't heard from him, hadn't expected to, for that matter. She hadn't had the courage to ask Cody's family for information. Her shame ran too deep.

There had been times when she'd considered being in the dark a blessing. It had kept her from chasing after him, from destroying what few shreds of pride and dignity she had left.

Now, though, she had no doubts at all that Cody would be coming home. She might have driven him away with her betrayal, but his mother's death would surely bring him back.

Had he changed much? she wondered. Had he lost the flirtatious, fun-loving nature that had charmed her and half the women who'd crossed his path? Would she have to live with regrets for the rest of her life for turning him into a bitter, cynical man?

"No good'll come of what you're thinking," Mabel Hastings advised, coming up behind her to peer over her shoulder at the front page of the newspaper.

"How do you know what I'm thinking?" Melissa asked defensively.

Mabel shook her head, her tight gray curls bouncing at the movement. When Mabel had a permanent, she meant it to last. She'd been wearing the exact same hairstyle as far back as Melissa could remember. It did not suit her pinched features.

"I been reading you like a book ever since you set eyes on Cody Adams way back in junior high school," Mabel informed her huffily. "You seem to forget how many times you sat right here at this very counter making goo-goo eyes at him."

Melissa chuckled despite her irritation at the unsolicited interference. "'Goo-goo eyes'? Mabel, exactly how old are you? A hundred, maybe? Not even my mother would use an expression like that."

The older woman, who was probably no more than sixty, scowled at her. "Don't matter what you call it, the point is you've been crazy about that boy way too long and just look where it got you."

Melissa sensed the start of a familiar lecture. Listening to it was the price she paid for having a job that paid enough in salary and tips to keep her financially afloat and independent. She didn't have to take a dime from her parents.

"Okay, I get your point," she said, trying to avoid the full-scale assault on her sense and her virtue. "Drop it, please. I probably won't even see Cody."

She was bright enough to know it would be far better if she didn't. Her life had taken some unexpected twists and turns since he'd left, but it was settling down now. She was at peace with herself. There were no more complications, no more tears in the middle of the night over a man who didn't love her—at least, not enough—and no more roller coaster ups and downs.

No way did she want to stir up old memories and old hurts. One look into Cody's laughing brown eyes and she couldn't trust herself not to tumble straight back into love with him. She'd clearly never had a lick of sense where he was concerned.

Now, though, the stakes were way too high. Now she had more than her own heart to consider. She had someone else to protect, someone more important to her than life itself—Cody's daughter, the child he didn't even know he had.

Chapter Two

The entire family was walking around in a daze. Cody had never seen them like this, not even when Erik died. He supposed they were all following Harlan's lead. His father hadn't spoken more than a word or two to anyone. He hadn't eaten. He wasn't sleeping. He had refused a sedative prescribed by the doctor. Not even his unusually subdued grandchildren, tugging on his sleeves and competing for his attention, drew so much as a smile. He looked haggard and lost.

On Saturday morning Cody found Harlan in his office, staring at nothing, his complexion a worrisome shade of gray. Cody walked over and perched on a corner of his desk.

"Hey, Daddy, are you doing okay?"

Harlan blinked, his gaze finally focusing. "Cody, have you been here long?"

The vague question startled Cody. Normally nothing went on at White Pines that Harlan didn't notice. "Actually, I got here yesterday."

His father's lips quirked for a fraction of a second. "Hell, I know that. I haven't lost my marbles. I meant now. Have you been standing there long?"

Relief sighed through Cody. "Nope. Just walked in. Everyone's been looking for you."

"Must not have been looking too hard," Harlan grumbled in a manner that was more in character. "I've been right here all night long."

Cody was dismayed. "You didn't sleep?"

"Off and on, I suppose."

"Daddy, you should have been resting. Today's going to be rough enough without facing it exhausted."

His father shrugged. "I couldn't go upstairs."

"Damn," Cody muttered. Why hadn't any of them thought of that? Of course it was going to be hard for their father to spend time in the suite of rooms he had shared for so many years with his wife. It was hard for the rest of them just being in the house where their mother had reigned over every last detail. "I'm sorry. I'll go upstairs and bring some clothes down for you. It'll be time to go to the church soon."

He had barely reached the door when his father's voice stopped him.

"How could a thing like this happen?" Harlan murmured.

His choked voice sounded too damned close to tears. Cody was shaken by that as he hadn't been by anything else in his life.

"We were supposed to have so many years left," Harlan went on. "I had promised your mother we'd travel, that we'd see all the sights she'd been reading about over the years." He glanced at Cody. "Did you know she gave up a trip around the world for her college graduation to marry me? I promised to make it up to her one day, but I never got around to it."

Guilt sliced through Cody. His departure had kept them from going on those trips. His father had had to take over the running of White Pines again, just when he'd been ready to indulge all of his wife's fantasies.

"You can't think about that," Cody told him, partly because he couldn't bear to think about it, either. "You'll make yourself crazy. Think about the years you did have. You made Mother very happy. She loved being your wife. She loved being mistress of White Pines. She was wild about all those fancy ancestors of yours."

"She loved you boys, too," Harlan added quietly. "Oh, I know she didn't pay you the kind of attention she did me. I regret that. I regret that you all thought that meant she didn't love you."

At Cody's expression of shock, he added, "Don't deny it, son. I know you boys couldn't help feeling that way. Catering to me was just your mama's way. When you were little, I don't think she knew quite what to make of you. She was an only child. She wasn't prepared for the chaos of four rambunctious boys. But she cared about you and she was so very proud of the way you all turned out."

"Even me?" Cody asked, unable to prevent the

question from popping out. He hated what it said about his insecurities. He had feared that turning his back on White Pines would cost him whatever affection either of his parents felt for him.

Harlan chuckled. ''Are you kidding? You were her baby. There wasn't a day since you've been gone that she didn't worry about you and how you were getting along, when she didn't tell me how she missed hearing you thundering down the stairs or raising a ruckus in the kitchen.''

''She hated it when I did those things,'' Cody protested.

''Only until they stopped,'' Harlan said softly. Sorrow had etched new lines in his face. The sadness behind the comment emphasized them.

Cody watched with amazement and new respect as his father visibly pulled himself up, gathering strength from some inner reserve that had been severely tested in the past few days. He stood, crossed the room and put a comforting arm around Cody's shoulders, sharing that strength with his son.

''Come on, boy. Help me figure out what to wear, so I won't put your mama to shame.''

Together they climbed the stairs and went to prepare for the funeral of the woman Cody had adored and on occasion admired, but until just this morning had never understood.

Melissa watched the clock above the soda fountain ticking slowly toward noon. She would not go to

Mary's funeral. She would not! If she did, she would be going for all the wrong reasons.

Drugstore owner and pharmacist Eli Dolan came out from behind the prescription counter, then peered at her over the rim of his reading glasses. "You going?"

"Going where?" Melissa asked.

He muttered something about women and foolishness under his breath. "To that funeral, of course. You ought to be paying your respects."

She didn't bother asking how Eli knew that she had been close to Mary at one time. Everyone in town knew everyone else's business. That's what had made staying here after her daughter was born so difficult. She doubted there was a single soul that didn't have their suspicions about the identity of Sharon Lynn's daddy, but as far as she knew only her own parents and Cody's brother Jordan and his wife knew the truth for certain.

She wouldn't have admitted it to Jordan and Kelly, but he had taken one look at the baby and guessed. She hadn't been able to deny it. Jordan had vowed to keep her secret and, as far as she knew, he'd been true to his word. She was ninety-eight percent certain that he'd never told Cody. Harlan had instilled a deep sense of honor in all of his sons. That included keeping promises, even when extracted under the most trying conditions.

She also had a hunch that if Jordan had told, Cody would have stormed back to Texas and raised a commotion that would have set the whole town on its ear. Or maybe that was just wishful thinking on her part.

''You'd better get a move on, if you're going to find a place in church,'' Eli prompted, clearly not intending to let the matter drop. ''It's bound to be crowded. Folks around here think mighty highly of Harlan and his sons. They'll be there for them, even if most of them found Mary a little high-falutin' for their taste.''

''I can't leave here now,'' Melissa hedged, taking another wipe at the already polished counter. ''It's lunchtime.''

''And who's going to be here?'' he shot right back. ''Everybody will be at the funeral. I don't expect we'll be doing much business. And you seem to forget that I was making milk shakes and sandwiches when you were still in diapers. I can handle things for the next couple of hours. If I make a mess of things, you can say you told me so when you get back.''

He glanced over at Mabel and nodded in her direction. ''Or she'll do it for you,'' he said with a sour note in his voice. ''Now, go on. Do what you know is right.''

Melissa didn't question the sense of relief she felt at being nudged determinedly out the door. If Eli didn't find it odd that she'd be going to the funeral, maybe no one else would, either. Maybe it would have been more noticeable if she'd stayed away.

Bracing herself against the brisk January wind, she rushed down Main Street, glad that she'd chosen to wear a dress to work rather than her usual jeans and

T-shirt. Obviously some part of her had known even when she'd dressed that morning that she would change her mind about going to the service.

It was a dreary day for a funeral. Leaden clouds, practically bursting with rain—or, given the rapidly dropping temperature, more likely sleet—hung low in the sky. She tugged her coat more tightly around her, but gave up on keeping her long hair from tangling as the wind whipped it around her face.

All the way to the church she tried to keep her mind off Cody and on the service that was to come. Her best efforts, however, were a dismal failure. She kept envisioning Cody, wondering how he was holding up, worrying how he and all of his brothers were doing and regretting more than she could say that she couldn't take her place with them and offer the support she desperately wanted to give.

She was so late that she planned to slip into the back of the church and stand in the shadows. Cody would never know she was there. The last thing she wanted to do today was add to his misery.

She ran up the steps of the old church just as the bells were chiming in the tall white steeple. The sun peeked through the clouds for just an instant, creating a terrible glare. Going from that sudden bright sun outside into the church's dimly lit interior, she was momentarily blinded.

Apparently, whoever was hard on her heels was having the same problem because he slammed smack into her, his body rock solid as he hit her at full tilt.

The contact almost sent her sprawling on the polished wood floor.

''Sorry,'' he said, gripping her elbows to keep her upright. ''You okay, darlin'?''

Melissa's heart climbed straight into her throat. She would have recognized that voice, that automatic flirtatiousness, even if she hadn't heard it for a hundred years. The firm, steadying touch was equally familiar and just as devastating. If she'd brushed against a live wire, she couldn't have felt any more electrified.

''Cody?''

She spoke his name in no more than a whisper, but at the sound of her voice, he jerked his hands away as if he'd just touched a white-hot flame.

''Excuse me,'' he said, his voice instantly like ice.

As if she were a stranger, he shoved past her to make his way to the front of the church. No, she corrected, if she'd been a stranger, he would have been less rude, more solicitous.

Trembling from the unexpected face-to-face meeting, Melissa watched him stride up the aisle to join his father and his brothers in the first pew. In that single quick glimpse, she had seen new lines in his face. His sun-streaked, normally untamed hair had been trimmed neatly in the way his mother had always wanted it to be.

It was his eyes, though, that had stunned her. Once they'd been filled with so much laughter. Naturally she had expected to find sorrow today in the dark-as-coffee depths. What she hadn't anticipated was the cold antipathy when he recognized her, followed by an emptiness that was worse than hatred.

Well, she thought despondently, now she knew. Cody hadn't forgiven her. He'd looked straight through her as if he'd never known her, as if he'd never teased her or made love to her or shared his deepest, darkest secrets with her.

"Oh, God," she murmured in what could have been the beginning of a prayer, but instead simply died before completion. Their relationship was clearly beyond even divine intervention. She'd known it all along, of course, but she hadn't wanted to believe it. The last flicker of hope in her heart died like a candle flame in a chilly wind.

Though a part of her wanted to flee, she moved into the deepest shadows and stayed through the service, grieving not just for the woman lying in the flower-draped casket, but for the death of her own dreams.

"You went to the funeral, didn't you?" Velma Horton asked the minute Melissa walked through her mother's doorway to pick up her daughter after work.

"How did you know?" she asked, though it was easy enough to guess. The grapevine had probably been buzzing all afternoon and her mother was definitely tapped into that.

Her mother sniffed. "You think I didn't know why you wore that dress today. I know what you said, some nonsense about all your jeans being in the laundry, but I'm not a fool, girl. I knew you wouldn't miss a chance to catch sight of Cody. So, did you see him?''

''Briefly,'' Melissa admitted.

''And?''

''And what? We didn't talk.''

''Then you didn't tell him about Sharon Lynn.''

Melissa shook her head. ''He wouldn't care,'' she said with absolute certainty that was based on the way he'd looked straight through her for the second time in their lives.

To her surprise, her mother breathed a sigh of relief and some of the tension drained out of her expression. ''Good.''

There were times, like now, when Melissa didn't understand her mother at all. When Velma had learned her daughter was pregnant, she'd been all for chasing Cody to the ends of the earth and demanding he take responsibility for his actions.

''I thought you wanted him to know,'' Melissa said, regarding her mother with confusion. ''There was a time you threatened to go to Harlan and demand that he drag Cody back here. You thought he owed me his name and his money. The only thing that stopped you was Daddy's threat to divorce you if you did.''

Velma rolled her eyes. ''Your father's got more pride than sense. Anyway, that was before Sharon Lynn was born, back when I didn't know how you'd manage by yourself. Seems to me you've done just fine. There's no sense in trying to fix what's not broke.''

It was a reasonable explanation for the turnaround,

but Melissa didn't entirely buy it. "There's something else, isn't there? Some other reason you don't want Cody to find out the truth?"

"There is," her mother admitted, an ominous note in her voice. "Harlan Adams is a powerful man."

"That's not news. What's your point? What does he have to do with this? It's between me and Cody."

"Not if Harlan gets it into his head to claim his granddaughter," her mother stated, a note of genuine fear in her voice. "There's no way we could fight a man like that."

Melissa was stunned by what her mother was suggesting. "Don't you think you're being a little paranoid? Jordan's known for almost a year now and he hasn't even spilled the beans. I suspect the rest of the family will react with just as much indifference."

Her mother didn't seem to be reassured. "Just watch your step. I'm warning you, Melissa, keep that baby as far away from Cody Adams as you can."

Though she didn't think the warning was necessary, Melissa nodded dutifully. "I don't think we have to worry about that. Cody will probably be gone before we know it."

Just then the sounds of her daughter's cheerful, nonsensical babbling echoed down the narrow hallway. Melissa smiled. Her heart suddenly felt lighter than it had all day. The baby had had that effect on her from the moment she'd been born.

"Did she just wake up?" she asked as she started toward her old bedroom.

"I doubt she's even been asleep. She didn't want

to go down for her nap. I think she sensed the tension in both of us. You go on in. I'm going to fix your daddy's dinner."

Melissa went to pick up her daughter from the crib her mother had put up next to the twin bed Melissa had slept in for most of her life. Sharon Lynn was standing on shaky, pudgy little legs, hanging on to the crib rail. Her eyes lit up when she spotted her mother.

"Ma...ma...ma."

"That's right, darling girl," Melissa crooned, gathering her into her arms. "I'm your mama."

She inhaled the sweet talcum-powder scent of her baby and sighed as tiny little hands grabbed her hair and held on tight. "You've got quite a grip, little one. You must have gotten that from your daddy. I'm the original hundred-pound weakling."

"Da?" Sharon Lynn repeated, echoing a sound Melissa had taught her while showing her a snapshot of Cody. Her mother would have pitched a royal fit if she'd known.

"Oh, baby," she murmured, tightening her embrace. "Your daddy's right here in town. He has no idea what he's been missing all these months. He has no idea that he has a precious little girl."

Cody would have made a wonderful father, she thought with a sigh. He would have been too indulgent by far, too readily conned by sweet talk and a winning smile, but, oh, how he would have cherished and protected a child of his. Her foolish actions had cost him the chance to prove that. Worse, they had cost her daughter a chance to be loved by an incredible man.

There were days when she almost made herself sick with regrets.

''We do okay by ourselves, though, don't we?'' she asked, gazing into round, dark eyes that reminded her too much of Cody. The baby returned her gaze with the kind of serious, thoughtful look the question deserved. Melissa wondered how many years it would be before that innocent contemplation turned to something far more accusatory because her mother had robbed her of any contact with her father.

''Don't,'' her mother pleaded, coming up behind her.

''Don't what?''

''Don't tell him.''

''Who said I was going to?'' Melissa asked.

''I know that look. You're making up pipe dreams about what it will be like when Cody finds out he has a baby girl. You're expecting him to declare he's never stopped loving you and sweep you off to get married.''

Her expression turned dire. ''It won't be that way, I'm telling you. If he cares about the baby at all, he'll take her from you. That's how much he hates you for what you did to him. You made a fool of him in front of the whole town by going out with his best friend. A man never forgets a betrayal like that. I don't care if it was just a bunch of foolishness on your part. The results were the same as if you and Brian had had something going.''

''You don't know anything about Cody's feelings,'' Melissa argued, even though she had just seen with her own eyes that Cody did despise her. She didn't want to believe he could be cruel enough to try to take their daughter away from her.

"Are you willing to take that chance?" her mother demanded.

The baby whimpered, either because she was picking up on the sudden tension or because Melissa was holding her too tightly. "No," she whispered, fighting the sting of tears as she kissed her daughter's silky cheek. "No, I'm not willing to take that chance."

She had been weaving pipe dreams, just as her mother had guessed. The risk of trying to make them come true, though, was far too great. Rather than winning back Cody, she could very well lose her child. She would die before she let that happen. Sharon Lynn was the most important thing in her life.

All the way home she assured herself that she only needed a few days. If she kept the secret just a few more days, Cody would be gone and that would be the end of it.

Later that night she sank into the rocker beside Sharon Lynn's crib and set it into motion, hoping to lull the baby to sleep and to quiet all those clamoring shouts in her head that told her she just might be making the second worst mistake in her life by keeping silent. As much as she hated to admit it, her mother was right about one thing. If Cody did learn the truth from someone else, there was no telling what he might do to exact revenge.

Chapter Three

For the past two days Cody hadn't been able to stop thinking about his brief meeting with Melissa at the funeral. She looked exactly as he'd remembered her, her long hair a tangle of fiery lights, her body slender as a reed except for the lush, unexpected curve of her breasts.

Even before he'd heard her voice, in that instant when he'd caught her to prevent her from falling, he'd known it was her just from the way his body had reacted to touching her. He had hated that reaction, hated knowing that his desire for her hadn't waned at all despite the months of self-imposed exile. That seemed like the cruelest sort of punishment.

Late that night after the funeral he'd been pacing downstairs when his father had come out of his office and caught him. Harlan had guessed right off that his agitation had to do with Melissa, though he'd been uncommonly cautious in broaching the subject.

"I thought I saw Melissa at the church today," Harlan had said casually after he'd pulled Cody into his office and they were both seated in comfortable leather chairs in front of a blazing fire, glasses of whiskey in hand. At the reference to Melissa, Cody had put his aside without tasting it. He'd feared if he got started, he'd never stop.

"She was there," he'd conceded, his voice tight.

"Did you get a chance to talk to her?"

"We have nothing to say to each other."

"I see," Harlan said. He'd let the silence build for a bit, taking a sip of his drink before adding nonchalantly, "I heard she's been working at Dolan's Drugstore, running the soda fountain for Eli. Doing a good job, too. Eli says business is up. The kids are hanging out there again instead of driving to the fast-food place out on the highway."

Cody hadn't even acknowledged the information. He'd just tucked it away for later consideration. Ever since, he'd been considering what to do about it.

He could drive into town, march into Dolan's and confront Melissa about what she'd done to him, something he probably should have done the very night he'd found her with Brian. He could raise the kind of ruckus that would be the talk of the town for the next year. It would go into the textbook of Cody Adams lore that had begun when he was barely into puberty.

If half the tales had been true, he would have worn himself out by the time he was twenty.

Sighing, he conceded he couldn't see much point to adding another wild exploit to his reputation. A scene would only rake up old news, embarrass Melissa—not that he cared much about that—and tell anyone with half a brain that Cody wasn't over her. Otherwise, why would he bother to stir up the cold ashes of their very dead relationship?

No, for the sake of his own pride if nothing else, it was better to stay the hell away from town. He repeated the advice to himself like a mantra, over and over, until he should have gotten it right.

Even as his old red pickup sped toward town late Tuesday morning, he was muttering it to himself, swearing that he'd have lunch with Luke and Jordan at Rosa's Mexican Café, then turn right around and go back to White Pines. A couple of beers and a plate of Rosa's spiciest food would wipe all thoughts of Melissa straight out of his head.

Unfortunately he hadn't counted on his brothers getting into the act. He'd been certain that they would leave the subject of his love life alone. He hadn't counted on the fact that both of them were now happily married and apparently intent on seeing that he took the plunge, too.

"Hey, Cody, why don't you drop by Dolan's as long as you're in town?" Jordan suggested after they'd eaten. He said it with all the innocence of Harlan at his matchmaking best.

''Any particular reason I should?'' he inquired, refusing to fall into Jordan's trap.

He lifted the cold bottle of beer to his lips and took a long, slow drink just to show how unaffected he was by the prospect of seeing Melissa, whom Jordan clearly knew worked at Dolan's. This was probably the whole reason his brothers had suggested meeting in town in the first place rather than gathering at White Pines. They'd been plotting behind his back to try to force a reunion between Cody and his ex-lover.

''They still have the best milk shakes in the whole state of Texas,'' Luke chimed.

''We've just eaten enough food to stuff a horse,'' Cody stated flatly.

Luke and Jordan exchanged a look.

''Worried about your handsome figure?'' Luke taunted.

Cody scowled at his oldest brother's nonsense. ''No.''

Luke went on as if he'd never spoken. ''Because if that's it, I'm sure they have diet sodas in there, served up by the sweetest gal in all of Texas, or so I hear.''

''I don't want a milk shake. I don't want a diet soda. There is nothing that drugstore has that I want,'' he said pointedly, scowling first at Luke and then at Jordan.

''Sounds to me like a man who's protesting too much,'' Jordan observed. ''What does it sound like to you, Lucas?''

''Definitely a man who's scared out of his britches,'' Luke agreed.

Cody drew himself up indignantly. ''Scared of what? A milk shake?''

''Maybe not that,'' Luke conceded. ''How about Melissa Horton?''

Ah, a direct hit. Cody sighed. ''I am not scared of Melissa,'' he said with extreme patience. ''I feel absolutely nothing for Melissa.''

''Cluck, cluck, cluck,'' Luke murmured, making a pitiful attempt to mimic a chicken.

The sound grated on Cody's nerves. He balled his hands into fists. He hadn't gotten into a rip-roaring fight with his big brothers in a very long time, but Luke was pushing every one of his buttons. And, from the teasing glint in his eyes, his big brother knew it, too. Even Jordan sensed that his patience was at an end. He eased his chair between them, a conciliatory expression on his face.

''Now, Luke, don't rile Cody,'' he said blandly. ''If he says he doesn't want to talk to Melissa, then who are we to interfere?''

Cody didn't exactly trust Jordan's sudden taking of his side. Jordan had a knack for sneak attacks that could cripple a business adversary before he even knew he was under seige. Cody eyed him warily.

''That's true,'' Luke conceded, his turnaround just as suspicious. ''Daddy meddled in our lives enough that we should be more sensitive to Cody's feelings. Besides, Melissa probably doesn't want to see him any more than he wants to see her.''

''Why? Is she involved with someone?'' Cody asked, regretting the words the instant they slipped out of his mouth. The triumphant expressions on Luke's and Jordan's faces were enough to set his teeth on edge.

Jordan stood as if he'd just recalled a business crisis that couldn't be put off. "Come on, Luke. We've obviously accomplished our mission here," he said blithely. "The man is on the hook. Let's leave him to decide whether to wiggle off or take the bait."

"A fascinating metaphor," Luke commented, joining Jordan. He glanced back at Cody. The teasing glint in his eyes faded. "Don't be a damned fool, little brother. Go see the woman. You know you want to. It's time you settled things with her once and for all. We want you back here for good."

Cody finished the beer after they'd gone. He thought about ordering another one, but decided against it. It would only be delaying the inevitable. Some sick, perverse part of him wanted to see Melissa, just as Luke had guessed. He needed to know if that reaction he'd felt at the church had been a fluke or the undeniable response of a man for the woman he'd belatedly realized that he'd always loved.

He paid the check—his damned brothers had stiffed him on the bill, on top of everything else—and then headed down Main Street. In the middle of the block he hesitated, staring across at the front of the drugstore that had been his favorite hangout as a teenager. His and Melissa's.

Little had changed. Dolan's Drugstore was still printed in neat black, gold-edged letters on the door. A display of toys sat on the shelf beneath the big plate-glass window, visible to any child passing by. A rack of comic books stood off to the side. Cody suspected they were the same faded editions that had been there a decade before. The toys looked suspiciously familiar, too. In fact, when he'd crossed the street for a closer look, he was almost certain that there was a ten-year layer of dust on the red, toy fire truck.

Telling himself he was fifty kinds of crazy for going inside, he found himself turning the knob on the door anyway. A bell tinkled overhead, alerting anyone working that a customer had entered.

The soda fountain was on his left, partially blocked by a section of shelves with first-aid supplies and a new display of condoms. Talk about times changing. He couldn't think of a better example. He recalled the first time he'd ever come into the store to buy condoms. They'd been behind the pharmacy counter then. He'd blushed brick red when he'd had to ask Mabel Hastings to give them to him. It was a wonder he'd ever gone back. His only consolation had been that she'd seemed even more embarrassed. After that he'd always made sure Eli was on duty when he'd returned for a new supply.

A half-dozen teenage girls were sitting on one side of the U-shaped soda fountain, probably discussing schoolwork, or, more likely, boys. An equal number of boys was on the opposite side, tongue-tied and uncertain. The sight of them brought back a slew of memories best forgotten.

There was no sign of Melissa, though clearly someone had served the kids their shakes and hamburgers. Cody fought a bitter feeling of disappointment. He hadn't wanted to come here, but now that he had gathered the courage, he wanted to get this encounter out of the way. He wanted to shove the past behind him once and for all. He doubted a meeting would be enough to keep him in Texas, but maybe it would buy him some peace of mind.

"Hey, Missy, customer!" one of the boys shouted as Cody slid onto a stool close to the cash register.

"I'll be right there," a voice capable of raising goose bumps on any man past puberty sang out from the back.

The door to the storeroom swung open. Melissa emerged, her arms loaded with two trays of glasses piled atop each other. Her gaze zeroed in on Cody with impeccable precision. Every bit of color washed from her face. The trays wobbled, then tilted. Glasses crashed to the floor. Her gaze never wavered from his, despite the sound of breaking glass.

Several of the teenagers sprang to their feet and rushed to clean up the mess. Cody couldn't have moved if his life had depended on it. Apparently Melissa couldn't, either. Not even the swirl of activity at her feet caught her attention. He felt as if he'd been punched in the gut.

This definitely wasn't the reaction he'd been praying for. In fact, it was exactly the opposite. He'd wanted to look into those soft, sea green eyes of hers and feel eighteen months of hurt and anger boiling into a fine rage. Or, better yet, he'd wanted to feel nothing at all.

Instead it appeared his hormones were very glad to see her. Obviously they had a different sort of memory pattern than his brain.

"Missy, are you okay?" one of the boys asked worriedly. He scowled in Cody's direction.

"Fine," she murmured.

The youngster, who looked all of fourteen, clearly wasn't convinced. Just as clearly, he had a big-time crush on Melissa. "Is he a problem?" he inquired, nodding toward Cody.

Apparently the boy's itch to slay dragons for her got her attention as nothing else had. She jerked her gaze away from Cody and smiled at the teenager.

"It's okay, David. Cody and I have known each other a long time." She patted his shoulder. "Thanks for cleaning up the glass, you guys. Your sodas are on me."

"Nah, you don't have to do that," David said, pulling money out of his pocket and leaving it on the counter. "Right, guys?"

The other boys dutifully nodded and pulled out their own cash. Unless costs at Dolan's had risen dramatically, they were very generous tippers, Cody noted as all of the teens departed.

"See you tomorrow," David called back from the doorway. He lingered uncertainly for another minute, as if he couldn't make up his mind whether Cody was to be trusted. When Melissa shot him another reassuring smile, he finally took off to catch up with his friends.

"Quite an admirer," Cody said. "I think he was ready to mop up the floor with me."

"David is just testing his flirting skills. I'm safer than those girls in his own class. He knows I won't laugh at him."

"Maybe you should. Better to hurt him now than later," he said with unmistakable bitterness.

Melissa looked as if he'd struck her. "I'm not going to hurt him at all. He's just a boy, Cody." She straightened her spine and glowered at him. "Look, if you came in here just to hassle me, you can turn right around and go back wherever you came from. I don't need the aggravation."

Cody grinned at the bright patches of color in her cheeks. Melissa had always had a quick temper. He suddenly realized he'd missed sparring with her almost as much as he'd missing making love with her.

"Actually, I came in for a milk shake," he said, coming to a sudden decision to play this scene all the way through. He propped his elbows on the counter. He waited until he'd caught her gaze, then lowered his voice to a seductive whisper. "A chocolate shake so thick, I'll barely be able to suck it very, very slowly through the straw."

The patches of color in Melissa's cheeks deepened. She twirled around so fast it was a wonder she didn't knock a few more pieces of glassware onto the floor with the breeze she stirred.

With her rigid back to him, Cody was able to observe her at his leisure. Her snug, faded jeans fit her cute little butt like a glove. That much hadn't changed, he noted with satisfaction. With every stretch, the cropped T-shirt she wore kept riding up to bare an intriguing inch or so of a midriff so perfect that it could make a man weep. Her long dark hair with its shimmering red highlights had been scooped up in a saucy ponytail that made her look a dozen years younger than the twenty-seven he knew she was.

And, to his very sincere regret, she made him every bit as hard now as she had as a teenager. He squirmed in a wasted effort to get more comfortable on the vinyl-covered stool.

When she finally turned back, she plunked his milk shake onto the counter with such force half of it sloshed out of the tall glass. Apparently she wasn't entirely immune to him, either, and she wasn't one bit happier about the discovery.

She grabbed up a dishrag and began scrubbing the opposite side of the counter, her back to him. Given the energy she devoted to the task, the surface was either very dirty or she was avoiding him.

"So, how've you been?" Cody inquired, managing the nonchalant tone with supreme effort.

"Fine," she said tersely, not even glancing around.

He frowned. Why the hell was she acting like the injured party here? She was the one who'd cheated on him. Getting her to meet him halfway became an irresistible challenge.

"How are you, Cody? It's been a long time," he coached.

She turned and glared. "Why are you here?" she demanded instead.

He could have shot back a glib retort, but he didn't. He actually gave the question some thought. He considered the teasing he'd gotten from Jordan and Luke. He considered his own undeniable curiosity. He even considered the size of his ego, which had found being cheated on damned hard to take. The bottom line was, he had no idea what had drawn him across the street and into the drugstore.

"I don't know," he finally admitted.

Apparently it was the right answer because her lush, kissable mouth curved into a smile for the first time since she'd spotted him at the counter.

"You mean to tell me that there's something that actually stymies the brilliant, confident Cody Adams?"

He nodded slowly. "It surprises the dickens out of me, too."

She leaned back against the counter, her elbows propped behind her. It was a stance that drew attention to her figure, though Cody doubted she was aware of it.

"You planning on sticking around?" she asked.

"A few more days, just till Daddy's got his feet back under him again." It was the same response he'd given everyone who'd asked. Now that he was right here with Melissa in front of him, though, he wondered if she might not be the one person who could change his mind.

At the mention of his father, her expression immediately filled with concern. "It must be horrible for him."

"It is."

"And the rest of you?"

"We're doing okay. Mostly we're worried about Daddy. He adored Mother. It's going to be lonely as hell for him with her gone."

"I'm surprised you're not staying, then."

He shook his head. "There's nothing for me here anymore," he said automatically, refusing to concede that he had evidence to the contrary in the tightening of his groin at the first sight of her.

She actually blanched at his harsh words. "I'm sorry," she whispered, looking shaken. "What about White Pines? You always loved it. You were building your whole future around running that ranch."

She was right about that. He'd fought tooth and nail to get Harlan to trust him with the running of the ranch. He'd spent his spare time building his own house on the property just to make the point that, unlike Luke or Jordan, he never intended to leave. Then in a matter of seconds after catching Melissa with Brian, he'd thrown it all away.

Now, rather than addressing his longing to be working that land again, he shoved those feelings aside and clung instead to the bitterness that had sent him away.

"There's no way I can stay here now," he said, unable to prevent the accusing note that had crept into his voice. "You ruined it for me."

Melissa swallowed hard, but she kept her gaze on

him steady. Some part of him admired her for not backing down.

"Maybe we should talk about what happened, Cody. Maybe if we could put it behind us, you'd change your mind about staying. Your decision to stay or go shouldn't have anything to do with me."

Talk about finding her in the arms of his best friend? Analyze it and pick it apart, until his emotions were raw? Cody practically choked on the idea. Once he got started on that subject, he doubted the conversation would remain polite or quiet. Eli would be bolting out from behind the prescription counter and Mabel, whom he'd spotted lurking over toward the cosmetics, would get a blistering earful.

No, he absolutely did not want to talk about the past. Or the present. And most definitely not about the bleak, lonely future he'd carved out for himself.

He slid off the stool and backed up a step. "There's nothing to say," he said, hoping his tone and his demeanor were forbidding enough to keep Melissa silent. He slapped a five on the counter, then tipped his hat.

"It's been a pleasure," he said in a tone that declared just the opposite.

He had made it almost to the door when he heard a soft gasp of dismay behind him. He stepped aside just as Velma Horton opened the door and pushed a stroller inside. His gaze went from Velma's shocked expression to the chubby-cheeked little girl who promptly reached her arms up toward him, a thoroughly engaging smile on her face. He stared at the toddler in stunned silence, then pivoted slowly to stare at Melissa. Her face was ashen, removing any doubt at all that the baby was hers.

For the second time in a matter of minutes Cody felt as if he'd been hit below the belt. He could count backward as quickly as anyone in Texas. That darling little girl with the big eyes and innocent smile looked to be a year old, which meant she was Brian's.

His blood felt like ice water in his veins, but he forced himself to walk back toward the soda fountain. "I see congratulations are in order," he said so politely it made his teeth ache. "Your daughter is beautiful."

"Thank you," Melissa said so softly that he could barely hear her.

"I guess you and Brian were meant to be, after all," he said, then turned on his heel and bolted for the door before he made an absolute idiot of himself.

He brushed past Velma and the baby without giving them a second glance. Damn, Melissa! She'd turned him inside out again. For a fleeting moment he'd actually wondered if he could put the past behind him and move on, maybe get something going with her again since his body was as hot for her now as it had been eighteen months ago. He'd allowed old feelings to stir to life, indulged in a few quick and steamy fantasies.

One look at that baby had shattered any possibility of that. He should have known that Melissa and Brian were together. He should have guessed that the betrayal was more serious than the one-night stand he'd tried desperately to convince himself it was. He should have realized that neither of them would have cheated on him for anything less than powerful emotions they couldn't control. He should have given them credit for that much at least. He couldn't make up his mind, though, if that should make him feel better or worse.

It wasn't until he was back at White Pines, riding hell-bent for leather across the open land trying to work off his anger and his pain that he stopped to wonder why Jordan and Luke would have set him up for such a terrible sucker punch. Couldn't they just have told him and saved him the anguish of making a fool of himself over Melissa all over again?

Instead they had taunted him into going into Dolan's. They had poked and prodded at all of his old feelings for Melissa until he could no longer ignore them. Would they have done that if they'd known about Brian? If they'd known about the baby? Harlan had done his share of nudging, too. He'd been the first to plant the seed about finding Melissa at Dolan's.

It didn't make a lick of sense. How could they not have known? It was a small town. Harlan sure as hell knew everything that went on. And yet they had sent him like a lamb to slaughter, straight back to Melissa.

He reined in his horse and sat for a long time contemplating the possibilities. For once in his life he was oblivious to the raw beauty of the land surrounding him. Since he knew damned well his brothers weren't cruel, their actions had to mean something. At the very least, he'd bet that Melissa and Brian weren't married, after all. At the most…

He thought of that cute little girl who'd practically begged him to pick her up.

He didn't even want to consider the astonishing, incredible idea that had just popped into his head. What if she was his? What if he was actually a father?

He tried the idea on for size and realized that a silly grin had spread across his face. A father? Yes, indeed, the possibility fit as well as those tight little jeans had caressed Melissa's fanny.

Then his grin faded as he considered all the time he'd lost if it were true. If that little girl was his, he resolved there was going to be hell to pay.

Chapter Four

Melissa stood over Sharon Lynn's crib and stared down at her sleeping child. The baby's cheeks were flushed, her dark blond hair curling damply against her chubby neck. Her blue nightshirt was sprinkled with tiny yellow ducks. A larger, stuffed duck was cuddled next to her. It had been her favorite toy ever since she'd been to a duck pond a few months before. She refused to go to bed without it.

A smile curved Melissa's lips as she watched her baby and fought the desperate need to pick her up, to cling to her. She hadn't been able to let her daughter out of her sight since that terrible moment in the drugstore when Cody had come face-to-face with his child. In that instant her heart had ricocheted wildly and her breath had caught in her throat as she'd waited for him to recognize Sharon Lynn as his, just as Jordan had the very first time he'd spotted her. She'd almost been grateful that the decision to tell Cody or not to tell him had been taken out of her hands.

But instead of promptly recognizing the baby as his, Cody had clearly leapt to the conclusion that someone else was the father. Given the cold glint in his eyes when he'd stepped back to the counter to congratulate her in a voice devoid of emotion and his comment about her relationship with Brian having been meant to be, he must have assumed the father was Brian Kincaid. It was a further complication in an already complicated situation.

She sighed as she considered the terrible mess she had made of things. She should have told Cody everything straight off, right then and there, but her mother's terrified expression and her earlier dire warnings had kept Melissa silent, too fearful of the consequences of blurting out the truth.

She couldn't imagine what her life would be like without her baby. As difficult as things had gotten after she'd learned she was pregnant, there had never been a single instant when she'd regretted having Cody's child. Every time she looked into that precious face, she saw a miracle that she and Cody had created together. Beyond that biological tie, however, Cody had no right at all to claim his child. She was the only parent Sharon Lynn had ever known. If only she could keep it that way.

Unfortunately, though, there was no way the truth could be kept hidden forever. Cody had already seen his daughter. His brother knew that Sharon Lynn was Cody's. Sooner or later the pieces of the puzzle would come together, and when they did, she didn't have a doubt in her mind what Cody's reaction would be. If he'd been furious when he'd thought she was cheating on him with his best friend, he would destroy her when he found out about the baby she'd kept from him. Maybe he wouldn't fight her for custody as her mother feared, but he would make her life into the hell she deserved for deceiving him in the first place.

She rubbed her knuckles against Sharon Lynn's soft skin and sighed again. There was so much of Cody in her daughter. She had the same stubborn tilt to her chin, the same dark blond hair that streaked with gold in the summer sun. And, for the most part, she had the same sunny disposition and laughing eyes Cody had had before he thought Melissa had betrayed him.

It had hurt today to glimpse the old teasing Cody, only to see him vanish in the space of a heartbeat at the first mention of the past. When he'd walked out of Dolan's, her heart had been heavy with the burden of guilt and fear.

"I have to be the one to tell him," she whispered finally, her fingers caressing that precious cheek. "I have to tell your daddy all about you."

Maybe by revealing the truth herself, before he learned it from someone else, she would have some small chance of earning his forgiveness. They could work out a solution together.

Tomorrow, she vowed. First thing tomorrow afternoon when she got off work, she would drive out to

White Pines and tell Cody everything. And then she would pray that it didn't cost her the only person on earth she held dear.

Too restless to stay in one place for long as he contemplated how to go about discovering whether Melissa's baby was his, Cody drove over to visit Jordan and Kelly. Six-year-old Dani was always a distraction and he just might get a chance to hold that nephew of his. He had a hunch it would be a bittersweet sensation given what he suspected about Melissa's child being his own.

"Uncle Cody!" Dani screamed when she caught sight of him. She ran and leapt into his arms, planting kisses all over his face. "I really, really missed you."

The weight of her in his arms, the peppermint-sticky kisses, filled him with nostalgia and accomplished exactly what he'd hoped for. "I really missed you, too, pumpkin. I'm sorry I didn't get to take those kittens you had for me awhile back."

She patted his cheek consolingly. "That's okay. Francie had more. Want to see? One is all black with a white nose. I think you'll really, really like him."

He grinned. "I bet I will," he agreed. "We'll go see him later."

"We'd better go now," Dani protested. "Later it will be my bedtime."

"Give me a few minutes inside to say hello to your mom," he negotiated. "I'm sure it won't be your bedtime then."

Dani braced her hands against his chest, leaned

back in his arms and studied him intently. "You promise you won't leave without going to see the kittens?"

"I promise," he said, solemnly crossing his heart as he put her down.

"Okay," she said cheerfully, and ran toward the house screaming, "Mommy, Uncle Cody's here and he says he's going to take one of Francie's kittens."

"Thank goodness," Kelly called back as she emerged from the house, a grin on her face. "Conned you again, huh?"

He chuckled. "If you're not careful, that child of yours is going to be the biggest scam artist in the entire United States."

"I prefer to think she'll have a career in diplomacy or maybe negotiating strike settlements," Kelly said. "Come on in. Jordan's still at the office, but he should be home soon."

His sister-in-law surveyed him closely. "How are you? You look lousy."

"Obviously Dani isn't the only one in the family with a silver tongue."

Kelly didn't bat an eye. "Did you see Melissa today?"

"I'm sure you know perfectly well that your husband and Luke badgered me into it."

"They said they were going to try. I wasn't sure if it had worked."

"I saw her," he admitted. "And her baby." He watched closely for Kelly's reaction. She remained expressionless.

''I see,'' she said blandly, keeping her attention focused on the vegetables she was chopping. ''How did it go?''

Cody thought she was working awfully darned hard to feign disinterest. ''Fine for the first few minutes, ugly after that.''

''Oh, Cody,'' she protested softly. ''Isn't it time you settled things with her and came home for good?''

Suddenly he didn't want to pursue the topic. He needed a break from it. They could get into it again when Jordan got home. Hopefully his brother would have answers that Kelly couldn't or wouldn't give him.

''I don't want to talk about Melissa right now. First I want to catch a glimpse of that brand new baby boy of yours,'' he declared just as Jordan came in and dropped a kiss on his wife's cheek.

''Hey, little brother, what brings you by?'' Jordan asked, sneaking a carrot from the pile Kelly had just cut up.

''He's going to take a kitten,'' Dani chimed in. ''Can we go see them now, Cody? It's later.''

Since going to see the kittens would keep him from having to deal with the subject of Melissa and her baby a little longer, Cody stood and headed for the kitchen door. Dani tucked her hand in his.

''You should probably take two kittens,'' she said on the way out. ''One might get lonely.''

''Listen, young lady, I said one kitten,'' he protested over the sound of Kelly and Jordan's laughter.

''But you were going to take two last time.'' Apparently she caught his stern expression because she gave a little shrug of resignation. ''I bet you'll change your mind when you see them.''

A half hour later he was back in the kitchen with two kittens in a box. Dani had been giving him very precise instructions on caring for them ever since they'd left the barn. Kelly's expression turned smug when she saw him.

''You are pitiful,'' Jordan said, shaking his head. ''Is there a female on the face of the earth you can resist?''

''Who are you kidding?'' Cody shot back, gesturing to the big tomcat that was curled in Jordan's lap purring contentedly. ''You always hated cats and now you're surrounded by them. I don't hear you complaining.''

''You may not hear it,'' Kelly said, ''but it is almost the last thing I hear every single night. He says 'Good night, I love you, no more cats,' all in one breath.''

''I do not,'' Jordan said, dislodging the cat and pulling Kelly onto his lap.

Cody listened to their banter and watched their undisguised affection with envy. Until he'd lost Melissa he'd never thought he wanted marriage and kids. He'd been as commitment-phobic as any one of those jerks who made the rounds of the talk shows. Ironically, ever since their breakup, all he'd been able to think about was settling down and having kids. He'd deliberately isolated himself in Wyoming so he'd be far from the temptation to try something at which he knew he'd inevitably fail.

After all, he hadn't appreciated Melissa when he'd had her and she was as sexy and generous, as kind and intelligent, as any woman he'd ever known. He'd had a roving eye, just the same. He'd taken her for granted, which everyone in the family had accused him of doing at one time or another. He suspected he'd do the same with a wife. What was the point of ruining some woman's life for his own selfish longing to have just a taste of the kind of love Jordan and Luke had found?

"How long are you sticking around? Have you told your boss when you'll be back in Wyoming?" Jordan asked after Kelly insisted Cody stay for dinner.

Kelly dished up a serving of stew for him and lingered at his shoulder. "You are not going back until after J.J. is baptized," she said emphatically.

Cody glanced up at her. "When is that again?"

"Next weekend, which you know perfectly well. I sent you an invitation. We're going ahead with it. Harlan insisted."

Something in his expression must have given him away because she frowned. "You ripped it up, didn't you?"

Cody recalled the scattered pieces of the pretty blue invitation and felt a tide of red rising in his cheeks. Was the woman a damned witch?

"Of course not," he fibbed.

The response drew a disbelieving snort. "So you'll be here at least that long," she said.

Cody had a feeling once he learned the truth about Melissa's baby, he wouldn't be able to get away from

Texas fast enough. He'd need to cool his temper for a good long while before confronting her with what he knew. He'd also need time to make up his mind exactly what he wanted to do about the baby she'd kept from him. He intended to learn that truth in the next twenty-four hours.

"Sorry," he said eventually. "I can't promise to stay that long."

Kelly glanced at Jordan, then back at him. "Your brothers said you were going to say no," she said.

"I had no idea I was so predictable."

"Lately you are," his sister-in-law said. "Lately, you've gotten downright boring."

He gave her a wry look. "More of that fatal charm, I see."

Kelly frowned at his teasing. "What if I told you that Jordan and I want you to be the baby's godfather?"

Something deep inside him shifted at the offer. He felt an unexpected warm glow. It was a feeling he told himself he didn't deserve, especially not if he had a real child of his own he'd never even acknowledged.

"I'd say you made a lousy choice," he responded.

"I told you he wouldn't even be gracious about it," Jordan chimed in. "Leave him be, Kelly. He's as stubborn as the rest of us when he digs in his heels. He'll change his mind, if we let the idea simmer long enough."

"I won't change my mind," Cody said. "Sorry."

"You say that a lot these days," Jordan observed.

"Maybe I have a lot to be sorry for."

''Well, this is one thing you can check off the list,'' Jordan said.

He spoke in that matter-of-fact way that indicated he'd reached a decision and wanted no further argument. It was a tactic that might have served him well in business, but it grated on Cody's nerves.

''I want you here, little brother,'' Jordan stated emphatically. ''And I want you to be the baby's godfather. It's settled.''

Despite his annoyance at Jordan's attempt to snatch the decision out of his hands, Cody could feel himself weakening, feel that odd, empty sensation in the pit of his stomach that always meant the loneliness was taking hold again.

''Did you check it out at the church?'' he inquired lightly. ''They'll probably be worried about lightning hitting the steeple if I show my hide in there.''

''There was some mention of that, but I believe there's a general consensus that your soul is still salvageable,'' Kelly said. ''Please, Cody. We've missed you. It's only for a few days more. How bad can that be?''

A few days, one hour, any time at all would be hell, especially if he discovered in the meantime that he had a baby of his own. Still, Cody had never been able to resist his sister-in-law. Kelly had been coaxing him into trouble since they were toddlers. Jordan had been too stuffy even at seven to fall in with some of her more outrageous mischief, though there had never been a doubt in anyone's mind that Jordan was the one she loved.

''I'll stick around,'' he said eventually. ''Long enough to get that nephew of mine in good graces with the Lord. Then I'm heading right back out. Understood?''

''Understood,'' Kelly said meekly.

Kelly meek? Every alarm bell in him went off. Before he could get too caught up in trying to figure out her angle, she was gone. He was left alone with Jordan, while Kelly went upstairs to tuck Dani into bed. Suddenly the questions that had been tormenting him earlier in the day could no longer be ignored.

''Kelly mentioned that you saw Melissa and her little girl today, after you left Luke and me,'' Jordan said, his gaze fixed on Cody's face.

The comment gave him the perfect opening. ''Why didn't you warn me?'' Cody asked, trying to keep the anger out of his voice. ''You knew about the baby, didn't you?''

Jordan sighed, then nodded. ''I saw her once, about eight months ago. She was just a baby.'' He scanned Cody's face as if looking for answers. ''What did you think when you saw her?''

''I figured Melissa and Brian had more going for them than I'd realized. I figured they were a happy little family now.'' Cody threw out the possibility to gauge his brother's reaction. If Jordan knew anything different, he'd find it out now.

The color washed out of Jordan's face. ''Did you say that to Melissa?''

''More or less,'' he admitted. ''Along with offering her my congratulations.''

''What did she say?''

''Nothing.''

''I see.''

Cody lost patience for the game. He knew darned well that Jordan knew more than he was saying. He could see it in his eyes. His brother was looking everywhere in the kitchen except directly at him.

''You might as well spit it out,'' he told him finally.

''What?''

''Whatever has you looking like you'd rather be in Kansas.''

A faint grin tugged at Jordan's mouth. ''Maybe Houston, not Kansas,'' he said. He sighed. ''How good a look did you get at the child?''

''Good enough,'' Cody said. He sensed that Jordan wanted him to reach a different conclusion than he'd just offered all on his own. He sucked in a deep breath. ''She's mine, isn't she?''

Once Cody had actually spoken the words out loud, Jordan nodded, confirming everything.

Cody's heart pounded. An uncommon mix of hope and dismay swirled through him. ''You know that for sure?''

''I saw it right off,'' Jordan admitted. ''She was the spitting image of your baby pictures. I confronted Melissa about it straight out.''

Cody felt an icy chill settle over him as Jordan's earlier comment came back to him. He stood and leaned down to look his brother in the eye. ''And that was when? About eight months ago, you said?''

''Yes,'' Jordan replied softly.

"And Melissa confirmed your suspicions right then and there?" he demanded, the hurt and anger of yet another betrayal slamming through him.

"Yes."

"Damn you, Jordan," he snapped, backing up to prevent slamming a fist in his brother's face. "How could you do that to me? How could you keep a secret like that? Didn't you think I had a right to know? Or was this another one of those big-brother-knows-best decisions?"

"She pleaded with me not to tell you," Jordan said simply.

Cody stared at him incredulously. "And your loyalty was with her and not me?"

"Why the hell do you think I've done everything in my power to get you back here? I didn't want to lay this on you when you were in Wyoming. I wanted you here, so you could see for yourself. I didn't want you to accuse me or her of making it up just to get you back here."

Cody wasn't buying it. "No, you were more concerned with keeping your promise to a woman who betrayed me than you were with doing what was right—giving me a chance to know my own child." He turned on his heel and headed for the door, the box of kittens in tow. "I can't believe you would do something like this. Maybe family loyalty doesn't mean anything once you're a big corporate executive. Is that it, big brother?"

"Cody, you have it all wrong," Kelly protested when she came back into the kitchen. Obviously she had overheard the tail end of the argument.

"I don't think so," he snapped, shooting her a look of regret. "Don't expect me at the baptism, after all. In fact, forget you even know me."

Kelly called out after him. He heard the screen door slam behind her, then Jordan murmuring something he couldn't quite make out. Whatever it was, though, it silenced her. When he looked back as he drove away, he saw them standing on the porch staring after him. He was sure it was only his imagination, but he thought he saw his brother wiping something that might have been tears from his cheeks.

He slowed the car momentarily and closed his eyes against the tide of anguish washing through him. Melissa had done it again. She had come between him and his family. He vowed then and there it would be the last time. This time he wouldn't run. He wouldn't let her control his destiny as he had before.

Forgetting all about his resolve to let his temper cool, an hour later he was in town, pounding on the Hortons' front door. Ken Horton, wearing a robe and slippers, opened it a crack. At the sight of Cody, he swung it wider, a welcoming smile spreading across his weathered face. Cody could see Velma's panicky expression as she stared over her husband's shoulder.

"Cody, what on earth?" Horton grumbled. "You trying to wake the whole neighborhood?"

"Where's Melissa?"

"She's not here," he said as his wife tugged frantically on his arm. When he leaned down, she whispered something in his ear, something that wiped any lingering expression of welcome from his face. "Go on home, Cody."

"Not until you tell me where she is."

"Don't make me call the sheriff."

"Don't make me pound the information out of you," Cody shot back belligerently.

Ken Horton regarded him sympathetically. "Boy, go on home and get some sleep. If you've got things to talk over with Melissa, do it in the morning, when you're calmer."

Despite his earlier promise to himself to think things through clearly, Cody realized he didn't want to be calm when he talked to Melissa. He wanted this rage to keep him focused, to keep him immune to the sight of her. He wanted to have this out with her while he was hot with anger, not lust.

"If I have to knock on every door in town, I'm going to talk to her tonight," he swore.

"There's nothing you have to say, nothing you need to know, that won't be settled just as readily in the morning," Horton repeated, still calm, still intractable.

Cody considered it as much as an admission that he and Melissa had serious issues to resolve, such as his relationship to that baby. He gathered from the warning look Horton shot at his now tearful wife that they didn't entirely agree on whether Cody had the right to know the truth.

"Where can I find her in the morning?" he asked finally, resigned to the delay. They all knew he wouldn't tear through town, creating yet another ruckus he'd never live down.

"She gets to work about nine," her father told him.

"I'm not talking to her at Dolan's," he said. "I don't want the whole town knowing our business."

Horton seemed about to offer an alternative when Velma piped up. "That'll just have to do," she said. "We're not telling you where she lives."

He couldn't decide if Velma was worried about him throttling Melissa or if she was simply being protective of her daughter's secret. Because he wasn't sure, he backed down.

"If you talk to her, let her know I'll be by the minute the doors open. Tell her to arrange with Eli for someone to cover for her unless she wants her personal life broadcast to everyone in town."

To his surprise, Ken Horton held out his hand. When Cody shook it, Melissa's father said, "For whatever it's worth, Cody, I think it's about time you two got everything out in the open. The two of you had something special once. Melissa's been punished enough for making one foolish mistake."

He gave his wife a defiant look. "And a man has a right to claim his child."

Velma Horton groaned and covered her face with her hands. Tears spilled down her cheeks. Cody wondered at the fear he'd seen in her eyes right before she placed her hands over them. She'd had the same terrified expression earlier in the day. He'd always thought Velma Horton liked him. Now she seemed to think he was some sort of a monster.

Was she blaming him for running out on her pregnant daughter? Or was it something more? He wondered what could possibly be behind the expression he'd read in her eyes.

Eventually, as he slowly walked back to his pickup, it came to him. She was actually afraid that he'd come home to take his baby away from Melissa.

Was that what he intended? He sat in his truck on the dark street in front of the Hortons' house, his head resting on the steering wheel. He honestly hadn't thought beyond discovering the truth and confronting Melissa with it.

Obviously, it was a good thing Ken Horton had prevented him from seeing Melissa tonight. He needed to get his thoughts in order. He needed to have a plan. For once in his life he couldn't act on impulse. Too many lives were at stake, his own, Melissa's, and that darling little girl's.

His heart ached every time he thought about his daughter. His arms felt empty, just as they did when Dani climbed out of them or he had to turn Angela back over to Jessie or Luke. He wondered about that vacant place he'd thought would always be inside him and realized that there was someone who could fill it, a child of his own.

Tomorrow he would claim her. He realized he didn't even know her name or how old she was or whether she could walk or talk. So many precious details. He sighed. Tomorrow he would fill in the gaps.

Tomorrow he would finally experience what it was

like to feel like a father. Right now it was all too abstract, but in the morning he would hold his child in his arms. Whatever else happened between him and Melissa, he vowed that nothing would ever rip his baby away from him again.

Chapter Five

Her mother had warned her. In fact, the first thing out of Velma's mouth when Melissa had dropped off her daughter for the day had been a detailed description of Cody's late-night visit. Based on Velma's panicked reaction, Melissa had been tempted to take Sharon Lynn and flee. She knew, though, that in his present mood Cody would only track her down.

Besides, hadn't she resolved just last night to tell him herself about Sharon Lynn? The decision on the timing had just been taken out of her hands. Of course, that also meant that his anger had had all night to simmer. She walked to work, dreading the confrontation that was clearly only minutes away.

She meant to ask Eli for an hour or so off to deal with a personal matter. She meant to be outside, on the sidewalk, when Cody arrived. She meant to do everything possible to ensure their conversation took place in private, away from prying eyes and potential gossip. She meant to be calm, reasonable, even conciliatory.

Cody took any chance of that out of her hands.

Before the door to the drugstore fully closed behind her, Melissa heard the bell ring loudly as the door slammed open again. Without even turning around, she sensed it was Cody. The air practically crackled with tension. She pivoted reluctantly and found him so close she could almost feel his breath on her face. She surveyed him slowly from head to toe, trying to gauge exactly how furious he was.

He looked exhausted. His mouth was set in a grim line. His shoulders were stiff. His hands were balled into fists. He also looked as if he'd slept in his clothes, perhaps in his truck, right in front of the drugstore. That would explain why he'd appeared right on her heels.

Despite all that, her heart flipped over. Her pulse scrambled. She had the most absurd desire to fling herself straight into his arms.

But she couldn't. More precisely, she didn't dare. It would only complicate an already impossible situation. She sucked in a deep breath and waited. The first move was going to have to be his.

As she waited, she was suddenly aware of every sound, every movement. She could hear the hum of the electric clock, the rattle of plastic bottles and *ping, ping, ping* of pills being counted out as Eli filled a prescription in the back, the swish of a mop as Mabel dusted the floor. Mabel rounded the aisle of shelves, caught sight of the silent tableau at the front of the store and stopped and stared.

Melissa felt like screaming. Mabel's presence was anticipated, but unfortunate. Of all the people in town, she was the most likely to spread word of every last detail of any encounter between Melissa and Cody. Her pale eyes sparkled as she watched the two of them.

Cody tipped his hat to Mabel, but didn't extend even that much courtesy to Melissa before latching on to her arm and practically hauling her into the storage room, past the startled gaze of Eli Dolan. Cody kicked the door shut behind them, plunging them into darkness.

"Dammit, Cody, what do you think you're doing?" Melissa demanded, trying to wrench herself free and reach the light switch at the same time. She couldn't succeed at doing either one.

"We need to talk," he declared, seemingly oblivious to the lack of light.

"Fine. Then let's do it like two civilized adults. There's no need for your caveman routine."

He was close enough that she could see that his eyes sparked fire, but he released his grip on her. Melissa felt along the wall until she found the switch. She flipped it on, illuminating the room that was small under the best of conditions, but claustrophobic with Cody pacing in the cramped space.

Somehow he managed to neatly avoid the stacks of

just-delivered boxes, metal shelves of inventory and a disorderly array of cleaning supplies. Melissa had the feeling that he was practically daring the inanimate objects to give him an excuse to knock them all to the floor. She couldn't recall ever seeing him quite so angry or quite so speechless. Cody's glib tongue was known far and wide, especially among women.

She kept silent and waited. Finally he stopped in front of her, his hands shoved in his pockets, legs spread, a belligerent expression on his handsome face.

"Whose baby is it?" he demanded in a tone that made her hackles rise.

Melissa made up her mind then and there that she wasn't giving in to his bullying or to any coaxing he might decide to try when that failed. Maybe that had been the problem in the past. She'd been too darned easy on him, too much in love to ever say no. She hoisted her chin a challenging notch.They were going to have a conversation on her terms for a change.

"Good morning to you, too, Cody."

Cody's gaze narrowed at the sarcasm. "Dammit, I asked you a straight question. The least you could do is give me a straight answer."

She wasn't sure where she found the courage to face him down, but she did. "Why should I, when you're acting like a bully?"

"I think I have a right to act any damn way I please."

"No," she said softly. "You don't. I told you before that we can discuss this like two civilized adults or I can go into the other room and go to work."

He raked his hand through his hair in a gesture that was vintage Cody. She'd always been able to tell exactly how frustrated or annoyed he was by the disheveled state of his hair.

"If that baby's mine, I have a right to know," he retorted, his voice starting to climb.

"I was under the impression that you already know the answer to that. You certainly carried on as if you did when you dropped in on my parents last night."

He didn't look even vaguely chagrined by the reminder of his outrageous behavior on her parents' doorstep. "I want to hear it from you," he snapped. "I want to hear why you kept it from me. If I am that child's father, I should have been told about her way back when you first discovered you were pregnant. I had a right to know. We should have been making decisions together."

Melissa met his gaze unflinchingly. "You gave up any rights the day you left town without so much as a goodbye. You never got in touch. I didn't know where you were. How was I supposed to let you know?"

"Jordan knew where I was, but you made damned sure he wouldn't tell me, didn't you?"

"Because your leaving town the way you did told me everything I needed to know about how you felt about me. What was the point of dragging you back so you could tell me to kiss off?"

She could almost see his patience visibly snap.

"Dammit, Melissa, you know that I had more than enough cause to go," he practically shouted, slamming his fist into a box and sending it crashing to the floor. Judging from the shattering noise it made, it was the glasses Eli had bought to replace the supply she'd broken only the day before.

Eli opened the door a crack and peered inside, his expression anxious. "Everything okay back here?"

"Fine," Cody and Melissa said in unison. The response wasn't very heartfelt from either of them.

Eli glanced at the box on the floor and shook his head wearily. He backed away without comment and shut the door.

Throughout the interruption, Cody had kept his gaze fastened on her face, sending color flooding into her cheeks. "You know I'm right," he said more quietly the instant they were alone again. "You cheated on me."

She had known from the beginning that that was what he believed. She had even wanted him to believe it…up to a point. Even so, it hurt to hear him say it. "Still jumping to conclusions, I see. That was always one of your worst habits, Cody."

He shoved his fingers through his thick hair again. "Jumping to conclusions," he repeated incredulously. "Did you or did you not sleep with my best friend?"

She was amazed at the speed with which the conversation had veered from the subject of their daughter to the real source of Cody's fury. He'd had well over a year to work up a good head of steam on the subject and clearly he intended to vent it now, unless she put a quick stop to it.

"I did not," she told him quietly.

"See—" he began triumphantly. His expression suddenly faltered as her reply finally penetrated his thick skull. "You didn't?"

"Never," she said emphatically, her gaze unflinching.

"But I saw..."

"You saw exactly what I wanted you to see." She shrugged. "Unfortunately, you leapt to the wrong conclusion."

He stared at her blankly. "I don't get it."

It was time—way past time—to spell it out for him. "Brian and I had one date. It wasn't even a date, really. It was a setup. Brian only went along with it because he knew I was crazy about you. You were supposed to get wildly jealous, realize you were madly in love with me, and propose. You were supposed to fight for me. You weren't supposed to haul your butt out of town without looking back."

"Jealous?" He stared at her in bemusement. "How the hell was I supposed to know that? You were in his arms. What was I supposed to think, that you were discussing the weather?" he asked in a tone loud enough to wake the dead.

"You're shouting again," she observed.

He scowled. "Well, so what if I am?"

Melissa chuckled despite herself. He was too darned stubborn to recognize even what was staring him straight in the face, much less the subtleties of the trap she had tried to spring on him. No wonder it had failed so miserably. She should have issued an ultimatum in plain English if she'd wanted him to marry her, not tried to trick him into recognizing his own feelings. As for right now, he obviously needed his present circumstances clarified for him.

"Mabel's probably taking notes," she stated patiently. "Eli may be calling the sheriff. Other than that, there's no reason to quiet down that I can think of."

Cody groaned and sank onto a stack of boxes. When he finally looked at her again, she thought she detected a hint of wonder in his eyes.

"Then the baby really is mine?" he asked quietly. "Jordan was right?"

"No doubt about it, at least in anyone's mind except yours."

His gaze honed in on hers and an expression of complete awe spread over his face. "I have a baby."

"Actually, you have a *toddler,*" she corrected. "She's thirteen months old."

"Whatever," he said, clearly unconcerned with the distinction. "Tell me everything. I want to know her name. How long you were in labor. What time she was born. I want to know what she likes to eat, whether she can talk, how many steps she's taken, if she has allergies, what her favorite toy is. I want to know every last detail."

The yearning behind his words struck her. He almost sounded as if he regretted missing out on so much. His eagerness was impossible to resist. Suddenly she couldn't wait to see him with his daughter.

It was something she'd dreamed about since the first moment the doctor had confirmed her pregnancy.

"Wouldn't you rather just go and meet her?" Melissa inquired softly.

He nodded, apparently speechless again.

"I'll speak to Eli and be right with you," she promised.

"Don't try ducking out the back," he warned, but he was grinning when he said it.

"I'm not the one who runs," she reminded him.

His comment might have been half-teasing, but hers was not. She wanted him to know that she was stronger now than she had been when he'd abandoned her. She wanted him to know that she was tough enough and secure enough to fight him for her daughter, if she had to.

But she also wanted him to see that she was brave enough to allow him into his child's life, if he wanted a place there. This wasn't about her any longer. It wasn't about her feelings for Cody, though those clearly hadn't died. This was about her daughter and what was best for her. It was about giving her child a chance to know her father.

Even so, as they walked down Main Street toward the tree-lined street where her family had lived her whole life, Melissa couldn't help the vague stirring of hope deep inside her. The past year and a half of loneliness and regret had been wiped out of her heart in the blink of an eye. Left in its wake was anticipation, the eager-to-start-the-day anticipation of a woman in love. As dangerous an emotion as that was, she could no more have prevented it than she could have held back the wildness of a tornado's winds.

Cody was back and she might as well admit to herself one more truth. Time and distance hadn't dulled her feelings for him a bit. She wanted him every bit as fiercely as she ever had.

Cody was in a daze. He was only marginally aware of the woman walking beside him. Instead he kept seeing images of the child that he now knew without any doubt whatsoever was his. Melissa's confirmation kept echoing over and over in his head. He was a father.

The realization was both incredible and scary. What if he blew it? What if his daughter took one look at him and rejected him? Okay, the latter was unlikely. Just the day before she had reached for him as if she already knew who he was. He recalled the eager stretch of her arms in the air and the sensation of tenderness that had welled up inside him at her innocent smile.

On the walkway at the Hortons' he paused, his hand on Melissa's arm. "Wait."

She turned a quizzical look on him. "Second thoughts?"

"No." He swallowed hard. "What's her name?"

"Sharon Lynn."

He repeated it softly, just to hear how it sounded on his tongue. "I like it."

"I'm not sure she'll tolerate being called by both when she gets a little older, but for now that's what we call her. My father tends to call her Pookie. I'm trying to break him of the habit. I will not have my child go through life being nicknamed Pookie. Missy is bad enough."

He smiled at her and barely resisted the urge to reach over and brush a strand of auburn hair from her cheek. "I never called you Missy."

"For which I was exceedingly grateful. That's probably why I let you get away with so much."

"You never let me get away with a thing," he protested.

"That baby inside says otherwise."

"I'll have to remember that," he said, grinning. "If I just whisper your name in your ear, you'll do anything I ask, is that right?"

She frowned, probably at the sudden provocative note in his voice. He knew she didn't want him to guess how easily he got to her. She was going to fight him tooth and nail.

"That was then," she said staunchly, confirming his guess. "This is now and the tide has turned, cowboy."

He readily accepted the challenge in her tone. "Is that so, Me...liss...a?" He deliberately drew her name out. Before she could react to the teasing, he lowered his head and dropped a quick kiss on her parted lips. "See, it still works."

The startled, slightly dazed expression on her face almost tempted him to try again. That brief brush of his mouth over hers had been just enough to tantalize him. Memories of warm, moist kisses and stolen caresses slammed through him, turning teasing into something very, very serious.

How had he ever walked away from her? Why hadn't he stayed and fought, just as she'd demanded earlier? Had it been the gut-deep sense of betrayal that had driven him all the way to Wyoming? Or had it simply been the even more powerful fear of the commitment to which fighting for her would have led? He'd never thought of himself as a coward, but suddenly he was taking a long, hard look at his actions in a whole new light.

"Cody?"

He blinked and gazed down into her upturned face. Before he could question himself, he scooped his hand through her silky hair to circle the back of her neck. With his gaze fixed on her turbulent sea green eyes, he reclaimed her mouth, lingering this time, savoring, remembering.

He felt her hands on his chest, tentative at first, then more certain as she slid them up to his shoulders and clung. Her body fit itself neatly, automatically, into his, the movement as natural as breathing and far, far more exciting.

Cody couldn't believe he had ever walked away from this. He couldn't imagine how he had lived without the sweetness of her kisses or the heat of her body pressed against his. The swirl of sensations was overpowering, demanding…and totally inappropriate for a sidewalk in plain view, he realized as a passing car honked and the teenage driver shouted out encouragement.

Melissa backed away as if she'd been burned. Her face was flaming with embarrassment. A warning flashed in her eyes, turning them the shade of soft jade in sunlight.

"That can't happen again," she stated emphatically.

"It can and it will," Cody said with just as much certainty. "Count on it."

Alarm flared in her expression. "No, Cody, this isn't about you and me anymore."

"Sure it is, darlin'. It always was."

"No!" She practically shouted it, as if volume might make her edict clearer. "You and I are over. You saw to that."

Cody dropped his own voice to a seductive growl. "We'll see," he taunted.

"Dammit, Cody, do you or do you not want to see your daughter?"

"Of course I do," he said, amused that she seemed to think the two concepts were diametrically opposed. "Meeting Sharon Lynn has absolutely nothing to do with my intentions toward you."

"Yes, it does," she said stubbornly.

"You're not keeping me from my daughter," he responded emphatically. "And you're not going to put up much resistance, once I set my mind to winning you back."

A scowl darkened her face. "You are the most arrogant, most infuriating man on the face of the earth. It's too late, Cody. You couldn't win me back if you courted me from now till we're both tottering around in orthopedic shoes.''

A grin tugged at his lips. ''Is that a challenge?''

''That's a guarantee.''

Chuckling at her sincere conviction that she could win a test of wills with him, he took her hand and headed for the house.

''You don't have a chance, sweet pea,'' he told her solemnly as he ushered her inside, where Velma was waiting, her gaze wary. He lowered his voice to taunt one last time, ''You don't have a snowball's chance in hell.''

Melissa never responded because her mother spoke up just then.

''You brought him,'' Velma said, her tone accusing.

''You knew I would,'' Melissa told her mother. ''Where's Sharon Lynn?''

''Down for her nap,'' she said, a note of triumph in her voice. ''There's no need to wake her.''

Cody was aware of the undercurrents between mother and daughter. Clearly, Velma was angry about his presence. Once again he had the sense that she feared him having any contact at all with his child.

Melissa shot him a vaguely apologetic look. ''I'll get her,'' she said.

He fell into step beside her. ''Don't wake her. I'll come with you. Let me just look at her for now. Your mother's right. There's no need to wake her yet.''

If he had expected the suggestion to gain Velma's approval, he failed. He should have saved his breath.

An expression of doom on her face, she trailed along behind them. He had the feeling she would have thrown herself across the threshold to the bedroom if she'd thought it would keep him away from her granddaughter.

He couldn't waste time worrying about Velma, though. From the instant he stepped into the room his gaze was riveted to the child asleep in the crib. She was sleeping on her stomach, her legs drawn up under her, her butt sticking up in the air. He couldn't imagine the position being comfortable, but she was sleeping soundly.

Awestruck, he moved closer to the crib. Melissa stayed a few steps behind him. Her mother never budged from the doorway. He studied the tiny, balled-up fists. Her skin looked soft as down and her light curls feathered around her face like wispy strands of silk. Her mouth curved like a miniature bow of pink. She was perfect. Adorable.

An overwhelming surge of protectiveness spread through him. This was his daughter. *His!* He'd seen Luke with the newborn Angela. He had watched Jordan hold J.J., but he had never guessed the depth of emotions that his brothers must have been feeling. He'd never experienced anything like it before in his life.

"She's so beautiful," he whispered, his voice choked.

"She has your eyes, your hair," Melissa said quietly.

"And your mouth," he noted. "I had no idea."

''No idea about what?''

''That it was possible to create anything so perfect.''

Melissa laughed softly. ''You haven't seen her throw a tantrum yet.''

He turned toward her and grinned. ''Ah, so she has your temper, too?''

''Oh, no,'' Melissa protested. ''You're not blaming me for that. Every ounce of stubbornness she possesses she got from you.''

Gazing directly into her eyes, he slipped an arm around her waist and pulled her close. ''Thank you.''

''For?''

He wasn't certain how to explain all that he was grateful to her for. For having the baby, even without him in her life. For keeping her healthy and safe. For loving her. So many things.

''For our daughter,'' he said simply.

''Oh, Cody,'' she whispered, tears welling up in her eyes and spilling down her cheeks.

''Shh, darlin', don't cry,'' he said, pulling her close. ''You're not alone anymore.''

To his astonishment, he realized that after the loneliest year and a half of his life, he was no longer alone, either. He was just a visit to the preacher away from having a family of his own. And nothing or no one was going to stand in his way.

Chapter Six

Still awestruck, Cody was knee-deep in mental wedding plans before he and Melissa walked out the front door of her parents' house. He was so caught up in thinking ahead to the day when Melissa and Sharon Lynn would move into his old house out at White Pines, that he almost forgot to ask Melissa to have dinner with him that night so he could officially propose and go over the details.

"Both of you," he told her as they stood in front of the drugstore a few minutes later. "You and Sharon Lynn. We'll go to DiPasquali's. I'll pick you up at your folks' place after you get off work."

Her lips set in a stubborn expression he knew only too well.

"Was there an invitation in there somewhere or did you mean it to sound like an order?" she asked.

He supposed they could quibble all morning over the difference, but he didn't see much point to it. They had far bigger issues to worry about, like setting a wedding date in the next week or so. Now that he'd seen his daughter, nothing was going to keep him from her. The prospect of instant parenthood scared the daylights out of him, but he was eager to get started, anxious to make up for lost time. He considered Melissa part of the package, of course.

"An invitation, of course," he said, wise enough to pacify Melissa. He wanted her in a receptive frame of mind tonight. He didn't want her stubborn streak kicking in. "Would you like to have dinner with me tonight at DiPasquali's?"

"I think your daughter is a little young for pizza."

Based on the spark of amusement in her eyes, she might have been teasing, but Cody took her comment seriously. He hadn't thought of that. In fact, what he really knew about babies would fit on the head of a pin. That was easily corrected. He would buy a book on parenting at the first opportunity. He was going to be the best-prepared father on the face of the planet, even if he was getting a late start.

"There must be something on the menu there she can eat," he said. "Or is there someplace that would be better?"

"DiPasquali's is fine," Melissa soothed. "I'll feed her first. She can chew on a slice of bread while we eat. She'll be perfectly content. She loves to eat out. She gets a lot of attention."

"Fine, whatever," he murmured distractedly, already thinking ahead to what he needed to accomplish between now and dinnertime.

He wanted to buy an engagement ring. And that book on parenting, of course. If he couldn't find one in town, maybe Luke or Jordan would have one he could borrow. He needed to call Lance Treethorn and tell him he wouldn't be returning to Wyoming. And he should sit down with his father and work out an arrangement for taking over his old duties at White Pines. Harlan would probably be relieved to be sharing the workload again.

"Cody?"

"Hmm?" He glanced up and caught Melissa's serious expression. "What's wrong?"

"Nothing. I'm just glad you want to be part of your daughter's life."

He stared at her, uncertain what would have made her ever suspect he'd do otherwise. "Well, of course, I do."

Melissa shrugged. "I wasn't sure how you were going to feel. And Mother, well, she had this crazy idea you were going to fight me for custody."

Cody couldn't imagine why he would have to fight for custody. He was going to claim his daughter *and* Melissa. If he'd known about the baby eighteen months ago, he would never have left for Wyoming in the first place. The incident with Brian might never have happened. He and Melissa would have been married. Custody arrangements would never have become an issue. At least, he finally understood Velma's reaction to him.

"That explains why she's been looking at me as if I'm about to steal the silver," he said.

"Yes."

"Well, she can stop worrying. We'll settle everything tonight." He leaned down and dropped a kiss on Melissa's lips. "See you later."

"Settle everything?" she repeated, a note of anxiety in her voice. "Cody!"

He turned back.

"What does that mean, we're going to settle everything?"

He smiled. "Not to worry, darlin'. We'll talk about it tonight."

"Exactly what did he say?" Velma fretted as Melissa bathed her daughter and got her ready for their evening with Cody.

"He said we'd settle everything tonight." She grabbed Sharon Lynn's rubber duck in midair as her daughter hurled it from the tub.

"What does that mean?"

Melissa sighed. "I don't know what it means, Mother. I suppose I'll find out shortly."

"I don't like it. I think your father and I should be there to protect your interests."

"I doubt Cody intends to pluck Sharon Lynn out of her high chair at the restaurant and carry her off into the night," she said as she toweled her daughter dry. "Anything other than that, I can cope with just fine on my own."

"What if he does decide to take her?"

"He won't," Melissa repeated, not sure how she knew with such conviction that Cody wouldn't do something so outrageous. "Stop worrying. I can handle Cody."

"You couldn't handle him two years ago," her mother commented. "What makes you think things are so different now?"

Melissa thought carefully about that before she answered. She used the struggle to get Sharon Lynn into her red corduroy pants and a cute little flowered shirt to buy some time.

"I'm stronger than I was then," she said eventually. "I've had almost two years to see that I don't need Cody Adams in order to survive. Sharon Lynn and I are doing just fine on our own."

Her mother regarded her skeptically. "Are you saying you're immune to him now?"

The kiss they'd shared on the front walk burned its way into her awareness. "No," she admitted. "I can't say that."

Velma groaned. "I knew it. I knew it the minute I saw the two of you playing kissy-face on the front walk."

"We were not playing kissy-face," Melissa retorted, blushing just the same. "Maybe you and Mabel have the same vocabulary after all."

"Mabel saw you kissing, too?"

"No, she just accused me of making goo-goo eyes at him way back in junior high."

"If only you'd limited yourself to that," Velma said dryly.

Melissa frowned. ''If I had, we wouldn't have Sharon Lynn,'' she reminded her mother quietly.

Velma retreated into silence after that. She was still looking anxious when Cody arrived to pick them up. Melissa had a feeling she had her father to thank for keeping her mother from racing down the driveway after them. He appeared to have a tight grip on her elbow and a glint of determination in his eyes as he waved them off.

The ride to DiPasquali's took only minutes. It was a wonder they didn't crash into a tree, though. Cody couldn't seem to take his eyes off his daughter. Sharon Lynn returned his overt inspection with shy, little peek-a-boo smiles. Apparently she'd inherited her father's flirtatious nature, too, Melissa thought with some amusement. Cody was clearly captivated. She should have been pleased, but the doubts her mother had planted kept her from fully relaxing and enjoying the way father and daughter were bonding.

At the small Italian restaurant where both she and Cody were well known, they were ushered to a back booth amid exclamations over Sharon Lynn's outfit and Cody's return. Melissa didn't miss the speculative looks sent their way by customers who knew their history only too well.

Though a high chair was set up at the end of the table for the baby, Cody insisted she was just fine beside him in the booth. Sharon Lynn stood on the vinyl seat next to him, bouncing on tiptoes and patting Cody on the top of his head.

He circled her waist with his hands and lifted her

into the air, earning giggles and a resounding kiss for his trouble. Melissa watched the pair of them with her heart in her throat. When Sharon Lynn climbed into Cody's lap, studied him seriously for a full minute, then cooed, "Da," Melissa felt the salty sting of tears in her eyes.

Cody's mouth dropped open. "Did she just call me Da?"

Apparently sensing approval, Sharon Lynn repeated the sound. "Da, Da, Da."

"She knows who I am," he whispered incredulously.

Melissa hated to disappoint him, but she knew that her daughter tended to call every man that. Besides, she refused to admit that she had tried to teach Sharon Lynn that very word while showing her a snapshot of Cody. She seriously doubted her daughter had actually made the connection between that blurry picture and the man holding her now.

She almost told him not to get too excited over it. Sharon Lynn might not even remember to connect that word with him tomorrow. The look in Cody's eyes kept her silent. He clearly wanted to believe that he and his child had made some sort of cosmic connection.

As she watched the pair of them, something shifted inside Melissa. Her earlier doubts fled. Maybe there really was some sort of instinctive bond between father and child. She wasn't sure what to make of this softer, gentler Cody. He had always been filled with laughter, but there was something incredibly sweet and tender in the way he teased his daughter and kept her giggling. Pride shone in his eyes at everything she did.

''She's brilliant,'' he declared every few minutes over the simplest accomplishments.

Sharon Lynn was clearly basking in the praise and the attention. Melissa held her breath, wondering just when exhaustion would overtake her daughter and turn that cheerful demeanor into far more familiar crankiness and tears. She couldn't help worrying about how Cody would respond to his child then. Would he turn tail and run again the instant the newness of this experience wore off, just as he had abandoned a long string of women once he'd tired of them? She was torn between anticipation and panic as she waited to see how the rest of the evening would play out.

They made it through their pizza without calamity striking. Sharon Lynn yawned a few times, grabbed a handful of the mushrooms Melissa had removed from her slice and squished them. When Cody tried to wipe her hands, she began sobbing as if she were being tortured.

Cody stared at Melissa helplessly as Sharon Lynn batted his hands away. ''What did I do?''

''You didn't do anything. She's tired.''

''Are you sure? Maybe she's hurt. Maybe there was a piece of glass and she cut herself.'' He unfolded her tightly clenched fingers and examined each one.

''Any sign of blood?'' Melissa inquired, barely hiding her amusement.

He scowled at her. "How can you be so calm?"

"Because this is a nightly ritual."

He blanched. "Nightly?"

She nodded. "Just about. She gets so tired she can hardly keep her eyes open, but she doesn't want to miss anything, so she fights going to sleep."

Cody was regarding the sobbing child as if she were an alien creature. "Want me to take her?" she offered.

"No," he said insistently. "I have to learn how to deal with this."

He lifted Sharon Lynn up and sat her on the edge of the table facing him. Huge tears rolled down her blotchy cheeks. "Okay, kiddo, let's try to figure out a solution for this little problem you have with bedtime."

"Cody?"

He glanced up at her. "Hmm?"

"I don't think reason and logic are going to work."

"Sure they will," he argued. "Just watch."

He began talking in a low, soothing tone, explaining very patiently that sleep was very important. He added a lot of nonsense about fairy princesses and treasures that didn't come from any storybook Melissa had ever read.

Whether it was his tone or the actual words, Sharon Lynn's eyelids began to droop. The next thing Melissa knew, she was cradled in Cody's arms, sound asleep.

"Amazing," she admitted. "I should hire you to do that."

"No need to hire me," he said, his gaze suddenly fixed on her in a way that had her pulse scrambling.

''I intend to be available for bedtime duty every night from now on.''

Melissa swallowed hard against the tide of panic that swept through her. Surely she hadn't heard him right. ''Excuse me?'' she whispered.

''Once we're married, I'll get her to bed,'' he said, making his intentions perfectly clear.

''Married?'' she repeated as if it were an unfamiliar concept.

''Well, of course,'' he said. ''What did you think was going to happen?'' He reached into his pocket, scooped something out and set it on the table between them.

Melissa stared at the small velvet box incredulously. She looked from it to Cody's face and back again.

''Go ahead,'' he encouraged. ''Open it. If you'd rather have something else, we can go together tomorrow.''

She shook her head, fighting the urge to grab that tempting little box and claim not only the ring inside, but the future Cody had obviously mapped out for them. This reaction of his to discovering he was a father wasn't even remotely what she had expected. Obviously he wasn't thinking clearly. He hadn't wanted to marry her two years ago. She was faintly insulted that it had taken a baby to drag a proposal out of him.

Actually, it wasn't even a proposal. It was another of those orders she hated so much. Issuing edicts was something he had learned at Harlan Adams's knee.

Considering how he'd rebelled against his father, she would have thought he'd be more sensitive to the crummy habit.

"No," she said flatly, meeting his gaze evenly. She was very proud of herself for getting the word out, for keeping her voice and her resolve steady.

He blinked and stared. "No what?"

She drew in a deep breath and, before she could change her mind, blurted, "I will not touch that box and I will not marry you."

A red flush climbed up his neck. "Of course you will," he said just as emphatically. "Don't be stubborn, Melissa. It's the sensible thing to do."

"Sensible," she repeated in a low, lethal tone. "I do not intend to get married because it is *sensible!*"

She stood and jerked on her coat, then moved to pick up Sharon Lynn. Cody held his daughter out of her reach.

"Sit back down and let's talk about this," he ordered. "You're causing a scene."

"I don't care," she said emphatically, though she didn't dare look around to see just how many people were fascinated by their argument. "There is absolutely nothing to discuss."

"Please," he said, sounding slightly more meek.

Since when had Cody cared about scenes? Melissa regarded him suspiciously, but she did sit on the edge of the seat. She did not remove her coat.

"How about another soft drink?" he coaxed.

"Cody!"

"Okay, okay." He leaned toward her intently. "Maybe I didn't go about this quite right."

"I'll say."

He reached awkwardly around his sleeping daughter and picked up the velvet box. He flipped it open to display an impressive emerald surrounded by diamonds. Melissa fought to pretend that the ring didn't just about take her breath away. The size of the ring and the sparkle of those stones were not important. A marriage based on obligation was the real point here. She wouldn't have it.

"It reminded me of your eyes," Cody said. He grinned. "The way they are right now, when they're shooting off sparks."

Melissa's resolve wavered. A little voice in her head gathered steam, repeating *no, no, no* so loudly she couldn't ignore it. Hadn't she told herself just a few hours earlier that she'd always been too easy on Cody? Hadn't she made a fool of herself over and over again by giving in if he so much as smiled at her?

And hadn't she learned that she could take care of herself? She no longer liked the idea of relying on anyone, either financially or, even more importantly, for her happiness.

"You're wasting your time," she told him emphatically before her resolve could falter. "The ring is beautiful. You're a fine man. I'm thrilled that you want to be a part of Sharon Lynn's life. But I will not marry you."

He looked absolutely dumbfounded. If the conversation hadn't been quite so difficult for her, too, she might have smiled at his flabbergasted reaction.

"Why?" he demanded, staring at her, indignation radiating from every pore.

"Because I will not get married for all the wrong reasons."

"What wrong reasons? We have a child. I intend to be a father to her."

"That's fine. It doesn't mean you have to be a husband to me. I'm doing just fine on my own. You were apparently doing so fine on your own that you saw no need to come back for almost two years."

"That's it, isn't it?" His gaze narrowed. "You're just doing this to get even because I left town and you had to face being pregnant all alone."

Melissa regarded him sadly. "No, Cody, I am not trying to get even. I'm just trying not to compound one mistake by making another."

He seemed thoroughly taken aback by the realization that anyone—and most especially the woman who'd always adored him—would consider marrying him to be a mistake. Obviously his ego hadn't suffered any during their separation. It was as solid as ever.

She reached across the table and patted his hand. "It's nothing personal."

He stared at her. "How can you say that? I think it's pretty damned personal."

"Once you've had time to think it over, you'll see that I'm right," she assured him. "Obligation is a terrible basis for a marriage."

This time when she stood and reached for Sharon

Lynn, he didn't resist. He pocketed the ring and stepped out of the booth. ''I'll take you home,'' he said, his voice flat.

Melissa directed him to the small house she'd been renting for the past year, since about a month after Sharon Lynn's birth. Cody showed no inclination to get out of the pickup, so she let herself out. She hesitated for a moment with the door still open.

''I'm sorry, Cody. I really am.''

He didn't look at her. ''I'll call tomorrow and we'll work out a schedule for me to spend time with my daughter.''

The chill in his voice cut straight through her. For the first time she wondered if she had made a terrible mistake in alienating him. Even though she knew in her heart that her decision was the right one, the only one to be made under the circumstances, perhaps she should have found a way to be more diplomatic about rejecting him.

''Fine,'' she said. ''Whatever works for you will be okay.''

She closed the door and started up the walk. An instant later she heard the engine shut off, then the slam of the driver's door behind Cody. He caught up with her before she could even make it to the front stoop.

Before she realized what he intended, he hauled her into his arms and kissed her so hard and so thoroughly that her head spun. Then, as if he suddenly became aware of the child she was holding or possibly because he figured he'd made his point, he released her.

"Give her to me," he said. "I'll carry her inside."

"Cody, she's fine," Melissa protested. She didn't want him inside, not when her knees were shaking and her pulse was racing.

"I said I'd carry her," he repeated, plucking her neatly out of Melissa's arms. "Open the door."

Following her directions, he made his way to the baby's small room. Angrily shrugging aside Melissa's offer of assistance, he fumbled with his daughter's clothes. He scanned the room, picked out a nightshirt from a small dresser, changed her, then laid her down gently.

Only then did a sigh shudder through him. His hand rested for a moment on the baby's backside.

"Good night, sweet pea," he murmured, his gaze riveted to his sleeping daughter as he backed toward the door.

The sight of Cody with their child, feeling his pain and his longing as he'd tucked her in for the night, had shaken Melissa. She was leaning against the wall outside the room, trying to gather her composure, when he finally emerged.

His gaze caught hers, burning into her. "It's not over," he said quietly. "Not by a long shot."

Trembling, Melissa stood rooted to the spot, staring after him long after she'd heard the truck's engine start, long after Cody had driven away.

Cody was right. It wasn't over. More than anything, she feared the struggle between them for their daughter was just beginning.

•

Chapter Seven

Cody didn't get a wink of sleep the entire night. When he wasn't overwhelmed by the amazing experience of holding his daughter, he was thinking about Melissa's astonishing transformation.

He had never noticed before how stubborn she was, nor how self-confident and independent. In fact, as he recalled, there had hardly ever been an occasion when she hadn't been thoroughly accommodating to his every whim. She'd picked a hell of a time to change, he thought, thoroughly disgruntled over having been shot down.

Sometime shortly after dawn, he finally forced himself to admit that he actually found the new Melissa ever so slightly more intriguing than he had the compliant woman he'd left behind.

Kelly, Jessie and the others had always warned him about taking Melissa for granted. It appeared he should have paid more attention to their advice. Melissa had used his time away to develop a very strong sense of who she was and what her priorities were. He was beginning to wonder if there really wasn't room for him in her life anymore.

Tired of his own company, he walked into the dining room at White Pines the minute he heard the rattle of breakfast dishes. Unfortunately, the housekeeper was very efficient. Maritza had already retreated to the kitchen, but she had left an array of cereals, a large pot of fresh coffee, a basket of warm rolls, and a bowl of berries, banana slices and melon. He noticed there were no eggs or bacon, no hash browns or grits. Obviously Harlan hadn't won his war to get what he considered to be a decent breakfast served during the week.

Cody was just pouring himself a cup of coffee when his father came in. He surreptitiously studied his father's face. Harlan looked tired and sad, but his complexion no longer had that unhealthy-looking pallor it had had when Cody had first arrived.

''You're up mighty early,'' Harlan observed, his expression sour as he surveyed the food the housekeeper had set out. ''Dammit, I can't seem to get a decent piece of meat in the morning anymore.'' He shot a hopeful look at Cody. ''Want to drive into town and get a real breakfast? Maybe a steak and some eggs?''

''And bring the wrath of Maritza down on my head? I don't think so. The fruit looks good.''

''I don't see you eating any of it.''

''I'm not hungry.''

''Late night?''

''Something like that.''

''I thought you were past carousing.''

''Who was carousing? I had dinner with Melissa.'' He paused and drew in a deep breath. It was time to test the words on his lips, time to test his father's reaction. It would be a good barometer of what others would have to say.

''And my daughter,'' he added.

Harlan merely nodded, clearly not startled by the profound announcement.

''About time,'' he said succinctly.

Cody stared at him, his blood suddenly pumping furiously. ''You knew, too? Dammit, Daddy, you're every bit as bad as Jordan,'' he accused. ''You kept it from me, just like he did. What is wrong with everyone in this family? I thought we were supposed to stick together.'' He was just warming up to a really good tirade when his father cut in.

''Settle down, son. Nobody told me, if that's what you're thinking. Didn't take much to add up two and two, once I'd seen that child. She's the spitting image of you at that age. I've got a picture of you boys on my desk that would have reminded me, if I hadn't seen it for myself.'' He shrugged. ''Besides, Melissa never had eyes for anyone but you.''

Cody couldn't think of a thing to say. Apparently

his father had been willing to stand on the sidelines and wait for Cody to show up and discover he had a daughter. It didn't fit with his usual manipulative style. Either his father was mellowing or he had some other kind of devious scheme up his sleeve.

Harlan speared a chunk of cantaloupe, eyed it disparagingly, then ate it. "So," he began, his tone one of such studied indifference that Cody immediately went on alert. "Is that why you took off? Did Melissa tell you she was pregnant?"

Cody was horrified his father could think so little of him. Was that it? Had Harlan thought he'd already made his decision about marrying Melissa and being a father to his child?

"No, absolutely not," he declared indignantly. "Do you honestly think I have so little backbone that I'd run from a responsibility like that?"

His father shot a bland look in his direction. "I wouldn't like to think it, but the evidence was staring me in the face."

"What evidence?"

"You were gone. Your girl was pregnant. She quit college. She had to take that piddly job at Dolan's to make ends meet, which suggested that no one was paying a dime to support her or the baby. Didn't take a genius to add it all together and figure out that one."

"Well, your calculator malfunctioned this time," Cody snapped. "She never said a word, never even tried to track me down. The first I knew about that baby was when Velma Horton brought her into Dolan's when I was there the other day. Even then, I thought someone else had to be the father. It never crossed my mind that Melissa would hide something that important from me.''

''I see.'' Harlan scooped up a strawberry, eyed it with disgust, then put it back. ''Now that you know, what do you intend to do about it?''

''I proposed to her last night.''

Harlan's eyes lit up. His expression was suddenly more animated than it had been in days. ''Well, hell, son, why didn't you say so? Congratulations! When's the wedding?''

''No wedding,'' Cody admitted dully. ''She said no.''

Harlan's openmouthed expression of astonishment reflected Cody's feelings precisely.

''She flat-out turned you down?'' his father said incredulously.

''Without so much as a hesitation,'' he said. ''It was downright insulting.''

Harlan chuckled. ''Well, I'll be damned.''

''You don't have to sound so amused,'' Cody grumbled.

''Sure, I do, boy. Seems tame little Melissa has grown up into a spirited young woman. The next few months or so ought to be downright interesting.''

Cody glared at him. ''Months? Forget it. I'm giving her a day, maybe two, to get over this contrariness. Then I'm hauling her to a justice of the peace.''

His father started to laugh, then smothered the sound with a napkin. ''Sorry,'' he mumbled, then gave up the fight and chuckled. ''Son, you're going to be able to sell tickets to that one.''

Cody's frayed temper snapped. He stood and tossed his own napkin back on the table. ''Well, get out your checkbook, Daddy. The best seats in the house are going to cost you. Melissa and I might as well start off our married life with a nice little nest egg.''

Melissa wiped down the counter at Dolan's after the last of the lunch crowd had left and eyed Cody warily. He'd been skulking up and down the aisles of the drugstore since noon, but he hadn't come near the soda fountain. He seemed unaware that Eli and Mabel were watching him with overt fascination. Thankfully, he was also unaware of what his presence was doing to her pulse rate. Who knew what he would do to capitalize on that little hint of a fissure in her resolve.

''Mabel, why don't you take the rest of the afternoon off,'' Eli suggested, playing straight into Cody's hands.

''What's wrong with you, old man?'' Mabel grumbled. ''You planning on shutting down business?''

Eli gave her a pointed nod in Melissa's direction. ''Go on, Mabel. You've been wanting to check out the new seeds over at the hardware store so you can get your garden in at the first sign of spring. Go do it.''

Melissa almost chuckled as she watched Mabel struggle with herself. She'd been talking about those seeds for a week, ever since the hardware store owner had told her they'd arrived. She also hated to miss out on something with the kind of gossip potential that Melissa's next confrontation with Cody was likely to have.

"Go," Eli repeated, shooing her toward the door and taking the choice out of her hands. "I might not feel so generous again anytime soon."

"Don't doubt that," Mabel retorted sourly.

Mabel got her coat and left, reluctance written all over her narrow, tight-lipped face. Cody inched a little closer to the soda fountain, as if an invisible barrier had been removed from his path.

"Melissa," Eli called. "I'll be in the storeroom, checking this morning's delivery. Call me if you need me."

"Traitor," Melissa mumbled under her breath.

Cody had moved close enough by now to overhear. "Nice talk," he commented. "He's just doing you a favor."

"Me?" She stared at him incredulously. "Oh, no. You probably paid him to get rid of Mabel and to disappear himself. I noticed the other night that you'd inherited Harlan's knack for manipulation."

Cody clearly wasn't crazy about the comparison, but he let the charge roll off his back. "I'm not desperate enough to be paying anyone to give me time alone with you," Cody said, his grin widening. "I'm still relying on my charm."

"Take it somewhere else," she muttered.

"Tsk-tsk, Me…liss…a," he drawled, tipping his hat back on his head as he settled on a stool at the counter. ''What does it take to get a little service around here?''

''More charm than you've got,'' she retorted. ''Or cold, hard cash.''

He plucked a twenty out of his wallet and set it on the counter. Then he winked. It appeared he was giving her a choice about which currency she wanted to accept. Melissa would have gladly taken the wink, if it meant she could shove that bill straight down his throat.

Since she couldn't, she snatched the twenty, tucked it into her pocket and withdrew her order pad and pen. ''What'll it be?'' she inquired in the same impersonal tone she used with other impossible customers.

Cody propped his elbows on the counter and leaned forward. ''A kiss for starters.''

''You wish.'' Her knees trembled despite the defiant retort. Why was it that temptation always entered a room right at Cody's side? Shouldn't she have been totally immune by now? Lord knows, she'd been lecturing herself on getting over him from the day he'd left town. Some of that advice should have taken by now. Apparently, though, it hadn't.

''Then I'll have a hamburger, fries and a shake,'' he said.

The mundane order was a disappointment. Melissa cursed her wayward hormones as she slapped the burger on the grill and lowered the fries into the hot grease. She sloshed milk into a metal container and out of habit added two scoops of chocolate ice cream, even though Cody hadn't specified the kind he wanted. Half of the mixture splashed out when she jammed the container into place on the automatic shaker.

"Nervous?" Cody inquired.

He spoke in a smug, lazy drawl that sent heat scampering down her spine. She scowled at him. "What on earth do I have to be nervous about? You're the one who doesn't belong here. You're the one making a pest of himself."

Sparks flared in his dark eyes. "Want me to ask Eli how he feels about you making a paying customer feel unwelcome?"

He didn't have to. She already knew that Eli would have heart failure if he heard her trying to run Cody off with her rudeness. He'd already taken Cody's side once today by slinking off to hide out in the storeroom to give them time alone. She'd never before noticed that Eli held Cody in particularly high esteem. His behavior must be part of some instinctive male support system that kicked in whenever one of them sensed that a woman might be getting the upper hand.

She turned her back on Cody, finished fixing his food, then set it down on the counter with a jarring thud.

He grinned at her. "Service with a smile," he commented. "I love it. You earn a lot of tips this way?"

Melissa closed her eyes and prayed for patience. When she opened them again, Cody hadn't vanished as she'd hoped. "Why are you in here?" she inquired testily. "Shouldn't you be out roping cattle or something?"

''We have plans to make, remember?''

''I told you just to tell me when you wanted to see Sharon Lynn. I'll make the arrangements so you can pick her up at my parents' anytime.''

''Not those plans,'' he said complacently, picking a pickle off of his hamburger and tsk-tsking her, apparently for not remembering that he hated pickles.

''Sorry,'' she said without much sincerity. She should have dumped in the whole damned jar. ''You could have eaten at Rosa's.''

''I prefer the spice here,'' he retorted. ''Now let's get back to those plans. I was thinking that a week from Saturday would be good.''

Melissa was surprised he wanted to wait that long before seeing his daughter again. Maybe his fascination was already waning. At this rate he'd be moving back to Wyoming in a month. Surely she could wait him out that long. She'd probably be a tangled heap of frustrated hormones, but presumably her sanity would still be intact.

''Sure, if that's what you want,'' she said more agreeably now that she knew he was likely to be out of her hair in no time. ''I'm off on Saturday, so you can pick Sharon Lynn up at my place.''

''Not just Sharon Lynn,'' he corrected. ''Can't have a wedding without the bride.''

Melissa dropped the glass she'd been rinsing out. It shattered at her feet. Eli poked his head out of the storeroom, saw the glass and shook his head.

''I hope to hell you two settle this quick,'' the pharmacist said. ''It's costing me a fortune in broken glasses.''

''Don't worry, Eli,'' Cody consoled him. ''I'll settle up with you.'' He fixed his unrelenting gaze on Melissa and added, ''I always accept my responsibilities.''

''Oh, stuff a rag in it,'' Melissa retorted, stripping off her apron and opening the cash register to shove in the twenty she'd pocketed. ''Eli, I'm leaving. Mr. Adams has already paid his check. Keep the change.''

She made it as far as the sidewalk, still shrugging into her coat, when Cody caught up with her. If her refusal to kowtow to his wishes for a second time had ruffled his feathers, he wasn't letting it show. He fell into step beside her, his expression perfectly innocent.

''Going to pick up the baby?''

Actually Melissa had no idea where she was going. She'd been so anxious to get away from Cody that she'd walked out of the drugstore without the kind of plan she should have had. It was an unfortunate sign of weakness, one she couldn't allow him to detect.

''No, actually, I have things to do.''

''Like what? I'll help.''

''No, thanks. I can handle it.''

''Come on, Me...liss...a,'' he coaxed, planting himself on the sidewalk in front of her, legs spread. He rocked back on the heels of his cowboy boots and peered at her from beneath the brim of his hat. It was a look that invited a woman to swoon. She ought to know. She'd done it often enough, flat-out making a fool of herself over him.

"Would spending a little time with me be so awful?" he inquired.

Awful? That wasn't the word she would have chosen. Dangerous, maybe. Stupid. Risky. There was a whole string of applicable words and none of them had anything to do with awful.

"I'd rather not," she said politely.

"Bet I can change your mind," he countered, grinning at her.

She scowled at him as he advanced on her step by step. "Don't try."

He shook his head. "I don't know. The temptation is pretty great. Your mouth is all pouty. Very kissable," he assessed, his gaze hot on her. He took yet another step closer, crowding her. "Your cheeks are pink. Just about the color of rose petals and twice as soft. It's all hard to resist."

As he spoke, her lips burned as if he'd kissed them. Her cheeks flamed, turning to what she was sure must be a deeper shade. Damn, it didn't seem to matter if he actually touched her or not. Her body reacted predictably just to the provocative suggestion.

"Go away," she ordered in a voice that was entirely too breathless.

His expression solemn, he shook his head. "I can't do that, Me…liss…a."

She sighed. "Why not?" she demanded far too plaintively.

He circled one arm around her waist and dragged her against him. She could feel the hard heat of his arousal.

''You know the answer to that,'' he whispered, his lips scant millimeters from hers. His breath fanned across her cheek.

''Cody.'' His name came out as a broken sigh, a protest that not even someone far less relentless than Cody would have heeded.

''It's okay,'' he consoled her. ''Everything is going to turn out just fine.''

He slanted his mouth over hers then, setting off fireworks in January. *Why, why, why?* her brain demanded. Why was her body so darned traitorous? Maybe it was like the tides. Maybe the way she responded to Cody was as immutable as the sun setting in the west.

She resisted the explanation. It meant she had no will at all to fight it. She put her hands on his chest and shoved with all her might. She might as well have been trying to topple a centuries' old oak. Cody didn't budge. He didn't stop that tender assault on her mouth.

For what seemed an eternity he coaxed and plundered, teased and tasted until she was shivering with urgent and almost-forgotten need. When she was weak with a desire she definitely didn't want to feel, Cody finally released her. She very nearly melted at his feet. In fact, she might have if he hadn't kept his hands resting possessively on her hips. Even through her coat, her skin burned at his touch.

''So, what are we going to do with the rest of the afternoon?'' he inquired. The gleam in his eyes suggested he had an idea of his own. His lips quirked up in the beginnings of a smile.

''Not what you're thinking,'' she said curtly.

His grin spread. "Don't be so certain of that, sweet pea. It sounds an awful lot like a challenge and you know I never could resist a dare."

Desperate for space, she backed away from him. "Give it a rest," she said crankily.

He reached out and rubbed his thumb across her lower lip. The sensation sent fire dancing through her.

"I'm just getting started, darlin'," he murmured, his gaze locked with hers.

Melissa held back a sigh of resignation. "You're not going home, are you?"

"When I can be with you? No way."

"Come on, then."

His expression immediately brightened. Once more he fell dutifully into step beside her. "Where are we going?"

"To buy groceries," she said, plucking a boring chore out of thin air. "And after that, we're ironing." She slanted a look at him to judge his reaction. He didn't bat an eye.

"Sounds downright fascinating," he declared. He captured her gaze, then added slowly, "I've always been particularly fond of starch."

She ignored the provocative tone. "Oh, really?" she said skeptically.

"Yes, indeed," he swore. "In my shirts and in my women. And you, sweet pea, are full of it."

Melissa had a feeling it would take her weeks to puzzle out whether he meant that as a compliment. For the first time, though, she had this funny little feeling she was going to have the time of her life figuring it out.

Chapter Eight

Somewhere in the middle of the grocery store, Melissa lost track of Cody. She was aware of the precise instant when she no longer felt the heat of his stare or the sizzling tension of his nearness. She almost sagged with relief, even as she fought off a vague stirring of disappointment. Clearly his attention span was no better now than it had ever been.

Worse, he was getting to her. Despite her best intentions, she was responding to his teasing, to the allure of his body. She could not let that happen. Steering totally clear of him, however, seemed to be the only way she was likely to be able to avoid succumbing to that seductive appeal. Now seemed like a good time to make a break for it.

All she had to do was get through the checkout line

and race home before he caught up with her. She could barricade the door. Or maybe just hide out in a bedroom until he was convinced she wasn't home.

She tossed a six-pack of soft drinks she didn't need into the cart, just in case Cody wasn't as far away as she hoped. She had to leave the store with more than a quart of milk or he'd know that this trip had been nothing more than a ploy to avoid being alone with him.

She had rounded the last aisle and was heading for the cashier when she spotted him. He was positioned in front of the baby food, studying labels with the intensity of a scientist in his lab. Apparently, though, he wasn't so absorbed that her presence escaped his notice.

"Which of these does Sharon Lynn like?" he asked, holding up competing brands of strained peas.

"Neither one."

His brow knit worriedly. "Doesn't she have to eat vegetables?"

"Yes, but she's past the baby food. She has her first baby teeth. She can chew soft food." She regarded him oddly. "Do you really care about this?"

"Yes," he said succinctly, and replaced the peas. "Fill me in on everything."

Melissa shrugged. "Okay. She can eat the junior brands. Like these," she said, plucking a couple of jars off the shelf. "There are some foods that don't have to be specially prepared. She can eat the regular stuff. Peas, for example."

To her surprise, he seemed to be taking in every

word as if she were delivering a fascinating treatise on something far more significant than baby food. In the past he'd reserved that kind of attention for very little besides ranching.

"What are her favorite foods?" he asked, studying the larger jars intently.

"Ice cream and French fries."

Cody stared at her. "That's her diet?"

"No," she said patiently. "Those are her favorites." She gestured to the junior baby food. "This is what she gets most of the time. When I have time, I even blend some myself from fresh fruits and vegetables. She's particularly fond of squishing bananas."

Cody eyed the jars of carrots and meats and fruits, seemed to struggle with his conscience, and then turned his back on them. "Let's go."

"Where?"

"To the ice cream section," he said as grimly as if he were going into battle and the enemy had pulled a last-minute tactical switch. "I'm not bringing home jars of that disgusting-looking liver or those limp little bits of carrot if she'd rather have ice cream."

"Cody, I do feed her. You don't need to stock my refrigerator, especially not with ice cream."

He stopped in his tracks and turned to face her. "Don't you see, this isn't about you. It's about me and my daughter. You've had her to yourself for thirteen months. Now I want a chance to be important in her life."

"By stuffing her with chocolate-fudge ice cream?"

Instead of taking her well-intended point, he seized

on the tiny sliver of information she'd imparted about their daughter. ''Is that her favorite? I'll buy a gallon of it.''

He sounded relieved to know that he wouldn't have to resort to another round of guesswork and label-reading. In fact, he was loping off to the frozen food section before Melissa could gather her thoughts sufficiently to argue with him.

Okay, she told herself, it was only a gallon of ice cream. So what? It wasn't as if he could buy their daughter's affection or ruin her health with one extravagant gesture of chocolate fudge.

She had a feeling, though, that this was only the beginning. Cody was not a man to do anything by half measures. His retreat to Wyoming, abandoning not only her but his beloved home and family, was a perfect example of that. He could have straightened everything out between them with a few questions or even by hurling accusations and listening to explanations. Instead he had leapt to a conclusion and reacted by impetuously fleeing to another state.

He was doing much the same thing now that he had discovered he had a daughter. He wanted to be in her life—completely—right this instant. He wanted to marry Melissa…right this minute. The concepts of moderation or patience had obviously escaped him.

She sighed as he appropriated the shopping cart. The two half gallons of chocolate-fudge ice cream had turned into four. And she didn't like the gleam in his eyes one bit as he turned the cart on two wheels and headed straight for the shelves of diapers.

She'd been right. He was going to take over and she had a sinking feeling in the pit of her stomach that there would be very little she could do about it.

Cody realized he had almost lost it there for a minute at the supermarket. He'd wanted to sweep entire shelves of baby food into the shopping cart.

As it was, in addition to the ice cream, they had left the store with five, giant economy-size packages of disposable diapers, a new toy duck for Sharon Lynn's bath, five storybooks he could read to her at bedtime and an astonishing selection of her favorite juices. Melissa had just rolled her eyes at the startled checkout clerk.

"New father?" the girl had guessed.

"New enough," Melissa had replied.

Let them make fun, Cody thought. He didn't care. This was the first step in his campaign to make himself indispensable to Melissa and his daughter.

"Where to now?" he asked when they'd piled all those diapers and the rest of the shopping bags into the back of his pickup.

"I'm going home to iron," Melissa said, sticking to that absurd story she'd told him earlier in a blatant attempt to get rid of him. "Unless, of course, you'd like to do it for me?"

He frowned at her. "What about Sharon Lynn?"

"She's with Mother."

"I'll drop you off and go get her," he suggested eagerly.

"She's probably still taking her nap," Melissa said.

She said it in such a rush he had the feeling she thought he intended to kidnap the baby and take off with her. As much as he resented the implication, he kept his tone perfectly even. ''She won't sleep forever,'' he countered reasonably. ''I'll bring her straight home. I promise.''

''You don't have a car seat,'' she noted pointedly.

Damn, but there was a lot to remember. ''We'll stop now and get one.''

''All of that ice cream will melt.''

He frowned at the obstacles she kept throwing in his path. ''Not in this weather. It's freezing out. And if it does, I'll buy more.''

''Couldn't you just drop me off at home?''

''No, you need to come with me. You can show me the best kind of car seat.''

Melissa sighed heavily. ''Cody, what's the point? They're expensive and you probably won't...''

He guessed where she was going. ''Won't what? Won't be here long enough to use it? You can get that idea right out of your head.''

He tucked a finger under her chin and forced her to face him. ''I've quit my job in Wyoming. I am home to stay, Melissa. Get used to it.''

She held up her hands. ''Sorry. I didn't mean anything. I was just trying to keep you from wasting money.''

''If it's for my daughter, it is not a waste of money,'' he said curtly. ''Now, can I find the kind of car seat I need at the discount superstore out on the highway?''

She nodded.

He turned the truck around on a dime, spewing gravel. He drove ten miles before his temper had cooled enough to speak again. He'd set out today to woo Melissa into changing her mind about marrying him. His first overtures, however, appeared to have gone awry. He'd lost his sense of humor, right along with his temper. It was no way for the two of them to start over. He sucked in a deep breath and made up his mind to mend fences.

"Truce?" he suggested, glancing over at her. She was huddled against the door, looking miserable. She shrugged.

"I'm not an ogre," he stated. "I'm just trying to fit into Sharon Lynn's life." Her gaze lifted to meet his. "And yours."

She sighed. "We don't need you," she repeated stubbornly. "We were doing just fine before you came back."

He ignored the tide of hurt that washed through him at the dismissive comment. "Maybe I need you."

Melissa frowned. "Yeah, right," she said sarcastically. "As if Cody Adams ever needed anybody. Didn't you pride yourself on staying footloose and fancy free?"

He saw no point in denying something she knew better than anyone. "I did," he agreed. He thought about the agonizing loneliness of that cabin he'd sentenced himself to in Wyoming. "Maybe being alone for the past eighteen months has changed me. Maybe

I'm not the selfish, carefree, independent cuss who stormed away from Texas.''

''And maybe pigs can fly,'' she countered.

He grinned at her. ''Maybe they can,'' he said quietly. ''If you believe in magic.''

''I don't,'' she said succinctly.

Cody heard the terrible pain in her voice, even if her expression remained absolutely stoic. Dear heaven, what had he done to her by running off and leaving her to face being pregnant all alone? He saw now what he hadn't observed before. Not only was Melissa stronger and more self-sufficient, she also had an edge of cynicism and bitterness that hadn't been there before. The blame for that was his, no one else's.

At the discount store, when Melissa would have grabbed the first car seat they came across, Cody stopped her, deliberately taking the time to read the package for every last detail on safety. If nothing else, he intended to impress on Melissa that he took his parenting responsibilities seriously. Nothing was too trivial, too expensive, or too complicated to tackle if it had to do with his daughter.

Nearly an hour later they finally loaded the new car seat into the truck.

''I think that salesclerk despaired of ever getting you to make a choice,'' Melissa said, the beginnings of a smile tugging at her lips.

''It wasn't for her kid,'' he retorted.

''Okay, forget the salesclerk. Should I point out that the one you ended up taking is exactly the same one I tried to get you to buy when we walked in?''

He scowled at her. "What's your point?"

"That I had already done the exact same research, reached the exact same conclusion. You insisted I come along because you claimed to want my advice. When it came right down to it, though, you didn't trust me."

Cody carefully considered the accusation before turning to meet her gaze. "You're right. I should have listened to you. It's just that this is new to me. I'm trying to get it right. I don't want to mess up with something this important."

Her expression softened. "Cody, I can understand that. Really, I can. I was just as obsessive when I first brought Sharon Lynn home from the hospital. Mother and Daddy thought I was a lunatic. I didn't trust a piece of advice they offered. I was convinced it was probably outdated. I had to do it all for myself. Talk about reinventing the wheel." She shook her head. "I wasted more time, only to find myself doing exactly what they'd suggested in the first place."

He grinned. "You're just trying to save me traveling over the same learning curve, is that it?"

"Exactly," she said. She reached over and patted his hand. "I'm not trying to keep you out of Sharon Lynn's life, or control your input, or anything like that. I promise."

The impulsive touch didn't last nearly long enough. Cody grabbed her hand and pulled it to his lips. He brushed a kiss across her knuckles and saw the instantaneous spark of desire in her eyes. "I'll try to watch the defensiveness, if you'll do something for me.''

She regarded him with conditioned wariness. ''What?''

''Bring Sharon Lynn out to White Pines this weekend,'' he coaxed persuasively. At the flare of panic in her eyes, he pulled out his strongest ammunition—her fondness for Harlan. ''I think seeing her would do Daddy a world of good. With Mother gone, he needs something positive in his life, something to cheer him up. You should have seen the look in his eyes this morning when I told him she was mine.''

The hint of wariness in her eyes fled and was promptly replaced by astonishment. ''You told him?''

''I did. But it wasn't news. He'd figured it out the first time he saw her, the same as Jordan had.''

Her mouth gaped. ''And he didn't do anything about it? I'm amazed he didn't haul your butt straight back here or offer to set up a trust fund for the baby or something.''

''Frankly, so am I. Maybe he's learned his lesson about manipulating.''

Melissa's expression was every bit as skeptical as his own had to be. ''Okay,'' he said. ''He probably has a scheme we don't know about yet. Even so, are you willing to take a chance? Will you bring her out? It's time she learned something about her father's side of the family.''

He was playing to her sense of fairness and it was clearly working. He could practically read her struggle with her conscience on her face.

"I'll bring her," Melissa finally agreed with obvious reluctance. "On one condition—no tricks."

Cody regarded her innocently. Now that he'd gotten her basic agreement, he could go along with almost anything she demanded. "What kind of tricks?"

"No preachers lurking in the shadows. No wedding license all signed and ready to be filled in."

He feigned astonishment, even though he thought she might actually have a very good idea, one that hadn't even occurred to him until just that minute. "Would I do that?"

"In a heartbeat," she said. "And even if you had an attack of conscience, Harlan wouldn't. No conspiracies, okay?"

"Cross my heart," Cody said, already wondering if there was some way to pull off such a wedding.

Melissa's gaze narrowed. "Why doesn't that reassure me?"

"And you accused me of a lack of trust," he chided.

"I'm not the one whose brother threw a surprise wedding in place of a rehearsal," she said, reminding him of the sneaky trick Jordan and Kelly had pulled on his parents to avoid the out-of-control celebration his mother had planned for their wedding. The whole town had gossiped about that little stunt for weeks.

"I'm glad you mentioned that," Cody taunted. "It does give me some interesting ideas."

"Cody Adams, I am warning you..."

"No need, sweet pea. I'm not fool enough to take a chance on getting rejected in front of my family and the preacher. When you and I get married, it'll be because you're willing and eager.''

'''When,' not 'if'?'' she chided.

''That's right, darlin'. Only the timing is left to be decided,'' he declared with far more confidence than he felt. He unloaded the last of their packages under Melissa's irritated scrutiny. Apparently, though, his certainty about their future had left her speechless. He considered that a hopeful sign.

''See you on Saturday,'' he said, escaping before he had a chance to put his foot in his mouth. ''Come on out about eight. You can have breakfast with us.''

Besides, he thought, if Melissa was there by eight, that gave him most of the day to convince her to have a wedding at sunset.

Melissa debated bailing out on her day at White Pines. Handling Cody was tricky enough without having to worry about Harlan's sneaky tactics at the same time. Still, she couldn't very well deny Harlan the chance to get to know the granddaughter he'd just officially discovered he had.

That was what ultimately decided her, or so she told herself as she dressed Sharon Lynn in bright blue corduroy pants, a blue and yellow shirt, and tiny sneakers. She brushed her hair into a halo of soft curls around her face.

''Ma? Bye-bye?''

Proud of Sharon Lynn's expanding vocabulary, she nodded. ''That's right, my darling. We're going to see your daddy and your granddaddy.''

Sharon Lynn's face lit up. She reached for the new toy duck that was never far from sight. "Da?"

Melissa shook her head at the instant reaction. Obviously Cody had had an incredible impact on his daughter in just one visit. Did he have that effect on all women or just those in her family? She tickled Sharon Lynn until she dissolved into a fit of giggles.

"Yes, Da," she told her approvingly. "We're going to see Da." And she, for one, was nervous as the dickens about it. Sharon Lynn clearly had no such qualms.

When Melissa pulled her car to a stop in front of the house at White Pines, she drew in a deep, reassuring breath, trying to calm her jitters. It was going to be just fine, she told herself, even as she fought the overwhelming sense of déjà vu that assailed her.

How many times had she driven out here, filled with hope, anxious to spend time with the man she loved, only to leave bitterly disappointed by his refusal to commit to anything more than a carefree relationship? Everything had always seemed more intense out here, the air crisper and cleaner, the terrain more rugged, the colors brighter. Similarly, her emotions had always seemed sharper, too—the bitter sorrow as well as the blinding joy.

Once she had dreamed of this being her home, the place where she and Cody would raise a family. Now with the snap of her fingers and a couple of "I do's," her dream could come true. But Cody's proposal, forced only by the existence of a child for whom he felt responsible, had tarnished the dream. She doubted it could ever recapture its original, innocent glow.

"Da, Da, Da!" Sharon Lynn screamed excitedly, bouncing in her car seat as Cody strode across the front lawn. He was wearing snug, faded jeans, a T-shirt that hugged his broad chest and worn cowboy boots. He looked sexier and more masculine than any male model ever had in *GQ*.

Before Melissa could fight her instinctive reaction just to the sight of him, he had thrown open the door and lifted his daughter high in the air, earning squeals of delight for his effort.

"Hey, pumpkin, I could hear you all the way inside the house," he teased the baby. "Your grandpa Harlan said you were loud enough to wake half the county. He's thinking of getting you geared up for the hog-calling contest at the state fair. What do you think?"

Melissa noted he reported his father's reaction with unmistakable pride. He glanced her way just then and the humor in his eyes darkened to something else, something she recognized from times past as powerful, compelling desire. Whatever was behind his proposal of marriage, the one thing she couldn't doubt was Cody's passion. He wanted her and he was doing nothing to hide that fact from her.

"Thank you for coming," he said, his expression solemn.

"I told you I would."

He shrugged. "You never know, though. Sometimes things come up."

Suddenly, for the first time Melissa was able to pinpoint the most devastating problem between them. Neither of them had so much as a shred of trust left for the other.

She didn't trust Cody not to leave again. She didn't trust him not to rip her daughter away from her.

And worse, to her way of thinking because she knew he had a right to feel as he did, he didn't trust her to keep her promises. She had kept the secret of his daughter from him. He had to wonder if he could trust her to be honest with him about anything.

All at once she was unbearably sad. Regrets for the open, honest relationship they had once shared tumbled through her, leaving her shaken.

Before she realized he'd even moved, Cody was beside her, Sharon Lynn in his arms.

"Are you okay?" he asked, his expression filled with concern.

"Of course. Why would you think I wasn't?"

"Maybe it has something to do with the tears."

She hadn't even realized she was crying. She brushed impatiently at the telltale traces. "Sorry."

"You don't have to apologize, for heaven's sake. Just tell me what's wrong."

"An attack of nostalgia," she said, knowing it was only partially true. "Nothing to worry about." She plastered a smile on her face. "Come on. Let's go inside before Harlan falls out of that window he's peeking through."

Almost as if he'd heard the comment, the curtains fell back into place and a shadow moved away from the downstairs window. Cody grinned at her.

"He can't wait to meet Sharon Lynn. If you think I'm bad, wait until you see the room he's fixed up for her visits."

The implications of the lighthearted remark sent panic racing through Melissa. If Harlan had fixed up a room, then he clearly intended for Sharon Lynn to be at White Pines a lot. Was this visit just a prelude to the custody battle her mother had warned her about? Cody might not be willing to fight her in court, but Harlan was another matter. With Mary dead and his life stretching out emptily in front of him, who could tell what kind of crazy notion he might get into his head.

Apparently her fears must have been written on her face, because Cody halted again. "Melissa, you don't have to worry," he reassured her. "It's just a room. You know Harlan. Everything drives him to excess."

"You're sure that's all it is?"

"Very sure. You don't have anything to worry about from Harlan." That said, he winked at her. "I, however, am another matter entirely. I've given up on winning you with diapers and juice and toys."

"Oh?"

"I intend to win you with my sexy, wicked ways."

He was up the front steps and in the house before she had a chance to react. When she could finally move again, her legs wobbled and her pulse was scampering crazily.

Suddenly any threat Harlan might pose dimmed in importance. Cody was the one she needed to worry about. Always had been. Always would be.

Chapter Nine

At the precise instant that Cody and Melissa entered the front door at White Pines, Harlan stepped into the foyer. His prompt presence indicated that he had indeed been watching for Melissa's arrival and was eager for an introduction to his granddaughter.

Cody studied his father's face closely as Harlan's gaze honed in immediately on Sharon Lynn. For the first time since the funeral, there was a spark of animation in his dark eyes. And when he glanced at Melissa that animation included her, only to be quickly replaced by questions, unanswerable questions Cody hoped he wouldn't get into right off.

To stave them off, Cody crossed the wide sweep of wood floor and woven Mexican rug to stand in front of his father, Sharon Lynn still perched in his arms.

"Daddy, meet your granddaughter, Sharon Lynn."

The baby responded to the cue as if she'd been coached. A dimpled smile spread across her face as she held out her arms to be transferred to her new grandfather's embrace. Harlan accepted her with alacrity.

"You are a mighty fine young lady," he told her, his expression sober, his eyes unmistakably welling up with rare tears. "I'm very glad to be welcoming you to the family." His gaze shifted then to encompass Melissa once more. "It's good to see you again, girl. We've missed you around here."

Cody saw the sheen of tears spring to Melissa's eyes and realized more than ever what he had cost them all by running off as he had. His parents had always accepted that Melissa would one day be his wife. They had approved of her spirit, her kindness and her unconditional love for him. Melissa had been present on most family occasions, welcomed as if their relationship had been sealed.

Though he'd never asked his parents if they had continued to see her, he had suspected Melissa wouldn't feel that same sense of belonging after he'd gone. He knew from his father's comment just now that she had indeed stayed away and that her absence had hurt them all, costing them a relationship they held dear. The severing of ties had been as complete as if he and Melissa had been married and then divorced in an incredibly acrimonious manner that had forced everyone to choose sides.

"Thank you, Harlan," she said, stepping closer to

be enveloped in a fierce hug that included Sharon Lynn. ‘‘I’ve missed you, too. And I’m so terribly, terribly sorry about Mary.’’

‘‘I know you are. Mary thought a lot of you, girl. She always hoped…’’ At a warning glance from Cody, he allowed his voice to trail off, the thought left unspoken.

It hardly mattered, though. The damage had already been done. Melissa’s cheeks turned bright pink. Cody could feel the blood climbing up the back of his neck, as well. His father surveyed them both, then gave a brief nod of satisfaction as if he’d learned something he’d hoped for.

‘‘Come on, then,’’ Harlan said, his voice laced with a telltale trace of huskiness. ‘‘Let’s go have some breakfast, before we all turn maudlin and start bawling.’’

To Cody’s relief, his father left the subject of the past untouched beyond that single, oblique reference. Either he was far too fascinated by the child he held or he recognized that it was not a conversation to be held in the baby’s presence.

There was no mistaking, though, that more questions lingered in his eyes. Cody guessed they would be as much about the future as the past. He also knew there were no answers his father would like hearing, not yet anyway. Harlan had the same impatience as his sons. He liked things settled to his satisfaction. Between Cody and Melissa nothing was settled at all.

Sharon Lynn patted her grandfather’s face, then

glanced to her mother for approval. ''Da?'' she questioned.

Cody scowled as he realized that he wasn't unique in his daughter's view. He caught Melissa's grin and realized how pitiful it was to be jealous of his own father.

Unaware, as Cody had been, that it was Sharon Lynn's universal name for any adult male, Harlan beamed at her. ''Damn, but you're a smart one,'' he praised. ''You and I need to have ourselves a little talk. What other words do you know?''

''Ma and bye-bye,'' Melissa offered. ''It limits the conversations tremendously.''

Cody noticed that his father didn't seem to mind. He seemed perfectly content to carry on a one-sided conversation with his granddaughter. It was probably the first time in years someone hadn't talked back to him.

The distraction also kept Harlan from touching the eggs and bacon he normally couldn't wait to eat on the weekends. Possibly that was the most telling indication of all of Sharon Lynn's power over this new male in her life.

''So, Sharon Lynn, have you ever seen a horse?'' Harlan inquired.

Cody chuckled as his daughter tilted her head, a quizzical expression on her face as she appeared to give the question serious consideration.

''I'll take that for a no,'' Harlan said. ''In that case, I think it's about time to fix that. Can't have a rancher's baby who doesn't know about horses. Maybe we'll even go for a little ride."

Cody glanced at Melissa to check her reaction to the instantaneous bonding between Sharon Lynn and his father. To his astonishment, the color had drained out of her face. Clearly the idea of Sharon Lynn going off with Harlan panicked her in some way. What he couldn't figure was why.

"Harlan, I really don't think—" she began.

"Don't worry about a thing," Harlan reassured her, cutting off her words. "I had every one of my boys up on horseback when they were no bigger than this. She'll fit right on the saddle in front of me. She'll be just fine. I guarantee I won't let her tumble off."

Harlan and the baby were out the door before Melissa could offer the firmer protest that was clearly on the tip of her tongue. Cody knew better than to argue with Harlan. He also knew that Sharon Lynn would be perfectly safe with his father. However, he could see that Melissa wouldn't believe it unless she witnessed their adventure on horseback with her own eyes. He put down his fork.

"Come on," he said. "You'll be worrying yourself sick, if you're not right alongside them."

"She's too little to be riding a horse," Melissa complained, her complexion still pale as she followed him outside. "She'll be terrified."

"I doubt that," Cody said. "You're projecting your feelings onto her. You never were much for horses. I guess you were more of a city girl than I realized."

She shot him a wry look. "Hardly that."

He grinned at her. "I don't know. About the only time I could get you into the barn was when I wanted to tumble you into the haystack."

"Cody Adams, that is not true," she contradicted, patches of bright color flaring in her cheeks. "Besides, that has absolutely nothing to do with Sharon Lynn and this crazy idea Harlan has of getting onto a horse with her."

"Stop fussing. She's just the right age to be introduced to riding. Kids her age have no fear. It's not like Daddy's going to put her on the horse, hit its rump and send her galloping around the paddock. He's going to be in the saddle, holding her."

"I suppose," Melissa said, but her gaze immediately sought out some sign of Sharon Lynn the minute the barn came into view.

The little cutie was hard to miss. She was squealing with delight from her perch atop the fence around the paddock. Misty, the oldest, smallest and gentlest of their mares, had come to investigate. Sharon Lynn's eyes were wide with excitement as she patted the white blaze on Misty's head.

"This is Misty," Harlan was explaining quietly, his grip firm on the horse's bridle. "Can you say that? Misty."

"Mi'ty," Sharon Lynn dutifully repeated, surprising all of them.

The horse neighed softly at hearing her name.

Cody glanced at Melissa and saw that she'd finally begun to relax. Her gaze was riveted on her daughter, though. He sensed that if Misty so much as shied back a step, Melissa was poised to snatch Sharon Lynn out of harm's way.

Just when he thought the worst of her reaction was past, she turned and looked up at him, anxiety and dismay clearly written all over her face. ''How can your father even think about getting on a horse ever again?'' she asked in a low voice, not meant to carry.

As if he'd been struck by a bolt of lightning, Cody finally realized why Melissa had been so upset by Harlan introducing Sharon Lynn to riding. The accident that had cost his mother her life hadn't even crossed his mind when Harlan had suggested bringing Sharon Lynn out to see the horses. But obviously the way Mary Adams had died had left an indelible image on Melissa's mind, as it might on anyone who didn't have the sensitivity of a slug, Cody chided himself. She had been fearful of horses to begin with. His mother's death could only have exaggerated that fear.

''Damn, no wonder you turned white as a sheet a minute ago when Daddy suggested bringing Sharon Lynn out here,'' he apologized. ''You were thinking about what happened to Mother, weren't you?''

''Aren't you?'' she asked, staring at him incredulously.

''No,'' he said honestly. ''There's no point in blaming the horse for what happened to Mother. It was an accident and not an uncommon one at that. The horse was spooked by a snake. Even then, the fall might not have killed her. It was the way she landed.''

Melissa shuddered. ''Still, how can either one of

you not think about it every single time you see a horse?''

''Because Daddy is a rancher, through and through. So am I,'' Cody said, trying to explain to Melissa what must seem inexplicable. ''There are some things over which a rancher has no control. Rattlers spooking a horse is one of them.''

He glanced at his father. ''If he blames anyone or anything for what happened to Mother, it's more than likely himself for suggesting that ride in the first place. He also knows that the only way to conquer the fear after what happened is to get right back on a horse. He's been out riding over that same stretch of land every single day since she died.''

Melissa clearly wasn't reassured. ''I don't care about conquering fear. All I see is that your mother's death should be a damn good reason for him not to bring his granddaughter anywhere near a horse,'' she argued. ''She's a baby, Cody.''

Cody was beginning to see there was no reasoning with her on this. It was too soon after his mother's tragic accident. ''If it's really upsetting you, I'll talk him out of it,'' he offered. ''But sooner or later, Sharon Lynn will ride. She can't have a cowboy for a daddy and not learn.''

Melissa rested her hand on his forearm. The expression on her face pleaded with him.

''Later, please,'' she said. ''Just the thought of it after what happened to your mom makes me sick.''

Cody could see that she wasn't exaggerating. Though he didn't agree with her, he could feel some compassion for the anxiety she was experiencing. He walked over and spoke to his father. Harlan shot a look over his shoulder at Melissa and gave an understanding nod.

"Of course," he apologized at once. "I didn't realize it would bother her so."

"Neither did I," Cody said. "But she's practically turning green."

"You take this little angel on inside, then. I'll be there in a bit."

Cody reached for his daughter, who let out a scream the instant she realized she was being taken away from the horse.

"Mi'ty!" she sobbed plaintively. "Mi'ty!"

"You'll see Misty another time," Cody promised. "Right now, I'm going to take you inside so you can see all of your new toys that Granddaddy bought you."

He wasn't sure if Sharon Lynn totally understood exactly what having Harlan Adams as a benefactor was all about until they reached the room he'd filled with everything from a set of white baby furniture with pink gingham sheets and comforter to every stuffed toy he'd been able to order straight from the biggest department store in Dallas. Even Cody had been bowled over by the assortment he'd assembled practically overnight. Melissa's mouth was agape as she surveyed the room.

"Did he buy out the store?" Melissa asked.

Before Cody could respond, Sharon Lynn was trying to scramble down, her gaze fixed on the rocking horse.

"Mi'ty, Mi'ty," she called joyously as she dropped from unsteady legs to her knees to crawl toward it. She pulled herself up beside it and tried to climb on. Cody lifted her up and settled her on the seat, keeping a firm grip on the waistband of her pants as she rocked enthusiastically.

He grinned at Melissa. "Told you she was going to be a natural on horseback."

"I think this one is a little more her size," Melissa retorted dryly. "The distance to the ground isn't quite so far."

Before he could comment on that, something else caught Sharon Lynn's eye and she twisted around and tried to clamber down. Cody lifted her off the rocking horse and set her back on her feet.

"How about you walk wherever you want to go this time?" he suggested.

Sharon Lynn clamped her fingers around his, wobbled precariously, then took an unsteady tiptoe step forward. With each step her confidence obviously mounted, though she kept that tight grip on his fingers.

"She's going to ruin your back," Melissa observed. "You're bent practically double."

Cody didn't give a hoot. This was the first time he'd witnessed his daughter's faltering, tentative footsteps. He'd bend over the rest of the afternoon and ache for a week, if she wanted to keep walking. With every minute he spent with her, every experience they shared, the powerful sense of connection he felt with her intensified.

Just then she stumbled and fell. Her eyes promptly filled with tears. Certain that she must have broken something to be sobbing so pathetically, Cody knelt beside her and gently examined ankles, arms, knees and elbows. He even checked for a bump under her hair or on her forehead, though he knew perfectly well she hadn't hit her head. She'd landed squarely on her well-padded button.

Finally satisfied that she was more scared than hurt, he scooped her up, only to find Melissa grinning at him.

"And you thought I was overreacting. At this rate, you're going to be a wreck in a month," she chided, sounding smug. "Either that or you'll drive the emergency room staff at the hospital completely wild. They'll flee when they spot you coming."

He lifted his eyebrows. "Is this another chunk of that learning curve you're trying to help me skip?" he taunted.

To his amusement, she blushed furiously. "Stop teasing. I only took her in twice," she admitted defensively.

"Oh? When?"

"The first time I thought she'd swallowed the toy from a box of cereal."

Cody shuddered. He would have had her in for X rays himself. "Had she?"

"No, I found it later in the crack between the refrigerator and the sink. I suppose she threw it across the room.''

''And the other time?''

''She fell and bumped her head,'' Melissa said, shivering visibly at the recollection. ''It terrified me. I'd never seen so much blood in my entire life. I was sure she was going to bleed to death before I got her to the hospital.''

Cody's heart skidded to a halt. He anxiously studied Sharon Lynn's face for some sign of such a traumatic injury. He smoothed back her hair to get a better look at her forehead.

''No stitches?'' he asked when he could find no evidence of them.

Melissa shrugged. ''Not a one,'' she confessed. ''They put a butterfly bandage on it and sent us home. Apparently head injuries just bleed profusely. There was no permanent damage done.''

Cody met her gaze and caught the faint signs of chagrin and laughter in her eyes. He also thought he detected something else, perhaps a hint of resentment that she'd been left to cope with such things on her own. Guilt sliced through him, even though part of the blame for his absence could be laid squarely at Melissa's feet.

''I'm sorry I wasn't here for you,'' he said, and meant it. He regretted every lost opportunity to share in the experiences—good or bad—of his daughter's first year.

The laughter in Melissa's eyes died at once. That

hint of resentment burned brighter. ''I handled it,'' she said abruptly, and turned away.

He watched as she walked over and knelt down by their daughter, listening intently to Sharon Lynn's nonsensical jabbering. The hard expression on her face when she'd turned away from him softened perceptibly. A smile tugged at her lips as she cupped her hand possessively behind her daughter's head, caressing the soft curls. Sharon Lynn looked up at her, an expression of adoration on her face.

In that instant Cody saw what it meant to be a family… and he wasn't a part of it. Melissa couldn't have shut him out any more effectively, any more deliberately, if she'd tried.

He stood there, so close and yet very much apart from them. Longing welled up inside him, longing to know all of these little details of Sharon Lynn's first months that Melissa shared so grudgingly.

There was so much more he yearned for, as well. He yearned to share their closeness, to have Melissa look into his eyes with something more than distrust.

He sighed then, because it all seemed so unlikely, so impossible, thanks to his own foolish decision to accept what he'd seen that fateful night at face value. If only he'd stayed. If only…

Wasted regrets, he chided himself. This was his reality—a child who barely knew him, a woman who wanted no part of him, who was willing to allow him glimpses of his child out of a sense of obligation, not love.

He thought then of the flicker of passion he'd

caught once or twice in Melissa's sea green eyes, of the heat that had flared when he'd touched her, and wondered whether her disdain ran as deep as she wanted him to believe.

Reality and circumstances could change, he reassured himself. Sometimes for the worse, of course. Harlan knew all about the dramatic, unexpected, tragic turns life could take. He'd lost a son and his beloved wife when he'd least expected it. Those losses had taught a lesson to all of them.

Harlan had also taught his sons that they could control most aspects of their lives if they set their minds to it and fought for what they wanted. In fact, he'd turned out a dynasty of control freaks, it seemed. Luke had built his own ranch from the ground up, rather than take the share in White Pines that Harlan had wanted him to have. Jordan had fought his father bitterly for a career in the oil industry. Cody had battled for a share of White Pines, and now, it seemed, he had an even more difficult war to wage.

Cody's gaze settled on Melissa and his daughter once again. They were worth fighting for. Harlan had given him years of practice at battling for everything from permission to go to a dance to the right to build his own house on White Pines' land. Apparently it had all been preparation for a moment like this.

His mouth curved into a slow smile. He'd just have to think of Melissa's rejection not as a setback but as a challenge. It was an opportunity to utilize all those lessons Harlan had not-so-subtly instilled in them. He would have to seize the initiative and keep Melissa thoroughly off kilter until she finally woke up and realized that this time he wasn't running.

This time he intended to be the steadying influence in her life and he meant to be there always.

Chapter Ten

The morning had been far too intense, Melissa thought as she finally escaped the house and settled gratefully into a chair on the patio with a tall glass of iced tea. The day had turned unseasonably warm and though she still needed her jacket, it was pleasant to sit outside in the fresh, clean air with the sun on her face while Sharon Lynn napped.

Her emotions were raw. Coming back to White Pines had been far more difficult than she'd anticipated. Part of that was because she felt Mary Adams's death here in a way it hadn't struck her even at the funeral. Some of it had to do with Harlan's warm-hearted welcome and the obvious delight he was taking in getting to know his new granddaughter. Most of it, though, undeniably had to do with Cody.

At White Pines she was on his turf. Like Harlan, he reigned over the operation of this ranch as comfortably as she served burgers at Dolan's. His self-confidence radiated from him in this environment. It always had.

Cody might have been wickedly flirtatious and carefree in his social life, but when it had come to work he'd been mature and driven to prove himself to his father. His early success as a ranch manager had smoothed away any insecurities he might have had living in Harlan Adams's shadow.

Cody's command of this privileged world, combined with seeing how easily Sharon Lynn had been accepted into it as Cody's child, had caused her to rebel. Earlier, as Sharon Lynn had taken a few faltering steps with Cody's help, Melissa had had this awful, selfish feeling that Cody was benefiting from having a daughter without having done anything to deserve it beyond making her pregnant in the first place.

He hadn't coached her through labor. He hadn't walked the floor with Sharon Lynn in the middle of the night. He hadn't fretted and cried trying to figure out a way to calm her, all the while convinced he was a failure at parenting. He hadn't been there to panic over the sight of the blood from that cut she had described to him earlier.

No, he had simply waltzed back into their lives and expected to claim his parental rights by flashing his charming grin and dispensing toys like some cowboy Santa. Well, she wouldn't have it. She wouldn't let it be that easy. He was going to have to earn a right to be a part of his daughter's life…and of hers.

That decided, she was troubled only by the realization that her demands were vague, that even she might not recognize when Cody had paid the dues she expected. Should she have a checklist? A timetable? Or would she finally know somewhere deep inside when she was through punishing him for being absent when she'd needed him the most?

"You okay?" Harlan asked, coming out of the house and studying her worriedly.

"Fine," she said, fighting not to take her annoyance at Cody out on his father.

Harlan was innocent in all of this. She had seen for herself the toll his wife's death had taken on him and she was glad that bringing Sharon Lynn here had given him some pleasure. She was sorry that she had so stubbornly resisted the temptation to announce to all the world long ago that her child was Cody's, just so that Harlan and Mary might have had the chance to know their grandchild from day one. The irony, of course, was that everyone in town had known it anyway.

"If you're so fine, how come you're sitting out here in the cold all by yourself, looking as if you just lost your last friend in the world?" Harlan asked.

"I didn't lose him," she said dryly. "I'm thinking of killing him."

Harlan's blue eyes twinkled at her feisty tone. "Ah, I see. Cody can be a bit infuriating, I suppose."

"There's no supposing about it. He is the most exasperating, egotistical..."

"Talking about me?" the man in question inquired. He spoke in a lazy drawl that sent goose bumps dancing down Melissa's spine despite her resolution to become totally immune to him. Obviously she still needed to work harder on her wayward hormones.

"Which part clued you in?" she inquired. "Exasperating or egotistical?"

Harlan chuckled at the exchange, then promptly clamped his mouth shut in response to a dire scowl from his son. "Sorry," he said insincerely. "You two want to be left alone, or should I stick around to referee?"

"Stay," Melissa encouraged just as Cody said, "Go."

"Thank you, Melissa," Harlan said, winking at her. "I think I'll stay. The show promises to be downright fascinating. This time of day, good entertainment's hard to come by. Nothing but cartoons on TV."

"Daddy!" Cody warned.

"Yes, son?"

"We don't need you here," Cody insisted rudely.

"Speak for yourself," Melissa shot back.

Cody strolled closer until he was standing practically knee-to-knee with her. He bent down, placed his hands on the arms of the chair and said very, very quietly, "Do you really want him to hear our private, personal, *intimate* conversation?"

The gleam in his eyes was pure dare. Melissa swallowed hard. Surely Cody was just taunting her. She couldn't imagine him saying anything to her that Harlan shouldn't hear. And the truth of it was, she wanted Harlan here as a buffer just to make sure that the conversation stayed on a relatively impersonal track. She didn't trust those slippery hormones of hers. They were liable to kick in when she least expected it.

She shot a defiant look at the man who was scant inches from her face. "Yes," she said emphatically.

Cody appeared startled by the firm response. His lips twitched with apparent amusement.

"Suit yourself, Me...liss...a."

The breath fanning across her cheek was hot and mint-scented. The glint of passion in his eyes sent her pulse skyrocketing. She tried to avoid that penetrating look, but no matter how she averted her gaze she seemed to lock in on hard, lean muscle. Temptation stole her breath.

She saw the precise instant when Cody's expression registered smug satisfaction, and it infuriated her. It galled her that she responded to him, annoyed her even more that he clearly knew it.

She gathered every last ounce of hurt and resentment she'd ever felt toward him to slowly steady her pulse. With careful deliberation she lifted her glass of tea to her lips and took a long, deep swallow. She kept her gaze riveted to his as she drank, determined to show him that this latest tactic no longer had the power to rattle her. He would not win her over with his easy charm.

Yet even as she did, even as uncertainty and then a flash of irritation darkened Cody's eyes, she quaked inside and prayed he would back off before she lost the will for the battle. She was weakening already, her palms damp, her blood flowing like warm honey.

Just when she was sure she could no longer maintain the calm, impervious facade, Cody jerked upright, raked a hand through his hair and backed off.

"Score one for Melissa," Harlan said softly, his voice laced with laughter.

Cody whirled on him. "Daddy, I'm warning you…"

Harlan's dark brows rose. "Oh?"

Cody frowned. "Dammit, how come you two are in cahoots?"

"Not me," his father protested, his expression all innocence except for the sparkle in his eyes that was quintessential Harlan. "I'm just a bystander."

"An unwanted bystander," Cody reminded him.

"Speak for yourself," Melissa retorted once again.

Cody scowled down at the two of them for another minute, then muttered a harsh oath under his breath and stalked off. Only when he was out of sight did Melissa finally allow herself to relax.

"Whew! That was a close one," Harlan said, grinning at her. "Another couple of seconds and the heat out here would have melted steel. Scorched me clear over here. You sure have figured out how to tie that boy in knots."

To her amazement, he sounded approving. "Shouldn't you be on his side?" Melissa inquired.

"I suspect Cody can take care of himself," he observed. "I'm just relieved to see that you can, too."

Melissa met his amused gaze and finally breathed a sigh of relief. She grinned at him. "It's about time, don't you think?"

"Way past time, I'd say," he said, and reached over to pat her hand. "You want some advice from a man who knows Cody just about as well as anyone on earth?"

"I suspect I could use it," she agreed, wondering at the turn of events that had truly put her and Harlan Adams in cahoots, just as Cody had accused. Maybe Harlan's wisdom would be more effective than his wife's advice had been.

"Despite all these centuries that have passed, the caveman instinct hasn't entirely been bred out of us men," Harlan began. "Now I know that's not so politically correct, but it's the truth of it. A man needs to struggle to claim what he wants. It builds up his passion for it, makes him stronger. Call it perversity, but things that come too easily don't mean so much. Don't ever tell 'em I said so, but I made every one of my sons fight me to earn the right to become his own man. They resented me at the time, but in the end they were better for it."

Sorrow flitted across his face as he added, "Except maybe for Erik. He wanted to please too badly. I made a serious miscalculation by forcing him to work in ranching, one I'll regret to my dying day."

Listening to his philosophy about men, Melissa wondered if Mary Adams had put up much of a struggle. Her adoration of Harlan, her catering to his every whim, had been obvious to anyone who knew the two of them. Given Mary's advice to her about making Cody jealous, Melissa suspected she had given her husband fits at one time.

"Did Mary make you jump through hoops?" she asked.

"She did, indeed," Harlan told her, chuckling even as his expression turned nostalgic. "I knew the first minute I laid eyes on her that she was the woman I wanted to marry. She was smart as the dickens, beautiful and willful. She claimed later that she fell in love at first sight, too. She didn't let me know it for a good six months, though. In fact, for a while there I was convinced she couldn't stand to be in my presence. It was a hell of a blow to my ego."

He shook his head. "My goodness, the things I used to do just to earn a smile. That smile of hers was worth it, though. It was like sunshine, radiating warmth on everyone it touched. For thirty-six years, I was blessed with it."

"You're missing her terribly, aren't you?" Melissa said softly.

"It's as if I lost a part of myself," Harlan admitted, then seemed taken aback that he'd revealed so much. He drew himself up, clearly uncomfortable with the out-of-character confidences. "Enough of that now. You didn't come all the way out here to listen to me go on and on."

"May I ask you a question?" Melissa asked impulsively.

"Of course you can. Ask me anything."

"Did you know Cody had asked me to marry him?"

"He told me."

"Did he also tell you I'd turned him down?"

Harlan nodded.

She looked over at this man who had always been so kind to her, who'd treated her as a daughter long before she had any ties to his family beyond her hope of a future with his son. Did she dare ask him what she really wanted to know, whether Cody loved her for herself or only as the mother of the daughter he was so clearly anxious to claim? She hedged her bets and asked a less direct question.

"Was I wrong to say no?"

Harlan regarded her perceptively. "Are you afraid he won't ask again?"

She drew in a deep breath, then finally nodded, acknowledging a truth that was far from comforting.

"What would you say if he does?"

"Right now?"

"Right now," he concurred.

She thought it over carefully. Given the unresolved nature of their feelings, she would have to give him the same answer. "I'd tell him no," she admitted.

"Then there's your answer," he reassured her. "Look, I don't claim to know what happened between you and Cody that made him run off to Wyoming, but it's plain as day to me that it wasn't a simple misunderstanding. You keeping that baby a secret from him proves that. Feelings that complicated take time to sort out. Take as long as you want, just don't shut him out of your life in the meantime. Silence and distance aren't the way to patch things up.''

Harlan's warning was still echoing in her head when she finally went in search of Cody. He was right, the lines of communication did need to remain open, for Sharon Lynn's sake, if not her own.

She suspected Cody was either in the barn or had taken off for his own place nearby. His father had promised to look in on Sharon Lynn and to entertain her if she awakened from her nap.

When she didn't find Cody in the barn, she set off across a field to the small house Cody had built for himself in defiance of his father's order that he should strike out on his own and work some other ranch, maybe even start his own as Luke had. Every board Cody had hammered into place, every shingle he had laid on the roof had been a declaration that he intended to stay and claim his share of White Pines.

Melissa had watched him night after night, at the end of long, backbreaking days running the ranch. She had helped when she could, bringing him picnic baskets filled with his favorite foods on the evenings when he'd skipped supper to keep on working until the last hint of daylight faded.

She had observed his progress with her heart in her throat, waiting for him to ask her opinion on the size, the style, the color of paint, anything at all to suggest he intended it to be their home and not just his own. Though he had seemed to welcome her presence and her support, those words had never come.

Even so, she had been there with him when the last

detail was completed, when the last brushstroke of paint had covered the walls. Though she had only spent a few incredible, unforgettable nights under that roof, she had always felt as if this was home. It was the place Sharon Lynn had been conceived.

As she neared the low, rambling white structure with its neat, bright blue trim, she thought she heard the once-familiar sound of hammering. She circled the house until she spotted Cody in the back, erecting what appeared to be a huge extension off what she knew to be the single bedroom.

The sight of that addition didn't snag her attention, however, quite the way that Cody did. He had stripped off his shirt, despite the chill in the air. His shoulders were bare and turning golden brown in the sun. A sheen of perspiration made his muscles glisten as they were strained and tested by his exertion.

Sweet heaven, she thought, swallowing hard. He was gorgeous, even more spectacularly developed than he had been the last time she'd seen him half-naked.

''Cody,'' she whispered, her voice suddenly thready with longing.

She heard the loud *thwack* of the hammer against wood and something softer, followed by an oath that would have blistered a sailor's ears. The ladder he was on tilted precariously, but he managed to right it and climb down without further mishap.

His gaze riveted on her, he muttered, ''Damn, Melissa, don't you know better than to sneak up on a man when he's halfway up a ladder?''

She knew his testiness had more to do with his injured thumb than her unexpected presence. She grinned at him. ‘‘I’ve been in plain view for the last half mile. You would have seen me if you were the least bit observant.’’

‘‘I’m concentrating on what I’m doing, not scanning the horizon for visitors.’’

‘‘Just what is it you’re doing?’’

‘‘Adding on.’’

She gave him a wry look. ‘‘That much is plain. *What* are you adding on?’’

‘‘A room for my daughter.’’

Surprise rippled through her. ‘‘Isn’t that room Harlan’s prepared good enough?’’

‘‘I want her to have her own room in my home,’’ he insisted, giving her a belligerent look that dared her to argue.

‘‘Seems like a lot of work for an occasional visit.’’

He climbed down from the ladder and leaned back against it, his boot heel hooked over the bottom rung behind him. His chin jutted up belligerently. It should have warned her what was coming, but it didn’t.

‘‘We’re not talking an occasional visit, Melissa,’’ he declared bluntly. ‘‘I expect to have her here a lot. You’ve had her for more than a year. I’m expecting equal time.’’

A year, here with Cody? Away from her? A sudden weakness washed through her. ‘‘You can’t be serious,’’ she whispered, thinking of the warning her mother had given her at the outset. Had Velma been right, after all? Would Cody bring all of the Adams influence to bear to get custody of his child?

"Dead serious," he confirmed, his unblinking gaze leveled on her.

This was a new and dangerous twist to Cody's driven nature. Clearly he intended to go after his daughter with the same singleminded determination he'd devoted to securing his place at White Pines.

"Cody, she's not a possession," she said in a tone that barely concealed her sudden desperation. "She's a little girl."

"A little girl who ought to get to know her daddy."

"I've told you—I've *promised* you—that we can work that out. I don't want to prevent you from spending time with her, from getting to know her, but to bring her to a strange house, to expect her to live with a virtual stranger...I won't allow it, Cody. I can't."

"You may not have a choice," he said coldly. "I don't want to get lawyers involved in this, but I will if I have to."

Melissa had no trouble imagining who would win in a court fight. As good a mother as she'd been, Cody and his family had the power to beat her. "There has to be another way," she said.

He nodded. "There is."

"What? I'll do anything."

His mouth curved into a mockery of a smile. "You make it sound so dire. The alternative isn't that awful. You just have to marry me."

The conversation she'd just had with Harlan echoed in her head. She couldn't marry Cody, not under these circumstances, especially not with him trying to blackmail her into it. What kind of a chance would their marriage have if she did? None. None at all.

She forced herself not to react with the anger or counterthreats that were on the tip of her tongue. Reason and humor would be more successful against the absurdity of what he was suggesting.

"Cody, half of the women in Texas would marry you in a heartbeat if you're anxious to have a wife," she said, refusing to consider the terrible consequences to her emotions if he took her up on what she was suggesting. "Why try to blackmail me into it?"

"Because you're the one who's the mother of my child," he said simply.

"But that's all I am to you," she replied, fighting tears. "It's not enough to make a marriage. At the first sign of trouble, what's to prevent you from bolting again, just like you did when you saw me with Brian? You don't trust me. You don't want me."

"Oh, I wouldn't say that," he said, straightening and walking slowly toward her with a look that flat-out contradicted her claim.

Melissa held her ground. If she backed down now, if she showed him any hint of weakness, he would win. The prize was more than her pride, more than her body. The prize they were warring over was her daughter.

Cody's advance was slow and deliberate. His eyes, dark as coal in the shadow of the house, seemed to sear her with their intensity. His lips formed a straight, tight line. Anger and frustration radiated from every masculine pore.

When he neared to within a few scant inches, the heat from his body enveloped her, tugging at her like a powerful magnet. And still she held her ground.

"I want you, Me...liss...a," he said quietly. "Make no doubt about that."

She shivered under his slow, leisurely, pointed inspection. Her skin sizzled under that hot gaze. The peaks of her breasts hardened. Moisture gathered between her thighs. Her entire body responded as if he'd stroked and caressed every inch of her. She ached to feel his fingers where his gaze had been. And still, unbelievably, she held her ground.

Her breath snagged, then raced. Her pulse skittered crazily. She longed for someplace to sit or lean, anything to keep her weak knees from giving away her shakiness.

"Tempted, Me...liss...a?"

"No," she squeaked, hating herself for not making the response firmer, more emphatic.

"Remember how it felt to have me inside you?" he taunted, hands jammed into his pockets, deliberately stretching faded denim over the unmistakable ridge of his arousal.

Her gaze locked on that evidence of his desire. A matching hunger rocketed through her. She swallowed hard, clenching her fists so tightly she was certain she must be drawing blood. But still she held her ground.

"In there, on that big, old, feather mattress," he

reminded her silkily. "Our legs all tangled, our bodies slick with sweat. Remember, Me . . . liss...a?"

Oh, sweet heaven, she thought, desperately trying to replace his images with other, safer memories of her own. Memories of being alone and scared, when she realized she was pregnant. Memories of staring at a phone that never rang as day after day, then month after month ticked by. Thinking of that, she steadied herself and held her ground.

She leveled a look straight into eyes that blazed with passion and said, "It won't work, Cody. We can't resolve this in bed."

He reached out then, skimmed his knuckles lightly along her cheek and watched her shiver at the touch. "You sure about that, darlin'?"

She wasn't sure about anything anymore except the tide of desire she was battling with every last shred of her resistance. Her breathlessness kept her silent, afraid that anything she said or the whispered huskiness of her voice would give her away.

His fingers traced a delicate, erotic path along her neck, circling her nape, pulling her closer and closer still until their lips were a scant hairsbreadth apart, their breath mingling along with their scents; hers, wildflower fresh, his, raw and purely masculine.

The touch of his mouth against hers, gentle as a breeze, commanding as the pull of the tides, sealed her fate. The ground she'd held so staunchly gave way as she swayed into the temptation of that kiss.

Cody gave a sigh that she interpreted as part relief,

part satisfaction. He coaxed her lips apart, touched his tongue to hers in a provocative duet.

Melissa bowed to the inevitable then. She had no power or will to resist this lure. She gave herself up to the sweet, wild sensations that had always been her downfall with Cody. He knew every inch of her, knew how to persuade and cajole, how to tempt and tease until her body was his as it had always been.

Her heart, she prayed, she could protect a little longer.

Chapter Eleven

The dare was backfiring. Cody knew it the instant he saw Melissa sprawled across his bed, her long auburn hair tangled on his pillow, her skin like smoothest satin, her coral-tipped breasts beckoning to him.

Until this moment it had only been distant memories that tormented him, fueling steamy dreams and restless nights. Now she was here and this throbbing hunger he felt for her was real. Powerful sensations he'd been telling himself that absence—and abstinence—had exaggerated were reawakened now with passionate urgency.

There might still have been a split second when he could have reclaimed sanity and reason, but if there was, he let it pass. His need for her was too great. His conviction that making love to her once again would bind her to him forever was too compelling.

The soft, winter sunlight spilled through a skylight above the bed and bathed Melissa in a golden glow. An artist might spend a lifetime searching for anything so beautiful, he thought as he stood looking down at her. An artist might spend an entire career trying to capture that same sensual vision on canvas and fail in the end. Cody certainly had never seen anything to equal the sight. He couldn't tear his gaze away.

Pregnancy had changed her body, gently rounding it, where before it had been all sharp angles and far more delicate curves. He swallowed hard as he absorbed the changes, regretting with every fiber of his being that he'd never seen her belly swollen with his child or her breasts when they were tender and engorged with milk.

He was aware of the instant when embarrassment tinted her skin a seashell pink from head to toe. She grabbed for a corner of the sheet, but before she could cover herself, he caught the edge and tugged it gently from her grasp. He stripped away his own clothes and sank down beside her, his gaze never leaving hers.

His breath eased out of him on a ragged sigh. "You are even more beautiful than I remembered," he said, touching his fingers to the pulse that hammered at the base of her neck, gauging her response. Her skin burned beneath his touch. Her pulse bucked like the most impatient bronco he'd ever ridden.

And her eyes, oh, how they pleaded with him. The delicate sea green shade had darkened with some inner turbulence. There wasn't a doubt in his mind that she wanted him with a desperation as fierce as his own.

He also knew with absolute certainty that she didn't want to desire him at all. Outside just now, she had fought her own passion valiantly, but nature and the inevitability of their mating were against her, just as they had been against him since his return to Texas.

He had always understood that internal war, perhaps even better than she did. Way back, when he'd waged his own battle to resist being hemmed in, when he'd struggled against commitment, his body had betrayed him, hungering for Melissa in a way he should have recognized as proof that they were meant to be. It had never been anywhere near as casual between them as he'd sworn to himself it was.

Now, with this second chance, his gaze intent, he skimmed his fingers over delicate skin, caressing new curves and exploring familiar planes. He scattered kisses in the wake of his touch, until her skin was on fire and her breath was coming in soft gasps and her eyes were the color of a stormy sea.

He wondered if he would ever understand the complex mix of raw, violent emotions she stirred in him. The primitive urge to claim and possess tangled with a more sensitive desire to awaken and give pleasure. He concentrated on the latter, judging the success of each stroke of his fingers, each dark and passionate kiss.

''Cody, please,'' she pleaded, her body arching upward, seeking his, seeking the very possession he held back.

''Not yet,'' he soothed, even as he intensified his touches, tormenting and teasing until he sensed that she was right on the edge of a shattering, consuming climax.

His own body was rigid with tension, his blood pounding hotly through his veins. He held his own satisfaction at bay with a will that was being tested beyond endurance. He had no idea if the torment was meant to incite Melissa or prove something to himself. Perhaps he was hoping for one last, tiny victory in his internal battle to demonstrate that she didn't have the power to captivate him so thoroughly, after all.

But of course, she did. And when her soft cries and his own demanding need could no longer be ignored, he slowly, *slowly* entered her, sinking into that moist, velvet sheath with a sigh of thrilled satisfaction. As the pace of his entry and retreat escalated, they rode each wave of pleasure together until willpower—his and hers—vanished in an explosion that made them one.

Afterward, still floating on the memories of that wild, incredible journey, Cody couldn't help thinking of the implication. Melissa was home at last, where she belonged...and so was he.

''I told you so,'' Cody murmured smugly sometime later, when the room was bathed in the last pink shimmer of a glorious sunset.

''Told me what?'' Melissa asked, her eyes closed, her body tucked against his side.

''That being married to me wouldn't be so awful.''

Her eyes blinked open and she rose up to lean on one elbow. ''This isn't marriage, Cody,'' she reminded him with a scowl. "It's an interlude, one afternoon, nothing more."

He was stunned that she could be so cool, so dismissive, in the aftermath of such all-consuming heat and passion. "Are you saying that this meant nothing to you?"

"I'm saying it's not enough to make a marriage," she countered stubbornly. "Cody, if sex were all that mattered, you would never have left for Wyoming and we'd have been married long ago."

His temper snapped at that. "I would never have left for Wyoming if you hadn't deliberately tried to make me think you were becoming involved with my best friend," he shouted, flinging her responsibility for his leaving back in her face.

Even as he hurled the accusation, he climbed from the bed and yanked on his jeans. He stalked out of the bedroom, not sure where he was headed until he found himself outside on the deck, standing at the rail gazing over the land he loved. Not even such natural beauty had the power to soothe him now, though. Fury made his insides churn.

The quick escalation of the argument forced him to admit that Melissa was right about one thing: making love hadn't solved anything. If anything, it had complicated matters, because now they both knew that the explosive chemistry between them was as volatile as ever. It was going to be harder than ever to work things out with reason and logic, when the temptation was going to be to fall into bed.

He sensed Melissa's presence before he felt her slip

up to the rail beside him. He glanced down and felt the sharp tug of desire flare to life all over again, proving the very point he'd just made to himself.

She had pulled on one of his shirts, which fell to midthigh, leaving her long, slender legs revealed. She'd cuffed the sleeves halfway up her arms. The sun turned her tousled hair to strands of fire. She looked part innocent waif, part sexy siren.

"It should never have happened," she said, meeting his gaze, her expression troubled.

"I don't—I *won't*—regret it." He studied her intently. "You do, though, don't you?"

"Only because it complicates everything," she said, echoing his own thoughts. "I want so badly to think clearly about all of this, to make the right choices this time. When you touch me, my brain goes on the blink. I'm all sensation and emotion and nostalgia."

"Stay here with me tonight," Cody blurted impulsively, suddenly wanting to seize the opportunity to force a resolution to their standoff. "Sharon Lynn will be fine with Daddy. Maritza will be there to help him look after her."

A wistful smile played around her mouth. "Haven't you heard a word I was saying?"

"All of them. I was just thinking, though, that we're both stubborn, strong people. Surely we could sit down and discuss all of this rationally and reach a sensible conclusion."

"Here?" she said doubtfully. "Within a few feet

of that bed in there? Within a few feet of each other, for that matter?''

She was shaking her head before the last words were out of her mouth. ''Forget it, Cody. It would never work. Besides, this isn't something we can resolve in a few hours or even a few days.''

He sighed heavily. ''So what do we do?''

''We give it time.'' Her expression turned rueful. ''Preferably in very public places.''

Cody wasn't wild about her solution. Now that he'd made up his mind to make the commitment he should have made two years earlier, Melissa's insistence on a delay was exasperating. He also feared that a decision reached on cold logic alone might not work in his favor. He wanted the heat of their passion on his side.

Of course, he reminded himself, their chemistry didn't necessarily confine itself to suitable locations. It could flare up just about anywhere, anytime, with the right look, the right caress. And there was something to be said for deliberately, provocatively stirring it up, when fulfillment was absolutely out of the question.

Yes, indeed, he decided with a renewed sense of anticipation, he could make things between himself and Melissa hotter than a day in the sweltering Texas sun. He could make it his business to drive her wild.

The plan had only one drawback that he could think of—it was very likely to drive him to distraction at the same time.

''Okay, you win,'' he said eventually, pleased when

he noted the faint hint of disappointment in her eyes. A less diplomatic man might have reminded her to be careful what she wished for. Getting her way obviously wasn't quite as satisfying as she'd expected.

"Let's get dressed and see what's happening up at the main house," he said, deliberately making it sound as if they'd just shared something no more personal than a handshake. "Sharon Lynn's probably awake by now. You shower first. I'll clean up the tools I left outside."

Melissa nodded at the bland suggestion and turned toward the house with unmistakable reluctance. Cody grinned at the dejected slope of her shoulders.

"Hey, Melissa," he called softly.

She glanced back at him over her shoulder, her expression uncertain.

"I'll be thinking about you in that shower," he taunted. "All wet and slippery and naked."

Color flared in her cheeks. The sparkle returned to her eyes. A pleased smile tugged at her lips as she turned and sashayed into the house with a deliberate sway of her hips.

Oh, my, yes, he thought as he watched her go. This was going to get downright fascinating.

If there was a decidedly knowing gleam in Harlan's eyes when they eventually returned to the main house, Melissa pretended to ignore it. What worried her more was that he might be getting ideas after their long absence that she and Cody had spent the time wisely and worked things out. Harlan believed strongly in family. He clearly wanted them to resolve things in a way that kept them all together. Despite what he'd said earlier about taking all the time she needed, hearing that they had not settled a thing would surely disappoint him.

"I think we'd best be getting back into town," Melissa announced within minutes.

"What's your hurry?" Harlan asked at once. "There's plenty of room here, if you want to stay the night. I'm rattling around in this big old place all by myself. It would be a pleasure to have company."

Melissa couldn't help thinking of another very recent invitation to stay at White Pines, one she had firmly declined. Her gaze caught Cody's and picked up on the gleam of anticipation in his eyes as he awaited her answer to his father's plea. She felt the web of Adams charm being woven snugly around her.

"No," she said, breaking free for now. "Another time."

She scooped up her daughter. "Time to get home, pumpkin."

Sharon Lynn promptly tried to squirm free, holding her arms out plaintively toward her grandfather. "Da?"

"You can come to see Granddaddy again very soon," Melissa promised, forcing herself not to see the equally wistful expression in Harlan's eyes as she refused to relinquish her daughter.

Harlan leaned down and kissed them both. "You're welcome here anytime," he told her. "Both of you.

Don't stand on ceremony. Come whenever you have some time.''

''I'll walk you out,'' Cody offered, falling into step beside her. ''Don't wait up for me, Daddy. I might spend some time in town tonight.''

Melissa didn't have to glance back to know that the comment had stirred a speculative glint in Harlan's eyes.

''Why did you say that?'' she demanded of Cody the instant they were out of earshot of the house.

He regarded her with his most innocent look, the one only a fool would trust. ''Say what?''

''That you'd be staying in town for a while?''

''Because it's true.''

''No, it's not,'' she said firmly. ''We did not discuss anything about you coming into town.''

''Who said I'd be with you?'' he inquired, leveling a gaze straight into her eyes.

''But you said... W-who?'' Melissa sputtered. ''Dammit, Cody, you did that deliberately.''

''Did what?''

''Let your father assume that you intended to spend the evening, maybe the whole night, with me.''

''Is that what I said?''

''It's what you implied.''

''You sure you're not projecting your own desires onto me?''

''No, I am not,'' she practically shouted, causing Sharon Lynn to begin to whimper. Melissa kissed her cheek. ''Shh, baby. It's okay. Your daddy and I are just having a discussion.''

Cody chuckled. ''Is that what it is? You sure do get riled up over a little discussion.''

''I am not riled up,'' she insisted, keeping a tight rein on her frayed temper.

''Could have fooled me.''

''Oh, forget it,'' she snapped as she put Melissa into her car seat and buckled her in. As she walked around the car, she heard the driver's door open and assumed Cody was simply being polite. Instead she found that he'd climbed in behind the wheel.

''Now what?'' she asked, regarding him suspiciously.

''I thought I'd hitch a ride.''

''Why would you want to do that? It'll leave you stranded in town.''

''Oh, I'm sure I can find someone willing to bring me home,'' he said, then winked. ''Eventually.''

He said it in a smug way that had her grinding her teeth. ''Is that a new technique you've learned for luring ladies out to your place?'' she inquired testily. ''You claim to need a ride home?''

''Let's just say I'm trying it out tonight.''

''And what if no one responds to your plight?''

''Oh, I don't think there's much chance of that,'' he said confidently. He shrugged. ''If it does, I'm sure you'd be willing to take me in for the night.''

''When pigs learn to fly,'' she retorted, irritated beyond belief that mere hours after they'd made love he was going on the prowl again. ''Get out, Cody.''

''I don't think so.''

"Cody Adams, do not make me march back into that house so I can borrow a shotgun from Harlan."

He chuckled. "I'm not real worried about that, darlin'. You'd never shoot a man in plain view of his daughter."

He was right, of course. But, lordy, how she was tempted. "Oh, for heaven's sake," she muttered, flinging open the back door. "If you want to behave like a horse's behind, go right ahead."

"Thank you," he said, and turned the key in the ignition.

Cody was the kind of driver who liked to tempt fate. Melissa clung to the door handle, while Sharon Lynn squealed with excitement as they sped around curves. She knew they were perfectly safe. Cody never tried anything unless he was confident of his control of the road, the car, or the situation. In fact, she suspected that was exactly the point he was trying to make.

Even so, she was pale by the time he finally pulled to a stop in front of Rosa's Mexican Café. She was faintly puzzled by his choice. It was hardly a singles hangout.

"This is where you intend to spend your night on the town?"

He shrugged. "I thought we could grab a bite to eat first."

"Uh-huh," she said, regarding him skeptically.

"Do you have a problem with that?"

"Not really, I suppose, but you could have asked."

"I just did."

"Funny, it didn't sound much like a question to me. Maybe I already have plans for the night."

His expression turned dark. "Do you?" he demanded, his voice tight.

She let him wonder for the space of a heartbeat, then shrugged. "No, but I could have."

"Melissa, I swear..."

"Tsk-tsk," she warned, enjoying turning the tables on him, albeit briefly. "Not in front of the baby."

He scowled at her, scooped Sharon Lynn out of her car seat and headed inside, leaving Melissa to make up her own mind about whether to join them or remain in the car and quibble over semantics. Sighing over this latest test of her patience, she reluctantly followed him inside.

On a Saturday night, Rosa's was crowded with families. Melissa spotted Jordan and Kelly with their kids right off. Cody apparently did not, because he was making a beeline for an empty table on the opposite side of the restaurant. He picked up a booster seat en route and was already putting Sharon Lynn into it by the time Melissa joined him.

"Didn't you see Jordan and Kelly?" she asked. "They were trying to wave us over. There's room at their table."

"I saw them," Cody said tersely.

Melissa studied the set of his jaw. "Okay, what's wrong?"

"I do not intend to spend the evening with my brother," he said. "If you can call him that."

"Cody," she protested. "Why would you even say something like that?"

He frowned at her. "Because he knew about Sharon Lynn and he didn't tell me."

Melissa flinched as if he'd struck her. "Because I swore him to secrecy," she reminded him. She didn't want this family split on her conscience.

"He should have told me," Cody repeated, his stubbornness kicking in with a vengeance.

Melissa regarded him with a mix of frustration and dismay. The last thing she had ever wanted was to cause a rift between the two brothers. Uncertain what she could do to mend it, she turned and walked away. Cody was on her heels in a flash.

"Where are you going?" he asked suspiciously, latching onto her elbow.

"To the ladies' room," she said.

"Oh." He released her at once. "Sorry."

Melissa rolled her eyes and continued on to the back, praying that Kelly would spot her and join her.

She was combing her hair when Jordan's wife came into the rest room. "What are we going to do about them?" Melissa asked at once.

"It's not Jordan," Kelly said. "He feels terrible about what happened. He doesn't blame Cody for being furious."

"Okay, then, how do I get through to Cody? It's my fault. I've told him that, but he says Jordan should have ignored my wishes."

"He probably should have," Kelly concurred. "I could have told Cody myself and I didn't. There's enough blame to go around. The point now is to make things right. I wanted it settled before the baptism tomorrow so that Cody could be J.J.'s godfather. But until this is resolved, Jordan and I have decided to postpone the ceremony. It was only going to be a small family gathering anyway.''

''Maybe if Jordan made the first move,'' Melissa suggested.

Kelly shook her head. ''It wouldn't work. This is Cody's call, I'm afraid. The trouble is, we're dealing with the stubborn Adams men here.''

''Can you all stick around?'' Melissa asked. ''I'll think of something.''

''Sure,'' Kelly agreed. ''Our dinner's just now being served anyway. I can't imagine what you can do, but let me know if you think I can help.'' She paused on her way to the door. ''By the way, it's good to see the two of you together again. How are things going?''

''Don't ask,'' Melissa said.

Kelly grinned. ''That good, huh? Does that mean you haven't signed up at the Neiman-Marcus bridal registry yet?''

''No, and I wouldn't be holding my breath for that if I were you. I am not inclined to marry a man who is as thoroughly, unrepentantly, exasperating as Cody is.''

''Interesting,'' Kelly murmured, a knowing twinkle in her eyes.

''Don't start with me. I've just been subjected to Harlan's knowing looks for the past few hours.''

"Not another word," Kelly promised readily. "Nobody understands the perverse streak that runs in this family any better than I do."

After Kelly had gone, Melissa slowly put her comb into her purse and headed back to their table. She saw at once that Cody had been joined by Kelly's precocious six-year-old, Dani.

"I came to see the baby," Dani announced when Melissa had joined them. "She's cuter than my brother. I wanted a sister, but somebody got mixed up and gave me a brother instead."

Melissa grinned at her. "I bet you'll be glad of that when you're older. I always wished I had a brother who'd look out for me." She shot a pointed look at Cody when she said it.

Cody rolled his eyes. Clearly, he didn't think Jordan had done such a terrific job of looking out for him when it counted.

Dani stood closer to the table and leaned her elbows on it, propping her chin in her hands as she regarded her uncle. "You know, Uncle Cody, I was thinking."

He visibly contained a grin. "What were you thinking, you little con artist?"

"Maybe Sharon Lynn should have a kitten of her own."

"Maybe she should." He glanced at Melissa. "What do you think?"

"I think you two were plotting this," Melissa charged, trying not to chuckle at the guilty expressions. "Sharon Lynn does not need a kitten. More importantly, a kitten does not need Sharon Lynn. She'd probably scare it to death."

Dani's brow knit as she considered the argument. "She's probably right, Uncle Cody. Babies don't understand about kittens. Francie thinks that my brother is a pest."

"A valid point," Cody agreed. "Maybe after Sharon Lynn gets to know how to behave around those kittens you talked me into taking, she can have one of her own."

"Good idea," Dani said. "Francie will probably have more by then."

"Over my dead body," Jordan said, arriving to stand behind his stepdaughter. "Hello, Melissa." He looked straight at Cody, who avoided his gaze. "Cody."

After a visible internal struggle, Cody nodded curtly.

Jordan stood there, looking uncharacteristically indecisive for another minute before sighing and saying, "Come on, Dani. Your dinner's getting cold."

When the pair of them were gone, Melissa said, "You were rude to him, Cody. He made an overture and you didn't even say hello."

Cody closed his eyes. When he opened them, his stubborn resolve seemed to be firmly back in place. "I had nothing to say to him."

"Cody, I'm the one who betrayed you, not Jordan. I'm the one you thought had cheated on you. I'm the one who kept it a secret that I'd had your baby. You're speaking to me. You've forgiven me."

She studied him intently. ‘‘Or have you? Are you taking all the anger you don’t dare express against me because of Sharon Lynn and projecting it on to Jordan?’’

She saw by the way his jaw worked and his gaze evaded hers that she’d hit the nail on the head. She sighed. ‘‘Don’t do this, Cody. Don’t let what happened between us come between you and Jordan. Please,’’ she pleaded.

When he didn’t respond, she gave up. ‘‘Just promise you’ll think about what I said, okay?’’

‘‘Yeah,’’ he said tersely. ‘‘I’ll think about it.’’

With great reluctance, Melissa finally conceded it was the best she could hope for. For now, anyway.

Chapter Twelve

Sometime well after midnight, Melissa woke to the sound of Sharon Lynn whimpering. She tumbled out of bed, flipped on the hall light and raced into the baby's room.

Sharon Lynn was tossing restlessly. Her skin was dry and burning up.

"Oh, baby," Melissa soothed as she scooped her up. "Are you feeling bad? Come with Mommy. I'll get you some water and check your temperature."

She had barely made it into the kitchen and flipped that light on when the front door burst open, scaring her half to death. She grabbed the frying pan and peeked through the kitchen doorway, prepared to do battle with a lunatic. Instead it was Cody, his clothes rumpled, his hair tousled, who stood in the foyer.

"Cody, what on earth?" she demanded, trying to slow the pounding of her heart. She set the frying pan down, though she wasn't entirely convinced he couldn't do with a good whop upside the head for scaring her so badly.

"What's going on?" he asked, casting worried looks from her to the baby and back. "I saw the lights come on. Are you okay?"

She ignored the question and tried to figure out what he was doing at her house in the middle of the night. The last time she'd seen him he'd been sitting at the bar in Rosa's. He'd declared his intention of starting his night on the town right there, clearly implying he intended it to end in someone's arms. She'd choked back her fury and tried to exit with some dignity, when all she'd really wanted to do was have a knock-down, drag-'em-out brawl with him. She was still itching for a fight, as a matter of fact, but right now Sharon Lynn's condition took precedence.

"Where have you been?" she asked, pleased that she was able to sound so cool when she was seething inside.

"On the porch," he admitted, taking his feverish daughter from her arms. As soon as he touched her, alarm flared in his eyes. "Good heavens, she's burning up. Have you taken her temperature?"

"I was just about to." She tried to remain calm in the face of his obvious panic and her own. She'd experienced rapidly spiking temperatures before and learned that it was a matter of course for children. Still, she'd never felt Sharon Lynn's skin quite so hot.

The thermometer registered one hundred and three degrees. Cody's face blanched when she told him.

''We're going to the hospital,'' he said at once, starting out of the kitchen.

Melissa blocked his way. ''Not yet,'' she said far more calmly than she was feeling. There was no point in both of them panicking. ''Let me give her a Tylenol and try bathing her with cool water to see if we can't bring that temperature down. If there's no change, then we'll call the doctor.''

Sharon Lynn patted Cody's stubbled cheek weakly and murmured, ''Da.'' She sounded pitiful.

Cody looked thoroughly shaken. ''Melissa, I don't think we should wait. Something's really wrong with her.''

''It's probably nothing more than the start of a cold or a touch of flu,'' she said. ''Stuff like that reaches epidemic proportions this time of the year.''

''Her temperature's over a hundred,'' he reminded her. ''That can't be good for her.''

''Babies get high temperatures. It's nothing to get crazy about,'' she insisted, amending to herself, *yet.*

She gave Sharon Lynn Tylenol, then ran cool water into the kitchen sink. ''Bring her over here and let's get her out of that nightgown. It's soaking wet anyway. Why don't you go back to her room and bring me a clean one, along with a fresh diaper. We'll need those after I've sponged her off a bit with cool water.''

Cody looked as if he might refuse to budge, but eventually he did as she'd asked. By the time he'd returned, Sharon Lynn was no longer whimpering. In fact she seemed to be relaxing and enjoying the cool water Melissa was gently splashing over her.

"Are you sure that's good for her?" Cody asked, worry etched on his face.

"It's exactly what the doctor and all the child-care books recommend. If you don't believe me, there's a book in the living room. Go read it." Anything to get him out of the kitchen again before he wore a hole in the linoleum with his pacing. Worse, she was feeling crowded with all of his hovering.

"No, no, I'll take your word for it," he said, standing over her shoulder and watching every move she made. "Maybe we should take her temperature again."

Melissa sighed and stepped aside to allow him to put the fancy new thermometer in Sharon Lynn's ear for a few seconds.

"It's a hundred and two," he proclaimed. "That's it. We're going to the hospital."

"It's down a whole degree," Melissa observed, blocking him when he would have snatched Sharon Lynn out of the bathwater. "The Tylenol's working."

"Not fast enough."

"Let's give it another half hour," she compromised.

Cody hesitated, then finally conceded grudgingly, "A half hour. Not a minute more."

He sat down at the kitchen table and fixed his gaze on the clock over the sink. Apparently he intended to watch each of those thirty minutes tick by.

"Da!" Sharon Lynn called out.

Cody was on his feet in an instant. "What's up, sweet pea? You feeling better?" he asked, caressing her cheek with fingers that shook visibly.

A smile spread across his daughter's face. "Da," she repeated enthusiastically.

A little color came back into Cody's ashen complexion. "She feels a little cooler."

Melissa agreed. "I'm betting when we check her temperature again, it'll be just about back to normal."

Twenty minutes later Sharon Lynn was no longer feverish. She was once again tucked into her crib. Cody, still looking shaken, stood over her.

"How do you stand this?" he murmured to Melissa. "I've never been so terrified in my life."

Melissa patted his hand. "It gets easier after you've been through it once or twice and know what to expect," she promised him, but he shook his head.

"I can't imagine it getting easier," he said. "What if her temperature hadn't gone down? What if you'd guessed wrong?"

"Then we would have called the doctor or gotten her to the hospital."

"It might have been too late."

"Cody, stop that," she ordered, not daring to admit that she'd been scared silly, too, that she always was, no matter what the books said. "It's over. She's going to be fine. It was just a little fever."

He closed his eyes and drew in a deep breath. "Okay, you're right. Just a little fever." He still sounded unconvinced. He definitely showed no inclination to budge from beside the crib.

Melissa grinned at him. ''Cody, everything really is fine. You don't have to stand there and watch her all night.''

''I am not leaving this house,'' he said, his jaw jutting out belligerently.

''Fine. You can sleep on the sofa.'' She yawned. ''Good night, Cody.''

''Where are you going?''

''Back to bed.''

''How can you possibly sleep?''

''Because I'm exhausted. You must be, too.'' In fact, he looked as if he hadn't slept in days.

''I won't sleep a wink,'' he swore.

''Whatever,'' she murmured, and headed for her room. At the doorway she recalled that they'd never really talked about why he'd been on her front porch in the first place. ''Cody, why were you here in the middle of the night?''

A sheepish expression spread across his face. ''I figured if you found me on your doorstep in the morning, you'd give me a lift home.''

She grinned. ''Couldn't find another taker for that fabulous Adams charm, huh?''

''Never even tried,'' he admitted, then shrugged. ''You've spoiled me for anyone else, Me...liss...a.''

She studied his face intently, looking for signs that the comment was no more than a glib, charming lie. He appeared to be dead serious. A little flutter of excitement stirred deep inside her. Was it possible that Cody really did intend to stick around through thick and thin, through good times and bad?

For the first time since he'd come home from Wyoming, she dared to hope that he really had changed. If he had…

No, she cautioned herself at once. It was too soon to leap to any conclusions at all about the future.

"Good night, Cody," she whispered, her voice husky with a longing she would never have admitted.

"Good night, darlin'."

Cody felt as if he'd slept on an old washboard. Every muscle ached like the dickens. Every vertebra in his back had either been compressed, twisted or otherwise maimed by Melissa's sofa. He suspected she'd made him sleep there on purpose, knowing what it would do to him.

He also had the distinct impression that there was a tiny wanna-be drummer in his head flailing away without much sense of rhythm.

He groaned and opened his eyes, blinking at the sunlight streaming into the living room. That was when he realized that the loud clanging wasn't in his head. It was coming from Sharon Lynn's room. If that was the case, it just might be something he could stop before his head exploded.

Moving inch by careful inch, he eased to his feet and padded down the hall to the baby's room. When he opened the door a crack, he found her bouncing in her crib, banging a wooden block on the railing. The instant she spied him, a smile spread across her face.

"Da," she enthused, and held out her arms.

Cody wondered if he would ever get over the thrill that sweet, innocent gesture sent through him.

"Morning, pumpkin. I take it from all the commotion in here that you're feeling better."

"Ya...ya...ya."

"That must mean yes," he decided as he plucked her out of the crib and took the toy block from her as a precaution. His head was feeling marginally better, but another round of Sharon Lynn's musical skills would be a killer.

Her temperature seemed to be gone. He quickly changed her, then carried her into the kitchen. Once there, he was stymied. Was she old enough for regular cereal? Or was there some sort of baby food she was supposed to have? He didn't recall discussing breakfast when he and Melissa had shopped for groceries.

He settled Sharon Lynn into her high chair, found a soft toy bear to entertain her, and searched through the cabinets. Nothing conclusive there beyond an assortment of frosted cereals that seemed more likely to appeal to a one-year-old than her mother. Then again, he didn't know much about Melissa's breakfast habits, either. On the rare occasions when they'd slept in the same bed before he'd left for Wyoming, breakfast had been the last thing on their minds first thing in the morning.

A glance in the refrigerator suggested that juice might be a good place to start. He recalled buying an awful lot of apple juice at the store. He filled a bottle and handed it over. Sharon Lynn tossed her bear on the floor and accepted it eagerly.

Scrambled eggs struck him as a safe bet. Besides, he and Melissa could eat them, as well. Fixing one meal for all of them appealed to him. It struck him as cozy; a family tradition of sorts. Their very first.

He started the coffeemaker, popped four slices of bread into the toaster, put butter and jelly on the table, then broke half a dozen eggs into a bowl and whipped them with a fork until they were foamy. Suddenly he heard the faint sound of footsteps behind him. He pivoted around and discovered Melissa leaning against the doorjamb.

''My goodness, you've been busy,'' she murmured, yawning and bending over to pick up the bear Sharon Lynn had tossed aside in favor of her juice. ''How long have you been awake?''

Goose bumps chased down his spine at the sleepy sound of her voice and the sight of that cute little fanny draped in a very short, very revealing, silk robe.

''Our daughter's better than any rooster I ever heard. She woke me at the crack of dawn.''

''Obviously she's feeling better,'' Melissa said, going over to touch her hand to the baby's forehead. ''No more temperature.''

''Seemed that way to me, too.''

''Did you take it?''

He shook his head, drawing a grin.

''Turning into an old hand already,'' she teased. ''No more panicking.''

''I wouldn't say that,'' he said, shuddering at the memory of that icy fear that had washed through him in the wee hours of the morning. ''But I am going to borrow that book of yours and read it from cover to cover.''

He reached for Melissa's hand and pulled her toward him. He was vaguely surprised that she didn't put up a struggle. Maybe he hadn't imagined the closeness between them the night before.

When she was standing toe-to-toe with him, he had to resist the temptation to tug the belt of her robe free. Instead he brushed a strand of hair back from her face and gazed into her tired eyes.

''You were wonderful last night,'' he said softly. ''Not only were you good with Sharon Lynn, but you kept me from freaking out.''

Her lips curved slightly. ''Having you here helped me, too,'' she said, surprising him.

''Why?''

''Staying calm for your benefit kept me from freaking out myself,'' she admitted.

He stared at her in astonishment. ''You were scared?''

''Terrified,'' she admitted. ''But I knew I couldn't let you see it or you'd have insisted on borrowing your father's plane and flying us all to some critical care hospital in Dallas in the middle of the night.''

''You've got that right.'' He grinned. ''We're quite a pair, aren't we?''

''Just typical parents, Cody.''

The simple words were no more than the truth, yet Cody felt as if he'd just heard something terribly profound spoken for the first time. He was a parent, a certified grown-up, with responsibilities he couldn't slough off. Responsibilities, in fact, that he actually yearned to accept.

He wanted more Sunday mornings just like this one, waking up to the sound of his daughter making some sort of commotion to get attention, fixing breakfast for all three of them, sitting at the kitchen table across from Melissa. He renewed his vow to himself to do everything within his power to convince Melissa they ought to be a family.

After they'd eaten and after he'd cleaned up most of the scrambled egg Sharon Lynn had managed to rub into her hair or fling halfway across the kitchen, he sat back with a sigh of pure contentment.

''Don't get too settled,'' Melissa warned, a teasing note in her voice. ''Your daughter needs a bath. I think I'll let you do the honors since that egg she's smeared everywhere was your doing.''

''You sound as if that's punishment,'' he said. ''What's the big deal?''

''You'll see,'' Melissa retorted a little too cheerfully to suit him.

She ran the inch or so of bathwater into the tub, then left him to it. It didn't take long for Cody to figure out why she'd had that smug expression on her face when she'd exited the bathroom.

Sharon Lynn really loved water. She loved to splash it. She loved to scoop it up by the handful and dribble it all over him. She loved to throw her toys into it, sending yet more splashes into the air.

She wasn't quite so crazy about soap. She wriggled and squirmed, trying to get away from him. Slippery as an eel, she evaded capture until she'd managed to soak him from head to toe. In fact, he was fairly certain that he was wetter and soapier than she was.

Melissa chose that precise moment to reappear. He heard her chuckling as he tried to towel his daughter dry.

"You find this amusing?" he inquired softly.

"Mmm-hmm," she admitted. "I sure do."

He dipped his hand in the scant remaining water that was actually in the tub and splattered it straight in Melissa's smug face. A startled, incredulous expression spread across her face.

"You brat," she muttered, turning on the faucet in the sink and scooping up a handful of water to pour over his head.

Sharon Lynn squealed with glee as water splashed everywhere.

Cody nabbed a plastic cup from the counter behind him, dipped it into the bathwater and soaked Melissa's front. Only after the damp bathrobe clung to her body did he realize the mistake he'd made. His breath snagged in his throat at the sight of her nipples hardening beneath that suddenly transparent silk. He swallowed hard, aware of the tightening in his groin and the flood of color climbing into his cheeks—and equally aware of the impossibility of pursuing the desire rocketing through him.

Melissa's gaze locked with his for what seemed an eternity, then dropped to the unmistakable evidence of his arousal. A smile slowly tugged at the corners of her mouth.

"Serves you right," she taunted as she turned and padded off to her room.

Cody groaned and wished like crazy that he knew Melissa's neighbors so he could plead with them to baby-sit for the rest of the morning. He wanted to finish what she had started with that provocative taunt.

Instead he forced himself to concentrate on getting Sharon Lynn dried off and dressed. The task was somewhat complicated by the soaked condition of his own clothes. He was dripping everywhere.

As soon as he had his daughter settled in her play-pen, he grabbed a towel, went into the laundry room, stripped, and tossed his clothes into the dryer. He wrapped the towel snugly around his waist and re-treated to the kitchen to drink another cup of coffee while he waited for everything to dry.

When Melissa wandered in a few minutes later her mouth gaped. "Where are your clothes?" she de-manded, her gaze riveted on his bare chest.

"In the dryer."

"Get them out."

"I can't wear damp clothes," he observed.

"Whose fault is it they're wet?"

"Yours, as a matter of fact," he said blithely. "You're the one who insisted I bathe Sharon Lynn. You obviously know what she's like in water."

She fought a grin and lost. "Yeah, I do," she ad-mitted. "But, Cody, you cannot sit around in nothing but a towel."

"You have any better ideas?" He didn't wait for

any suggestions from her before adding, ''We could go back to bed.''

''In your dreams.''

He deliberately caught her gaze. ''Absolutely,'' he said softly. ''You have no idea how vivid my dreams have become lately.''

From the fiery blush in her cheeks, he had the feeling, though, that he'd been wrong about that. He got the distinct impression that Melissa's dreams had been just as erotic as his own lately. He vowed that one day soon they'd compare notes...and make them come true.

Chapter Thirteen

The rapport between them lasted all the way back to White Pines. In fact, Cody had high hopes that he was finally beginning to make progress with Melissa. He was convinced that his presence during the previous night's medical crisis had started the difficult process of convincing her that he wasn't going to bolt out of their lives at the first sign of trouble.

It had been such a small thing, being by her side during those tense moments, but he'd heard the gratitude in her voice this morning, seen the first faint flicker of renewed faith in her eyes. He couldn't allow anything to shake that trust again, not until he'd had time to strengthen it.

As they drove up the long, winding lane at White Pines he was startled to see his father emerge from the house. It appeared Harlan had been watching for them and, from the too cheerful expression on his face and the contradictory worry in his eyes, Cody could only guess that there was bad news.

He stepped out of the car and faced his father warily. "Hey, Daddy, everything okay?"

"Fine, just fine," Harlan said too heartily. He darted a worried look at Melissa, then added, "You'll never guess who's here to see you, son."

Cody shot a desperate glance toward Melissa and saw that she was hanging on his father's every word. He couldn't imagine who might have turned up at White Pines uninvited, but experience with his father's demeanor suggested he was right to be concerned. He regretted more than he could say having Melissa here at this precise moment. He should have walked home, even if it was twenty miles. He would have if he'd had any idea that trouble was going to be waiting on the doorstep.

He drew in a deep breath and braced himself. "Who?" he asked just as the front door creaked open and a slight figure with cropped black hair and a pixie face emerged. Shock rendered him speechless.

"Janey? What the hell?" He looked to his father, but Harlan merely shrugged. Cody turned back to the teenager who'd apparently tracked him down and come after him all the way from Wyoming. "What are you doing here?"

Even as he sought answers for Janey's unexpected presence, he heard Melissa's sharp intake of breath behind him. Before he could turn around, the car door slammed with enough force to rock the sturdy vehicle on its tires. He knew what that meant. He forgot all about Janey as he tried to get to Melissa before she got the wrong impression and took off in a snit. Correction, she already had the wrong impression. He just had to stop her.

''Melissa,'' he protested just as the engine roared to life. ''Dammit, we need to talk. Don't you dare drive away from here!''

He might as well have been talking to the wind. The order was wasted. She'd already thrown the car into gear, then backed up, spewing gravel in every direction. He slammed his fist on the fender as she turned the car, shifted again and headed away from the house at a pace that would have done an Indy 500 driver proud.

''Terrific,'' he muttered. ''That's terrific. Not five seconds ago, I actually believed she was starting to trust me and now this!''

''Cody,'' his father warned, nodding toward the girl who had stopped halfway down the sidewalk.

Sure enough, Janey looked as if he'd slapped her. Cody raked his hand through his hair and tried to get a grip on his temper. It wasn't the teenager's fault that his personal life was a mess. He crossed to Janey Treethorn in three strides and looked into a face streaked with tears and eyes that were as wide as a doe's caught in the cross hairs of a hunter's gun. His anger dissipated in a heartbeat.

''Janey, don't cry,'' he said softly, pulling her into a hug. ''Shh, baby, it's okay.''

"I'm s-sorry," she stammered. "I didn't mean to mess up everything."

"I know," he soothed, awkwardly patting her back as he cast a helpless look at his father. Harlan shrugged, clearly as bemused by this turn of events as Cody was.

"It's not your fault," he told her, even though he very much wanted to blame her for ruining his fragile truce with Melissa. "Come on, let's go inside and you can tell me why you came all this way. Does your dad know you're here?"

"Ye-es-s," she said, sniffling. "Your father called him last night."

Cody's heart sank. Obviously, Janey had run away from home, if last night was the first Lance had heard of her whereabouts. His former boss was probably fit to be tied. Janey was the least rebellious of his daughters. If she had pulled a stunt as crazy as this, the other two were likely to drive him completely over the edge. Lance needed a mother for those girls and he needed her in a hurry.

Inside, Cody suggested that Harlan go and see if Maritza could rustle them up some hot chocolate. He knew it was Janey's favorite. There had been many cold winter nights when she'd fixed it for him and her father, then lingered in the shadows listening to them talk.

Before he sat down, he went into the closest bathroom and gathered up a handful of tissues and brought them back to her. He was careful to sit in a chair opposite her, since he had the terrible feeling that her crush on him was what had brought her all the way to Texas. He'd never done a thing to encourage it, except to be kind to her, but apparently that had been enough to cause this impulsive trip to Texas.

''Feeling better?'' he asked after a while, when she appeared to have cried herself out and had finished the mug of hot chocolate Maritza had served with barely concealed curiosity.

Janey nodded, but wouldn't meet his gaze. Her cheeks were flushed with embarrassment. She tucked her jeans-clad legs up under her and huddled on the sofa like a small child expecting to be scolded. She looked so woebegone that Cody was having a difficult time maintaining what was left of his dying anger.

''Janey, tell me what this is all about.''

''I c-can't,'' she whispered.

''There must be a reason you left Wyoming and came all the way to Texas. How did you know where to find me?''

''I found the address in Dad's papers.''

''Did something happen at home?''

She shook her head, looking more and more miserable. Finally she lifted her chin and met his gaze for barely a second, then ducked it again. ''You left,'' she said accusingly. ''One day you just weren't there anymore and you never said goodbye.''

Even though his reason for leaving had been an emergency, he could see how it might look from her perspective. He knew that in her reserved way, she counted on him.

"Didn't your dad tell you why I had to come home?" he asked.

"He said your mother died."

"That's right."

"But I thought you'd be coming back," she whispered. "But then you never did. And then Dad said you'd called and that y-you'd q-quit."

Her tears started all over again. Cody went for more tissues and brought back the whole box to buy himself the time he needed to figure out how to explain things to this shy, young girl who'd so badly needed someone that she'd chosen a miserable, cynical cowboy from Texas who already had a lousy track record for reliability.

"Janey, when I got here there were things that I realized I had to do. I couldn't come back. I explained all of that to your father."

"But…not…to me," she choked between sobs. "I thought you were my friend."

Cody sighed. "I am. I always want to be your friend."

"Then you'll come back as soon as things are settled here?" she inquired, hope written all over her tear-streaked face.

"No, sweetie, I can't come back."

"Why not?" she asked.

Not sure how she was likely to react, he drew in a deep breath before admitting, "Because I found out that I have a little girl and I have to be here for her."

Dismay darkened her eyes. "A baby?"

"Not so much a baby anymore," he confided. "She's over a year old."

"And you didn't know about her?"

"No."

Despite herself, she was apparently fascinated. For the first time since he'd arrived home, there was a sparkle in her dark eyes.

"How come?" she asked, her expression alive with curiosity.

"It's a long story."

"Was that her mom in the car just now?"

Cody nodded.

"Uh-oh," she murmured. Guilt and misery replaced the sparkle in her eyes. "I'm sorry if I messed things up for you, Cody. I really am."

He grinned ruefully. "Oh, the list of my sins is pretty long as it is. One more thing won't matter all that much."

"Want me to tell her you didn't know I was coming here?"

He had a feeling that the less Melissa saw of Janey, the better for all of them. Janey might be only fifteen, but she was a beautiful young girl who looked older than her years. It was the very fact that her body had blossomed so prematurely that had contributed to her shyness.

Ironically, he suspected she had been drawn to him for the very reason that he hadn't acted like the over-sexed teens who attended school with her. She'd felt safe with him, free to talk about her dreams, and she had magnified that feeling into a giant-size crush.

"No, sweetie, I'll take care of Melissa. Now, let's think about getting you back home again. How'd you get here?"

"I used my savings for a bus ticket. Then when I got to town, I called the ranch. Your dad came and got me."

Cody shuddered when he thought of her traveling that distance alone by bus. He also suspected that Harlan had deliberately not tried to track him down when Janey turned up to give him more time with Melissa before throwing a monkey wrench into things.

"I'll talk to Daddy about having his pilot fly you back to Wyoming," he told her.

Her eyes lit up. "Really?"

Her instantaneous excitement told him that her heart was already well on its way to healing. Maybe all she'd really needed was closure, a chance to say goodbye and make sure that she hadn't lost a friend. If he'd been half so insistent on closure before he'd taken off from Texas, maybe he and Melissa would have been married by now, instead of trying to rebuild their shattered trust.

Janey would be okay. He was sure of it. In the meantime, though, he had another heart to worry about. He had a feeling patching up the holes in Melissa's trust wasn't going to be nearly so easy to accomplish.

Melissa broke three glasses during the breakfast rush at Dolan's on Monday. As each one shattered, she heard a heavy sigh of resignation from Eli. She knew exactly how he felt. She'd had her fragile hopes shattered—again—the day before when she'd arrived at White Pines to find an adorable, sexy woman waiting on the doorstep for Cody.

As she swept up the debris from her latest round of clumsiness, she wished it were even half as easy to tidy up the aftermath of a broken heart.

When she finished sweeping, she glanced up and discovered Mabel sitting at the counter, curiosity written all over her face. To try to forestall the questions that were clearly on the older woman's mind, Melissa grabbed the coffeepot and poured her a cup.

"How about a Danish, Mabel?" she asked. "We have cheese and cherry left."

"No, thanks. So, did you and Cody have another fight?" Mabel inquired point-blank.

"No," Melissa replied honestly. They hadn't fought. She had taken off before her disillusionment could come pouring out in a wave of accusations.

"Now, why is it I don't believe that?" Mabel murmured. "You never broke a glass until that boy came back into town. Since then, you've been smashing them up so fast poor Eli's liable to go bankrupt."

"I'm going to reimburse Eli for the glasses," Melissa told her stiffly.

"No need for that," Eli called, proving that he'd heard every word of the discussion of her love life. "Maybe Mabel and I ought to sit that boy down and give him a stern talking to, though."

Mabel shot their boss a sour look. "What would

you know about straightening out a lovers' tiff, old man?''

''As much as you do about starting one,'' Eli shot back.

Melissa stared at them. For the first time she noticed that their bickering carried the unmistakable sting of two former lovers. *Eli and Mabel,* she thought incredulously. Surely not. Then again, why not? She knew of no one else in either of their lives. Maybe that was so because they'd spent years carrying the torch for each other, unable to heal some foolish rift.

''Maybe I'm not the one who needs an intermediary,'' Melissa suggested, observing their reactions intently.

''You don't know what you're talking about,'' Mabel snapped. She shot a venomous look at the pharmacist. ''Neither does he, for that matter.''

''I know what I know,'' Eli countered. ''Besides, we're not talking about you and me now. We're talking about Melissa and Cody.''

''I'd rather talk about the two of you,'' Melissa said hurriedly, dying to know the whole story of two people who'd worked together as far back as she could recall without giving away so much as a hint that there was anything personal between them.

''No,'' Mabel and Eli chorused.

Melissa winced. ''Okay, okay. We'll make a pact. You stay out of my personal life and I'll stay out of yours.''

Mabel gave an obviously reluctant nod. Melissa

waited for Eli to concur, but instead he muttered, ''Too late. Yours just walked in the door.''

Melissa's gaze shot to the front of the drugstore. Sure enough, Cody was striding in her direction, a glint of pure determination in his eyes.

''Go away,'' she said before he could settle himself on one of the stools.

''Is that any way to greet a paying customer?'' he inquired.

He slapped a twenty on the counter. At the rate he was throwing them around, he was going to go broke.

''I'm not leaving until I've spent every last dime of that or you and I have talked,'' he announced. ''You pick.''

Melissa poured him a cup of coffee, snatched the twenty and tucked it in her pocket. ''The coffee's on me. I'll consider the twenty a tip for services rendered.''

Flags of angry color rose in Cody's cheeks. His grip on his coffee cup tightened, turning his knuckles white. ''There's a name for taking money for that, darlin'.''

Mabel sputtered and backed off her stool so fast it was still spinning a full minute after she'd gone. Melissa had a hunch she wasn't all that far, though, more than likely not even out of earshot.

''How dare you!'' Melissa snapped.

''You started this round, not me,'' he said tightly. ''Care to back up and start over?''

''We can't back up that many years,'' she retorted.

Cody visibly restrained his temper. Melissa watched

as he drew in several calming breaths, even as his heated gaze remained locked on her. Her blood practically sizzled under that look. No matter how furious he made her, she still seemed to want him. It was damned provoking.

"Believe it or not, I came in here to apologize," he said eventually, his voice low.

"What's to apologize for? Just because you didn't mention that you were involved with another woman—a woman who apparently traveled quite some distance to be with you—that doesn't mean you owe me an apology."

To her annoyance, amusement sparkled in Cody's eyes. "I don't have a thing to hide, sweet pea. Want me to tell you about Janey?"

Melissa did not want to hear about the gorgeous creature with the exotic features, elfin haircut and sad, sad eyes. Cody had probably broken her heart, too.

"I can see that you do," Cody said, taking the decision out of her hands. "First of all, yes, Janey is from Wyoming. Second, I had no idea she was coming. Third, our relationship—then and now—most definitely is not what you think it was."

"Yeah, right," Melissa said sarcastically.

"Fourth," he went on as if she hadn't interrupted. "Her father was my boss, Lance Treethorn."

He leveled his gaze straight at her, until she felt color flooding into her cheeks. "Fifth, and most important, she is a fifteen-year-old kid."

Melissa stared at him. "Fifteen," she repeated in a choked voice. "Cody, that's—"

He cut her off before she could finish the ugly thought. ''What that is, is a shy, lonely teenager with a crush on the first guy who didn't slobber all over her due to adolescent hormones,'' he insisted adamantly.

Melissa wanted to believe him. In fact, she did believe him. Cody was far too honorable a man to do anything so despicable. Harlan might have raised stubborn, willful, overly confident sons, but he'd instilled a set of values in them that was beyond reproach. She was the one who ought to be horsewhipped for even allowing such a thought to cross her mind.

She moaned and hid her face in her hands. ''God, I'm sorry.''

Cody shrugged. ''Well, she does look older than she is. That's been her problem. The guys ahead of her in school think she's a lot more mature than she is and try to take advantage of her. She's coped by hiding out at the ranch.''

''And you were kind to her, so she developed a crush on you,'' Melissa concluded, feeling like an idiot. ''Why didn't you do something to put a stop to it?''

''For one thing, I had no idea it would go this far. The most overt thing she ever did before was leave food for me. She bakes a brownie that makes your mouth water.''

Melissa grinned. ''You always were a sucker for brownies.''

''It was the first thing you learned to bake, remember? You were twelve, I think.''

She remembered all right. Even back then she'd been trying to woo Cody by catering to his every whim. She wondered if it was ever possible to get beyond past history and truly have a new beginning. She'd been facetious when she'd snapped earlier that they couldn't go back far enough to start over, but maybe it was true. Maybe there was no way to ever get past all the mistakes and the distrust.

Despondency stole through her as she considered the possibility that they would never be able to move on.

"Melissa?" Cody said softly.

"What?"

"What's wrong?"

"Nothing."

"I don't believe that. You looked as if you were about ready to cry."

She tried to shrug off the observation. "Don't mind me. It's probably just Monday blues."

"I know how to cure that," he said. "Come out to White Pines tonight. We'll have a barbecue. It's warm enough today."

Melissa didn't think spending more time with Cody was such a good idea, not when parting suddenly seemed inevitable. Maybe Janey Treethorn's presence had been innocent enough, but sooner or later some other woman would catch his eye. They always did.

"The temperature's supposed to drop later," she said by way of declining his invitation. "It might even snow overnight."

Cody's expression remained undaunted. "Then I'll wear a jacket to tend the grill and we can eat inside."

"You never give up, do you?"

"Never," he agreed softly, his gaze locked with hers. "Not when it's something this important."

"What is it that's important, Cody?" she asked, unable to keep a hint of desperation out of her voice. "What?"

"You, me, Sharon Lynn," he said. "I want us to be a family, Melissa. I won't settle for anything less this time."

She heard the determination in his voice. More important, she heard the commitment. He sounded so sincere, so convinced that a family was what he wanted.

"Will you come?" he asked again. "You and Sharon Lynn?"

Melissa sighed. She'd never been able to resist Cody when he got that winsome note in his voice, when that thoroughly engaging smile reached all the way to his dark and dangerous eyes.

"What time?"

"Five-thirty?"

"We'll be there."

"My house," he said. "Not the main house."

Thoughts of making love in that house flooded through her. Melissa shook her head. "No," she insisted. "Let's have dinner with Harlan, too."

"Scared, Me...liss...a?"

"You bet, cowboy. You should be, too." She lowered her voice. "The last time we were alone in that house, we made love and we didn't take precautions. I'm not risking that again.''

Cody grinned. ''Hey, darlin', that's something I can take care of right here and now,'' he offered. ''I'm sure Eli can fix me right up.''

Melissa's cheeks flamed at the prospect of having Eli and Mabel know any more of her business than they already did. ''Cody, don't you dare. Besides, we decided that sleeping together only complicated things.''

''Did we decide that?''

''You know we did. We have dinner at Harlan's or you can forget it.''

''Okay, darlin', I'll let you win this round,'' he said, startling her with his lack of fussing. ''See you at five-thirty.''

It wasn't until she arrived at White Pines that she discovered the reason for Cody's calm acceptance of her edict.

''Where's Harlan?'' she inquired suspiciously the minute she stepped into the too silent foyer of the main house.

Cody's expression was pure innocence as he gazed back at her. ''Oh, didn't I mention it? Daddy's gone to spend a few days with Luke and Jessie.''

With Sharon Lynn already happily ensconced in her father's arms, with a huge stack of ribs just waiting to be barbecued, Melissa bit back the urge to turn right around and flee. This round, it appeared, had gone to Cody.

Chapter Fourteen

For the next two months, Cody won more rounds than he lost, much to Melissa's chagrin. Though she'd turned down his proposals every time he made them, he took the rejections in stride. He just redoubled his efforts to change her mind. Her resistance was in tatters. Her senses were spinning just at the sight of him. She was clinging to the last shreds of pride and determination she had left.

There were moments, she was forced to admit, when she couldn't even remember why she was so staunch in her conviction that marrying Cody was positively the wrong thing to do. He had done absolutely nothing since his return to indicate that he wasn't thoroughly absorbed in his relationship with her and their child. He was sweetly attentive to her. He doted on Sharon Lynn.

And still, for reasons she was finding harder and harder to fathom, she kept waiting for some other woman to come between them, for some blowup that would send Cody racing away from Texas, away from them. It didn't seem to matter that his roots at White Pines ran deeper than ever. He'd left his home and her once before. She never forgot that, wouldn't let herself forget it.

She put more obstacles in their path to happiness than championship hurdlers had ever had to jump. Cody, just as determinedly, overcame each and every one, without criticism, without comment. He just did whatever was asked of him.

The truth of it was that his thoughtfulness and consideration were beginning to wear on her. She figured it was an indication of the depths of her perversity that she longed for a good, old, rip-roaring fight.

She was already working herself into a confrontational state when she reached her mother's after a particularly exhausting day at work, only to find that Sharon Lynn wasn't there.

"What do you mean, she's not here?" she demanded, staring at her father. Her mother was nowhere in sight, which should have been her first clue that her life was about to turn topsy-turvy.

"Cody came by," her father admitted. "I let him take her."

"You what?" Her voice climbed several octaves. Was everyone in town on Cody's side these days? She'd thought for sure at least her parents would stick up for her. Instead her father had joined the enemy camp.

"Why would you do that?" she asked plaintively.

Her father regarded her with amusement. "He's the child's father, for starters. He wanted to spend some time with her. He said he'd drop her off at your house and save you the trip. I guess he didn't tell you that, though."

"No, he did not," she snapped. "Which is a pretty good indication of why Cody Adams is not to be trusted."

"If you ask me, he's been jumping through hoops to prove he can be trusted. Why don't you give the guy a break?" He patted her cheek. "Come on, lady-bug. You know you want to."

"I can't," she said simply.

"Why not?"

"Because he'll leave again at the first sign of trouble."

"He left before, because you provoked him into it. I can't say I blame him for being furious about finding you out with Brian. Going out with him was a danged fool idea to begin with."

Melissa's anger wilted. "I agree, but Cody should have stayed and talked to me. He shouldn't have run."

"Don't you think he knows that now?" her father inquired reasonably. "Don't you think if he had it to do all over again, he would make a different choice?"

"I suppose," she conceded reluctantly. "He says he would anyway."

''And aren't you the one who made things worse by refusing to tell him about the baby?''

She scowled at her father, the man who had stood by her even though he disagreed with her decision to keep Cody in the dark. ''What's your point?''

''He forgave you, didn't he? Isn't it about time you did the same for him?''

Melissa was startled by the depth of her father's support for Cody. ''How come you've never said any of this before?'' she asked.

Her father's expression turned rueful. ''Because your mother seemed to be saying more than enough without me jumping in and confusing you even more. Watching you getting more miserable day by day, I finally decided when Cody showed up today that enough was enough. I told her to butt out.''

Melissa couldn't help grinning. ''So there'd be room for you to butt in?''

''Something like that. Go on, cupcake. Meet Cody halfway, at least. For whatever it's worth, I think he's a fine man.''

Melissa sighed. ''So do I.''

She made up her mind on the walk to her own house that she would try to overcome the last of her doubts and take the kind of risk her father was urging. There was a time when she would have risked anything at all to be with Cody. The pain of losing him once had made her far too cautious. It was probably long past time to rediscover the old Melissa and take the dare he'd been issuing for months now.

She found him in a rocker on her front porch, a tuckered out Sharon Lynn asleep in his lap.

"Rough afternoon?" she queried, keeping her tone light and displaying none of the annoyance she'd felt when she'd discovered he'd absconded with her daughter. She sank into the rocker next to him and put it into a slow, soothing motion. She allowed her eyes to drift closed, then snapped them open before she fell completely, embarrassingly, asleep.

"Playing in the park is tough work," he said, grinning at her. "There are swings and seesaws to ride, to say nothing of squirrels to be chased." His gaze intensified. "You look frazzled. Bad day?"

"Bad day, bad week, bad everything," she admitted, giving in to the exhaustion and turmoil she'd been fighting.

"I know just how to fix that," Cody said, standing. He shifted Sharon Lynn into one arm and held out a hand. "Give me the key."

Melissa plucked it from her purse and handed it over without argument. As soon as he'd gone, she closed her eyes again. The soothing motion of the rocker lulled her so that she was only vaguely aware of the screen door squeaking open and the sound of Cody's boots as he crossed the porch.

"Wake up, sleepyhead," he urged. "Here, take this."

She forced her eyes open and saw the tall glass he was holding out. "Lemonade?" she asked with amazement. "Where'd you get it?"

"I made it."

Her eyes blinked wider. ''From scratch?''

He grinned. ''I didn't bake a chocolate soufflé, sweet pea. It's just lemonade.''

They sat side by side, silently rocking, for what seemed an eternity after that. The spring breeze brought the fragrance of flowers wafting by. Hummingbirds hovered around the feeder at the end of the porch.

''This is nice, isn't it?'' Cody said eventually.

''Not too tame for you?'' Melissa asked.

''Don't start with me,'' he chided, but without much ferocity behind the words.

She thought of what her father had said and of her own resolution to start taking risks. ''I'm sorry. I didn't mean to say that. I guess it's become automatic.''

''Think you can break the cycle?'' he inquired lightly.

Melissa met his gaze. ''I'm going to try,'' she promised. ''I do want what you want, Cody.''

''But you're scared,'' he guessed. At her nod he added, ''Can't say that I blame you. I spent a lot of years hiding from the responsibilities of a relationship. Once you make a commitment, there's a lot riding on getting it right. I never did much like the idea of failing.''

''Can I ask you something?''

''Anything, you know that.''

''What makes you so certain we can get it right now?''

He grinned at the question. ''You know any two more stubborn people on the face of the earth?''

Her lips twitched at that. ''No, can't say that I do.''

''I pretty much figure if we finally make that commitment, neither one of us will bail out without giving it everything we've got.'' He slanted a look over at her that sent heat curling through her body. ''Nobody can do more than that, sweet pea. Nobody.''

He stood, then bent down to kiss her gently. ''Think about it, darlin'.''

''You're leaving?'' she asked, unable to stop the disappointment that flooded through her.

''If I stay here another minute with you looking at me like that, I'm going to resort to seducing you into giving me the answer I want. I think it'll be better if I take my chances on letting you work this one out in your head.''

He was striding off to his pickup before she could mount an argument. She actually stood to go after him, but a wave of dizziness washed over her that had her clutching at a post to keep from falling.

What on earth? she wondered as she steadied herself. Suddenly she recalled the occasional bouts of nausea she'd been feeling that she'd chalked off to waiting too long to grab breakfast in the mornings. She thought about the bone-deep weariness that had had her half-asleep in that rocker only a short time before. And now, dizziness.

Oh, dear heaven, she thought, sinking back into the

rocker before she fainted. Unless she was very much mistaken, every one of those signs added up to being pregnant—again.

How could this have happened to them a second time? Melissa wondered as she left the doctor's office in a daze the following morning. How could she be pregnant from that one time they'd made love at Cody's? They'd been so darned careful not to repeat the same mistake. She'd held him at arm's length, refusing to make love again for that very reason, because neither one of them used a lick of common sense once they hopped into bed together. It was better not to let their hormones get out of hand in the first place.

She had no idea what was going to happen next, but she did know that this time she would tell Cody right away. There would be no more secrets to blow up in her face later.

Dammit, why couldn't everything have been more resolved between them? They were so close to working things out. She had sensed that last night in their companionable silence, in the way Cody had vowed to give her the time and space to reach her own conclusions about their relationship.

She knew exactly how Cody was going to react. Forget about time and space for thinking. He was going to demand they get married at once. She wanted that, wanted it more than anything, but not if he was only doing it because of the baby. Okay, both babies.

He was a fine father. He'd accepted his responsibility for Sharon Lynn wholeheartedly. That wasn't the issue. He'd been proving that over and over since the day he'd learned the truth about Sharon Lynn. She had seen the adoration in his eyes whenever he was with his daughter. She had watched his pride over every tiny accomplishment.

He had even behaved as though she were important to him, too. But never once, not in all these months, had he said he loved her. She would not marry a man who could not say those words. She would not marry at all just because she was pregnant.

It created an interesting dilemma, since there wasn't a darn thing she could do about being pregnant. There was nothing on earth that meant more to her than being a mother to Cody's children. And she knew from bitter experience that she could do it just fine on her own, if she had to.

Still, she had to tell him sometime....

She managed to hold off for a couple of weeks, but her symptoms were cropping up when she least expected it. She didn't want him guessing when he found her practically swooning in his arms.

After thinking it over, she chose the storeroom at Dolan's to tell him. Eli and Mabel were getting used to her dragging Cody into the back to talk. They'd probably heard enough muffled arguments and full-scale screaming matches to last them a lifetime.

At least, though, they would be there to intervene if Cody decided to try to drag her off by the hair to the preacher. At home she'd have no such protection. She doubted even her parents would stand up to him. Her father was already on Cody's side and her mother had maintained a stoic silence ever since her father's edict that she butt out of Melissa's and Cody's business.

She had one other reason for choosing the storeroom. She had noticed that Eli and Mabel were off by themselves whispering who-knew-what at the oddest times. Melissa had the feeling that the two of them were patching whatever differences had separated them years before. Maybe the very visible ups and downs of her relationship with Cody had set an example for them. They might as well be in on the denouement.

When Cody walked through the door as he'd gotten into the habit of doing around closing every day, Melissa's hands trembled. This time nothing on earth could have persuaded her to so much as touch a glass in Cody's presence.

Not even giving Cody time to get settled, she drew in a deep breath. ''We need to talk.''

''Okay,'' he said, giving her that crooked smile that made her heart flip over. ''What's up?''

''In the back,'' she said.

Cody groaned. ''Not again.''

She glanced at Eli and Mabel, who were both suddenly extremely busy, their backs to the counter. ''Will you just come on?'' she muttered, holding the door open.

Cody trailed along behind her and propped a booted foot onto an unopened shipment of new glasses. ''What now?''

Melissa tried to gather her courage. Finally she blurted, "I'm pregnant."

Cody's eyes widened incredulously. "You're going to have a baby?"

She nodded, watching him carefully, not quite able to get a fix on his reaction.

"A baby?" Cody repeated.

"Yes."

"Oh, my God." He sank down on the box, which gave way just enough to shatter the two dozen glasses inside.

At the sound of all that cracking glassware, Melissa started to chuckle. Cody bounced to his feet, but there was no hope for the crushed shipment.

"You okay?" she inquired between giggles. "No glass in your backside?"

"Forget my backside. It's just fine. Tell me more about the baby. When is it due?"

"You should be able to figure that one out. We only slept together that once since you got back."

"I can't even add two and two right now. Just tell me."

"A little over six months."

He nodded. "Good. That's plenty of time."

Melissa regarded him suspiciously. "Plenty of time for what?" she asked, although she thought she had a pretty good idea of the answer.

"To get married," he said at once. "Finish fixing up my house at White Pines, decorate a new nursery."

Melissa held up her hands. "Whoa, cowboy. Who says we're getting married?"

A mutinous expression settled over his face. ''I do. No baby of mine is going to be born without my name. It's bad enough that we haven't taken care of getting Sharon Lynn's name legally changed. I'm not doubling the problem.''

''Okay, say I agree to get married—which I haven't,'' she added in a rush when she saw the instant gleam in his eyes. ''Then what?''

He stared at her blankly. ''What?''

''Are you planning for us to live happily ever after? Are you intending to get a divorce as soon as the ink's dry on the birth certificate? What?'' *Please,* she thought to herself, *let him say he loves me. Please.*

''You know better than that,'' he said.

It was a wishy-washy answer if ever Melissa had heard one. ''Do I?'' she shot back. ''How? Just because you've been here a few months now and haven't taken off?''

He raked his fingers through his hair. ''Yes.''

''Not good enough, cowboy,'' she said, exiting the storeroom and emphatically closing the door behind her.

Mabel and Eli were suspiciously close to the door, though their attention seemed to be thoroughly engaged in their work. Of course, Mabel was sweeping the exact same spot she'd swept not fifteen minutes earlier and Eli was dusting off a shelf, a task that usually fell to Mabel.

''I'm leaving,'' she announced, grabbing her purse and heading for the door.

Mabel trailed her outside. "Don't be a fool, girl. Marry that man and put him out of his misery."

"I can't," Melissa said, sounding pretty miserable herself.

"Why the devil not?"

"He's only thinking about the babies. He's not thinking about us at all."

"If that's all he cared about, he could file for joint custody, pick them up on Friday afternoons and send you a support check," Mabel countered. "I don't hear him talking about doing any of that. He's talking about marriage, has been ever since he got back into town."

"Because it's the right thing to do," Melissa insisted stubbornly. "The Adams men are nothing if not honorable."

Mabel shot her a look of pure disgust. "Maybe you ought to be thinking about doing the right thing, too, if that's the case. Those babies deserve a chance at a real home. Cody's willing to give them that. Why can't you?"

Mabel's words lingered in her head as she walked over to pick up Sharon Lynn. They echoed there again and again as she fought every single attempt Cody made to persuade her to change her mind.

She told herself she wasn't the one making things difficult. All it would take to make her change her mind was three little words—I love you. They were about the only words in the whole English language that Cody never, ever tried.

Chapter Fifteen

From the instant he discovered that Melissa was pregnant again, Cody tried to persuade her to marry him. He coaxed. He wooed. He pitched a royal fit on occasion and threatened to hog-tie her and carry her off to the justice of the peace.

For six solid months he did everything but stand on his damned head, but Melissa seemed to have clothed her heart in an impenetrable sheet of armor. He surely didn't remember the woman being this stubborn. The whole town was watching the two of them as if they were better than any soap opera on TV. He found it mortifying to be chasing after a woman who acted as if he didn't even exist.

He also discovered that this new side of Melissa was every bit as intriguing as it was vexing. He realized that he'd always taken for granted that sooner or later she would admit she loved him and accept his oft-repeated proposal. That she was still turning him down with another baby on the way shook him as nothing else in his life ever had. Maybe this was one time when his charm wasn't going to be enough.

And the truth of it was, she seemed to be getting along just fine. He'd seen that for himself ever since he'd gotten back from Wyoming. She had made a nice life for herself and Sharon Lynn. She would fit a new baby into that life without batting an eye.

She was strong and self-sufficient, downright competent as a single parent. She had her job at the drugstore. She had friends who were there for her. She had parents who supported her in whatever decisions she made, though he sensed that her father was not quite as thrilled with this independent streak as her mother was.

In short, Melissa had a life, while Cody was lonelier than he'd ever imagined possible even in the dead of a rough Wyoming winter.

The thought of Melissa going into that delivery room with anyone other than him as her labor coach grated. The prospect of his baby—a second baby, in fact—being born without his name made him see red. He wanted to be a part of that baby's life so badly it stunned him.

What flat-out rocked him back on his heels, though, was the fact that he wanted to be with Melissa just as badly. Maybe he'd started out just saying the words, asking her to marry him because of Sharon Lynn and more recently this new, unborn baby. But sometime, when he hadn't been paying attention, he'd gone and fallen in love with the woman. Mature, adult love this time, not adolescent hormones and fantasy.

How the hell was he going to get her to believe that, though? Nothing he had done in the past eight and a half months since he'd come home to Texas had done a bit of good.

He'd been steady. He'd been reliable. He'd even managed to seduce her, which was what had gotten them into this latest fix. Melissa, however, had kept a stubborn grip on her emotions. She had refused to concede feeling so much as affection for him, much less love.

Cody was at his wit's end. He'd decided, though, that it was tonight or never. He was going to make one last, impressive, irresistible attempt to convince Melissa to be his wife. If it failed, he would just have to resign himself to this shadow role in the life of his children. Up until now he'd turned his back on his pride, but it was kicking up a storm for him to stop behaving like a besotted fool and give up.

He took hat quite literally in hand and went to visit Velma. He needed her help if his plan was to work. Responding to his knock on her door in midafternoon, she regarded him with her usual suspicion.

''What do you want?'' she inquired ungraciously.

Cody lost patience. ''I am not the bad guy here,'' he informed her as he stalked past her and stood in the middle of the foyer.

He could hear Sharon Lynn chattering away in the

guest room. It sounded as if she were having a tea party. He longed to go down that corridor and spend some time with her. She was changing in one way or another every day and he hated to miss a single one. Today, though, he was on a mission here and he couldn't afford to be distracted.

"I came by to see if you could keep Sharon Lynn here tonight," he said.

"Why?" Velma asked bluntly.

"So that Melissa and I can have an evening together alone."

"Seems to me you two have found enough time to be alone without my help in the past. She's about to have a baby again, isn't she? She didn't get that way in public, I suspect."

Her sarcasm grated. Cody held back the sharp retort that came to mind. If this was going to work out, it was way past time he made peace with Melissa's mother. "Exactly what has she told you about our relationship?"

Velma didn't give an inch. "She doesn't have to say a word. I can see plenty for myself."

"What do you think you see, then?"

"That you think your money and your power give you the right to be irresponsible. You've used my daughter, left her, then come back here and used her again without ever giving a thought to the consequences."

"Are you aware that I have been trying to persuade

your mule-headed daughter to marry me since the very first instant I got back into town?''

Velma blinked, but she didn't back down. Talk about stubborn pride. Velma had it in spades, which probably explained Melissa's streak of it.

''Too little, too late, if you ask me,'' she retorted.

Cody started to tell her he hadn't asked her, but of course he had. ''Look, I don't blame you for resenting me, but the fact of the matter is that I love your daughter, stubborn as she is, and I want to marry her and be a father to our children. I think she loves me, too, but she thinks she's a fool for doing it.''

He saw from the set expression on her face that Velma had probably reinforced that belief. Maybe if he could win over the mother, she'd change her tune with Melissa and give him a fighting chance.

''You want her to be happy, don't you?''

''Of course I do,'' she said indignantly. ''What makes you think I don't?''

''Because I think she's taking her cue from you. I think if she and I had just a little time alone, we could work this out, preferably before another one of our children is born without my name. Will you give us that chance?''

Velma spent the next minute or two in an obvious struggle with her conscience. ''What is it you want, exactly?''

''Keep Sharon Lynn here tonight. Don't interfere with my plans. That's all.''

''You think you can convince her in one night, when you haven't made any progress at all in the past nine months?'' Velma inquired with a shake of her head. ''You don't know Melissa half as well as you think you do.''

She sighed heavily. ''Okay, I'll keep Sharon Lynn for you,'' she relented to Cody's relief. ''But it'll have to be for the whole weekend. If you ask me, it's going to take you that long, maybe even longer, to turn that girl around. She's scared spitless she'll admit she loves you and you'll turn around and leave again.''

''I won't,'' he swore. He circled Velma's waist and spun her around. ''Thank you. You're an angel.''

She kept her lips in a tight line, resisting him to the bitter end, but Cody thought he detected a spark of amusement in her eyes. ''See that you do right by her, young man, or I'll have your hide.''

He kissed her cheek. ''Not to worry, Velma. This is going to be a weekend to remember.''

He was already making plans to sweep Melissa away to a quiet, secluded cabin for a romantic weekend by the time he hit the driveway.

His first stop was her house, where he managed to sneak in without being caught by the sheriff or a neighbor. He rummaged through her drawers and closets to find lingerie and the prettiest, sexiest maternity clothes she owned. He packed them, along with perfume and cosmetics, praying that he got the right ones. He didn't want her dissolving into tears because she couldn't find her blush or her mascara. Her hormones had her reacting in the most bizarre ways these days. He figured he ought to get a whole lot of points for just managing to stick by her anyway.

He'd considered taking her off to someplace fancy, maybe the most expensive suite in Dallas, but then he'd decided that would put her too close to taxis or planes or other means of escape. He wanted her all to himself.

He fought all of his old past resentments—most of them, as it had turned out, unwarranted—and tracked Brian down in San Antonio, where he was practicing law. He pointed out that his former best friend owed him one for the scam he and Melissa had tried to pull on Cody years before.

''I'm just grateful that you didn't come after me with a shotgun,'' Brian said. ''Anything you want is yours.''

''Does your family still have that cabin by the lake?''

''You bet.''

''Can Melissa and I borrow it for the weekend?''

''It's all yours,'' Brian said at once.

He told Cody where to find the key, offered some unsolicited advice on taming the reluctant Melissa, then added seriously, ''I'm glad you called, buddy. I've missed you.''

''Same here,'' Cody said. ''Next time you're down this way, we'll have to get together. You do have your own woman now, don't you?''

Brian chuckled. ''Do I ever. Good luck. You and Melissa should have worked this out long ago. I'd have told you the truth myself, but Melissa swore me to secrecy.''

"Secrets are her specialty, it appears," Cody said. "Anyway, thanks again for the cabin."

Those arrangements made, Cody loaded groceries, flowers and nonalcoholic champagne into the back of the truck, then swung by Dolan's. He marched straight to the soda fountain, ignoring the startled gazes of the teens gathered there.

"Cody? Is everything okay?" Melissa asked as he rounded the corner of the counter and headed toward her.

"Just dandy," he confirmed, tucking one arm under her legs and the other behind her waist. He scooped her up, amid a flurry of outraged protests from her and that same pimply faced kid who'd defended her honor once before.

"It's okay, son," Cody assured him. "She wants to go with me."

"I do not!" Melissa protested.

"Eli, call the cops or something," the boy shouted, his face turning red as he bolted after Cody.

"Not on your life," Eli said, and kept right on filling prescriptions. Mabel held the door open, grinning widely.

Melissa huffed and puffed a little longer, but by the time Cody had driven to the outskirts of town, she'd retreated into a sullen silence.

"Was that caveman approach entirely necessary?" she inquired eventually.

"I thought so."

"I would have come with you, if you'd asked politely."

He shot a skeptical look in her direction.

"At least, I would have thought about it," she amended.

"That's why I didn't ask. You've been thinking entirely too much."

"Are we going to White Pines?"

"Nope."

"Luke and Jessie's?" she asked hopefully, the first little sign of alarm sparking in her eyes.

"Nope."

"Cody, where the hell are you taking me?"

"Someplace where we can be alone."

"Where?" she repeated.

"Brian's cabin."

Her eyes widened. "You talked to Brian?"

"I figured drastic measures were called for, and he promised the best and quickest solution." He glanced over at her. "I was willing to do anything it took to make this happen, sweet pea."

"Oh," she said softly, and settled back to mull that over.

It wasn't more than half an hour later when he noticed she seemed to be getting a little restless.

"You okay?" he asked.

She turned toward him, her lower lip caught between her teeth as she shook her head. Instantly, Cody's muscles tensed.

"Melissa, what's wrong?" he demanded. "Tell me."

"It's not a problem," she said. "Not yet, anyway. It's just that..." Her eyes widened and turned the color of a turbulent sea. She swallowed visibly. ‘‘Don’t panic.’’

Cody panicked. ‘‘Melissa!’’

‘‘It’s okay, really it is. It’s just that it’s entirely possible that I’m in labor.’’ She sucked in a ragged breath, then announced, ‘‘Cody, I think we’re about to have a baby.’’

Chapter Sixteen

Cody found his father already pacing the waiting room when he got Melissa to the hospital. He'd called him on his cellular phone, right after he'd spoken to the doctor. He'd asked Harlan to alert the rest of the family.

''Even Jordan?'' his father had asked cautiously, aware of the friction between them.

Cody decided then and there it was time to get over the rift between him and his brother. This was a time for healing.

''Even Jordan,'' he'd confirmed.

He turned now to his father. ''Did you reach everyone?''

''They'll be here in a bit. How is she?'' Harlan demanded at once as the nurse wheeled Melissa away to prep her for delivery. ''Is everything okay?''

Cody wiped a stream of sweat from his brow. ''She says it is, but I don't know. You had four sons. Is labor supposed to be so painful?''

''How should I know? Your mama wouldn't let me anywhere near the delivery room. She said having babies was women's work.'' He glanced at Cody with an unmistakable look of envy. ''Wish I'd had a chance to be there just once, though. Seems to me like it must be a flat-out miracle. You going in there with Melissa?''

''If she'll let me,'' Cody said. ''She's still making up her mind whether to be furious at me for kidnapping her this afternoon.'' He moaned. ''I must have been out of my mind. I didn't even think about the fact that she might go into labor.''

''Cody, you weren't at the other end of the world,'' Harlan reassured him. ''You'd barely made it out of town. You got her here in plenty of time. The only way you could have gotten here much faster would have been to park her in a room upstairs for the last month of her pregnancy. Now, settle down.''

''It's easy for you. It's not your baby she's having.''

Just then the nurse came out. ''Mr. Adams, would you like to step in for a minute? We're getting ready to take Melissa to the delivery room.''

Cody shot a helpless look at his father. ''It sounds like she's not going to want me in there.''

''Maybe it's time to stop bullying the girl and tell her how much you want to be there,'' Harlan advised.

Cody doubted it would be as simple as that. Indeed,

Melissa shot him a look of pure hatred when he walked into her room. Of course, that might have had something to do with the whopper of a contraction she appeared to be in the middle of.

He accepted a damp cloth from the nurse and instinctively wiped Melissa's forehead with it.

"You're doing great," he said.

"How would you know?" she retorted.

He grinned at the fiery display of temper. "Okay, you got me. I have no idea. No one's running around the halls panicking, though. That must mean something."

"They're used to this," she retorted. "I'm not. Besides, they're just observers. I'm doing all the work."

"If you'd let me take those natural childbirth classes with you, I'd be more help about now."

She latched onto his hand just then and squeezed. It was either one hell of a contraction or she was trying to punish him by breaking all of his knuckles. As soon as the pain eased, she glared at him again.

"Go away."

"I don't think so," he countered just as stubbornly. "I want to share this with you."

"You want to see me writhing around in agony," she snapped.

"No," he insisted. "Having a baby is a miracle. I missed out on Sharon Lynn's birth. I'm going to be with you for this one."

"Why?"

He regarded her blankly. "Don't you know?"

"Cody, I don't know anything except that you've

been making a pest of yourself ever since you got back into town. What I don't know is why.''

Before he could answer, the orderlies came to wheel her down the hall to the delivery room. He could tell by the set of her jaw that she was going into that room without him unless he could find the courage to tell her what was in his heart.

''Dammit, Melissa, I love you!'' he shouted after her, just as they were about to roll her out of sight.

''Stop!'' Melissa bellowed at the orderlies between contractions.

Cody reached her side in an instant. Even with her face bathed in sweat, her lower lip bitten raw, she looked beautiful to him. She always had, always would.

''What did you say?'' she demanded, then grabbed onto his hand with a grip so fierce he could have sworn that more bones broke.

He grinned through the pain—hers and his. ''I said I love you.''

A slow, satisfied smile spread across her face. ''It's about time, cowboy.''

''Haven't I been saying that for months now?'' he asked, vaguely bemused that she hadn't heard it before.

''Not the words,'' she told him. ''How was I supposed to believe it without the words?''

''Someone once told me that actions speak louder than words. I guess I was putting it to the test. I thought you needed to see that I wasn't going anywhere.''

''I also needed to hear why that was so,'' she told him, wincing as another pain started and then rolled through her. ''I didn't want you with me out of a sense of obligation.''

Relief swept through him as he realized he'd risked everything and finally gotten through to her. ''Does that mean you'll marry me?''

''Whenever you say.''

Cody turned and motioned to the preacher he'd had Harlan call for him. He'd also had Harlan make a call to a judge to cut through the legal red tape. ''Get to it, Reverend. I don't think this baby's going to wait much longer.''

The minister had never talked so fast in his life, quite possibly because he was conducting the ceremony in the doorway of a delivery room. Cody figured as long as they didn't cross that threshold, the baby would have sense enough not to come until his or her parents were properly married.

The ''I do's'' were punctuated by moans and a couple of screams. And not five minutes later, Harlan Patrick Adams came into the world with an impeccable sense of timing, just as the minister pronounced his mama and daddy man and wife.

Melissa was beginning to wonder if she was ever going to be able to hold her own baby. Between Cody and his father, she'd barely gotten a look at him. Cody had finally disappeared a half hour before, but Harlan was still holding the baby with a look of such pride and sadness in his eyes.

"I wish Mary could have seen him," he said softly as a tear spilled down his cheek.

"Wherever she is, I think she knows," Melissa told him. "And I'll bet Erik is right beside her, watching out for all of us."

Her father-in-law gave her a watery smile. "I can't tell you how proud it makes me to have you in this family finally."

"I'm glad to be a part of it finally," she told him. "Though given the way my brand new husband scooted out of here after the ceremony, I'm not so sure I made the right decision. Any idea where he went?"

There was no mistaking the spark of pure mischief in Harlan's eyes. "Can't say that I know for sure," he said.

Melissa didn't believe him for a second. The old scoundrel and Cody were clearly up to their ornery chins in some scheme or another. Before she could try to pry their secret out of him, the door to the room slid open a crack.

"Everyone awake?" Cody inquired lightly.

"Come on in, son," Harlan enthused. "We were just wondering where you'd gone off to."

Cody stepped into the room and winked at her. "Should I take that to mean that you suspected I'd run off on you already?"

"It did cross my mind," she admitted. "You turned awful pale there in the delivery room. I figured you might be having second thoughts about marriage and fatherhood."

"Not me," Cody retorted indignantly. "I just figured the occasion deserved a celebration. You know how this family likes to party. You up for it?"

She stared at him as he watched her uneasily. "What if I say no?"

"Then that's it. I send everyone away."

"Everyone? Who is out there?"

"Sharon Lynn, first of all. She wants to meet her new baby brother."

Melissa grinned. "Bring her in. Of course I want her to see the baby."

Cody opened the door and Sharon Lynn barreled in and ran toward the bed. Over the past few months she'd grown increasingly steady on her feet. In the final weeks of her pregnancy Melissa had had a heck of a time waddling after her.

"Mama! Mama!" Sharon Lynn shouted.

Cody lifted Sharon Lynn onto the bed beside her. "Harlan, bring the baby over so Sharon Lynn can get a look," Melissa said.

As Harlan approached with the baby, her daughter's eyes grew wide. "Baby?"

"That's right, pumpkin. That's Harlan Patrick, your baby brother."

As if she knew that newborns were fragile, Sharon Lynn reached over and gently touched a finger to her brother's cheek. "I hold," she announced.

"Not yet," Melissa told her just as there was a soft knock on the door.

Cody reached for the handle, but his gaze was on her. "You ready for more visitors?"

''Who else is out there?''

''Your parents,'' he said.

''Luke and Jessie,'' Sharon Lynn chimed in, clearly proud that she'd learned two new names. ''And Jordie and Kelly.''

Melissa chuckled as she imagined straight-laced Jordan if he ever heard himself referred to as ''Jordie.'' She gave her husband a warm smile, silently congratulating him for ending the feud that never should have happened.

''Let them in,'' she instructed Cody. ''If I'd known you were inviting half the town, I'd have insisted on that private VIP suite they have upstairs.''

As the family crowded in, a nurse came along, wheeling in a three-tiered wedding cake. Melissa stared at it in amazement. ''When did you have time to order that?''

''Right after you said 'I do' and delivered our son,'' he said. ''I told the bakery it was an emergency.''

Kelly leaned down to kiss her cheek. ''You should have seen the look on their faces when I stopped to pick it up. Obviously, they'd never heard of an emergency wedding before.''

Melissa swung her legs over the side of the bed and prepared to go over for a closer look.

''Stay right where you are,'' Cody ordered, looking panicked.

''I'm not an invalid,'' she informed him.

''It's not that,'' he admitted, casting a worried look at the cake. ''Actually, it was a little late to come up with an emergency cake. Fortunately, they had a cancellation.''

Melissa stared at him, torn between laughing and crying. ''That is someone else's cake?''

''They got the other names off,'' Kelly reassured her. ''Almost, anyway.''

Sure enough, when Melissa managed to get near enough for a closer look, she could spot the traces of blue food dye across the white icing on the top layer. Love Always had been left in place, but below it were the shadowy letters unmistakably spelling out Tom And Cecily.

Melissa grinned. ''Get on over here, Tom,'' she said pointedly. ''Give old Cecily a kiss.''

Cody didn't hesitate. He gathered her close and slanted his lips across hers in a kiss that spoke of love and commitment and all the joy that was to come.

''Okay, that's enough, baby brother,'' Luke said. ''Give the rest of us a chance to kiss the bride.''

Cody relinquished his hold on her with obvious reluctance. He stood patiently by as she was kissed and congratulated by all the others. Harlan grabbed a paper cup and filled it with lukewarm water from the tap.

''A toast, everyone,'' he announced.

When they all had their own cups of water, he lifted his cup. ''To Cody and Melissa. This marriage was a long time coming. There were times I despaired of the two of you ever realizing that you belong together. Now that you have, we wish you every happiness for all the years to come.''

"Hear, hear," Jordan and Luke echoed. "Much happiness, baby brother."

"Now it's my turn to kiss the bride," Harlan declared, giving her a resounding smack on the cheek.

Cody stole between them. "Get your own bride, old man. This one is mine."

"Maybe I will," Harlan said, startling them all.

Cody, Jordan and Luke stared at him in open-mouthed astonishment while their wives all chuckled with delight.

"Do it," Melissa whispered in his ear, standing on tiptoe to give him a kiss. "Find a bride and live happily ever after. No one deserves it more. Mary would want that for you."

She had a feeling that when Harlan Adams set his mind to finding a woman to share his life, he was going to set all of Texas on its ear. And his sons were going to have the time of their lives getting even for all the grief he'd given them over their own love lives. Melissa was thrilled that she was going to be right in the thick of it all, where she'd always dreamed of being.

Her mother and father came over to her then. "You happy, ladybug?" her father asked.

She clung tightly to Cody's hand and never took her gaze from his as she whispered, "Happier than I thought possible."

"About time," her mother huffed.

Cody leaned down and kissed her soundly. "Stop fussing, Velma." He grinned unrepentantly at her mother's expression of shock. "One of these days you're going to admit it," he taunted.

"Admit what?"

"That you're crazy about me."

Her mother scowled. "You're too sure of yourself, Cody Adams. Somebody's got to keep you in line."

He turned his gaze on Melissa then. "And I know just the woman to do it," he said softly.

"What if I don't want to keep you in line?" Melissa asked. "I kind of like your roguish ways."

"Told you she didn't have a lick of sense where that boy was concerned," Velma announced loudly.

Melissa glanced at her mother just then and winked. After a startled instant, her mother chuckled despite herself and winked right back. She tucked her arm through her husband's and added, "Married one just like him myself."

"Then I guess Cody and I are going to be okay, aren't we, Mother?"

Her mother glanced pointedly at Sharon Lynn and the new baby. "Looks to me like you've got quite a head start on it."

Cody brushed a kiss across her cheek. "Indeed, we do."

Everyone began leaving after that. Finally Melissa was alone with her husband. "I love you," she told him.

"I love you," he echoed. His expression turned serious. "Do you really think Daddy's going to start courting?"

"Sounded to me as if he meant what he said. How would you feel about that?"

Cody hesitated for a minute, then grinned. "Seems like a damned fine opportunity to get even with him, if you ask me."

"That's what I love about you Adams men," Melissa taunted. "You are so supportive of each other."

"You don't think he deserves to be taken on a merry chase?"

"By some woman," she admonished. "Not by you, Luke and Jordan."

He sighed and folded his arms around her middle from behind. His breath fanned across her cheek. "I suppose standing on the sidelines and watching him fall will have its moments," he agreed. "He sure seemed to get a kick out of watching that happen to the rest of us."

"Then I suggest you prepare yourself for the ride," she told him. "Knowing Harlan, it's going to be a bumpy one."

"As for you and me," Cody proclaimed, "from here on out it's going to be smooth sailing."

* * * * *

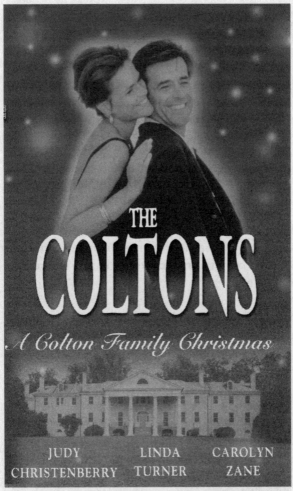

Maitland Maternity

Where the luckiest babies are born!

Her Best's Friend Baby
by Vicki Lewis Thompson

Just good friends? Sharing a house…
Carrying a child!

Mary Jane Potter works in the café next to the clinic and has seen many an expectant mum come and go. She knew she'd like to be a mother herself one day—but never thought she'd be carrying a baby for somebody else first!

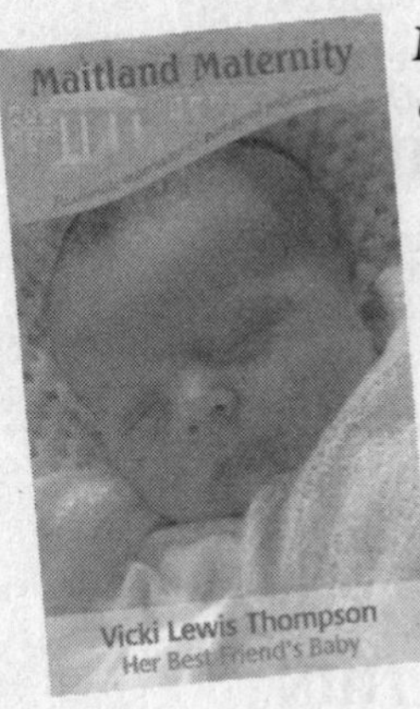

Morgan Tate: He was sure he could distance himself from the woman having his baby. But now he can't seem to leave her side...

Sara works with Mary Jane and is suffering from amnesia. Lately, she's begun to hope her memory might be coming back...

MAITLAND/RTL/9

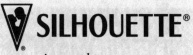